# FAMILY PRACTICE

## A THORNTON VERMONT NOVEL

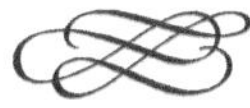

## CAMERON D. GARRIEPY

*For my parents.*

# WHAT'S IN THIS BOOK?

## CONTENT INFORMATION

*Dear Reader,*

***Family Practice*** *is the second book in the Thornton Vermont Series. While it works best in series order, it can be read as a stand-alone or out of order. It contains an HEA, open-door, sweet-with-heat sex scenes, occasional coarse language, and alcohol consumption. The heroine has an abusive relationship in her past which is referenced, and which spills into her present. Child endangerment, gaslighting, and difficult parent dynamics are part of the narrative. If these topics are sensitive to you, please read with caution.*

***Tropes/themes you'll find inside:***

- *second chances*
- *teenage crushes*
- *friends to lovers*
- *H is a lawyer; h is a single mom and event planner*
- *competence is sexy*
- *H/h over 30*

# FAMILY PRACTICE

# CHAPTER 1

*A*nneliese Thompson's back ached from painting but, come hell or high water, tomorrow Chloe would have a big-girl bedroom, in a home of their own. The rented cottage next door to the Fletcher Hotel—with its wild garden and faded picket fence that faced the town common—needed some love and a five-year-old's laugh to come back to life.

In that way, she and the cottage were a lot alike.

Her phone buzzed from the canvas-covered bed behind her. She kept rolling pale turquoise swaths, hoping to finish the last wall before the real world interrupted.

Her voicemail alert pinged, then her email. Someone wanted her attention.

She navigated the maze of her childhood furniture, crammed into the room at odd angles, holding her paint-smeared hands up for her own inspection.

The phone rang again. Twice in a row usually meant her mother. A brief worry for Chloe fluttered in her chest, but she quashed it and jogged down the stairs to the kitchen. She didn't want paint on her phone screen, and she hadn't yet unpacked soap for the bathroom.

The missed call from California set her heart racing afresh. Her hands felt dirtier somehow. The only person she knew in California was the last person she wanted to hear from. She nudged the kitchen tap open with one wrist, waiting for water hot enough to scald away the crawling sensation, then scrubbed away the paint.

Throat tight, she tapped through to the message.

"Anneliese, hi. My name is Kirsten Letourneau. I'm putting together an event, and from what I hear, you're the best planner in your area. The timeline is tight, and there are some unique concerns. Would love to talk to you about it. Give me a call as soon as possible." Kirsten left her phone number and signed off.

The name didn't ring a bell, but at least it wasn't Chad. Anneliese set the phone down on the drainboard and braced her hands on the sink. Three thousand miles, plus the better part of five years, and just the thought of her ex-husband still tipped her world off its axis.

Doing her best to relax, braced in front of the kitchen window, she saw her neighbor and landlord—and half owner of the Fletcher Hotel—wave. Jeremy, in his straw hat and Bermuda shorts, was tending the butterfly garden he maintained in the hotel's sunny side yard. She smiled and waved back.

Time to finish Chloe's room; Kirsten Letourneau's return call could wait.

By the time Anneliese had rolled the walls and cleaned the brushes, the morning was gone, and part of the afternoon with it.

She pulled out her client notebook and opened a fresh page. Kirsten Letourneau answered on the third ring.

"Hello. Kirsten here."

"Hi, Kirsten. Anneliese Thompson. I'm returning your call."

"Awesome. Hi. Thanks for getting back to me, and sorry if I sounded like a complete nutcase. My brain is still fried from the red-eye."

"Not at all." A red-eye flight sounded important. "What's the event?"

"A wedding. I have a client who wants a magazine-worthy party; her fiancé wants a New England wedding. It's my job to make that happen. I need someone in the area to partner with, and you come highly recommended."

"Who's your client?"

"That's confidential, for now. She's particular about controlling her message. There would be an NDA if you decide to work with us. For now, though, I'd love to come up there… Thornton, it's called? See some potential locations, that kind of thing."

What could it hurt? "Sure. When do you plan to be in the area?"

"I can take a train up tomorrow. Or rent a car. How far is it?"

Anneliese laughed. "You'll want to rent a car. The train station's a ways from here. Is this number your cell? I can text you the name of a cafe where I meet clients. It also happens to be the home of the best wedding cakes in the state."

And if she'd known the owner for most of her life, that was just a quirk of small town life. Growing up, Kate Pease was a pigtailed shadow trailing her brother, Jack. Anneliese spent most of her childhood with Jack and his best friend Joss Fuller—who just happened to be a second cousin of hers on her mother's side. Another small town quirk.

Like Jack, Kate grew up gorgeous and ambitious. Unlike Jack, Kate returned to town, becoming a fixture in Thornton.

"Now we're talking," Kirsten said. "I'm going to say late afternoon, since I literally have no idea how far Manhattan is from Vermont."

"Sounds about right." Anneliese laughed again. Despite the mystery—or maybe because of it—she liked this effervescent voice on the phone. "Text me when you get to town. My day is pretty flexible."

"Great. I totally have a feeling about this."

Kirsten had hung up before Anneliese thought to ask who referred her. She didn't know anyone who rated a non-disclosure agreement.

Time enough to worry tomorrow. For now, she was on her own in her newly rented house. No mother to question her parenting choices, or to remind her she was single and on the other side of thirty. No daughter with bottomless curiosity and rapid-fire questions.

Time for tea and reading on the screened porch, and supper when she felt like it.

She plugged in her new electric teakettle and filled the reservoir, humming to herself. She fussed over the tea leaves while the water boiled, then took her mug out to the porch.

Beyond the shabby screen, the garden was in unruly, riotous bloom. It had gone too long without a caretaker. Leggy purple phlox leaned against the pickets. A climbing rose had fallen over and was creeping along the flagstones. Crabgrass sprouted anywhere there wasn't something hardy to hold it back, and the daylilies were crowding the brown remains of spring daffodils and tulips.

She had her work cut out for her. Tea first, but some weeding before she curled up with her book.

It was nearly sunset when Jack Pease wrapped up his last meeting of the day. Boston Harbor glimmered below his 38th floor window; what the view lacked in early starlight, it made up for with the twinkle of air traffic from Logan International.

A quick knock sounded. His office door swung open, and his co-counsel stuck his head in. "Jack, we're headed to Elephant and Castle. You coming?"

Jack turned, giving Barry an easy grin. "Maybe in a few. I'll text you. Don't wait."

"Hot date?" Barry's face lit up. "Say it's a hot date."

There was no hot date, but no need to burst Barry's bubble. "Yeah. Hot date."

"I'm glad. Emily said she hadn't heard about a new girlfriend in a while. Starting to wonder if you were hiding some serious relationship from us." Barry folded his suit jacket over one arm. "I'll tell her you're still out there breaking hearts."

The door swung shut behind Barry, leaving Jack with the ghost of the conversation still in the room. Barry's wife didn't know the half of it. He hadn't been seriously involved with anyone since Iris, and that was nearly three-year-old news.

Since there was no hot date, and drinks with the team didn't appeal to him at the moment, Jack tidied his desk and loosened his tie. He'd walk home, maybe text Iris on the way and see what she was up to.

You around?
*IB: leaving hot yoga. You?*
Leaving the office. Have you eaten?
*IB: it's after 8. Go home*
On my way now
*IB: I'm a sucker. Meet me at Vitto's*
I didn't ask
*IB: 20 minutes*

Vitto's Ristorante hid on the outskirts of Boston's North End, in the basement of a residential building. The only sign was over the door, and most tourists passed by in favor of the flashier places on Hanover Street. Jack arrived first and snagged a booth near the bar. Iris was moments behind him, carrying her yoga mat on her back and looking not at all like someone who just sweated in an upside-down pretzel shape for an hour.

"Hey, gorgeous."

Iris settled in her seat, picking up her menu. "How's the water thing going?"

"They'll settle. It's not quite there yet." Jack glanced at the chalkboard over the bar to read the specials. "What about your arsonist?"

"Plea bargain." Iris set down her menu. "Celebrated with tickets to see my sister in Barcelona."

Barcelona with the Björnsdóttir sisters sounded far better than Boston with the usual suspects, even during Sox season. "Take me with you."

Before Iris could answer, a waiter came to take their order. After he left, she fixed her shrewd eyes on him. "What you're looking for isn't in Spain."

"Who says I'm looking for something?"

Iris unfolded her napkin and laid it alongside her cutlery. "This is me, Jack. Not one of your flings."

The waiter returned with their drinks. Jack gave his Campari and soda his full attention while he recovered. Iris always saw through him. "I still say I was one of *your* flings."

Iris sipped serenely from a glass of Prosecco. "I don't have flings. I take lovers. There's a difference."

Jack chuckled. "There is."

"I'm not the only one who sees it."

"That you take lovers?"

Iris laughed. "No. That you've been...unsettled. I'd say unhappy, but I think you're mostly content. It's like you're looking over your shoulder, like something is following you, but you can't see it when you look. It began around when we stopped seeing one another, though I don't flatter myself I'm the cause."

Jack reached for a roll. "So, I'm haunted?"

Iris took one too, her eyes serious over the bread. "In a way. You're only half here. You and I talk like we always have, but you barely go out with Barry and the team any more. I see more of your friends than you do. You haven't shown up with some fetching woman at your side in ages. You're not yourself—or who yourself is has changed."

"My own mother isn't this concerned about my social life."

"I assume your mother didn't recently run into another old flame of yours. Rachel's the general manager at Beast now, by the way. She hadn't seen you there in so long, she assumed you'd settled down."

Jack busied himself with buttering his roll. Iris's insightful nature was always intense, but she rarely turned her laser intuition on him. At least to his face. "Did you rehearse this?"

"It's been on my mind for a while."

"Remind me never to leave you alone with my sister."

Their server returned with their appetizers, giving Jack a moment to collect himself, but Iris was undeterred.

"You gave me an opening. I'm taking it." She pushed a radicchio leaf through the Burrate and citrus vinaigrette mingling on her plate. "I want you to find what you're looking for."

Jack took a deep breath, focusing on his truffled *arancini*. "Maybe I'm not looking for anything right now. My career is on track; I have good friends; my apartment is worth twice what I paid for it, and the Sox are leading the AL East."

"An embarrassment of riches." Iris's smile turned down at the corners, just enough to let him know she wasn't fooled.

Time to change the subject. "So, when are you and Pippa going to Barcelona?"

After dinner, Iris walked with Jack as far as the State House, leaving him alone with his thoughts as he crossed the Common. The sky was hazy, pink around the edges despite the darkness. Boston would eventually sleep, but the light pollution never allowed full darkness. The breeze drew the salt air inland, mingling with the scent of hot asphalt, trash, and kitchen vents rising from the cooling city.

He didn't lie to Iris. He loved his job; his team at the firm was the best at what they did. He had good friends and a great apartment, and the Sox really were having a decent season.

He stopped at the pedestrian crossing on Charles Street to buy a bottle of water from a vendor cart. "Hey, Gus."

"Hey, man. Thanks for the tickets. I think Fenway's got a fan for life."

"I had it on the radio in my office. Sounded like a great game. Glad Gabriel had a good time."

Gus's wife, Wanda, had been cleaning Jack's apartment for five years; their son, Gabriel, was eleven. It took some convincing to get Wanda to accept a pair of his season seats on the third baseline, but Jack felt better about giving them to her husband and son than passing them off to one of the guys he worked with.

"Night, Jack." Gus waved him on his way, already making change for his next customer.

Technically speaking, Jack's apartment was a straight shot across the Public Garden and up the Commonwealth Avenue Mall, with a slight left turn onto Gloucester to access his building's front door, but Jack detoured right, around the duck pond. His favorite bench was empty, and somehow that was more appealing than an empty apartment.

Iris was rarely wrong about people. It made her a successful—and terrifying—attorney. In the relative stillness of a soft Boston night, Jack felt the creeping sensation she was right about him, too.

He'd been going through the motions for a long while, although not unhappily. Iris was correct about the timing. He'd gone home to Thornton for a weekend the summer Nan opened the Damselfly Inn, only to find Anneliese had come home.

Anneliese, Joss, and Jack grew up exploring the woods and streams of their postcard town. She was simply a part of the fabric of his life; his affection for her was carefree and simple.

He didn't notice her complexities when they hit high school, nor how beautiful she was until another guy got there first. In the whirl of college and law school, Jack lost track of her, hearing years later she had married and moved to California.

The Anneliese who returned—divorced and with a baby—had cautious eyes, and no time for him. Though they reestablished the shell of a friendship in the years since, Anneliese treated him like a primed explosive.

It irritated him. He wanted to make her smile, find her laughter, and, if he was being wholly honest, to kiss the lips that smiled so easily for him when they were younger. The endless supply of attractive, interesting women in the city paled in comparison to the memory of a girl he once knew and the challenge of a woman he didn't know anymore.

What he wanted wasn't in Spain; *she* was in Thornton, Vermont.

"Mama!"

Anneliese leaned against the jamb of Chloe's new room, stretching the kinks out of her shoulders and grinning while her daughter twirled around in a bar of sunlight.

"Feesh and me love our new room!"

"Feesh and *I* love our new room." Her English teachers would be proud.

"'kay, Mama." Chloe stopped twirling and hopped onto the white-washed wrought-iron bed that had been Anneliese's as a girl, brought from the attic at her parents' house during the move. Her little girl wriggled into the down comforters like a puppy—despite the heat—and grinned back up at her. "Where will you sleep?"

"Right across the hall." Anneliese gestured toward the open door to the other bedroom on the second floor. For now, she had an air mattress and her suitcase propped against the wall, but there would be time to make the space her own.

Chloe hopped out of the bed and swam Feesh—her beloved stuffed clownfish—past walls the color of a tropical sea. The second floor rooms were charming at best, small and awkward with slanted ceilings and dormer windows. For Anneliese, however, Chloe's room felt like a fairytale, with lace curtains from the thrift shop, bleached and hung on the line at the Damselfly to whiten them, and a vintage crystal chandelier Joss painted and rewired.

Anneliese heard the snap of the screen door.

"Anneliese, are you upstairs?"

Her mother.

"Coming, Mom."

She left Chloe to explore the canvas bins tucked into the eaves, and trotted downstairs to meet her mother in the kitchen.

Jane Thompson stood in the kitchen, looking uncomfortable in her daughter's space. "I had your father look at that loose downspout. Are you certain the roof is sound?"

Anneliese swallowed a sigh. "Joss looked everything over before I signed the lease. He's sure Jeremy and Glenn aren't trying to fleece me. They'll have everything spruced up and painted this year."

Her mother took the defensive, her back straight, the worry lines around her eyes deepening. "I just wanted your father to look at it."

Anneliese knew from Aunt Molly that her mother had always been serious and practical, but Molly's stories hinted at a playfulness Anneliese had never seen. Her mother had always expected Anneliese to walk a narrow path. It was Aunt Molly she went to for sympathy and exuberant hugs. "I know, Mom. But Joss is a pro. And family. And Dad is—"

Her father chose that moment to come through the door. "Dad is what, Sunshine?"

Anneliese couldn't help but smile. Her father's expectations of her were no different, but she thought affection came more easily to him. "Dad is here to see Chloe's new room, not stare at my gutters."

"That he is." He placed a gentle hand on his wife's back. "Let's go see what our granddaughter's up to."

Anneliese waited for their footfalls on the stairs before she let herself relax. They loved her. They loved Chloe. They couldn't always hide their disappointment in her divorce, or the way she'd tumbled, broke and broken, back into Thornton after following Chad all the way to Sacramento and giving him too many years of her life.

Living in their home had reduced her to errant teenage status, even as she was mothering her own young daughter. She had respected their rules, been truly thankful for their help and support, but she wanted more. Flying the nest was everything she needed; she was determined not to let their overprotective skepticism affect her decisions anymore.

Her mother reappeared at the bottom of the stairs. "I asked your father to move that toy chest away from the dormer window. Chloe could easily fall out the window screen if she climbed up on it."

Anneliese pasted on a grateful smile and decided not to mention the safety latches Joss installed for her. Or that the windows were currently open from the top down for just that reason. "Thanks, Mom."

So much for not letting them affect her decisions.

Anneliese followed her mother back upstairs. "I appreciate you guys staying here with Chloe while I take this meeting."

Jane paused at the top of the stairs, disapproval in the furrows between her brows. "What is this anyway? It doesn't seem like the kind of client you usually work with."

"I have no idea, but I'm curious, and it doesn't hurt to sit down with this woman for an hour."

"That it doesn't." Her father was juggling three homemade yarn poufs Chloe rescued from her toy bins. "We're going to hold down your new fort while you meet this mystery client."

# CHAPTER 2

$\mathcal{A}$nneliese recognized her mysterious appointment the moment Sweet Pease's cheerful bell jingled the unfamiliar arrival. Kirsten's brunette-to-emerald ombré hair, sexy cat-eye liner, and flaunted curves spoke of a woman with strong opinions and fiercely independent style.

She caught the young woman's eye and waved.

Kirsten slid into the booth across from Anneliese and dropped her phone on the table. "I had to stop an hour ago and ask—" She broke off before speaking the name of her mystery client. "And double check I was still the U.S., but I get the appeal. This place is adorable." Kirsten offered her hand over the table. "Kirsten Letourneau."

"Anneliese Thompson." She handed Kirsten a laminated list of drinks and pastries. "Specials are on the board if you're hungry, but save room for wedding cake."

"Mmm, wedding cake." Kirsten pushed the menu away. "I'd better stick to coffee."

Moira, who'd worked for Kate as long as Anneliese had been home, arrived to take Kirsten's coffee order.

"Why don't you tell me what your client needs," Anneliese said.

"I've got some ideas already, but it's all based on local availability and trends I'm watching."

Anneliese's iPad was already on the table between them. She silently thanked the gods of Pinterest and WiFi as she pulled up her hastily prepped style boards.

"Basically," Kirsten said, "she wants about a hundred people; some will be celebrities, and their families, of course, so flawless accommodations, unique experiences, that kind of thing. Like I said, you come with a glowing recommendation, and I've spent some time on your social media channels. You've got great style." Kirsten trailed a manicured finger over one of the pinned images. "I love this for her. You're good. Can you do it in three months?"

"With the right budget."

Kirsten pulled a typed page from the large tote next to her. On it were some firm numbers, including the budget. There were two more zeroes at the end than Anneliese was used to. Her stomach fluttered in anticipation.

"That's definitely the right budget."

Kate chose that moment to push through the swinging doors from the kitchen. Anneliese hadn't seen Kate in her signature fuchsia chef's jacket and cap in months; her friend was too busy managing her two bakeries and house hunting with Ewan, but the promise of a mysterious wedding cake client with a message to control was more than enough to tempt Kate into hand-delivering in uniform.

"Hi Anneliese," Kate said, crossing to them with a trio of miniature fondant-wrapped cakes, each topped with a buttercream rosette in pale lilac, rich brown, and amber, respectively. Kate wore her charisma as easily as she did the chef's jacket. It was, Anneliese thought, when she most resembled Jack. "You must be the mysterious Kirsten. I'm Kate Pease, owner and executive chef at Sweet Pease; welcome to Thornton."

Kate set the plate between them. "Anneliese promised you a taste of what we offer. This is my standard tasting trio: vanilla-bean sponge cake with a lemon cream filling and lavender-infused Earl Grey buttercream; dark chocolate torte with a coffee cream filling and espresso chocolate ganache; and almond, brown butter cake with raspberry cream filling and Amaretto buttercream. The full wedding cake menu is on our website, and we can do a tasting and consult with the bride and groom as soon as we have a timeline."

Kirsten tucked into the cakes. "This is amazing. God, how do you not just eat these every day?"

"The threat of needing all new chef's jackets," Kate said with a grin. "Is there anything else I can do for you?"

Kirsten closed her eyes, savoring a bite of the chocolate torte. "Marry me?"

Laughing, Kate excused herself back to the kitchen, leaving Kirsten and Anneliese to talk about the big picture. Kirsten's questions about the style boards, the weather, and the transportation options were punctuated with hums of cake-induced pleasure.

"What's next then?" Anneliese said, "I think I'd be crazy to turn an opportunity like this down—assuming it's offered, and there's no time to waste, anyway."

"My boss gave me nearly carte blanche to do the legwork. She wants to come in, make final decisions, and be wowed." Kirsten set her fork down. "I'm staying in Burlington. I'll email you tonight with the standard agreements you'd need to sign before working with her, and you can email me your contract and an estimate. Be generous with it. Seriously. Above all, she wants this to be an unforgettable event."

Anneliese confirmed her contact details as she walked Kirsten to her car. "I'm looking forward to hearing from you. Enjoy Burlington."

"Will I be able to see Canada from there? I feel like I should after this drive." She grinned. "We must be nearly to the North Pole by now."

Anneliese watched the taillights of Kirsten's car vanish, then she permitted herself a little victory dance before setting out for home. A contract like this could be a game changer.

Her landlords were inspecting the wisteria vining the hotel's front porch when Anneliese got home. Glenn caught her eye before hurrying down the front steps and over to the low picket fence surrounding the carriage house.

"We've got a late robin's nest. Come see."

Anneliese set down her bag on the porch and made her way out of the front garden and around to the Fletcher House's grand front entry. The couple had pulled up a four-foot ladder and Jeremy was angling his phone to get pictures of the nest without getting too close to the babies.

"Hey, Anneliese." He peered back over his shoulder. "We didn't see the nest before because of the flowers, but Mama's nesting late, so we didn't miss the action!"

Anneliese laughed, touched by their enthusiasm. "I can see living next door to you two is going to be an adventure."

"Maybe almost as fun as watching you nest in our cottage."

Anneliese looked back at her new home. "I'm crazy about it."

Glenn regarded the house with hands on hips. "We'll hire someone to fix that fence and paint the exterior by the end of the summer."

"And put new screens in the porch," Jeremy added.

"I can live with faded paint." Anneliese couldn't believe her luck. Landlords who suggested repairs.

"But you shouldn't have to, and we have a reputation to uphold." Jeremy stepped down. "Go on up and take a look. Glenn will spot you. I've got to get back to the front desk."

Anneliese gave his departing back a wry look. "I think I can handle a glorified step-ladder."

"You're no fun," Glenn teased, with a smoldering glance at his husband. "Holding the ladder is my duty as the man of the house."

"I heard that," Jeremy said as he retreated into the hotel.

Three tiny blue eggs and one wet, skinny fledgling occupied the carefully constructed nest. She felt a kinship with the absent mother—hoping her fledgling would thrive, though she was grateful she had more than a few weeks to launch her baby into the world.

"Nests are happy things, Anneliese." Glenn watched her with open concern as she stepped off the ladder.

"Oh, I know." She smiled at him. "I was just thinking about babies flying the nest and…"

"You're entirely too sweet." Glenn gathered her into a hug, tucking her head under his chin. His tee shirt was impossibly soft and smelled like Old Spice. "And you have mail."

Anneliese stepped out of Glenn's arms and looked back at her garden gate, where the letter carrier was closing the mailbox.

"Mail! My own mail," she said, clapping her hands like Chloe in front of an ice cream sundae. "I didn't even think about getting my own mail."

Anneliese left Glenn to the bird's nest and gathered a small stack of generic solicitations addressed to "Resident" from the box. She gleefully sorted the junk mail into the recycling bins near the porch, stopping abruptly at an official-looking envelope from Pacific Western Bank.

Her fingers trembled as she tore it open. It was addressed to her at the cottage, but how? The meager state-mandated checks came quarterly to her parents' house since her return to Thornton, and her move had come together over the course of the last two weeks through sheer luck and timing. How had Chad gotten her address so quickly?

The check was, as it had been since the divorce was finalized—just shy of Chloe's first birthday, the bare minimum her ex-husband could get away with and still claim he hadn't abandoned Chloe. Not out of paternal duty, not out of care for their daughter's well-being. His apathy when she'd decided to leave California cemented his lack of love for the child they'd made together. Chad used child support to remind Anneliese he still held some power over her.

Anneliese buried the check in her purse. Her friends were due shortly, and she didn't intend to let Chad interrupt her first girls' night in her own home.

Chloe came home from school full of songs and clapping games. Anneliese handed her daughter a bowl of fresh peas from the farm share, hoping Chloe's version of shelling yielded enough edible peas for the pasta salad.

Chloe's whole body concentrated on splitting the pods at the seams. "Mama, I was line leader today, and at share time I said I had a new house."

"Oh yeah?" Pride swelled in Anneliese's chest. "What does line leader do?"

"Stands in front and follows Miss Jordan when we go to library and swimming, and I get to count everybody." Chloe popped a pod and scattered the peas across the table, giggling at Anneliese's frantic legume-wrangling. "Miss Cora said she had a headache and went home early."

Miss Cora was Kate and Jack's mother. "I hope she feels better," Anneliese said.

In the end, there were enough peas, and Chloe went out to draw on the driveway with her brand new sidewalk chalk. From the kitchen, Anneliese could hear Chloe singing to herself.

The singing was cut short by a joyous announcement.

"Kate-Kate! Nan!"

Anneliese met her friends and led them through the gate and onto the porch. Kate carried a huge basket wrapped in cellophane and a yellow bow. Nan held a bucket spilling over with hosta. Chloe was drawn to Nan like a magnet, pressing her face to their friend's midsection.

"Nan, is the baby listening to me? Hi, baby!"

Anneliese drew Chloe back, hugging her. "The baby can hear you, kiddo. I bet they're excited to meet you, too, but right now? I need you to run upstairs and put your toys in the baskets so we can show off your room."

Chloe dashed off, leaving the three women alone. Anneliese turned to her pregnant friend. "How are you feeling?"

"Done with morning sickness, I think. Ready for a long weekend away." Nan touched her belly, and Anneliese's hands reflexively came to rest on her own.

Kate handed over her basket. "We brought you presents."

"Kate brought treats. The hostas are from the inn. They'll look great in the shady spots out front." Nan hugged her. "This place is so sweet. I can't wait to see how it all comes together."

Anneliese took the basket from Kate. "Sit. No, wait. Come see Chloe's room. It's the only thing I've finished. Then we'll sit. I made iced tea."

Kate took in the plain walls and bare floors on the first floor with a hopeful eye. "You're allowed to paint?"

"They're *reimbursing me* for the paint. I started upstairs."

They followed her up the narrow stairs to the small landing between her room and Chloe's.

Chloe was sitting in the center of a pile of plastic food and stuffed animals. "We started to clean up, Mama, but Feesh and Bear and Bubbles were hungry."

Nan crouched down. "I'm always hungry. Maybe it's the baby."

Chloe offered her a plastic bunch of grapes.

"What's the color?" Kate asked.

"Pearl Reef. And that's all my old furniture from my parents' place."

"I love it. When I was her age, I would have given my entire Cabbage Patch collection for a room like this." Kate wandered onto the landing between the bedrooms to peer at Anneliese's nearly empty room with a delicate lift of one brow. "Your space needs a little *something*."

From anyone else, Anneliese might have felt hurt, but she knew Kate better. "I know the mattress on the floor isn't much, but…"

Kate pursed her lips. "It'll do, but you are going to have to upgrade for proper booty calls."

"Shh," Nan said, with a furtive glance behind them where Chloe played. "Little ears."

"I'd rather she didn't take the term 'booty call' to school, thanks." Anneliese sighed dramatically. "My lack of them has probably been noted anyway."

Kate slung an arm around Nan's shoulders. "We need to get our girl laid."

Nan laughed. "Give her five minutes to get settled."

"Fine, but I'm going to think about it." Kate shrugged. "In the meantime, you need curtains…"

"I have ideas about curtains." Anneliese had never had a booty call in her life. Heavy make-out sessions were about as exciting as things ever got before she met Chad, and… Anneliese let that thought go. He held that over her as well. "Let's go enjoy the porch. I want to hear what you and Joss have planned for your babymoon, and I can show you my ideas for the rest of the house."

Kate headed downstairs first. "I'll put together a tray. Do you have a tray?"

"I have some moving boxes. Just drag one onto the porch for now," Anneliese called down.

Nan laid a hand on her arm, holding her back from going down the stairs. "Are *you* okay?"

"What? Yeah." Anneliese avoided meeting Nan's eyes for a beat. "I'm fine."

"You didn't look fine for a minute there. Is there something with the house?"

"No, the house is great." That she could say without hesitation. "It's just—"

The sound of shattering glass interrupted anything she might have said to Nan about Chad's check.

"Kate? You okay?" When Kate didn't automatically curse and reassure in the same breath, Anneliese started down the stairs, Nan hot on her heels.

Kate's face was bone white, her eyes frantic. She clutched her phone to her ear.

"I'll be there in five minutes. Hang on, Daddy." Kate's voice broke over her father's name. She hung up the phone but seemed to stare at the broken glass as if she wasn't seeing it.

"What happened?"

"My mom…something happened. She was non-responsive when they put her in the ambulance. I have to go." Kate started to leave, and then patted the pockets of her skirt, looking to Nan. "You drove."

Nan pulled her keys from her bag. "I'll take you over there now. You need to call Ewan."

"Right." Kate was trembling; her voice wobbled and cracked. Tears spilled over her lashes and she squinted at her phone. "I can't."

Anneliese touched her shoulder. "I'll call and tell him to meet you there. It's going to be okay."

Nan was already bundling Kate out the door and down the garden walkway.

"Where's everybody going?" When Chloe spoke, Anneliese started. She hadn't heard her daughter come downstairs.

Anneliese scrambled for a simple, truthful answer. "Miss Cora's not feeling well, honey. Nan's going to take Kate to see her."

Anneliese watched them go with a heavy heart. The Peases were a tight-knit clan, and Kate's mom Cora was the heart of it.

*Jack.*

Kate's brother would know by now, too. Was he already making plans to come north? For all his expensive habits and city living, Jack was fiercely devoted to his family. She pictured him, white-knuckling the wheel of his sleek car, pushing the engine to get him home to his mother before—

It didn't bear thinking about, and she'd made promises to her friend. Time to call Kate's husband.

Anything to take her mind off worrying about Jack Pease.

# CHAPTER 3

$\mathcal{I}$t didn't matter how many cars Jack passed, how many lane-shifts he wove through, the drive north unfurled endlessly ahead. Miles of hazy mountain horizon, periwinkle against the pale July sky, flew by unnoticed.

*Your mother's on her way to the hospital.*

He gripped the steering wheel and nudged the accelerator toward the floor. The Audi's engine responded, leaping ahead as Jack passed a tractor-trailer on the right and pulled into a stretch of open road along the curve of a hillside.

*I'm in the ambulance now. Your sister's on her way.*

In his haste to be on the road, he'd rushed from a late lunch with Barry with just the clothes on his back. Hopefully there was a spare toothbrush in the bathroom at his parents' house.

*We're not sure what happened.*

Jack checked his mirrors and streaked by a rusty pickup and a minivan. Below him, the Connecticut River wound down from Canada, dividing Vermont and New Hampshire. Typically, he would have dropped the top and let the sweet rush of summer wind into the car, enjoying the valley and the peaks of the still-distant Green Mountains. Today, the miles between his car and the hospital in his home-town were nothing but obstacles.

It took another hour and a half to make his way along state high-ways between the interstate and his family. He was shaking by the time he stepped out of his car, and the thick, wet punch of humidity nearly flattened him.

Ewan waited for him in the lobby. "They're upstairs."

He followed his brother-in-law into the elevator. "What's going on?"

"They did a bunch of tests—I'm sorry, I don't know which ones, probably a CT?" Ewan's eyes were shadowed with worry. "Some kind of emergency treatment, too. I guess they're waiting to see how she responds."

The elevator doors opened to a small, antiseptic waiting area. Kate was perched on a scratchy chair, and she leapt at the sight of him.

"I hate hospitals," she whispered in Jack's ear as he hugged her tight.

Ewan was in a serious accident of his own in their early months together. Kate declared it enough time in the hospital for the rest of her life.

"How is she?"

"It was a stroke." Kate let him go, drifting backward instinctively to land at Ewan's side. "They're saying this anti-stroke protocol might prevent irreversible brain damage, but she's still not awake, and it's going to be a long road, whatever happens."

"But she's alive." It wasn't a relief exactly, but a weight lifted. The shaky feeling in his extremities began to settle.

"First door on the left. Dad's in there, but I'm sure he'll let you have a minute."

The pale, intubated shell in the hospital room bore no resemblance to the woman who raised him.

His father didn't move from the seat by his mom's bed. He acknowledged his son with a slight nod. Jack couldn't summon words. He only stood there, drowning in mechanical clicks, whirs and beeps, the chemical scent of illness thick in his nostrils.

He slipped out as quickly as he'd come in, brushing past a nurse on her way in.

His father followed a moment later, his expression weary and shell-shocked. "They're saying we should go home for the night."

Kate and Ewan exchanged quiet words before Kate looked at Jack. "Can you drive dad home? He rode over with Mom."

"Of course."

Every fear, every question, every hope bottled up in his throat on the drive back to his parents' Chapel Street house. Easier to let it be for now.

His father spoke first. "I'm glad you came."

"Dad. Of course I came."

"Maybe your mom will be awake tomorrow."

"I have to head back tomorrow. I left my team in the middle of something." Jack squeezed the steering wheel. "But I'll be back Friday night after work."

They climbed out of the car in the last fading light of the day.

"We'll go together to see her again in the morning. Before you head back." His dad took a deep breath and fished in his pocket for house keys, then let them both inside. "Let me help you get your things. I think we can manage to get sheets on your old bed. More or less."

"I didn't bring anything with me. Not even a toothbrush."

"Your mom always keeps extra—" His dad's chin trembled at the mention of his wife.

Jack squeezed his father's shoulder. "I'll figure it out, but I might need some help finding the spare sheets."

Twenty minutes later, Jack was forced to agree with his father's assessment of the bed situation. More or less, with the emphasis on less.

He'd gotten soft. Wanda was a master of hospital corners, and his clean sheets always smelled of cedar. He couldn't remember the last time he'd made a bed, never mind tugged at the corners of worn, extra-long twin jersey sheets.

He found his father downstairs, holding an empty glass under the tap and staring out the window. Jack rummaged around in the fridge, but nothing said *easy dinner for two shattered men.*

"Want me to grab some dinner at the co-op?"

His father set the unused glass down in the sink. "I think I'm just going to try to get some sleep."

"Dad, when's the last time you ate?" His own stomach was well aware he hadn't eaten since his interrupted lunch.

"I'm not hungry. I think I'll just to go to bed." His father left the kitchen as if on autopilot.

Jack stayed in the kitchen until he heard the snick of the master bedroom door. He was starving, and in no mood to cook.

The prepared foods case at the co-op was a welcome sight. Jack packed compostable containers with a small fortune in cold sesame noodles, grilled Jerusalem artichokes in vinaigrette, Castelvetrano olives, and a couple miniature ciabattas.

He wasn't sure who he expected to eat it all with him, but take-out was at least something he could control.

"Jack Pease," the woman at the register gasped and reached for his hand. "What brings you home midweek?"

"Hi…" He should have been able to place the woman's face, it had been a hard day.

"Anneliese didn't say anything about seeing you."

*Anneliese.* He flushed when he finally recognized Anneliese's mother. Jane had stopped coloring her gray hair since his sister's wedding. Had anyone told him she was working at the co-op and not for the family's antiques shop?

He'd been away too long.

"She doesn't know I'm here. I—" *What the hell should I say?* "My mom's in the hospital. I drove up this afternoon."

"Oh, Jack. What happened?"

"It was a stroke." He pulled out his wallet. "We were at the hospital all day. I'm sure Dad would have called…"

"I'm sure he will. When he's ready." Jane's eyes were soft with sympathy. She'd known his mom all their lives.

Jack's throat tightened. "Thanks, Mrs. T. How are Anna and

Chloe?" He asked both to deflect the conversation from his mother, and because curiosity threatened to consume him. He hadn't been home in months, and when he had, Anneliese and her daughter had been conspicuously absent from any festivities.

A slight shadow crossed Jane's face. "They're well. We're going to miss having Chloe around every day, though."

"Are they moving out?" A thousand scenarios flashed through his imagination, each populated by a faceless man who claimed Anna as his own. A faceless man Jack wanted to pummel.

"Anneliese didn't tell you?" There was disbelief in her tone, and it rattled uncomfortably between them.

"I guess not." Jack hoped he sounded casual.

He swiped his card for the food, hoping Jane might elaborate. He suddenly needed to know where—and with whom—Anna had landed.

Mrs. Thompson started to bag his groceries, but Jack took over.

"You know she's been saving to move out since she came back. We expected her to get her feet under her again, but we didn't expect to get so used to having our granddaughter with us." Jane sighed. "It isn't as if they're going far. A ten minute drive and Anneliese will still need us to watch Chloe…"

She trailed off as she tore the receipt from the register and handed it to Jack.

"So she's downtown?" He hadn't fished so obviously in a long time.

"Oh!" Mrs. Thompson laughed. "Yes. She's rented the cottage next door to the Fletcher Hotel. Those young men who bought it last year just snapped up the cottage, too. Anneliese has been over there every night for a week painting and fussing."

"I had no idea." The cottage by the hotel. He was embarrassed at his relief at hearing there was no man involved in Anneliese's decision to move. His manners kicked in again. "It's good to see you, Mrs. Thompson. I wish it were under better circumstances."

"You too, Jack. Bobby and I will look in on your father this week, and I'll bring a casserole. You'll be in our prayers."

Jack stepped out of the co-op in a daze. The urge to see Anneliese was irresistible. The sticky day had given way to a heavy, soft evening, though heat still radiated from the sidewalks as he turned the wrong way around the common.

The wrong way to get home, but the right way to call on the cottage.

He had loved the whimsical house all his life. It sat just below the grand Edwardian mansion once owned by the wealthy Fletcher family. He thought he remembered the Fletchers had brought a housekeeping couple to live there and maintain the property. At some point, the property was split apart, and the cottage fell into disrepair. He always thought it was a little sad—a little romantic—the way the house faded deeper into its overrun gardens over the years.

It needed someone to love it. He couldn't think of anyone better for the task than Anna.

Jack approached the gate wishing he had flowers, but the garden reminded him she didn't need them. She had always loved being out in the woods and fields; she probably loved a garden to tend to. He resolved to bring her a watering can instead, and maybe some good garden tools.

*She wouldn't refuse a housewarming gift from an old friend, would she?*

The truth was, he didn't know.

His hand was on her gate when he heard the creak of chains on the front porch.

"Jack?" Anneliese appeared at the screen door. The setting sun lent a rosy tint to her fair skin, but it shadowed her familiar gray-blue eyes.

Her expression was cautious as she opened the door and started down the walkway. "Have you been here long?"

"I just got here. Thornton, and the gate. I was at the co-op and I saw your mother…" Suddenly inspired, he lifted the bag from the co-op. "Have you eaten? I have dinner."

"I haven't. I only got Chloe tucked in a little bit ago." Anneliese regarded the bag in silence. Jack could almost see her weighing the decision to let him in. "I don't have a table, but the porch floor has worked okay so far."

"Then it works for me," he said, following her up the two stairs and through the wooden screen door. "I didn't know you'd rented this place."

"I'm surprised Kate didn't mention it," Anneliese said. "I'll be right back."

She disappeared inside the house. Jack tried not to be irritated she didn't invite him in.

Only a moment later she returned to set plates and silverware on the porch floor before wrapping her arms around him. "I'm so sorry about your mom."

She fit under his chin, her cheek against his chest. He watched the pink light play over the seemingly endless shades of blonde in her messy bun; her hair smelled of mint and sunshine. She held him for a blissful moment before stepping back to regard him with that wary look. He wanted her to stretch her body up against his again, for her to hold him again; he wanted to bolt. Instead, he set down the bag still dangling from his hand.

"I hope you like cold sesame noodles."

*Cold sesame noodles?*

Anneliese's palms tingled. Her emotions fought to spill over, but she mastered them. The day was weird and fraught enough without Jack Pease at her gate. Jack Pease with dinner in his hands. Jack Pease in her arms.

He smelled expensive. He looked expensive, with his dark hair fashionably trimmed, and his lean, long-limbed frame filling out a small fortune in subtle designer labels.

When you'd been half in love with someone since you were a teenager—when you'd failed at puppy love, failed at marriage, and finally accepted romance was something for others—it did no good to lose your head when he turned up on your doorstep looking for a friend—and a friend was always how he'd seen her.

It had never been Jack's fault he was too cool, too casually arrogant, to notice how she felt. How could he have known? She'd never told him; she'd only quietly resented every girl he'd squired around their small Vermont town, his effortless success, the money and leisure time to enjoy his city of choice. To enjoy the women there, she knew. You couldn't be friends with his sister and not know.

She'd reached for Jack with the mixture of camaraderie, awkwardness, and unrequited desire that had haunted her for more than a decade. Though she'd meant to comfort him, she felt anything but comfortable.

Her meeting with Kirsten seemed a million years ago. Her parents, a mystery client, Chad's check, and then poor Mrs. Pease. She'd been sitting on the porch swing with a book, but her eyes had been skimming the same paragraph for an hour.

Anneliese busied herself setting the plates out and rummaging through the take-out bag. Better to keep her hands occupied than to dwell on the clean, woodsy scent of Jack's skin. Still, she was achingly aware of him as he took the containers from her and laid out a picnic between them. Then he sat with his back against the railing.

"How is your mother? Any news?" she asked.

Jack looked up from his plate of food. His eyes, the dappled deep brown she'd always known—still too extravagantly lashed to be fair—were full of pain. "They told us to go home. There was some kind of emergency therapy to stop the damage, and she's still in intensive care. I don't know exactly..."

She sat opposite him, leaning against the wall of the house. "She's going to make it through this."

"What if she doesn't?" Jack's voice was small.

Anneliese's heart clenched. Jack was always confident, often to the point of annoyance. Seeing him adrift opened doors in her heart she preferred to keep closed. She jabbed her fork at an olive, but the bright green fruit skidded away under one of the chairs.

He didn't say anything more. Crickets and night breezes filled the silence while they picked at the food.

Anneliese hated to ask, but speculation wouldn't do anyone any favors. "Kate didn't say much to Nan about what happened."

"A stroke. Apparently, she's had a couple of mini-events in the last few weeks. TIAs, they're called. Dad says once she passed out, and another time it was dysphasia."

He said the medical terms so clinically; Anneliese's chest tightened. "I had no idea. Kate never said."

"She didn't know. They didn't tell us." His tone turned bitter. "We weren't supposed to worry."

"Whatever you need, Jack. We're all here." It didn't matter that she'd gone out of her way to keep a safe distance between them. Before her unruly emotions, they were old friends. He needed her as much as Kate did.

*Maybe more*, her heart whispered. *He doesn't know how to cope with the fear of loss.*

He might need her, but he'd never love her. Not the way she wanted.

"Thanks, Anna." He reached out to touch her folded knee. "Really."

If it were Kate sitting on her porch, she'd have poured them both a drink. She withdrew from the casual contact and stood. "You know what; I think I have a bottle of wine around here. Hang on."

There was a halfway decent bottle of red Glenn and Jeremy had left for her. She grabbed it and two pint glasses from her measly kitchen supplies, and turned back toward the porch door.

She found Jack watching the Fletcher Hotel. In the golden glow of the porch light, a dozen people in ties and dresses milled around carrying champagne flutes. There was soft music and easy laughter on the humid night air.

"There's a wedding this weekend." Anneliese sat down with the wine and glasses. "That's the bride and groom's out-of-town guest reception."

Jack's voice was nearly a whisper. "Do you remember Mr. Cartwright's stories about the Fletchers?"

Anneliese pulled the cork and poured a couple of fingers of Beaujolais into each of the glasses, handing one over to Jack. She did recall their high school English teacher's stories about his youth in 1950s Thornton. He told the students about coming home from Korea, dances at the Legion Hall, and the way downtown used to look when he courted his wife.

"I mostly remember how he talked about Mrs. Cartwright."

Jack took the glass with a small smile. "I wonder what the Fletchers would think of their grand house turned into a boutique hotel."

"If they were as savvy as local legend suggests, they'd see it's the best way to preserve their legacy."

"Maybe." Jack leaned his head back against the rail and closed his eyes.

Anneliese sipped, watching the play of light and shadow on his face. In the soft light, she could still see the boy he'd been at seventeen. When he opened his eyes, Anneliese saw a hint of the Jack she'd loved as a girl sparkling back at her.

"Joss had Mrs. Donovan for English. Mr. Cartwright retired before Kate was a senior. You're the only one who remembers this stuff the same way I do."

Anneliese snorted. "I don't think we remember senior year the same way at all."

Jack drank from his pint glass of wine and picked an olive from his plate. "I remember the way you and Joss and I hiked all over the county, the notebook you had with a list of the best swimming holes. I remember all the years before we were seniors, when the three of us were friends."

His wistful tone found every chink in her armor; it also brought her own memories to the surface. *I remember how happy I was to tag along with you and Joss on all those adventures, how stupidly thrilled I was to be by your side. I remember how you asked Jenna Christensen to be your prom date. I remember how much I hated you for never seeing me until another boy wanted me.*

Anneliese forced the heavy memories away. "I haven't forgotten, Jack."

"It feels like you did." He reached for the bottle to pour more wine for them both. "Ever since you came home, you've kept me at arm's length. You and Kate and Nan are thick as thieves, Joss is family, even my brother-in-law gets to dance with you at weddings, but you hardly ever speak to me."

"I'm not keeping you at arm's length." She doused the fire that crept into her tone. "*You're* hardly around."

The denial burned. Truthfully, she *had* done her best to keep Jack at a safe distance. As if any distance were safe.

Wine washed some of the ashy dishonesty from her mouth.

JACK STRETCHED, BOTH TO RELIEVE THE CRICK FORMING IN HIS NECK from sitting on the floor and to pour the last of the wine into their glasses. The easy-drinking red, cool and juicy, was an unexpected antidote to the tension that bloomed between them. When Anneliese leaned away from him as he topped off her glass, he wondered if there was enough wine in the world to restore what they'd had as kids.

She was right. He wasn't always around.

She was wrong. She was definitely keeping a wall between them. A wall he wanted to scale, though he couldn't exactly say why.

The music still played at the hotel next door, but the party was moving inside. The porch lights went out, leaving them in velvet half-darkness. Jack knocked back the last of his wine. Anneliese's glass stayed where it was; she studied the view of the garden and the street over his shoulder.

It was time to go.

He pushed himself to standing. "Can I bring anything in? Help you clean up?"

Anneliese blinked up at him from the other side of the porch floor. "You're going?"

"I don't want my dad to worry if he wakes up." He laughed at the absurdity of it. And the truth.

She scanned the plates, glasses, and empty food cartons before standing up herself. "I'll clean this up. Don't worry about it."

"Are you sure?" He didn't want to impose, not now. Not when there was a ghost of a rapport forming.

"I am." The look she gave him was stern, but softened when he leaned over to bag up the containers.

He craved that softness from her. "Thanks for letting me hang out."

"You're welcome. I'm glad you dropped by." He wondered if it was a platitude, but—as she had when he'd first arrived—she stretched up to hug him.

When she moved to step back, he didn't let go right away. In his moment of hesitation, the shadows obscured her face. Only the curve of her lips and the dusky fringe of her eyelashes caught the ambient light from the street.

Her lashes lifted, her lips parted, and Jack succumbed to the spellbound sweetness. When she didn't pull away, he closed his eyes and tasted the wine on both their lips,

His hands splayed out over her back, rasping over stripes of dried paint on her shirt. The heat of her skin warmed the cotton. She leaned into him; her closeness was more vibrant than the wine, but he could feel her holding back.

He angled his head, seeking more, wanting more.

And then getting more.

Anneliese tightened her hold on him, drawing snug the distance between them. Her lips parted; she invited him in. Her kiss demanded, even as she sagged back against the porch wall, pulling him with her, letting the house take their weight. Time flowed like honey; there was only the feel of her.

His fingers threaded in her thick, silky hair; his hands traced the swell of her hips and then the length of her neck while they each explored, tasted, lost themselves in a kiss more than a decade in the making.

The porch light at the hotel snapped on and a quartet of party-goers spilled out into the night, their laughter jangling. The magic vanished. Anneliese ducked out of his arms and backed up against her screen door.

Jack held fast to the wall, looking at his feet. His blood raced, his head swam. The air cooled where she had been.

Anneliese's expression was dizzy when he sought out her eyes, but behind the pleasure, what he saw knocked the air from his lungs.

Shock, and fear?

*What had he done?*

"Anna…"

She bit her lip, then reached for the screen door handle and slipped inside, leaving Jack still holding himself at arm's length from the clapboards, with the wreckage of the evening at his feet.

*A*nneliese idled in her parents' driveway the next morning, running her finger along the jagged edge where she'd opened the envelope from Chad's bank.

The split-level ranch on the cul-de-sac north of Thornton was her childhood home. Her parents bought it just after she turned three, and with the exception of an update to the wallpaper in the early nineties, and her father's ever-expanding landscaping efforts, it was much the same as it had been in 1984.

Somewhere in one of the albums her mother kept tidily arranged in the living room, there were photos of places her parents lived before. Places where they'd laughed and been silly with their friends. Aunt Molly—actually her mother's cousin—and Uncle Walt, Jack's parents... When had they stopped being silly? Or more specifically, when had they become so consumed with appearances and good behavior?

Her mother and Molly Fuller had always been close, and Anneliese envied Joss his calm, affectionate, playful mother. She'd envied Jack his steady, fair parents, so obviously besotted with one another. Neither Anneliese nor her younger brother James had given them any trouble, but the specter of trouble seemed to haunt her mother especially.

Anneliese cherished the freedom found hiking and exploring as a child with Joss and Jack. Their status as family—or nearly so—excused their maleness, and between the boys and Anneliese's two best friends, Michelle and Sarah, she'd had everything she needed.

Anneliese heard the snap of a nearby screen door and for a moment was reminded of Jack's mouth on hers, his hands in her hair. Despite being just this side of drunk and obviously hurting, he kissed like a romance novel hero. Like she'd longed to be kissed for more years than she liked to admit.

Not at all like a childhood friend.

Half a restless night and a morning spent wrangling a soon-to-be kindergartener for her summer program hadn't banished the heat of that kiss. Her current errand was a splash of cold water.

Her mother's car was in the garage; Anneliese had called the night before to make sure her mother wouldn't be working this morning. This wasn't laundry she wanted aired at the co-op.

Anneliese let herself in, leaving her purse slung over the newel post on the landing just inside the door. "Mom?"

"In the kitchen."

Her mother stood in front of the kitchen sink, glasses perched on the tip of her nose, reading a magazine. She folded it back to save the page, and set it down next to a glass of water on the counter. Otherwise, the kitchen was spotless and photo-tidy.

"Chad's check came yesterday," Anneliese said.

"Oh, did it? That's good." Jane opened an upper cabinet and began pulling out cans and spice jars. "The bank was quick to get your information updated."

"About that…" Anneliese forced herself to stay calm. Nothing was ever gained by getting her mother's hackles up. "I haven't been in contact with Chad since before Jeremy and Glenn offered me the cottage. Almost three weeks ago. I haven't told him I moved yet."

"Oh, I did." Her mother said it casually, as though she were talking about Aunt Molly, Mrs. Pease, or any of her church group friends. "He called last week."

Anneliese's pulse throbbed beneath her breastbone. "What do you mean, 'He called last week?'"

"He's called once a month or so since the beginning of this year." Jane set down the last of her ingredients from the cabinet. "When he told me you weren't taking his calls, I thought he ought to at least know what his daughter was doing."

"He. Doesn't. Call. Me." Anneliese bit out each word to keep from screaming. "Not unless it's to tell me the quarterly check will be a biannual check instead, or that first year, that I wouldn't be getting anything until he filed his taxes. And even when he does call, he doesn't care what Chloe's doing."

"Calm down, Anneliese. He's Chloe's father, and he's taking an interest. If you don't want to talk to him, fine, but he's been nothing but pleasant with me."

"Please." A sudden wave of panic washed over her. Anneliese gripped the nearest chair back. "Please. Tell me you haven't let Chloe speak to him."

"He always calls while she's at school, so she hasn't talked to him." Her mother's mouth tightened, two brackets of disapproval forming around her lips. "If this is how you behaved when you were married, no wonder it didn't work out."

"Didn't work out?" Anneliese pushed the chair, making it rock on its legs. "He left us. Vanished for two weeks. A suite in Vegas while I coped with colic and no money for groceries. He backed me up against a wall with our daughter in my arms and told me I was lucky he hadn't put the baby down as collateral." She was shaking, her lungs heaving for air; the memory would never leave her. "Before Chloe, he just manipulated and belittled me until I didn't recognize myself anymore. Unless he decided he wanted sex."

Her mother remained cool. "There's no need to speak to me like that."

"There is if you're going to side with that monster."

"I am not taking sides." Jane breathed in deeply through her nose.

"It's just easier for me to see how you let your husband down. He made mistakes. Men do."

Anneliese fixed her mother with a hard stare. "Has Dad?"

Jane blinked. "Has Dad what?"

"Pushed you around? Gambled with your grocery and mortgage money? Threatened me or Jamie?"

"Of course not."

"*Men* don't." Anneliese backed up, leaning into the door frame to release some of the awful tension. "My ex-husband did. And when I told him I wouldn't stand for it anymore, he walked out for good. Served me with divorce papers, and took half of what little we had while he lied about his commissions to screw the child support."

Her mother's expression shuttered. "I don't appreciate that kind of language."

"What, *screw?* Trust me, Mom. He said a lot of far uglier things to me before it was over."

*You were a pity fuck, Anneliese. Too uptight. I didn't mean to get saddled with a fat wife and a screaming kid, but I was a sucker for the way you looked at me. At least you used to have great tits. You don't like me anymore? Fuck off. Fucking alimony would be better than your sad sack routine.*

Her mother dug around in a drawer for the can opener. "I'm only saying a marriage takes work and commitment. You were always a dreamer. I can see how you might misinterpret things."

"I didn't misinterpret, Mom. And please. I am begging you. Do not tell that man anything without asking me first."

"Fine." Jane snapped the drawer closed, the only indication her measured judgment verged on anger. "Now, I need to get a chili started for John Pease. He says Jack is coming back up this weekend, and they'll need food in that house."

Anneliese lost all her fight, deflating like a burst balloon. If not for the tremors in her fingertips and her pounding heartbeat, she'd have wondered if she'd imagined the whole argument. "That's kind of you. I'm sure Jack and Mr. Pease will appreciate home cooking."

She turned to leave her mother to the chili, but her mother had the last word. "It could be worse, you know. At least he sends you child support at all. Terri Beaudette's husband left and he never sent her anything."

Life barreled forward, regardless of ex-husbands, scorching kisses, or fights with your mother.

Haley Perkins's Sweet Sixteen was only a week away. Marian Muse was organizing a charity book signing with Ewan in November, and Kirsten Letourneau's name waited in her work inbox.

Anneliese took a mug of tea out to the porch to read Kirsten's email, which contained the non-disclosure agreement and the contract. All that remained was to get everything signed and collect the deposit, so she could start spending the mystery client's money.

Kirsten hadn't been kidding about a tight turn around. Anneliese shot a quick message to Nan about availability at the Damselfly. Might as well keep the event in the family, as it were. It was a long shot during prime foliage time, but a nearly bottomless budget might buy some extra wiggle room. Anneliese could rely on Kate for the cake, but the catering... She doodled a question mark in the margins of her notes.

She watched the whorls of steam rise off the surface of her tea. There were bees in the roses. Even a few blocks from the playground, Anneliese could hear happy noise from Cartwright Primary School. She was frankly envious of Chloe's days at the pilot full-year pre-school program. During the summers, the children were outside all the time, trundling to the public pool for swim lessons, holding their loops on the walking rope, or playing on the massive play structure in the campus courtyard. They were explorers, playing and learning in the fields and along the edge of the woods bordering the campus. And come September, Chloe would hopefully seamlessly transition to traditional kindergarten in the same familiar corridors and grassy expanses she'd been a part of for two years already.

*Focus, Anneliese.*

Easier said than done. The argument with her mother was close to the surface, along with worry for Cora Pease. Jack's kiss whispered against her lips in idle moments. Chad's sinister interest in their lives lingered in her shadows.

There was the mysterious client, and whoever referred her.

Once she'd whittled down her event to-do list, what remained meant cleaning her house. After years of shuffling her book club in and out of her parents' house, cringing when they left crumbs or dirty footprints on the carpet, and ignoring her mother's disapproving glances at the dirty wine glasses, she was hosting her first bookclub meeting.

She sang along with Grace Potter while she swept and dusted, crooned with J.D. McPherson while she cleaned the bathroom. She knew eventually the shine would wear off chores, but for now she was happy to take care of her own space.

She'd splurged on craft sodas and a tray of French macarons from Sweet Pease. She chose a book she loved, a lesser-known Daphne du Maurier novel whose book jacket read like a paperback romance, but whose wisdom touched a different part of her heart every time she read it.

Anneliese set out her mismatched glassware with pride, knowing that when her guests left, she had every intention of leaving the glasses by the sink. She would have the whole weekend to clean them.

When the first of her book club friends arrived at the porch door, there were flowers on her kitchen table, and enough seats cobbled together on the porch to allow the group to sit together and catch the breeze without offering themselves as a mid-summer feast to Vermont's seemingly horse-sized mosquitoes.

JACK SAT WITH HIS FATHER ON SUNDAY EVENING, AFTER VISITING HOURS, poring over his parents' schedule of benefits from the insurance company, their savings and retirement account statements, and his laptop, open to a dozen tabs' worth of information about stroke rehabilitation.

Two bowls of Jane Thompson's chili steamed untouched between them.

"She's awake and responding," John said. "The rest we'll figure out."

"Dad, her rehab could be months. She might need a nursing home, or long-term home care. I know you've been careful, but I'll feel better knowing you can handle this without losing your savings." Jack reached for the beer condensing on a coaster. "You focus on Mom; let me wrap my head around this stuff."

John's eyes crinkled. Relief had returned some of his humor. "I think I can handle it."

"I don't doubt it, Dad. I just worry."

His father nudged a bowl in his direction. "Jane's a fair cook. You haven't eaten since that stale bagel at the hospital this morning."

Jack's phone rang before he could get the spoon from bowl to mouth. It was Joss. "Hey."

"Kate called. Heard your mom's awake. That's great."

"Yeah." Jack tried to banish the way the left side of her face drooped, and the way her lips started to form words, but her eyes told him she couldn't get them out. "She's got a long road. Dad and I are looking at stuff now."

"Take the kid out, Joss," John called to the phone.

Joss laughed. "Tell your dad he got it in one. Ewan and I are taking you out for a beer. Meet us at Temple in half an hour."

Jack disconnected the call, and his father motioned to his bowl of chili. "Eat up. You don't want to collapse on the bar."

"Are you sure it's okay? I can stay."

"Jack, I'm going to eat, maybe watch the Sox game, take a look at my inbox. I'm sure Evangeline has everything organized, but I'm falling behind at the office after a long, weary week. Your mother's still with me, and I'll see her first thing in the morning. I'm going to be grateful for small mercies. Go have a beer with your friends."

Aside from the idea of calling his dad's formidable secretary, Mrs. Drake, by her given name, Jack couldn't find anything wrong with that argument, and twenty-five minutes later, he walked into Temple to grab a table.

"Jacky!" Deirdre Temple, the owner of the restaurant, was seating guests. She kissed his cheek enthusiastically, but there was sympathy in her eyes. "Heard about your mum. Give her our love, will you?"

"Course, Dee. Is my brother-in-law here yet? Or Joss?"

Deirdre pointed to the far corner. "'Round the other side of the bar in the corner booth. If you're hungry, have the lamb sausages. If not, have them anyway."

Jack laughed. "I'll take that under advisement."

He found Ewan and Joss. Ewan shifted over on the bench to make room.

Small talk busied them for a while. Ewan had been gone for a month of speaking engagements over the spring, and during one, Kate had visited her husband on the road and was approached by a publisher about a cookbook. Ewan took the inevitable ribbing about her good fortune with a wry shrug. Joss was bidding on a restoration project at Thornton College. Nan's second trimester was going more smoothly than the first, but she was still tired.

He'd missed so much.

"How's John holding up?" Joss asked.

"Practically dancing around the house because she squeezed his hand." Jack hated the bitter edge to his words, but worry and fear for his mother crowded out any optimism.

"He's been running on adrenaline for days. I'd be on a roller coaster, too."

"I guess." Jack flipped a coaster between his fingers. "To me, it's more like sprinting into a wall."

"Have her doctors said anything about what comes next?" Ewan asked.

"Only that we need to manage our expectations. She's not coming home right away." Jack ordered another round. "I'm a little worried about Dad trying to balance it all. His practice, Mom's rehab, the scale of what this could cost…"

Ewan nodded. "Scares the crap out of me, and Kate and I have a decent nest egg going."

Joss picked at the label on his beer bottle. "Try coming at it from a one-man small business. Or a family farm. Sucks."

"It's not like my parents weren't planning, but shit." Their server dropped a round of drinks off. "This could change their entire retirement."

"What if they hadn't been?" Joss said. "Planning, I mean."

"Adulting sucks." Ewan raised a glass. "To Cora and her swift recovery."

Jack and Joss clinked their bottles. A seed of an idea formed in his head. An idea that would take some of the pressure off his father. A week before he'd have have laughed out loud at the suggestion of coming home for an extended stay, but a week before he hadn't almost lost his mom.

A third round and a plate of lamb sausages later, Jack said goodbye to his friends and struck out for home.

At the common, he paused. He hadn't seen Anneliese the entire weekend, but he'd thought about her.

So once again, Jack took the wrong way home. The way that led around the common and past the Fletcher Hotel. The cottage was dark, as it had been the week before, save for a low light on the porch.

Jack unlatched the garden gate—no squeak, someone had oiled it—and made his way along the path, the leaning heads of delicate purple flowers brushing against his hip. He'd made a mess of things with her the week before. That kiss...the memory of which crept into his thoughts at inopportune moments during the work week. Between the dull ache of worry over his mother and the searing memory of Anneliese warm in his arms, it was a wonder the managing partner hadn't asked for his resignation.

The sound of whispers met him as he raised his hand to knock. His cheeks went hot; he hadn't lost his head over a woman since the last time he'd lived in this town.

Anneliese's whisper was telling a story. "But when the princess cut him free, all he could say was..."

A little girl's laugh answered, along with a big stage whisper, "Your dress is all dirty!"

He realized mother and daughter were on the porch. Anneliese's reply had the lightness of familiarity. Just as Chloe's laugh had. "So, the princess turned around and marched right home without him."

Jack heard the unspoken "the end" in Anneliese's voice.

"Can I have a song, too?" Chloe asked.

He'd meant to knock, to let them know he was there, but then Anneliese started to sing. Jack didn't know that he'd ever heard her sing before, and the notes stole his chance to announce himself. It wasn't that her voice was perfect, though he wouldn't have known if she was a little out of tune. It was the startling intimacy of listening when she didn't know she had an audience beyond her daughter. The song was pretty, melodic and tender, and she sang it sweetly, without pretense. He heard how it was a gift for Chloe, and he felt awful and awkward, lurking there in the shadows.

When the song ended, he turned to slip silently away, but children's toys were notorious tattletales. He kicked a stray piece of sidewalk chalk on the flagstones, and sent it skittering over the stones and into the flowers.

"Hello?" Gone was the husky, gentle whisper. Anneliese's tone was cool and sharp. "Is someone there?"

He stepped away from the door. "It's me. Jack."

Anneliese materialized from the deep shadows. She wore men's pajamas and her long blonde braid hung over one shoulder. His body tightened in response.

"What are you doing here?"

"Mama?" Chloe emerged behind her mom.

He'd interrupted story time, and now he was lusting after someone's mom in her pj's. "I was at Temple with Joss and Ewan. I thought I'd...I didn't think about bedtime. I'm sorry."

"Me and Mama are having a porch sleep," Chloe said.

He looked between them. Chloe was so like Anneliese, small and blonde, with gray-blue eyes, but since he'd seen her last—could it have been a year?—her hair had grown and she seemed more like a small person.

Anneliese relaxed a fraction, but didn't move to open the door. She turned, revealing a makeshift tent made from a sheet slung over some clothesline. Underneath, a camping lantern and a cozy nest of pillows and blankets waited. "Like a slumber party and camp out, but with fewer bugs."

"I'm sorry I disturbed the porch sleep," Jack told Chloe, whose attention was waning. She drifted back to the blanket fort, where her stuffed clownfish waited.

Anneliese answered by changing the subject. "How's your mom?"

"Awake, responding." Jack said. It had become rote, automatic and both true and a gross oversimplification of the situation. "She'll be able to have more visitors next week."

"I'll come by as soon as it's okay."

"Thanks, Anna."

Anneliese glanced at Chloe, then back to him. "Good night, Jack."

"Good night," he said, backing down the stairs and mustering what remained of his dignity, wincing when he stumbled over a forgotten stick of sidewalk chalk.

So much for dignity.

# CHAPTER 5

Kirsten Letourneau met Anneliese at the empty granite chapel on the shore of Seven Sisters Pond.

"The college owns all of this land, including the barn we're going to tour later. It's available for rentals." Anneliese turned in the cool dim air of the chapel. "Imagine it full of candles and flowers and rented chairs. It'll look like a fairytale."

Kirsten's eyes sparkled. "You don't even know who you're working for, and you're already ninety-percent there."

"When *am* I going to find out?" Anneliese asked. "I signed everything."

"I know," Kirsten tapped her phone, swiping a couple times before turning the screen to face Anneliese. "Anneliese, meet Lela Tan, social media queen and style icon."

Smiling through the video call was a young woman with golden skin, ink-black hair and dark eyes. "I'm so glad to meet you, finally. I'm sorry I can't be there, but I'm doing a photo shoot in Cabo today, and then Grant and I are going to be at Frankie and Buffy's launch party. They've got this new boutique distillery opening in Jackson Hole…"

Frankie and Buffy were names Anneliese recognized—stars of a celebrity property makeover show focused on outdated homes of former celebrities. Lela Tan's name she knew from magazine shoots of young celebrity weddings. "It's a pleasure, Ms. Tan."

"Lela, or Lee," Lela insisted. "Where are you? I love the vibe."

"It's a ceremony site I'm suggesting for you." Anneliese switched into professional mode, painting over the bare walls and empty space with her nascent ideas.

Lela clapped. "Kirsten, I'll send you the drawings from Monique. You two can start on the concept for this place right away."

Kirsten flipped the phone back to herself. "Anything else you need for Wyoming?"

With practiced taps, Kirsten switched the call to voice-only, giving Anneliese the "hang on a sec" hand wave.

Anneliese drifted outside to sit on a rock by the water.

Seven Sisters was a glacial depression three miles off the state road near the crest of the Green Mountains, a droplet of crystal water in a deep expanse of green. In the bare seasons, you could see the tops of the college's ski lifts from the chapel doors, but now the canopy over-head shaded the clearing around the building.

They would arrange for luxury transport for the guests, keep the cars on the access road to a minimum. Bring in the high-end mobile restrooms the college hired for functions—here, and at Frost Barn on the Mountain Campus.

"Anneliese?"

Kirsten sat next to her. "I put Lela back on video for a last look. She says to go ahead."

"Just like that?"

Kirsten shrugged. "Lela trusts her intuition—and she likes you."

"Based on a moment of FaceTime?"

"Intuition." Kirsten stood, taking in the near-perfect roundness of the pond. "It's like a painting came alive up here. Will we be able to bring in a few conveniences?"

Anneliese turned the notebook where she'd been writing her thoughts to face Kirsten. "Something like these?"

"You are good."

"I am." Anneliese stood. "Should we drive over to the barn? I'll talk you through my plan."

～

"Dad?" Jack stepped onto his parents' deck. His dad was hooking up a propane tank to the grill.

John Pease rocked back on his heels. "What's up?"

"How many hours would you say you'll spend with Mom next week?"

His dad didn't answer right away. A cloud passed overhead, shadowing his father's face; Jack couldn't read his expression.

The idea that had taken root at Temple had grown. Jack had run his version of the numbers, and he wasn't sure how his father would be able to keep up with his caseload and his wife's care. He could retire—close the practice or sell to someone younger and local—but that hadn't been in the cards for at least another five years.

"I don't want you worrying about all this, Jack. We'll work it out." John closed the aluminum doors concealing the tank. "You and Katie have lives to lead."

Jack had lain awake considering that very thing. On paper, he did have a life to lead. The race to make partner, the endless grind of briefs and trials and client drinks, the Sox games, the box seats at the Harbor Pavilion. His life had been very good to him. And he had generous leave accumulated. He hadn't yet used any of his annual four paid weeks of vacation. There hadn't been time between cases to jet off the way he'd always assumed he would.

His family, his best friends...Anneliese... They were all here. Even Seth, his oldest friend who wasn't from Thornton, spent less time in New York and more time at his Church Street gallery in Burlington.

*Could he be useful here?*

He could apply to the Vermont bar for reciprocity; his Massachusetts and New York bars would suffice. How hard could it be to run a family legal practice for a few months?

"I have about twelve weeks of leave I can use, Dad. Let me handle the practice for a while. Take the pressure off you and Mom."

"Son," his father began, "I can't ask—"

"You didn't ask. I offered."

"I don't know, Jack. That's a lot for you to give up, and a lot to take on."

The slight softening in his father's tone told Jack the idea was taking root. "Let me be the judge of that." Jack ignored the little ball of flat-out panic in his chest and focused on the warmth in his dad's bear hug.

It turned out, in addition to being comfortable and pleasurable, his life was also easy to set aside. Including the time to drive back to Boston, it took a matter of days to box up—literally and metaphorically. That truth put Jack's life into harsh perspective.

Saying goodbye to his office hurt more than the idea of turning over the keys to his apartment.

The apartment existed to support basic bodily necessities: showers, sleep, sex. His office was where he felt most grounded.

Jack paused, watching the airborne ballet of planes beyond the glass. There was more to him than his Juris Doctor—wasn't there?

A knock on his office door startled him. Iris didn't wait to be invited in.

"I thought we might get lunch. I'll miss you while you're away."

They left the building in easy quiet, both turning without discussion to their noodle shop.

Over a split hot sake, Jack inferred the question she didn't ask. "Twelve weeks. To help out with my dad's law office and my mom's recovery." Jack finished checking off their choices on the tear-away order sheet.

Iris laid her slim, slightly chapped hand over his across the table. Jack regarded her ragged cuticles. They'd bonded learning to paddleboard on the Charles, but rowing was her first passion. He'd always liked the way she smelled of river water and sweat, after taking her scull out in the morning.

"She's going to be okay." Again, it wasn't a question.

"That's what everyone keeps saying, so I'm choosing to believe it."

Jack steered the conversation to Iris's Barcelona plans. It wasn't until their bowls appeared in front of them that she brought up his leaving again.

"You're a good son, Jack." She dipped her spoon into her broth, regarding him with a twinkle in her eyes. "Some poor girl who secretly loved you in high school is going to run into you at the grocery store and lose her mind."

A rusty laugh escaped Jack's throat; it sounded more like a cough. "Not likely. My prom date is married and living outside DC, and except for—"

*Anneliese. That was complicated.*

He gave Iris a wry smile. "Let's just say I was kind of a dick in high school."

"So, you've always been a player." Iris appraised him, lips pursed. "I'm sure there's someone who recalls you fondly."

He plucked a whole shrimp from the nest of noodles. "I'm not."

Later, when lunch and the rest of his meetings to arrange his leave of absence were through, he met Iris again in the lobby.

"Come have a drink at my place before you have to face yours."

He didn't think there was much to face. He'd need some of his clothes, but everything else that mattered would be packed away until his return. That didn't stop him from walking Iris through downtown and up the hill to her Pinckney Street apartment.

They took a bottle of wine to her roof deck.

"Tell me about your town. I want to imagine you there, reliving your glory days."

"It's gorgeous. It's also small and far from anything resembling a city. The college is about as close to civilization as you'd recognize."

"I grew up in a village on the Icelandic coast, Jack. I'm a city girl by choice, but small towns are in my blood," Iris reminded him.

"Those were hardly my glory days. If I've had them, they were here, maybe the first couple years after law school, before my stint in the New York office."

"Maybe it wasn't football..." Iris scrutinized him over her glass.

"But you were definitely the captain of some sports team, and I'm certain there were girls draped all over you. I bet you even made a few of them feel like princesses. One of them," she draped a long arm over the back of her wicker settée, the bowl of her wineglass titled just so, "must be pining away for you."

"Jesus. You make me sound like an ass."

Iris's wide smile glinted and a chorus of honking from the street below punctuated her point. "You are, Jack. A kind, handsome, charming ass."

She sipped, set her glass down, then leaned on her knees. "It's so lovely, being with you. An adventure, with none of the drama of not knowing where you stand. That's always quite clear. Lust, enjoyment. *Joie de vivre*, but never love."

"I never lied about that." He disliked the defensive whine in his voice.

"No, you never do. It's decent, but infuriating. And I think no woman until now has had the heart to tell you, because you always take such care."

"It's not like I've broken anyone's heart."

As soon as the words were spoken, he saw Anneliese in the dim light of her porch, watching him warily. Anneliese keeping her distance since her return from California. Anneliese on prom night, suddenly so much more than a childhood friend or his best friend's cousin. Suddenly so far out of reach in the arms of that guy...what was his name?

"I think you have." Iris's voice was soft, punctuated by a rare inquiry. "Who is she?"

"Anna. Anneliese."

"Is she in Vermont?"

Jack nodded.

Iris stood, picking up the half-empty bottle and her glass. "Then we have work to do."

Jack followed Iris into the apartment where she was already unfolding a slim laptop. He wasn't surprised when she found him a sub-letter in less than forty-eight hours.

# CHAPTER 6

*J*ack prowled the office while his dad collected a few papers from his desk and pondered the list—along with a mug of milky coffee—left by Mrs. Drake. The fearsome secretary was at her desk, having ruthlessly filed everything—likely twice—and straightened Jack's collar by way of welcome.

He'd arrived in Thornton the night before, so late he'd missed seeing anyone, even his dad, but that hadn't stopped him driving by the Fletcher Hotel.

Anneliese's lights had been out.

Now it was time to put his degree where his mouth was, and relieve his father of the burden of work.

Pease Family Law occupied a tiny house down the road from the co-op. The nineteenth-century, single-story four-square home was creaky and drafty, with hand-hewn floorboards and crooked door-ways from more than a century of settling. Jack had always loved it, though he'd never wanted it for his own.

"Mrs. Drake looks well." Jack studied a photograph of his family at the West Family Tree Farm, matching pom-pom hats and goofy smiles flanking a seven-foot blue spruce. Kate's adult front teeth had come in, dwarfing her childish face. Jack's hair was buzzed ruthlessly short. He couldn't recall which year it had been taken.

John looked up at his son through tortoise-shell bifocals. "She's been wonderful. You'll be glad of her when you get into my cases. She's got an impeccable memory for every case I've ever handled."

Jack turned back to the photo to hide his nerves regarding both this decision and his father's secretary. "I'm sure she does."

He heard his father sigh behind him. "I can't imagine this was an easy choice for you, Jack. I am grateful."

Jack replied without turning around, hoping he sounded more confident than he was. "I know, Dad. You just focus on Mom for now. I've got this."

"Why don't you head over to the hospital? I'll finish up a few things here and join you later."

His father's somewhat distracted dismissal stung. He'd expected to feel more like the hero of the hour, and less like an interloper. There was no room in the small space for his bruised ego, though, and with a brisk farewell from Mrs. Drake, Jack struck out for Main Street.

The previous evening's mugginess had given way to a mild, sunny morning, the kind that picked up your step whether you meant it to or not, and Jack let the buoyancy of blue skies and river song carry him the mile to the hospital. He passed a group of Thornton College summer students carrying leftovers from Rick's Diner; their laughter harmonized with traffic and birdsong.

Unless you counted the few blocks between his parents' Chapel Street house and Temple or Rick's, Jack hadn't roamed the center of the town alone since before he left for Williams. His increasingly rare visits home were busy ones, occupied by family dinners, drives to Burlington, nights at Joss's cabin with his friends or late nights catching up with his sister.

There were houses newly painted, houses grown shabby, fresher sidewalks, and a new park where College Street joined Main. The hospital had a new wing, and a garden in front, full of flowers, vegetables, and a buzzing, fluttering cloud of butterflies and bees.

His mother had mentioned in passing her work on fundraising for the garden. Jack hoped, as he approached the reception desk, she would enjoy it again soon.

Armed with directions to his mother's room, Jack made his way down the elevator corridor. Crammed with plush bears and cats, Mylar balloons, and a small cooler full of floral arrangements, a small gift shop stood vigil nearby. He jabbed the third-floor button between the two sets of doors, then noticed a spray of white daisies at eye level in the floral cooler.

He ignored the ping of the arriving elevator car to buy his mother flowers.

He hadn't considered that she might be asleep. Or that she would have a roommate. Or a roommate's visitors.

"Excuse me. Sorry, I'm just here to see my mother."

A woman scarcely ten years older than he was, if he had to guess, was propped up watching a cooking show with the closed captions on while a man sat next to her bed with a little boy on his lap. The boy buried his face in the man's shirt. Jack understood the impulse. The woman's arm was in a sling, and like his mother, she was hooked up to a number of monitors and fluids.

"Hey. Let me pull the curtain," the man said kindly, shifting the boy and standing to slide the privacy curtain on its ceiling track.

Jack nodded. "Thanks. Appreciate it."

The metallic scrape let him know he was unobserved.

Every surface near Cora Pease's bedside was covered in flowers and cards, awaiting his mother's smile when she woke. There wasn't room for the ones he brought, so Jack pulled the wilted stems from the existing bouquets and replaced them with his fresh daisies. When he was done, he tossed the dead blooms in the trash can and pulled up the hard-backed chair.

For a long while he just sat quietly, watching the rise and fall of his mother's chest, lulled by the clicks and whirs of the machinery around him. The ashen, hollow look was gone from her face, but she still seemed half a stranger.

His attention strayed to the conversation from the other bed. They were expecting the woman to be released by week's end. Jack gathered there had been some kind of car accident that landed her in the hospital.

After saying a long goodbye, the man and boy behind the curtain parted the blue fabric and ducked out. Jack returned the little boy's solemn wave over the man's shoulder.

"She has wonderful friends." The voice behind the curtain was gentle and weary.

Jack got up and peered around the curtain to where his mother's roommate still sat up in bed, the TV remote under her hand. "She does. A less wonderful son, I'm afraid."

"You're here. And you brought her fresh flowers." She turned off the television. "You're Jack."

Jack smiled. Thornton was so small. "I am."

"I'm Gwen. I've heard your name a lot since they moved her in."

Jack reached to shake her uninjured hand. "Jack Pease. It's a pleasure to know someone kind is sharing her room."

Gwen took his hand. Her grip was firm and warm. "You have a nice voice. You should read to her."

"Read?" He blinked, looking around the room. "What?"

Gwen fished around on her nightstand, shuffling aside a pile of magazines until she found a copy of *Vermont Life*. "There's an article on farming families. I tried to read it, but I hit my head in the accident, and it still hurts my eyes…"

Jack chuckled. "I see."

Gwen waved the magazine in front of Jack with a grin, gesturing toward the seat near his mother's bed. "I think you do."

He read three articles to Gwen before his father arrived.

"Still sleeping?"

Jack nodded, offering Gwen's magazine. "You can keep reading."

His father took the magazine, but Gwen shook her head. "I've imposed enough for one day."

"Beats daytime TV." John flipped the magazine open and picked up reading a book review.

"Anything you need from the office, Dad?"

"No, son." John barely looked up. "Tell Evangline thank you for the flowers."

Back at the office, Mrs. Drake nodded brusquely over her glasses when Jack thanked her.

The only person who seemed genuinely glad to see him was a stranger in a hospital room. It was shaping up to be a hell of a first day home.

Jack was reading through a real-estate transfer for a couple from two towns over, making sticky notes to email a colleague at Kearney-Mulligan about the finer points, when his sister cruised into the office.

"Don't you knock?"

"I don't need to." Kate was unapologetic. "Mrs. Drake likes lemon scones."

"You bribed Dad's secretary?"

"I did." Kate plopped into the chair opposite him and deposited a hot pink paper bag between them. "I brought you a treat, too."

Jack snatched the bag before Kate could take it back. Her lemon scones were light, tangy, and never too sweet. "What's up?"

"I haven't seen you since you pulled a prodigal and moved back into your boyhood bedroom." She pouted. "You used to call me when you came home."

"I got in late last night."

"You do look tired." Kate leaned back in the chair and scrutinized him.

Jack raked a hand through his hair. "I don't know what I was thinking." He pushed away the contract paperwork and the sticky note dispenser, knocking over the bag of scones. "I've been doing the same kind of work for a while now, it's pretty specialized. What I know about real-estate law, or wills, or any of the stuff Dad handles fits in that paper bag."

Kate straightened the bag. "Easy on the baked goods."

It was all too much, the prospect of new clients and their problems, broken up by quiet evenings at home with his father, while his mother faced an uncertain prognosis he couldn't fully grasp yet. He'd picked up the phone to text Joss, to call Kate, a hundred times since the night before, and found himself at a loss. Joss and Nan were nesting at the inn. Kate and Ewan were house-hunting, attending book signings, and managing Kate's two bakeries.

And Anneliese...

Kate waved her hand in front of his face. "Earth to Jack?"

"Sorry."

"You need full immersion therapy. STAT." Kate stood, whipping her phone out of her pocket. Her fingers flew over the screen, answered by a series of pings. "The Damselfly. Tomorrow night at five. Nan says, 'bring beer.'"

"How do you do it?"

"What?" Kate's forehead wrinkled. "Plan stuff? Hi. Have you met me?"

"No, Katie. Stay so positive. With Mom and everything..."

Kate pushed her phone into the back pocket of her jeans. She came around the desk and leaned down to wrap her arms around him. "Mom is going to be okay. I just keep believing that. And hanging on to you and Dad and Ewan and Nan when I forget. There's too much good in my life to give up on her. Like she says," she released him and mustered her best impression of their mother, "joy is a verb, Jack."

ANNELIESE WAS THE FIRST TO ARRIVE AT THE DAMSELFLY INN. THE front door was open, but the office was empty. The heat of the day was giving way to a gentle, warm evening, so she opted to go through to the terrace and leave her things in the screened-in porch.

Nan was already there, feet propped up on the chaise in the corner. "Kate's on her way. We'll have time for some planning before Joss and Ewan get back."

*What about Jack?* Anneliese bit her lip to keep from asking. "Where are the men off to today?"

"Ewan wants to learn some basic carpentry. They went on a field trip to the lumberyard."

Anneliese tried—and failed—to envision Kate's husband swinging a hammer. "Ewan's going to build things?"

"He says it's for book research, but between you and me—"

Kate pushed the screen door open. She carried a huge wicker picnic basket. "Between you two what?"

Nan laughed. "I think Ewan might be domesticating."

"Oh, totally. The moment we decided to buy a place, he was all, 'Alasdair is hiring a contractor, so I should ask Joss about carpentry.' Mmhmm." Kate rummaged in the basket, pulling out a glass container. "I made marshmallows, so we have to have a campfire."

Anneliese watched Kate unpack containers, bags, even a pitcher. "Are there six other people coming?"

"It's not all for tonight," Kate said. She set a travel platter with a snap-on cover on the glass table in the middle of the seating area. "If we're going to bombard you with baby shower planning, you should get to sample snacks."

"We're baby shower planning? When are we thinking?" Anneliese took the lid off the platter. "Ooh, is this the lavender thing we had the other day?"

"Yep. I needed a distraction." Kate dropped into a seat opposite and cut a slice of tasting cake onto a plate for Nan. "Did she tell you about her big meeting?"

Nan leaned forward to grab a fork. "No."

"I have a gig doing a celebrity wedding in three months. It's all super-secret, except for the part where I'm hoping she'll hire you both, and you can be in on it. I love the bride's P.A. already."

"A celebrity bride with a personal assistant. Ooh." Nan's eyes went wide. "So, that's why you emailed about occupancy."

"We're definitely going to need to talk. I want to do it at the Thornton College Mountain Campus. But it would take some crazy planning, and I want to book the inn for the bride and her entourage if we can find a weekend on short notice."

"So," Kate said, "we should plan the shower for September, so Nan has all her baby stuff well in advance of crazy town."

Nan checked the calendar on her phone. "I can do the shower in early September. If you want me to hold the inn for a weekend, we should decide that soon. People are going to start booking foliage trips."

Kate giggled. "Leaf-peepers."

"Okay," Anneliese got her notebook out of her purse and dog-eared a page. "Now, where are we thinking for the shower?"

"Let me guess," Nan said to Kate. "You've been house hunting, and there's one there with real potential." She turned to Anneliese. "I'm betting she wants to have it there."

"Anna, you have to see it," Kate said. "If we can close in time, we could totally do it. There's this open floor plan…"

Nan grinned at Anneliese. "She's smitten."

Anneliese wrote down *Kate's house*, but also *Molly's?* and *Sweet Pease?* "Have you decided if you're going to find out the gender, or should I be thinking about a neutral color scheme?"

Nan's expression went soft, and her hand drifted to her belly. "We're going to let it be a surprise."

"How am I going to buy baby clothes in *neutrals?*" Kate teased.

Nan cocked an eyebrow. "You'll manage."

Anneliese closed her notebook. "How's your mom, Kate? Any change?"

"None so far." Kate stretched out her feet. "My dad is keeping his head above water, but it's Jack I'm worried about. He's not himself. I mean, none of us are exactly, but he's been holed up at the house and Dad's office or the hospital for two days. He hasn't really talked to anyone. That's why I called an emergency hang-out."

"Your dad's office?" Anneliese forgot to keep the naked curiosity out of her voice.

"Oh my gosh, I completely forgot to tell you," Kate said in a rush. "He offered to use some of his paid time off to take over for my dad for a few months while Mom's recovering. Living in his old room and everything."

From the lack of surprise on Nan's face, Anneliese figured she was out of the loop on her own.

Her thoughts turned to the night he arrived on her porch—the stilted conversation, the sparks, and the flashes of old anger. He'd talked to her a little about his fears then, but he'd never said anything about coming home.

She considered revealing he'd been by to talk, but she'd always worn her heart on her sleeve. To confess the sweetness would confess the rest.

"You're quiet over there." Nan was watching her with concern.

Anneliese shook her head. "Just woolgathering."

"I'm telling you," Kate said, "we need to get her a man, pronto. She needs to christen her new bedroom."

"I'm practically a born-again virgin, Kate. There's no rush."

"What about the guy who raises the Highland cattle?" Nan asked. "What's his name?"

"Nick." Kate reached over to slice the next tasting cake. "He's nice. But maybe too old? Oh, I know. Rashid, the head chef up at that bistro in Bristol. Last time I flirted a recipe out of him, he was single."

"I know Rashid," Anneliese said. "He moonlights catering small parties. He's not interested in me."

Kate tilted her head. "How do you know that?"

"He asked if he could fix me up with a cousin of his who's moving up here from Atlanta to help him with the catering side of things. His cousin won't mind about Chloe, either. Pretty sure that means Rashid doesn't want me for himself."

Nan giggled. "Fair enough."

"I wish we could find a guy like Jack," Kate said. "Just not so much like Jack. Basically, I need another brother, so we can keep you in the family."

"I've already got her in the family," Nan said.

A text message from her mother chimed on her phone, and Anneliese seized the opportunity to change the subject. To anything but Jack.

"Mom's on her way to drop Chloe and her sleepover things at Molly and Walt's. I'm going to walk over there in a sec to say hi and bring Chloe here for a while." Anneliese looked pointedly at Nan's belly. "She equally excited about s'mores and visiting the baby. So, if

Rashid is a no-go, tell me about this Nick who raises Highland cattle."

~

LATER, WHEN JACK PARKED AT THE DAMSELFLY, THE ONLY SPACE LEFT was between a pickup from Delaware and a Beetle from South Carolina.

The inn rested in the broad canopy of a maple tree, surrounded on three sides by the Fuller Dairy's pastures and a stand of fir trees. He followed music and laughter around the house, a welcome sound after the distracting quiet of his father's office and the endless buzzing and beeping at the hospital.

Jack took a moment to admire Joss's handiwork. He'd been busy with additions to the innkeeper space. New gables blended seamlessly with the Victorian's existing lines, and a new semi-private screened-in porch occupied the space under the expanded second floor. Safe from late summer mosquitoes, Kate and Ewan were talking about the house they were putting an offer on.

It all seemed so painfully normal.

Jack rapped on the door as he pulled it open. He'd picked up a growler of something seasonal from the local brewery and a four-pack of crisp hard cider, and these he deposited on a potting bench that served as a sideboard.

Nan patted the seat next to her on the wicker sofa.

Jack dropped next to her and leaned over to kiss her cheek. "Hey, beautiful. How're you feeling?"

Nan rubbed the slight swell of her pregnancy with a smile. "Tired, a little seasick in the mornings, but good. How are you?"

He considered the truthful answer: frustrated, sad, frightened, distracted and confused. Instead, he adopted his usual cheer. "You know me, life of the party."

Nan laughed, but he swore he saw understanding in the small crinkles at the corners of her eyes. "It won't be for too long. You'll be back to your urban delights before you know it."

Jack took in the stargazer-scented air, his sister's musical laughter, and the golden light of the sinking sun. As he watched the shadows lengthen across the lawn, Anneliese appeared from the breezeway, hand in hand with her daughter.

Some delights were Thornton's alone.

Joss followed, stepping ahead to hold the door open for her. He was balancing a stack of bowls in his hands. Anneliese was laughing at something he'd said, unaware she was observed. The carefree laughter floated around her; the slanting light gilded her hair and the fluttering sleeves and skirt of her dress. Chloe broke away and skipped across the patio to the screen door.

"Nan! Is the baby still inside?" Chloe let the door bang shut and jumped across Jack to burrow in close to Nan's midsection, laying her ear on the baby bump. "She wants me to be her big sister."

"You're going to be the best big cousin." Nan ruffled Chloe's curls —the same color as her mother's but a tumble of ringlets like a wild Shirley Temple. "What if the baby's a boy?"

"Boys are okay, too." Chloe clambered down and met her mother at the door. "Can I have my ponies?"

Anneliese motioned to a monogrammed tote bag. Chloe immediately dug through, triumphantly producing three plastic ponies in improbable colors.

"Chlo', did you say hello to Mr. Pease?"

*Mr. Pease?* Anneliese's reminder made him sound like a stranger.

Chloe stopped short, and turned to Jack, ponies clutched between her hands. "Hi, Mr. Pease. I brought Applejack and Cupcake and Rainbow Dash."

Was he really such an infrequent visitor in the little girl's world? He tried to remember if he'd spent any real time with her since Kate's wedding. Before that, she'd been a chubby toddler who hadn't needed a name for him.

"I like the orange one, and," he sought out Anneliese's eyes, "if it's okay with your mom, call me Jack."

Chloe looked to her mother, who nodded tersely.

"The orange one is Applejack. You can be her because your names are the same." Chloe deposited the small orange horse on his leg. "I'll be Cupcake and Rainbow Dash. It's time for flying school."

Jack picked up Applejack and inspected the plastic horse's apple tattoos before looking it square in its enormous green eyes. "Hey there, namesake. Let's learn to fly."

Chloe danced her two ponies over his bent knees. The one with the rainbow hair had wings, and was trying to teach the others. Chloe's optimism was infectious, as were the giggles he got for letting Applejack cheerfully fail at flying.

He glanced up during a break in Chloe's narrative to find Anneliese watching him with an unreadable expression. She held a bottle of cider loosely in one hand and was ostensibly listening to something the others were discussing, but for a moment he held her gaze. He desperately wanted to find approval there.

"Applejack, it's not nap time." Rainbow Dash was scolding Applejack for lying down on the job. Jack straightened the pony and returned to the task at hand, painfully aware of his awkward emotions.

When Anneliese interrupted flying lessons to sit Chloe down in front of a bowl of grilled chicken, tomatoes, and cucumbers, Nan handed Jack a plate piled high with the same, dressed with a tangy yogurt dressing, feta cheese, onions, and Kalamata olives.

"You've got a new friend," she said with a smile.

Jack took the food. "She doesn't really know me, huh?"

Nan handed him a fork. "You're not around as much as you were when she was a toddler."

He paused to enjoy fresh, homemade food—a commodity sadly lacking in his life. It was tastier than the defensive flavor of guilt on his tongue. "I was here for your wedding, and Kate's."

Nan was kind, but firm. "Which were six months apart. And Kate's been married a year and a half."

"I've been here since then." He reached across Nan to grab a crusty piece of garlic toast from the basket on the coffee table.

"But have you seen Chloe much?"

"Fine." Jack sighed. Nan was right. He still thought of the funny, imaginative little girl as Anneliese's baby, and Anneliese had made herself scarce around him since Kate and Ewan's wedding.

A stained-glass sunset drew them outside to the fire pit. Chloe announced that the pony crew was sleepy and packed them away, trading them for a Tupperware with graham crackers and Hershey bars visible through hazy plastic.

Joss lit a fire in the fading light and Anneliese helped Chloe skewer one of Kate's marshmallows. The first one flamed and charred, and Jack volunteered to eat it, rather than watch Chloe's lip tremble.

"The trick is to find a spot between the logs where it's glowing, but there's not so much fire," he said, guiding Chloe's hand with the toasting fork, looping a casual arm around the bouncy little girl to keep her from tumbling into the fire on his watch. The sugar was just beginning to toast and droop on the fork when Joss's mother's voice called out across the yard.

"That looks like quite the marshmallow, young lady."

Chloe waved it in greeting, and the fork caught Jack in the ear, smearing hot marshmallow into his hair as Chloe dropped it in his lap. He sucked in a breath at the brief pain, but the marshmallow hadn't been hot enough to do any real damage, save to his pride.

"Oh, Chloe!" Anneliese was on her feet in an instant with a napkin in hand, but Molly Fuller was laughing as she caught her niece in a hug.

As much as he loved Anneliese's hands on his shoulder, the scent of her soap so close, Jack stopped Anneliese with a gentle hand on her arm. "Anna Banana, it's fine."

Jack pulled melted sugar from his hair with one hand and threaded a new marshmallow onto the fork with the other. While Chloe told Molly about her day at the state park with her grandparents and Applejack's flying lessons, Jack toasted another marshmallow for Chloe's s'more.

Anneliese took the toasting fork from him and assembled her daughter's treat. She voluntarily met his eyes for the first time that evening. "Thank you."

With a casualness he didn't feel, Jack wiped his sticky fingers on his shorts. "Any time."

~

Extracting Chloe from the campfire only went smoothly because Molly promised pancakes and baby cows the next morning, and because Anneliese agreed to walk back with them to say goodnight. Chloe was quite the negotiator. Maybe Jack would mentor her in a legal career, despite the hot marshmallow incident.

After returning from Molly and Walt's, Anneliese hid in the Damselfly Inn's downstairs powder room instead of returning to the fire pit. She couldn't bring herself to go back to the party.

Her chance to stay up too late, have a little too much to drink, and crash in another of Molly's guest rooms was slipping away because she couldn't cope with Jack being kind to her daughter.

More than kind. He'd been friendly, interested. Indulgent.

*Anna Banana.*

He hadn't called her that in almost fifteen years. Not since she'd called him on it at prom in a hormone-charged moment of confidence. She'd almost thought he wanted to kiss her.

Maybe he had wanted to kiss her on that long-ago night. She'd seen the same look on his face the night he turned up on her porch. And kissed her nearly senseless.

He'd toasted her daughter a replacement marshmallow. He hadn't so much as yelped when Chloe whacked him in the ear with a hot sugar grenade.

He'd laughed.

Her traitorous heart squeezed so hard she couldn't breathe.

Anneliese pressed the heels of her hands into her eyes and rubbed. How was she expected to shake off their kiss when he sat opposite her on a humid July evening with their dearest friends, watching her with something wistful and wanting in his gaze? And then being sweet with Chloe?

She wasn't a fool. She'd dodged Jack's idle flirtations in the years since she came home, but Jack was…Jack: her childhood friend, or what remained of him after years of privilege and charmed existence had chiseled away the boy she'd known. A player. A city dweller with a flashy car and devil-may-care eyes. He flirted the way his sister did, like breathing, taking the attention for granted.

In fairness, he was also generous, kind, and loyal to his friends and family.

So much so that he'd set aside his charmed life for a time to run his father's office and let his dad be present for Mrs. Pease, so much so that he hadn't even considered asking Kate to be the one to shoulder the family responsibilities as well as her growing business and her new marriage.

A knock on the powder room door startled her.

Nan was in the foyer when Anneliese unlocked the door. "You okay? When you didn't come back, I got worried. It's pretty dark between the farm and here."

Anneliese wilted under Nan's concern. "Sorry. I was…"

Nan's answering smile was understanding. "I get it."

"I wish I did." The truth slipped out, and Anneliese blushed like fury.

"I don't know the whole story, and you don't have to tell me, but if I had to guess…" Nan slipped an arm around Anneliese. "It's got to be hard to see Jack being kind to your daughter when her father can't be bothered."

Tears prickled in Anneliese's eyes. Nan's perception was always so sharp, but even Nan didn't know how close to the mark she was.

"Come on." Nan offered her a tissue. "We're figuring out a time to go see Kate and Ewan's place."

Anneliese leaned into Nan's embrace as they walked through the back door together, bolstered by her friend's sympathy. When Nan squeezed in next to Joss by the fire, Anneliese took the spot between Jack and Ewan, offering Jack a wan smile as she did.

One kiss. It was one kiss over too much wine. His presence was a reality for the time being, and she needed to learn how to share space with him.

# CHAPTER 7

On Wednesday, summer rainstorms rolled through in waves, drenching the entire area, and leaving a wet, green humidity in their wake. By the time Anneliese left her last appointment, she was ready to ditch her rain jacket entirely. Her friends wouldn't care if her hair was wet, and the slicker wasn't making much of a difference.

Kate had texted the address earlier. She and Ewan were moving fast on the farmhouse, and they wanted to show their friends the property now that the purchase and sale contract was signed.

Nestled in a small valley ten miles southwest of town, hidden from the main road by new-growth woods and neighboring homes, the elegantly sprawling farmhouse waited around the last bend of a winding dirt driveway.

Anneliese parked near the whitewashed barn, alongside Ewan's vintage Scout.

And Jack's Audi.

A wet cloud broke overhead. Kate and Ewan sheltered from the fat summer raindrops on the porch. Anneliese dashed for cover, joining them under the blue ceiling.

"This is gorgeous." She ran a hand along the smooth railing. "Can I see the rest?"

"Of course. Just leave your shoes on the porch. The owners didn't mind if we brought some family through, but I don't want to leave a mess." Kate was all wide-eyed innocence on the word "family." "Our realtor's inside. Jack couldn't wait. He's already poking around somewhere."

"Are Nan and Joss coming?" She'd assumed there would be reinforcements.

Ewan opened the front door for her. "Nan had a doctor's appointment. They're on their way."

There was no graceful way to wait for them, not without drawing Kate's attention.

Anneliese slipped through the open door and promptly forgot Jack entirely. The first floor had been renovated into one huge room with a stone fireplace anchoring its center. The back of the house, a kitchen and dining area addition, was all glass, with an unexpected view of the Green Mountains in the distance, but it was the décor that stopped her breath: every wall was pale chartreuse, every textile a shade of vivid rose. Lace and brocade competed with velvet and linen. Every available surface was cluttered with vases, statuettes, and little dishes.

Anneliese heard the creak of steps.

"I thought I heard the door." Jack chuckled. "It's a lot, right?"

In his pale gray dress shirt and dark tailored slacks, he was a welcome respite from the vivid color scheme. Anneliese blinked. "It's atrocious."

"You should see upstairs." Jack swept an arm up the staircase. He looked like the hero on the cover of a bestseller. It was unfair how much she'd always wanted him.

She passed him, close enough to brush her hand across his stomach if she dared, but she walked on, dismissing those thoughts and coming to a complete standstill in the upper hallway. She let out a strangled laugh.

Jack followed. "They're getting a great deal on the property, but Kate will spend a fortune redecorating."

The upstairs was a riot of ruffles and competing floral patterns. Three bedrooms and a bathroom, plus a master bedroom with an ensuite bath, all wallpapered in bold geometrics, hothouse roses, gold foil, and heavy curtains. Anneliese drifted into the master suite.

"I can't imagine—" She meant how to begin redecorating on that scale, but Jack launched into a more literal interpretation of how his sister could afford the house.

"Ewan sold his apartment in New York, they're going to rent out Kate's place in town. I don't think it will be a problem. Property values here are so low."

"Spoken like someone with an apartment in an expensive city." She tried to bottle up the bitterness, but it bled through.

"I'm sorry. I didn't mean to sound like that." Jack rested his hand on her shoulder. "It's all relative, I guess. This place is a steal, though."

She examined a particularly blowsy rose on the wallpaper. "I can't even see a future where I could buy a place for Chloe and me."

"You'll get there, Anna—" He stopped just shy of the *Banana*, but she heard it.

It should have sounded patronizing, but he was gazing at her with a boyish earnestness that softened the platitude.

He spread his hands and spun slowly. "If you're lucky, you'll find a place that's as ready to live in as this."

"From your lips…" Her laughter dried up as she considered those lips.

"Really, though." Oblivious, Jack walked into the master bathroom. "Would you stay in town? I could see you out here, too."

"Want to hear something silly?" Anneliese followed him and promptly forgot what she'd been saying. A huge, jetted soaking tub held court in front of a picture window with unblemished views of the garden and barn, the forest, and the Green Mountains beyond. "This bathroom is amazing. Look at the tub. Look at that *view*."

"That's not silly." Jack's expression had gone from playful to wanting. "I can think of a few great ways to enjoy the view."

She needed him to take back the desire in his eyes; it released a thousand butterflies in her belly. "I was going to say that I always wanted to live on Chapel Street. I loved your family's house as a kid."

"I always wanted—"

She never heard what he'd always wanted, because Kate chose that moment to come bounding up the stairs.

"Just ignore everything but the bones. I've already talked to a painter. And did you see the barn? Joss says he can convert it into a test kitchen for me and a studio for Ewan. There's even a cart road that cuts in from the main road and ends at the barn. We can have it widened for deliveries or extra parking—"

"Or friends and family VIP access?" Jack teased. "It's a house, Katie, not a nightclub."

"Says you." Kate launched into her plans for the master bath.

Anneliese heard more footsteps, and peered out a front window to the rainy scene outside. Nan and Joss had arrived; the official tour could begin.

WHEN ANNELIESE GOT HOME FROM KATE'S HOUSE, THE PAINTING CREW Jeremy and Glenn hired were scraping the back side of the house, and the fence had been repaired. She found her mother and Chloe hanging pictures in the kitchen. They'd strung twine along the wall, and were using binder clips to attach Chloe's artwork and some photographs Anneliese had left out.

"Mom," she said. "I love it."

"I saw it in one of my magazines, and I thought it might be fun." She straightened a crooked drawing. "I hope you don't mind."

"It's great." She squeezed Chloe's shoulders. "And you can be in charge of the art."

Chloe ran upstairs calling out, "I know one!"

Anneliese shared an indulgent smile with her mother. "I can't wait to see what she comes up with."

Her mother busied herself tidying away some dirty dishes on the counter. "I got the twine and clips from the shop.

"I saw Ted," her mother continued. "You know, his divorce has been final almost a year now."

Anneliese wished she had—just once—rolled her eyes at her mother when she was younger. If she tried it now, Jane might have a…

*Well, that was in poor taste.*

Ted Plante worked for her father. Fortyish, not unattractive, but not exactly inspiring, Ted started out as a picker of sorts, finding treasures in attics, rummage sales, and flea markets to sell to her father. Now he was gradually taking over the business in advance of her father's retirement.

"Stop, Mom. Ted's too old." Anneliese started unpacking lengths of yellow and black tulle she'd picked up earlier in the day.

"He's not too old, and he knows how to be a father." Jane fixed her daughter with a firm look while she dried a mug. "His children are wonderful."

"I'm sure they are." If she'd met them, Anneliese couldn't picture them. "He's nice, Mom, but he's not my type."

"Your type doesn't exactly have a great track record."

Anneliese's cheeks heated, but her mother was only winding up.

"I know you think you were sneaking around with that boy in high school, just like I know you've been mooning over Jack Pease since he grew whiskers."

"I was not—" *His name was Chris.*

"But he was no good for you, and you couldn't hold on to the man who was your type enough to marry…"

Anneliese kept her tone level. "Mom."

"Even Jack was always a little fast, though I still think he'll grow out of that. Look how well Katie turned out."

Jack was a subject she was not going to get into with her mother. Better to stick to Kate's triumphs. "Married, you mean?"

Her mother crossed the room to investigate the tulle. "Settled down, and I heard from John they're looking at a house."

"More than looking." Anneliese welcomed the change of subject. "I got a tour just now. It's a gorgeous property."

"You know Ted kept his house in the divorce. It's in a nice little neighborhood in Addison. Your father and I had dinner out there in the spring."

"I'm sure Ted's house is lovely." She pulled a couple pieces of the fabric up and wrapped them around her hand. "What do you think about these for Chloe's Founder's Day pageant costumes?"

Chloe thundered down the stairs. "I found it on your bureau, Mama. This one." She held it up for her mother and grandmother.

Anneliese took the photo. A group photo taken at Nan and Joss's wedding, it showed a much younger Chloe in her flower girl dress and the six of them—Anna, Nan, Joss, Kate, Ewan, and Jack—together on the Damselfly Inn's front steps.

"It's perfect."

"I know, Mama. It's got everybody. Even Applejack."

*Even Applejack.*

"Applejack?" Her mom looked at her with a curious tilt to her chin.

"Jack Pease. He and Chloe were playing ponies the other night at the Damselfly."

Her mom turned her attention to Chloe. "Is that the blue one with the rainbow hair?"

"No, Mere, that's the one with apples on her tush."

"How could I forget?" Jane took the tulle from Anneliese and layered it before scrunching it up. "Come here. Let's see if you look like a bee in this."

LATER THAT EVENING, JACK LAID OUT A FEAST OF CO-OP GOODIES IN front of his father. They were committing his mother's cardinal sin and eating dinner in front of the TV, but the Sox were on and the kitchen didn't have a fan.

"Are you going to see Kate's new house?"

His dad wasn't really watching the game. Jack could see his lids half-closed when he leaned back against the sofa cushion.

"Dad?"

His father blinked. "Mmm?"

"Is Katie taking you by the house?" Jack said.

Wherever he'd been, his dad returned quickly. "I'm going on a walk-through with them on Friday. I want to make sure it's only the paint colors that need updating."

Jack laughed. "Did she show you pictures?"

"No, but she told Mom all about it the other morning." John sighed. "I wish your mom were stronger. I know Katie's upset this is happening without her."

Jack closed his eyes for a moment to gather himself. His father's optimism was flagging as the days wore on. "Mom's getting better every day."

"Speaking of real estate." John changed the subject. "Did Ivy Brennan get in touch? She called about having her fiancé added to the deed on her house."

Jack flipped open a box of orzo and feta salad and handed it to his dad. "She did call. We have an appointment coming up. Mrs. Drake handled that part."

"How are you two getting along?" There was a touch of amusement in his father's eyes that sparked an answering hope in Jack.

"Most days I'm not sure why I'm here. She tells me where to be and what to do. All I had to do was give her my CV for the website." Jack filled his own plate with the orzo and reached for the cold pulled pork. "She's terrifying. She knows more about web design than I do, never mind your cases."

"I'd be lost without her, and she knows it." John followed Jack to the pork, and added marinated mozzarella to his plate. "She stays sharp picking up new office technology. She taught herself the website stuff, the bookkeeping software, the answering service…"

"Dad," Jack said, "I'm glad I came home."

"You don't have to say that. I know my caseload isn't what you're used to."

"No. I mean, yeah. But I am glad, too. Today, meeting up with Katie and Ewan and everyone, to see their new house. I would've missed it." He traded his plate for a sweating glass of iced tea. "They would have made a return trip if I'd come up on a weekend, but I would have missed that first glimpse."

He would have missed Anneliese's flushed uncertainty when he flirted, missed her honesty, even when it reminded him how blind he was sometimes.

He'd been about to tell her how he'd always loved the cottage she now called home.

With the exception of his parents' place, the fanciful little house was Jack's favorite house in Thornton. He couldn't have said exactly why he was so drawn to it, and not even his sister knew each time he returned home since it had been empty, he'd simultaneously hoped and feared that someone had taken up residence there.

It was about as opposite his efficient, well-appointed apartment as a place could be. Kate would never let him live down a crush on a whimsical little house like that.

Falling into genteel shabbiness, veiled in wisteria and lilacs, trimmed in fading gingerbread and clapboards, the cottage had waited empty for more than a year this time.

That Anneliese was making a home there with her daughter was perfect.

"Your mother would like that you found something to be happy about. I know it isn't easy, banging around your childhood home with your useless father." John smiled and, for a moment, his son was certain things would be just fine.

"I love you, Dad. Even when you're useless."

That brought a real smile to his father's face.

"Speaking of your mother, did I tell you Anna Thompson came by with flowers again this morning?"

"You didn't." *Neither did Anna.*

"I remember how she used to tag along after you and Joss all the time. Your mother always liked her. Between you and me, she thought Jane and Bobby were too strict with her, but they probably thought we let you and Katie run too wild."

Anneliese's parents had been strict, but she'd run just as wild as he and Joss when they'd played together as kids. She could hike as far, climb as high. Right on through high school. Until she stopped tagging along.

The inning changed, and Jack settled in to watch baseball. His dad fell asleep before the game ended; Jack left him on the sofa and went to rummage in the spare bedroom, where all the photo albums from the eighties were.

He pulled them out, leatherette spines gone stiff with age, cellophane protecting the images crinkling as he flipped the pages. It took some searching—full dark fell outside the house on Chapel Street, but Jack found the one he wanted.

It began with a family party in the backyard at the Fuller farm. He paged along, past rolls-worth of photos of the elder Fullers, Thompsons, and Peases as young parents, their friends all toasting some forgotten celebration, Molly brandishing a casserole dish for the camera. He and Joss and Anneliese had all been in kindergarten—just about the age Anneliese's daughter was now—and it was the first memory he had of the three of them together.

He'd gotten a Fisher Price camera, blue with black bumpers, and the kind of flashbulb tower that clipped in, a hand-me-down from an older cousin. It had been a bit of a relic even then, but he'd carried it everywhere for most of a year, begging his parents to buy more film and flashbulbs. His mother archived his efforts right alongside her own.

He turned a page and there it was, the photo he was sure he'd taken. Anneliese on the old rope swing over the swimming hole at Fuller Creek. The three of them had followed Joss's older cousins down to the creek when their parents wanted some peace. The bigger kids had pushed them on the swing—and had gone into the creek to tow them back when they'd come up sputtering.

The photo was foggy, a remnant of poor exposure and old photo paper, but it was real. They'd gone from two grubby boys and a tagalong girl cousin to three best friends, and the finding of hidden trails and swimming holes had been their secret language, even into high school.

Five-year-old Jack had accidentally captured the moment the swing flew away from him, the O of surprise on five-year-old Anneliese's summer-tanned face, her golden hair fanning out around her. A perfect moment of joy and thrill, too young to fear.

Too young to regret.

# CHAPTER 8

The weekend came and, with it, boredom.

Jack didn't do boredom well. In Boston, there were cases to work, Red Sox games to go to. Clubs, bars, restaurants, movies, concerts. Rowing on the Charles, museums. Pick up softball games, the firm's box at the Garden. Long, idle brunches in the sun on Newbury Street.

People came from all over the world to while away a sunny Vermont Saturday morning. He wanted to crawl out of his skin.

He texted his sister. *Anything going on?*

Kate's reply came quickly. *En route to Montreal with Ewan. Back in the AM xx*

He took a bowl of cereal out to the front porch. The daylilies needed deadheading. The beds needed weeding. There were bare spots in the mulch by the driveway. Without his mother, everything at home suffered, even the gardens.

He wanted to get Anneliese a housewarming gift.

"Dad," he called out to the house. "I'm going to pick up some stuff at Coulson's. Do we need anything else?"

Jack heard his father in his study. He came out into the front hall bearing a page of notebook paper with his mother's handwriting on it.

"She wrote this right before…" His dad's voice trailed off. "Anyway, if you're going, we should try to keep things up. She'll be in a temper if we let her gardens suffer."

Jack took the list. "Right. Can I take your car?"

He'd need something more practical than his car to get the job done. His dad's reliable station wagon was the soul of practicality.

His father read his mind. "Keys are on the peg by the door."

Ten minutes later, he parked at Coulson's. His mother's garden supply list was daunting. He might have grown up pulling weeds and listening to his mother talk flowers and shrubs, but the closest his apartment came to a garden was the terrarium of succulents on his coffee table—which Wanda watered for him.

*I'm sorry if I screw this up, Mom.*

He folded the list carefully and tucked it into his shorts' pocket. Maybe it was a small-town cliché to run into the owner before he'd crossed the parking lot, but there she was, waving to him.

Penny Coulson purposefully wove her way around pallets of bagged soil and fertilizer. "It's good to see you. How's your mom?"

"Same. Thanks, Penny."

"Need help with anything?"

Jack pulled out the page from his mother's notebook. "I've got a list."

Sorrow tugged the corners of Penny's smile. "Go on into the yard. Danielle'll help you out with all of this."

Danielle turned out to be a teenaged girl in combat boots and cargo pants with a ponytail that faded from turquoise to silver. He squinted slightly. Something about her was familiar.

The young woman was all business. "You'll need a flatbed to haul all of this." She spun on her boot heel and headed down an aisle of plant pots, leaving Jack to grab one of an untidy herd of wheeled carts and follow.

In for a penny, in for three hundred dollars in plants and gardening supplies, starting with a pair of decorative planters for the porch. To welcome his mom home.

Jack let his teenaged guide fill up a flatbed cart with mulch and soil, plants and flowers she promised him would "thrill, spill, and fill," whatever that meant, and a set of tools for Anna, with a galvanized watering can he could already picture on the porch.

And then he saw the child-sized set of tools and the sunny yellow watering can dappled with ladybugs.

They were adorable, and Chloe would love having her own things.

Danielle added a photocopied tip sheet for arranging his new planters. "I tagged the plants according to where they go on the chart."

"Thanks," Jack said. "I'm sorry, but do I know you?"

She ducked her chin slightly, pushing her hair off her face. "I sometimes work for Ms. Grady at the Damselfly."

Danny Beaudette. Nan's erstwhile vandal. "Jack Pease. I'm Nan's lawyer."

"I remember." She finished processing his credit card and handed Jack the receipt. "Have a nice day, Mr. Pease."

Jesus, he felt old.

When he pulled up alongside Anneliese's fence, Chloe was shuffling her purple bicycle up and down the garden path in front of the porch. Her huge turquoise helmet and matching knee pads brought a smile to his face.

Jack put a hand on the gate; it was tightly latched. "Hey, Chloe. Is your mom around?"

Chloe stopped her bike, dragging it with her as she turned. "She's inside talking on the phone. I'm supposed to be quiet for a little bit."

Anneliese was in the kitchen. He could see her through the porch window, her phone clenched against her cheek. He waved. She put up a hand in cursory greeting, then waved him through impatiently.

Jack returned his attention to Chloe. "You look like you need a spotter."

"What's a spotter?"

"How about I just hold on?" His father had done this for him and Kate in turn. It couldn't be that hard. Jack hooked his fingers under the back of the seat. "I'll walk along while you pedal so you can see what it feels like to balance on your own."

Chloe nodded. Jack held the bike steady.

"Okay, put your feet on the pedals. I won't drop you. Promise."

With her feet in place, he started walking, giving the bike the extra steadiness Chloe didn't have yet. The garden path petered out into a strip of balding grass and pine needles between the house and the hotel. He let Chloe steer around the corner of the house. His lower back twinged, but when he loosened his grip on Chloe's seat, he could feel she was starting to balance herself a little.

He looked up to see one of Anneliese's neighbors pruning an azalea. They exchanged awkward waves as he and Chloe wobbled their way around the perimeter of the house.

"Jack, I got all the way!"

"You did." She put her feet down, and Jack released her seat and put up his fist. "Knuckles."

Her fist bump packed a feisty punch. She let the bike fall, swinging one leg out of the way and not quite losing her balance, only to stand there inspecting him like a museum exhibit. What else did you talk about with a five-year-old?

"So," he said, choosing the same opening that worked with colleagues, "got any big plans for the weekend?"

"I'm a bee in the pageant for Founder's Day." Chloe enunciated the words slowly, as if she'd memorized them recently.

His mother nagged every summer, asking him to come home for Thornton's summer celebration. Every summer he dismissed it as a hokey relic. This year she'd miss it.

"Cool," he said. Would people expect him to attend Founder's Day?

Anneliese had retreated to the table. Through the porch window, her profile was bent into one hand, fingers pinching the bridge of her nose.

"Chloe, I need some help. Does your mom like to work in her garden?"

She dropped her bike. "She does, but Mere has all the shovels."

Jack smiled. "Hang tight."

He opened the back of the car, pulled out the plants, and carried them back through the gate, presenting them to Chloe. "Do you think she'll like these?"

"I like the red ones."

Jack broke an impatiens free from the plastic flat. "This one's yours."

She held the red flower in her cradled hands while he returned for the tools.

"What do you think?"

Chloe peered into the box. Her face lit up at the small yellow watering can and the ladybug-themed trowel and rake. "Are those for me?"

"Yep. Should we plant your flower?"

The screen door slapped against the frame about the time he realized they would need some water for their new transplant.

Anneliese picked her way around Chloe's discarded bike and the gardening supplies. "What's all this?"

Her smile was welcoming, but there were wary shadows in her eyes.

"I went to Coulson's for some stuff to spruce up Mom's gardens." Jack held up grimy hands. "I think I must be an easy mark. Danny Beaudette sold me a small fortune in plants, then I saw the little gardening set, and I had to get it for Chloe. I hope she gets a commission."

"Danielle," Anneliese said.

"Hmm?"

Anneliese crouched to pull a weed, squinting at him as she stood. "She doesn't go by Danny anymore. It's Danielle."

More things he didn't know. "I'll remember that. Anyway, when I got here I found a lost princess in your front yard, so I tried to teach her to ride her bike so she could find her way home."

"I'm a ninja frog," Chloe said. "And ninjas never get losted."

"Lost, not 'losted,'" Anneliese corrected her.

Jack gathered up the set for Anna. "I got some things for you, too."

"You shouldn't have." She took them with a wistful smile.

"It will all be worth it if this little thing survives." Chloe's impatiens was starting to droop a little.

"I'll bring out some water. I don't have a hose yet."

While Anneliese was inside, a woman walked by with a boy about Chloe's size and a baby snoozing in one side of a double stroller. Chloe ran to the gate, chattering to the woman and the boy about her flower and her bike. Jack pocketed his hands and waited either to be noticed or for Anneliese to return.

He was noticed by the woman first. "Are you Chloe's dad?"

"Oh," Jack stammered. "No, just a friend of Anna…Anneliese's."

"Oh, well…" The woman kicked the brakes on her stroller and gave him a frank once-over. This, he sensed, was a woman who supplied the healthy gossip trade in town. "Is Anneliese home? Jax wanted Chloe to come over to play."

"Hi, Grace." Anneliese appeared with a plastic water pitcher in hand. "Sure, Chloe can play with Jax for a while this afternoon. How about I come by and pick her up before supper?"

Chloe and Jax jumped around, chanting something Jack couldn't follow.

"That's perfect." Grace glanced significantly between him and Anneliese, then her gaze settled on Jack. "I'm sorry, I didn't catch your name."

"Grace," Anneliese interjected, "this is my old friend Jack Pease. Kate's brother. Jack, this is Grace Mackie. Jax and Chloe go to school together."

"Nice to meet you." They spoke over one another, and Jack wondered if Grace was also in a rush for the entire encounter to end.

Her answering smile was toothy; he suspected that if she was, it was for very different reasons.

Chloe ambled off with Jax and his mother and sibling without saying goodbye. He and Anneliese were left standing together at the garden gate with a pitcher of water and a drooping annual between them.

"Sorry about that," Anneliese said. "Grace is nice, but she's a bit of a gossip."

"I suspected. Sorry." Jack said. "About the gossip anyway."

"Right." Anneliese tipped the pitcher's contents around the freshly turned earth. "You didn't have to do all this."

"I wanted to."

She stood, and wiped her cheek with the back of her hand, leaving a pale smear of soil behind. "Thank you."

He couldn't help reaching up to smudge the dirt away with his thumb. Just the feel of her skin set his blood humming. "You're welcome."

Her phone rang, reminding him he'd lingered too long. She pulled it out, peering at the screen with a small frown.

He watched in wonder as something shifted in her. She squared her shoulders, stood a little straighter. Even her normally husky voice took on a smoother quality when she said, "Hello."

After a beat of silence, she looked at the screen.

"What was that?" he asked.

She locked the screen and slid the phone into her shorts' pocket. "I thought it was work because of the California area code, but..." She trailed off, then drew in a sharp breath. "Doesn't matter. Telemarketer. But I do have work. I was on a call with a client before."

"That's why Chloe said she was supposed to be quiet for a while."

Anneliese's expression softened. "I'm glad Grace came by. I bet she was getting bored."

"I feel her pain," Jack said, gesturing to his Coulson's haul. "To the tune of all this."

Anneliese laughed. "Welcome back to small-town Saturdays."

"Yeah." Jack closed the hatch of his dad's car. "I should let you get back to it. I've got planters to thrill, spill, and fill."

She laughed again, this time reaching out to lay her hand on his forearm. "Danielle really did sense an easy sale, didn't she?"

He climbed into the car and turned the key. If that was all it took to make Anneliese smile, he'd spend a dozen fortunes on mulch.

# CHAPTER 9

*T*hrill, spill, and fill worked. Jack vowed never to reveal how much time—or how many Google searches—it had taken him to get the planters done before he'd moved on to mulching and weeding, but by Sunday afternoon, the front yard looked almost up to his mother's standards.

He managed a shower and a cold beer in front of a baseball game before his father and sister ganged up on him.

"Jack, come *on*."

Kate actually picked up his hand and tugged, just like she had when they were kids.

"Katie, if he'd rather sit on his rear and watch a baseball game…" John's even tones from the foyer tugged at Jack's reluctance.

"He's coming." Kate turned her sweetest smile on him. "Because all your friends are going to be there, and Chloe's class is putting on a pageant, and I provided the pies for the contest. Even Ewan is playing along."

That got his interest; Jack muted the game. "Poor bastard. What did you do to him?"

"Ha!" Kate perched on the sofa arm. "He helped Joss build the stage for the pageant, and he volunteered to run the inn's vendor table for an hour so Nan could see Chloe dance."

"Oh, fine." He hit the power button on the remote and stretched. Kate wouldn't give him a moment's peace if he stayed home. "Give me a sec."

"Told you he'd come," Kate called to their dad in the front hall, tossing Jack a teasing grin as she went out.

Grumble as he might, the afternoon was soft, humid and hazy. He could hear a calliope and the happy noise of a crowd on the common from the front porch.

Kate looped her arms through his and their father's and the three of them walked down Chapel Street to where it joined Main, just off the common. He'd driven past the prep all week without considering his friends would be part of it.

"So, Ewan really helped Joss build something?"

"He's nesting." Kate beamed. "I could just squish him."

The tents and tables were alive now with bright banners and local goods. The high school jazz band played from the gazebo, and lights were strung from the maple trees that ringed the green, just waiting for darkness to fall.

Kate stopped them both. "There's my man."

Ewan was, as promised, sitting behind a table in the vendor's row. A banner bearing the Damselfly Inn's logo ruffled in the breeze, and the wind battled brightly colored stone paperweights for control of a stack of brochures. A small crowd circled the table—mostly female.

"Go be social. I'm going to stake my claim." Kate nudged her father and brother. "Go. If you hustle, Chloe's class is doing the first of two performances."

"Did my daughter just flounce?" John watched Kate head off in the direction of Ewan and his groupies.

"More like pounce." Jack shrugged; Kate was a force of nature. "You up for some pageantry?"

His father chuckled. "I can't think of anything else I'd rather do."

～

CHLOE WAS FOURTH IN LINE IN THE FRONT, A BUMBLEBEE IN A CLOUD OF yellow and black tulle, with a pair of lace wings worn like a backpack over her black leotard. Anneliese sat in the front row, coordinating the hand motions along with Grace Mackie. Jax was waiting just off stage in his blueberry costume.

Mrs. Blondin, a retired piano teacher kind enough to volunteer her aging hands for the festival, launched into the intro with gusto, and the class fell somewhat into step. Anneliese snuck a covert glance at Grace, who was biting her lip to keep from giggling when the strawberries started circling around the blueberries to lead the bees to them.

Even if it wasn't biologically correct, they sure were cute.

Eight bars from the end, a strawberry went left when she should have gone right, and Chloe stumbled against one of her fellow bees. There were tears in her eyes when she stood up again, and a tell-tale quiver around her lower lip. Anneliese's heart hammered in her chest for a moment, but Chloe found her spot for the last pose and scooted into it just in time.

Mrs. Blondin made a grand production of the final bars, and the small crowd gathered around the stage erupted into enthusiastic applause, including a perfect whistle of approval from the back—one which made her daughter light up like Christmas.

Anneliese turned back to look, expecting Joss to be the culprit. Instead, there was Jack, standing with his father, clapping like a fool and cheering Chloe by name. There was no time to moon over Jack's behavior, though. She and Grace jogged behind the painted backdrop to help the teachers organize the class before releasing them to the festival until the second performance.

With the props and set pieces—such as they were—stowed until the second run, and Chloe changed from her tutu into a comfy dress she could play in, Anneliese made her way out to find her parents.

She and Chloe found them waiting with Jack.

"Mere, Pep! Did you see me fall?"

Chloe seemed to have put her stumble behind her. Anneliese wished it were always that simple.

Jane gathered Chloe in for a hug. "You did great, sweetie. We can't wait to see you do it again later. Now," she said, gesturing to Jack, "say hello to Mr. Pease."

"Hi, Applejack," Chloe said. "Did you see me fall?"

Jack crouched down, and Anneliese saw he was holding a pink rose in one hand. "You should always bring a dancer flowers for her opening performance."

"Chloe, you should thank Mr. Pease for the flower," Jane reminded her granddaughter.

Anneliese caught a rare mutinous gleam in Chloe's eyes.

"Thank you," Chloe said. It was rote, but Anneliese noticed it satisfied her mother.

Jack offered Chloe the flower. "I saw you dance, Chlo'. It was awesome."

Chloe raised her knuckles for a first bump, holding her rose in the other hand. "Are you coming for hot dogs?"

Anneliese felt as though every eye in the crowd was on her, but the only one waiting for her to answer was Jack. She nodded. It wasn't as though she could refuse him without explaining the way she felt to her five-year-old.

"I'd love to." Jack looked around. "Maybe I can invite my dad along, too? I'm guessing he's hungry."

"Okay." Chloe grabbed her Pep's hand, still carrying the pink rose, and pulled him in the direction of the grill manned by members of the Methodist church.

Her mother joined Chloe and her father, leaving Anneliese to fall in step with Jack.

"Thank you for making a fuss over her." She laced her fingers behind her as she walked, conscious of the way their bodies brushed as they navigated the crowded common. All around them, Thornton celebrated. "I should have thought of flowers."

Jack shrugged. "We passed the Coulson's table on the way over. They were handing them out. How could I not?"

It was the sort of thing a father should be there to do.

Jack didn't notice when her smile soured. "They were cute, but I think their biology curriculum needs review."

Anneliese laughed in spite of herself. "The strawberries were leading the bees to the blueberries to help them grow. The kids sort of planned it themselves. A couple of the parents helped corral them into something that looked like choreography, and bless Mrs. Blondin for having a song about summer blueberries in her arsenal."

"To think I almost didn't come."

He said the words casually, but there was a wistfulness in his voice that sent a warm thrill down her spine.

"I'm glad you did."

"Mama!" They were trailing Chloe and her grandparents, and Chloe turned to holler back at them. "Come on!"

Jack slung an arm around her then, leaning in conspiratorially. "Kate sounds just like that when she's about to get her way."

Anneliese allowed herself to relax into the friendly contact. "I'm done for."

They found the Fullers on a quilt near the bandstand. Nan, Joss, and his parents shifted to make room for the Thompsons, while Jack went to find his father and procure enough hot dogs for the crowd.

"I see Kate and Ewan," Nan said, leaning over to Chloe. "Go invite Paul Bunyan to join us."

"Who?" Jane's frown lines bracketed her mouth.

"Nan means Ewan, Mom," Anneliese spoke quietly to her mother under the collected laughter at the inside joke. "The first time Chloe met Ewan, she thought he was Paul Bunyan and asked him if he'd brought Babe the Blue Ox to town with him. Nan still gets a kick out of it."

Her mother's expression softened, but she didn't join in the fun.

Chloe scrambled off to get Kate and Ewan. Jack returned, balancing two boxes piled with hot dogs. A handled brown paper bag hung from one arm, and his father carried a cardboard tray of paper cups.

"I didn't know what people wanted," Jack said, "so I got some of everything."

They ate and talked while the sun started its arc toward twilight. Watching Chloe with this family she'd made—some related, some chosen—Anneliese felt another handful of grief and rage fly free.

That was how she thought of it. Every time small joys and triumphs found her, little bits of the weight she carried from the wreckage of her marriage, her lost twenties, and her broken heart flew away. She could let them go, leaving more room for joy in her soul.

She felt Jack's gaze, and found him watching her, looking lost and far away.

"What is it?"

"My mom loves this festival. My dad was going to go anyway. And I was going to skip it." He sighed. "She should be here. She'd have loved the berries-and-bees number."

Anneliese reached out to him, just a tentative touch. "She'll be here next year."

"When you say it, I believe it."

"Anneliese." Her mother popped the fragile soap bubble of their connection. "Isn't it about time to get Chloe back to the stage?"

Anneliese checked her phone. So it was. "Finish your dog, Chlo'. Tutu time."

"We're coming to this show," Kate called after them. "Break a leg, Chloe!"

"Why do people say that?" Chloe asked. "It sounds mean. I know it's not mean, cause Mrs. Blondin says that's what people say when you're in a play…"

Anneliese let Chloe's chatter flow over her as they walked away. If she stopped to think, she'd have to consider that her heart wasn't making it easy to stay in friendly space with Jack.

THE SUN SANK VIOLET AND GOLD OVER THE DISTANT MOUNTAINS, BUT the heat stayed, settling into the soft summer darkness. The lights strung around the common were hazy with satiny night air. Walt and

Molly Fuller's quilt became a home base for all of them as the evening lengthened. The pleasure of good company eased Jack's restlessness, though he was acutely aware of Anneliese's every move.

He stayed with the picnic while everyone else went to watch Chloe's second pageant performance, drifting on popcorn and cotton candy-scented air. Every Founder's Day he'd found an excuse to stay in the city suddenly felt like a loss.

His phone disturbed his melancholy. Iris's name lit up the screen.

*Ran into Barry and Jen at Beast. Your team landed a new client tonight.* Words that typically gave him an adrenaline jolt.

He tapped a quick reply. *Will there be fireworks?*

*?*

Her puzzled, single character reply drew a smile. Catching Iris off-guard had once been one of his favorite games. *I'm waiting on the town common for the Founder's Day fireworks.*

*Of course,* she replied. *I can't compete with fireworks.*

Jack put away his phone without replying. There really wasn't anything to say.

By the time the pageant crowd returned, a jug band was playing, and an informal square dance had formed up.

"Do you remember any of that?" Kate asked of the Thornton natives, tossing Ewan a get-out-of-jail-free look. "From P.E.?"

"This Brooklyn bookworm knows a *do-si-do* from a *swing-your-partner.* I went to summer camp in the Catskills, thank you very much." He squeezed Kate close. "Are you brave enough?"

Her answering smile was brilliant. "Who needs toes?"

Nan shook her head, and Joss gathered her back against his chest. Molly coaxed Jack's dad out for a spin, and Jack caught Anneliese watching their laughing footwork with pure envy.

Jack leaned over. "I'm game if you are."

"Really?" Her head tilted, a confused wrinkle forming between her eyes. He wanted to kiss it away.

"Really. How hard can it be?" *Famous last words.* He stood and offered her a hand. "Chloe's working on half her weight in ice cream. Joss and Nan will keep an eye on her."

For at least the first thirty-two counts, Jack was so focused on following the calls, he had no time to enjoy the light in Anneliese's eyes. When he finally relaxed enough not to feel ridiculous, he could have kicked himself for missing out. She was a vision. Her hair fanned out behind her as she spun, her eyes sparkled like the fearless girl she'd been in his photo. They came together to link arms and turn; that gentle touch alone sent a shockwave through him.

He'd never win any square-dance competitions, but they stayed on the raised dance floor for another two songs, returning breathless and laughing to the quilt.

"Mama," Chloe said seriously, "you are a very good dancer."

"Isn't she?" Jack couldn't help the naked admiration in his gaze. The way Anneliese dropped her eyes and twisted her hands told him she'd noticed.

Anneliese's father checked his watch. "Chloe, the fireworks are about to start."

As if set by Mr. Thompson's watch, the lights flashed twice and flickered out. And as it had every Founder's Day Jack could recall from his youth, the Thornton Union marching band launched into the fireworks music.

The pyrotechnics bloomed over the common to "America the Beautiful." His first cynical thought was that the town had a bigger budget than when he was a kid, but the crowd *oohed* at the first big display, and Jack gave himself over to wonder.

He found himself joining the crowd in singing along to the state song, surprised that the lyrics of "These Green Mountains" still lived in a pocket of his memory. He was no more a singer than a square dancer, but he could hold the basics of a tune, and his childhood self had sung them for a dozen summers.

By the time the last booms echoed over the town and the smoke began to drift away on the night air, the crowd had already thinned. With the ease of familiarity, his friends and family packed up the Fuller's quilt and said their goodbyes. Somehow, his father slipped away with Kate, leaving him with Chloe, Anneliese, and the Thompsons.

"Anneliese," Mrs. Thompson said, "do you need your dad to help get Chloe home? You've got all the dance stuff to carry."

"I can help with that, Mrs. T." Jack surprised himself with the offer—and the Thompsons, too, if their expressions were to be believed. He dropped to one knee in front of Chloe. "Want a lift home, ma'am?"

Chloe giggled, then wrapped her arms around his neck. He straightened, groaning slightly at the weight of the sleepy little girl on his shoulder.

"Good night, then." Mrs. Thompson exchanged a look with her husband, then they each kissed Chloe in turn. "Anneliese, we'll see you tomorrow."

It was barely two blocks from their spot on the common to the cottage's garden gate. He carried Chloe's dance bag in his free hand, and they pointed out the flickering fireflies in the gardens they passed.

"I never see fireflies in the city," he said, setting Chloe down inside the porch.

"That's sad," she said. "It's good you live here now."

He didn't know how to answer her. Was it better to lie? To explain it? To let the question blow away with the ashy clouds from the fireworks?

Anneliese saved him from answering. "Go on up and brush your teeth, Chlo'. I'll be up in a minute to tuck you in."

Chloe dragged her heels, but after a stern threat of no cartoons the next day from Anneliese, they were alone, together, on the porch. The atmosphere thickened around them, but there too was Chloe's statement, its inverse truth and the little girl herself, only a narrow flight of stairs away.

"I'm glad I came out tonight."

"Thank you for carrying her home. And helping with her stuff."

They each stopped, tripping over each other's words.

"Anna—"

"Jack—"

Before he could talk himself out of it, he kissed her. Just a brush of lips, a sweet good night.

Anneliese stepped back. "Better not."

"No." He put a hand on the porch door. "You're probably right."

"I'm glad you came to Founder's Day, too."

He pushed the door open, and the noise of the fading celebration came flooding in. He knew the screen hadn't kept the world at bay, but it felt that way.

"Good night, Anna Banana. Give Chloe a first bump for me."

# CHAPTER 10

His mother's roommate had long since been released from the hospital, but Jack kept up the reading. His mom was more alert every day, and her speech was returning. He bought all Ewan's books at Vellichor, and while he told the hospital staff he was reading for his mom, the truth was he was enjoying the hell out of his brother-in-law's stories.

Cordelia Dirham-Sears, the feisty Victorian scientist heroine—whose wit definitely reminded him of his sister—was about to be attacked by urchins in an alley, after a visit to hero Alasdair Sledge's laboratory, when a cacophony of alarms burst from the monitoring equipment.

He reached out to the nurse who bustled in. "What's going on?"

"I'm sorry, sir, but you need to make room."

Jack flattened himself against the wall to make room for a small army of doctors and nurses. Someone took his arm—gently—and led him from the room to a seat in an empty lounge nearby.

The next hours passed in a blur of uncertainty. Ewan drove Kate over, and along with their father they waited together for news. When Nan and Joss brought a picnic cooler full of dinner, Jack was hit with a wave of gratitude so huge it threatened to crush him.

When the doctor finally spoke to them, the words rattled in Jack's exhausted brain: cardiac event, complications, monitoring. They were all sent home, and the doctor promised to call if there were any significant changes. Nan and Joss left for the inn, Kate and Ewan rumbled out of the parking lot in Ewan's red truck, and Jack rode home in anxious silence with his father, who fled upstairs as soon as they got home.

Rather than lurk in the kitchen feeling helpless in the face of his father's fears, Jack took a glass of iced tea out to the porch. The crickets struck up a tune as the air settled around the neighborhood. The lights winked out one by one upstairs at the Cartwright's house next door.

Rosie and Tim Keller owned the place now. Rosie's father—Jack's former English teacher—had grown up there. Only in a place like Thornton would a family still own a house for generations.

Jack's heart rose in his throat, but his emotions held fast, dammed behind his eyes. Rosie and Tim's romance might not have been the stuff of legends like Rosie's parents, but it was part of the fabric of Jack's earliest memories. They were younger than his parents, but still old in the eyes of his teenaged self when Rosie got married. He was beginning to see now how many quiet love stories flourished around him, and it made him miss Anneliese. He wondered if anyone had let her know the afternoon's dismal news.

Abandoning the tea to condense on the porch floorboards, Jack walked down Chapel Street to where it intersected with Main and kept going, his conflicted heart carrying him across the shadowy common, under the spire of the Congregational church. Toward the Fletcher Hotel and Anneliese's cottage.

His steps slowed as the cottage came into view. Anneliese was reading on the porch swing to the low, aching tune of a blues song he didn't know. The woman's voice, the weeping brass, and the slow beat went straight to the dammed-up place in his chest and the tears came. Swiping at them, he unlatched the garden gate and made his way to Anneliese's porch door.

He could see her, drifting slightly with the motion of the porch swing, her bare legs illuminated by her reading lamp, her face in shadow. She laid her book against her lap when she saw him.

He knocked, watching her though the screen and holding his breath until her bare feet touched the floor and she set the book down to open the door.

"What happened?" Her voice was husky; she spoke quietly and Jack was reminded that her daughter was sleeping upstairs. Anneliese searched his face in the glow of her porch light.

Jack tried to blink back the tears, but he couldn't hide from her.

"She…" The words hitched on his tongue. "My mom…" The welling tears spilled over and he choked on a sob.

Anneliese paled, her lips compressed in shock and worry.

"Something happened, a heart attack, I think…"

"Oh, Jack," Anneliese opened the door. "She's not…" The unspeakable faded between them as he stepped inside.

Jack sucked in a breath, swiping at his cheeks with the back of his hand. "She's stable, but it was a setback."

"I'm so sorry."

Anneliese wrapped her arms around him and held on, crooning a gentle, unintelligible stream of words Jack didn't need to understand. Comfort was language enough. He pressed his cheek against her temple and let his tightly wound emotions unspool while the crickets' symphony played from the garden.

It was like dancing, he realized, the way their bodies gave in to the gravity of closeness, sinking and swaying together—though Anneliese's music had stopped. He hadn't come to her seeking the heat that had built up between them, knotted up in his more immediate concerns, but it was there now. Jack felt at once hollowed out, and achingly aware of the fragile weight of desire between them.

Anneliese worried at her bottom lip, peering up at him. For the longest time, she looked at him with a thousand questions in her eyes. He resisted the urge to seduce, to talk his way around her doubts. He left his doors open, let her look into him while he lost track of where he ended and she began.

He wanted her, yes, but he needed her to issue the invitation.

"Come inside," she said, voice jagged. Her fingers trailed down his arm as she turned from him, but it wasn't a tease or a seduction. She simply let her hands drift along his skin.

He waited while she picked up her phone, a glass and her book, desire tightening his body, uncertainty skittering warily in his veins. The kitchen door was heavy against his palm when he held it open.

She went to leave the glass in the sink, so to slow his racing heart, Jack took in the details of the room.

Her kitchen was long and narrow, with the sink and drainboard at one end, and the stove and refrigerator along the inner wall. The floor was vintage checkerboard linoleum. At the other end of the room, a round table and four mismatched chairs waited for morning breakfast. The table was surrounded by windows, including the one that looked through the screen porch to the driveway. Chloe's ponies mingled with a binder and a stack of wedding magazines. A bright pink booster seat occupied a yellow spindle-backed chair, and a spray of marigolds in a coffee mug stood as a centerpiece.

Twine was hung with clothes-pinned photographs and drawings along the long wall opposite the porch, and Jack crossed the room to look.

In the center was a black and white photograph taken at Nan and Joss's wedding. They'd ended up sitting on the front porch after the guests had all gone home. He remembered the June stars and the luminaries along the Damselfly's front walk. Ewan and Kate, wearing their secret-engagement smiles, Chloe gathered up between Nan and Joss, half-dozing against Joss's shoulder in her flower girl dress, Jack and Anneliese perched against the railing—near to one another, but apart.

He glanced over at her, rinsing the glass in the sink, then back to the picture. He didn't have a single displayable image of these beloved people in his stored possessions. The apartment on Gloucester Street had been devoid of personal effects for the most part. All the goofy college and law school photos, all the high school ephemera and the rare shots of these people, his decorator had made them seem immature. His sister, his best friend, his new brother, two women he loved dearly.

"Isn't that a great shot?" Anneliese had come up beside him and taken his hand. "Chloe picked it."

He squeezed her fingers and sighed. "I wish I had a copy. I'll have to ask Nan and Joss."

Anneliese released his hand. "Jack, I—"

He'd presumed. Presumed and taken her for granted. Tucked her away in his hometown and only taken her out when he was there himself. No wonder she kept her distance.

"I know. I should go." She started to say something, but he rushed through his own words, trying to avoid lingering and spoiling the sweetness. "I'll talk to you tomorrow. Let you know what's going on."

"Of course." Two bright spots had risen on her cheeks.

He leaned down and pressed a kiss to her lips, then fled into the night, to make his way alone across the common and home, pursued by thoughts about love and friendships, photographs and his misguided decorator, and his own miserable shortsightedness.

*I HAVEN'T DONE THIS IN A WHILE.*

She'd started to say it, to confess that what they were about to do felt almost new again. For a few wild moments, she'd been ready to… She took a deep breath and left the kitchen before she whipped the freshly rinsed glass at the wall just to hear it shatter.

Anneliese threw herself down on the old sofa, wincing at the groan of protest from the worn springs. *Stupid her, stupid Jack.* If he hadn't been an idiot, they'd be half-naked and tangled on this very couch.

Which would be the most action it had seen since she and Chris Greene made out on it high school, when it had been in her family's living room.

She pushed up from the sofa, unable to relax with the ghosts of her mistakes, and went back to the porch to turn off the lights and lock up. She would do what she did every night. She would latch the gate, leave the light over the kitchen sink on, and check Chloe's covers before she read herself to sleep, alone on her air mattress.

Chloe was sprawled sideways on her bed, Feesh's tail clutched in her hand. Anneliese padded into her room, a spray of nightlight stars patterning the ceiling and lighting her way from a battery-operated turtle on the floor. She scooped up Chloe's sleep-heavy body and set her down again so she wouldn't slide sideways off the bed. Her daughter never let go of her stuffed clownfish.

Anneliese left Chloe's room feeling less scattered, less angry.

*Had she really been about to have sex with Jack Pease on a twenty-year-old, hand-me-down couch while her soon-to-be kindergartener slept upstairs?*

Anneliese turned on the cold tap, running her toothbrush under the water while she put Chloe's pink, sparkly toothpaste away and got her own out of the medicine cabinet. While she brushed, she set her face wash and moisturizer on the sink edge. The evening ritual settled her further, and she began to plan out the next day, making mental lists full of items to check off and trying to remember if her favorite casual dress was clean or dirty.

The problem was, it was easy to check if her dress was clean. She knew she had a lot of emails to send, and two appointments the next day. What she didn't know—what wasn't easy, was how to lie in her bed on a sultry summer night, her body humming from Jack's kisses, her heart banging in her chest at the memory of his back walking out her door, and her head furious with him for rejecting her, furious with herself for forgetting her own words when Jack had kissed her the evening of the Founder's Day Festival: *Better not.*

# CHAPTER 11

The longer Jack stayed, the more humbling it was to admit he underestimated the scope of his father's practice. Unlike his specialized focus back in Boston, his father carried a robust client load full of concerns Jack hadn't given a thought to since law school. He might have started out bored, but it hadn't lasted long.

Worse, Jack underestimated the scope of care his mother would need, even once she was transferred to the rehab facility. In the quiet moments, he wondered what would have happened if he hadn't offered to step in for his father. Kate would have picked up some of the slack, but his dad's practice would have suffered along with her new ventures. Money and time would have gotten tight; for all Jack knew, his father would have landed in the hospital, too.

There had to be a better way to handle all of this.

In the last three days alone, his father had consulted with therapists, specialists, pharmacists, and Joss—about making some changes to the house. John's entire existence zeroed in on regaining his wife's quality of life.

Joss appeared in the doorway as though summoned. "Quitting time."

Jack glanced at the timestamp on the computer. It was after five. "Did Mrs. Drake just let you through?"

"She loves me. I built her a mudroom cabinet and bench a few years ago. Her grandkids have cubbies, and her husband has no excuse not to hang up his coat." Joss knocked on the doorjamb for luck. "I can do no wrong."

Jack rubbed his temples. "She doesn't even let *me* in here without an appointment."

Joss sat in one of the client chairs. "She's tough on you because she likes you."

"If you say so. So, what's the plan?"

Joss leaned back. "You grab some boots and we hike Acadia Falls, then we stop at Temple and thrash Robbie at darts."

"How'd you get the night off?"

"Nan and Anneliese are driving to Bristol to some catering event." Joss pushed himself up out of the chair. "I feel like hitting a trail, and you look like you need to thrash someone in a way that won't get you arrested."

"Yeah." Jack started the process of shutting down his dad's computer and habitually returned the desk to his father's preferred order.

"You miss it, don't you?"

"What?"

"What you left behind." Joss gestured around the office. "I figure this has got to be pretty small-time after what you're used to."

"You know, it's a lot more than I was expecting. To be fair." Jack pushed in the chair behind the desk and turned off the lamp. "I didn't give the old man the credit he deserves. He works hard at this."

"You think they're invincible—fathers, I mean. Then one day they're just men who are doing their best, and you're one too. That hit me when I moved back from New York." Joss shrugged. "Let's get out of here."

Jack waved a quick good night to Mrs. Drake, who was already tidying up to go home.

There were no other cars at the trailhead; they had the woods to themselves.

Joss pushed him on the trail, setting a decent pace for the brief ascent.

Jack was winded when they got to the summit, but the view down the falls was worth it. The whole valley spread out at their feet. If he used his imagination, he could follow Route 7 north, turn off into Thornton and over the college campus, all the way out to the Damselfly and Fuller Dairy.

He took the valley and the town for granted, just like he did Anneliese. And his friends. "It's probably been ten years since I came up here."

"It took you about ten years to get up here this afternoon." Joss laughed. "You're getting soft."

"Screw you." There was no bite to the insult; Joss was a brother in all but name. Their parents had been friends long before either of them were born. Their friendship was as much a part of him as the color of his eyes.

"So, you're gonna be a dad." Jack leaned back on a rocky shelf and nudged his boots and socks off to dangle his feet in the stream that fed the falls.

Joss crouched by the water. "Nan says she wants a boy first, but I don't know. Chloe presents an excellent case for little girls. Even if I don't get to play ponies very often." He shot a look back at Jack. "Speaking of which, the flower at Founder's Day was a nice touch. If she's decided to love you, you're in for life."

Jack rolled his eyes. "I'm just a novelty. You guys are her family."

"You talking about Chloe, or Anneliese?"

"Both, maybe."

"What happened there?"

Jack wondered if Joss was asking about high school, or this summer. He chose the past.

"I think I didn't see her when it mattered."

"Sounds about right. We were pretty ignorant at seventeen. She's my cousin. It never would have occurred to me that she might have feelings for you back then." Joss sat down on a nearby rock. "I'm no expert on women, but you make her nervous. Ever since she got back."

Jack considered confessing what had happened between them more recently on her porch, but he didn't kiss and tell.

"I treated her like I do Nan, like a friend of Kate's—a pretty woman. Or at least that's what I told myself, but there's part of me..." Jack sat forward, watching his pale feet below the water's surface. It was still bone-chillingly cold, despite the summer heat. "That thought of her as mine. Part of a collection, or something. Jesus, I sound like an asshole."

"Yeah, but I get it." Joss was gentle about the brutal truth. "It's all play when you're in town, but when you go back to your real life, so do we. Here."

"Fuck. I am an asshole."

"So, you didn't see her when it mattered, when we were kids."

Jack pulled his feet out of the stream. "Now I see her, but it doesn't matter."

"Do you, though? See her?" Joss was serious now, gray eyes troubled as he squinted over the sunny water. "Her ex wasn't the type who knocked her around, I don't think, but he did enough damage."

"What did he do?" Jack felt his chest tighten. The rage was instant and frightening.

"You'd have to ask her. She doesn't talk about it. Nan probably knows more, but I think he just took her apart and it was all she could do to drag her pieces home afterward."

Jack felt a thousand different responses—most violent—bottle up in his throat. "It's none of my business, is it? Not unless she wants it to be."

Joss sat back. "Do you want her to make it your business?"

"Shit, I don't know." Jack picked up a stray stone and chucked it into the stream. "Impending parenthood turned you into a regular philosopher."

Joss closed his eyes. "Nah, that's just getting old, Pease."

"Speak for yourself, Fuller."

∽

"YOU LOOK WEIRD." ANNELIESE'S FRIEND MICHELLE SQUINTED AT HER through video chat. "Why are you weird?"

"I'm not weird," Anneliese said. "I'm sitting on my porch."

"Like a weirdo." Michelle tilted her head and examined Anneliese through her computer's camera. "Anyway, let me see if I can get the conference thingy working and bring Sarah in on the call so we can sort out the deets."

"You didn't just say, 'Deets?' Did you? Now who's weird?" Anneliese waited on the third empty box on her screen, silently thanking social media for helping her find her two best high school friends in the bleak aftermath of her divorce.

Chad had taken his things and left while she was at work and their infant daughter was at daycare. She'd come home to a few pieces of thrift store furniture and their clothes. He'd left $72 in their joint checking account and no forwarding address. When the paperwork was served through an attorney, there was nothing more to be done but pick up the pieces and move on—first to an acquaintance's apartment, then home to Vermont.

Chad never so much as asked to see his baby again, sending his mandated child support as infrequently as he could get away with. They almost never spoke, though he apparently called her mother to keep someone in the family well and truly gaslit. Likely just for the power trip.

Michelle and Sarah's unswerving support—if only through texts and endless video chats—helped her cope with moving home again. While she'd found true friendships after her return, including Nan and Kate, she and Sarah and Michelle had survived the awkwardness of adolescence together. And now they were planning a mini-reunion.

She rocked the swing, thinking back to letters she'd sent to the lawyer, telling Chad she was taking Chloe to Thornton. Thinking of the recent brace of phone calls from an unrecognized California phone number. A number that didn't belong to Kirsten Letourneau.

"Stop it, you're making me seasick." Michelle said. "And come back from wherever you just were."

Anneliese reached out to stop the swing's rocking. "Sorry. Didn't mean to give you porch swing motion sickness."

"Yes, rub it in my face that you work from a porch swing in our postcard hometown."

"You work from a gorgeous apartment in the nation's capital and have drinks with the most powerful people in the world."

"I have drinks with the people who work for the most powerful people in the world. It's like Six Degrees of Kevin Bacon, only with jowly white dudes and policy wonks."

Anneliese was still laughing when Sarah joined the chat.

"Did I miss anything good, or just Miche's antics?"

Sarah was in her office. Anneliese could see her framed degrees behind her. "Antics. How was your class?"

"You know how they say the hardest part about Harvard is getting in?" Sarah rolled her eyes.

Michelle peered at the screen. "Anneliese looks weird. I think she's not telling us something."

Sarah's eyes flicked to the corner of her screen. "I have ten minutes until a meeting with an advisee."

"Yes, you're very important, and I'm not wearing pants." Michelle leaned to one side, waving a bare foot and leg. "For reals. Freelance, no pants."

When Anneliese burst into giggles, Sarah's prim smile turned up. "Are you sure you still want us both in your house? Around your child? Miche is practically feral."

"I can't wait. Really." Anneliese grinned at the two of them. "And it's already all *This Is Your Life* around here, so you'll fit right in."

"*Now* we're getting somewhere." Michelle zeroed in on the buried lede, and Anneliese made a mental note to never let her get to be friends with Kate. She'd never have another private thought. "Who's back in town?"

*Out with it, then.* "Jack."

She'd expected Michelle to be the one to respond first, but it was Sarah. "I heard from my dad his mother had a stroke."

Michelle diffused the somber note. "So, Jack came home for a few days to check in and you guys finally got it on like bunnies?"

"You're awful." Sarah frowned, but there was a twinkle in her eye.

Anneliese straightened a pillow. "No! But he came over. One thing started to lead to another…" Sarah and Michelle both blinked at her from their corners of her laptop screen. "And then he left."

"What a jackass." Michelle's response was swift and direct.

Sarah's was more tempered. "Sounds like an adult decision."

"It was," Anneliese said. "Once I picked my ego up off the floor, I realized that. Thing is, he's going to be around for a while, and I don't know what to do about it."

"I think this is where you two put all your stuff behind you. How many people actually get to do that?" Sarah said. "You can catch us up in a couple weeks."

"And text every detail until then," Michelle added.

Sarah signed off when her advisee arrived. Michelle waggled her ruthlessly maintained brows. "Sarah's the designated grown-up, so I can safely say *I* think you should do the nasty and get him out of your system."

"Thank goodness you're not the designated grown-up." Anneliese was still laughing when the chat ended.

JACK WAS ON HIS WAY FROM THE PHARMACY TO HIS FATHER'S OFFICE when Nan called. He was carrying an envelope from the one-hour photo counter with two copies of the childhood photo of Anneliese inside, thinking one would look good clipped to the twine with the group picture on Anneliese's wall. He wondered if Nan's ears were burning—then wondered if his mother's were, too. The saying was one of her favorites.

He told Nan they were keeping his mother in rehab until she was strong enough to go home.

She turned the conversation to him. "How are you adjusting?"

"I have a...friend...in Boston who's referring to me as a 'country solicitor.' Which feels more accurate than I'm comfortable with." Unexpected heat flushed his neck. What he wasn't telling Nan was that Iris checked in regularly, asking if he was *courting* Anna yet.

"A *friend*?" Jack heard teasing in Nan's tone, but chose to ignore it.

"Don't tell anyone, but it's harder than I expected."

"I won't. Client privilege."

"That's not how that usually works," Jack said.

"It is why I called, though." Nan said. "Do you have a few minutes this afternoon? I'd like to talk to you about some things."

Jack was taken aback. "Sure. I don't have any appointments."

A half-hour later Mrs. Drake announced Nan's arrival over an intercom that had been state of the art when the real Mad Men had been hard at work, but which gave Jack a retro thrill he would deny hotly in public.

He stashed the photos in the desk, along with his research on family leave for parental care. After his conversation with Joss and Ewan, he'd been thinking about the unfairness of it all. He didn't know what to make of it yet, but he'd lucked out. It turned out Thornton's representative in Montpelier was a crusader for family care legislation. He left himself a note to call Noah Hawes's office.

Nan waved from the doorway. He'd had a soft spot for his sister's friend since the first time Kate dragged Nan along for a visit to the "big" city. He got up and came around the desk to hug her. "How's my favorite pregnant lady?"

She sank into his spare chair with a sigh. "My ankles are swollen and I can't eat fruit until after noon or I throw up, but I'm happy."

"Can I get you water or tea or anything?"

"Nope. Just a couple minutes of time." She absentmindedly rubbed her belly. "I don't have a will."

"Oh." Maybe he should have, but he hadn't expected that. "It's not my forte, but I can certainly look into it for you. Dad does them, so if it's okay with you, we'll partner on it."

"That's fine. I—" She pursed her lips in thought. "I've never had people to leave anything to. I was an only child. My mom died young. I didn't know my father. You know my grandparents raised me, and I lost them too young, too."

Jack had known some of that and pieced together the rest.

"What they left me made the difference between working for someone else, and having my own place. I just…" Her voice hitched and she swiped tears from her eyes. "Hormones. I swear, I can't watch a toilet paper commercial without weeping."

Jack pushed a box of tissues across the desk. "So, you want to make sure the Damselfly goes to Joss?"

"To the baby," she said. "I want to set things up so I can name them as the beneficiary, but I want to do it somehow so Joss isn't saddled with it if that's not what he wants."

The idea alone tightened his lungs. "Hey. You're not going anywhere for a long time."

She gave a watery laugh. "I hope not."

"What does Joss think about this?"

Nan blushed. "I haven't asked him. I wanted to find out what my options were, so I could present him with some ideas. It's a weird thing to be thinking about, but I can't help it." Again, her hand drifted to her belly. "I mean, he might not want to own an inn without me." Her smile wobbled.

Jack made some notes while Nan blew her nose. He hoped she would speak to Joss soon about all of this. He knew his best friend, and Joss's pride could be prickly. "I'll see what Dad has to say, do some research, but no more maudlin thoughts, okay?"

"Okay." Nan rolled her eyes, but she held tight to him when he hugged her goodbye.

Jack walked her into the baking heat, watched her cross the road and climb into her SUV, wondering idly when she'd upgraded from the replacement VW she'd been driving for a couple of years, and feeling like he'd missed everything when he couldn't recall.

"Mrs. Drake?" He turned to speak from the open doorway. "I'm going over to the hospital."

"Give Cora my best." Mrs. Drake took off her reading glasses, and set them down on her blotter. Jack knew she would rinse the coffee pot, tidy her desk and his father's, wipe down the sink in the powder room, and lock up before she left, as she had every day she'd come in to work.

They'd moved his mother to a new room. She was propped up while a nurse checked her vitals. The remains of supper lingered on a tray by the window.

He knocked lightly on the door to let the nurse know he was there. "I hope she's not giving you too much trouble?"

The nurse turned with a smile. "I think you have a visitor, Mrs. Pease."

Jack went around the bed and pressed a kiss to his mom's forehead. "Hey, gorgeous."

"Jack." There was a downward turn to his mother's smile, and a droop in her eyelid on the same side, a shake in her hands, but she was whole and awake, and her eyes told him everything he needed to know. His mother's spirit was undiminished.

"Your father was here all afternoon." She spoke slowly and carefully, the words slurred. "You just missed him."

"I figured." Jack took his mother's hand. "Dad said he was meeting Uncle Bill tonight, that I shouldn't wait up."

"He hasn't…" Cora Pease blinked at her son. She struggled between words, as if they were log-jammed on her tongue. "…been taking care of himself."

"I'm keeping an eye on him. Promise."

"That's good."

Jack took stock of the new room. It was less sterile than the previous room—still full of flowers, cards, and a drawing of green amoebas signed by Chloe. Jack was pleased to note the window looked out over the garden his mom worked to fund. "Do you need anything?"

"To go home?" Her lopsided smile squeezed his heart.

"Soon. Just rest and get stronger so they can fix you up."

She touched her hand to his cheek. Her skin was cool and soft. "Thank you for reading to me. It was nice to wake up to."

He blushed. "You had a roommate at the beginning, a sweet woman who couldn't read because it strained her eyes. She conned me into reading to both of you."

"You always were a sucker for the ladies." She patted his cheek, then gestured to the bedside table. "You read Ewan's books. They moved them all with me."

"He's good."

"Katie did well."

Jack laughed. "Doesn't she always?"

Cora smiled, but her lids fluttered.

"You're tired. I should let you rest."

"Mmhmm." She was drifting.

Jack stood, kissed his mother's cheek and tucked her covers around her. "I love you, Mom."

The sun was low in the sky behind him as he walked back into town. He stopped on the bridge, leaning his elbows on the stone to let the mist from the spray float around him. Peepers sang from the banks downstream. Foam pooled where the river bent on its journey north, carrying twigs and leaves as it swirled. Jack watched the detritus spin, helpless in the will of the current.

"Thinking about the Cartwrights?"

Jack didn't turn. It seemed too perfect for Anneliese to be there just then; he didn't want to spoil the daydream. "Thinking I know how those leaves and sticks feel."

She joined him, elbow to elbow. "You're not the leaves, Jack. This isn't even your river."

"What am I then?" He turned to her. She was wearing shorts and a U2 tee shirt she'd had for at least fifteen years. He knew, because he'd gotten it for her when he and Joss saw the band in Albany. The Thompsons hadn't let their daughter go along.

Her hair was braided down her back. In the gilded daylight, she could have been the girl who'd hiked and explored with him for years before some slick jerk from out of town had taken her away from him.

Anneliese laughed. "I don't actually know."

Jack leaned slightly, so their arms touched, but he continued to watch the current. "I was just at the rehab wing."

"Kate mentioned they were moving your mom. How's the new room?"

"Nicer. She was tired."

"She's been through a lot."

Anneliese's simple statement brought him up short, was embarrassed by his own selfish brooding. Pausing his career for a few months hardly left him helpless.

"Jack?"

"Yeah?"

"I was on my way home with my farm share. Do you have dinner plans?"

He snapped out of his reverie. Anneliese carried a pair of mesh sacks, overflowing with dark leafy greens. "Yes. Sorry. Can I take something?"

"Sure." She handed him a bag. "Does that yes mean you're having dinner with me?"

"I was somewhere else for a minute there." An invitation to dinner in a sleepy town with Anneliese and Chloe was the perfect cure for his self-pity. "I'd love to join the prettiest girls in Thornton for dinner."

"Oh." Anneliese's eyes widened. "Just me, I'm afraid. Jamie's kids are at my parents' tonight, so Chloe's there for a cousin slumber party."

"Oh." Dinner alone with Anneliese was a different thing altogether. Jack couldn't remember the last time he'd given a thought to Anneliese's younger brother, but he was glad at this moment the man had kids. "Are you sure?"

Her half-smile faltered. "I promise I can make a decent dinner out of this."

"Banana, I'm sorry. That's not what I meant." He realized what he'd called her and dialed back. "I'm sorry about that, too."

Anneliese put a hand on his arm, where moments ago they'd leaned together. "Don't worry about it. Let's have dinner."

At the cottage, she put him to work washing arugula and chopping Brussels sprouts. She tuned into the college radio station, put away a pile of clean dishes, preheated the oven and pulled out half her pantry. By the time he finished his task, she had a huge salad bowl waiting for the arugula, with a tangy mustard dressing redolent of garlic in the bottom. She tossed the sprouts in oil and sea salt, spread them on a tray, and slid it into the oven.

She handed him a bulk container from the co-op. "Slivered almonds. Toss in a big handful, then you can shred these." The almonds were followed by two carrots, still wearing soil from the farm.

She added dried cherries and poured two mismatched glasses of white wine while Jack peeled and shredded. It took him longer than he'd expected, but Anneliese had picked up her phone. He watched her work, swiping and tapping with the same focus he recognized from his team at the firm.

Jack pushed the scraps into her composter. "Do you always cook like this?"

"Only on farm share Fridays." Anneliese sampled the wine. "Most nights it's Chloe's leftovers, cheese and crackers, or cereal."

Jack washed his hands. On Anneliese's wall was a new set of Chloe's drawings, including one that looked a lot like the one in his mother's room. "Did Chloe do a series?"

"Hmm?" Anneliese followed his gaze. "Oh. She did. Tadpoles. Her class found a little pool near the school, just full of them. She's obsessed, and decided your mom, my mom, Aunt Molly…everyone needed one."

"Would she do one for me if I asked nicely? I could use some happy tadpoles at the office."

Jack wanted to memorize Anneliese's smile in that moment.

"Now you've done it. She'll create an entire series for you. And Mrs. Drake."

The oven timer beeped, and Anneliese moved to take the sprouts out. She scraped the roasted vegetables into the salad bowl and tossed it all together.

Jack stacked the glasses on the plates she'd left out. "Should I bring this stuff to the porch?"

Anneliese hip-checked the door open. "Perfect."

# CHAPTER 12

$J$ack Pease was on her porch swing, eating roasted Brussels sprout salad and listening to her plans to have Sarah and Michelle and their kids stay over Labor Day weekend.

Anneliese's fingers smelled of garlic. She hadn't washed her hair in three days. She was sitting on the floor in ratty shorts and an ancient tee shirt. It shouldn't matter. It was just Jack.

There was nothing *just* about it. She'd known since the moment he kissed her good night after Founder's Day—since the moment he pushed open her garden gate the night he came home—that there was nothing *just* about it.

Her heart was on a collision course. Maybe she was tired of pushing him away, but her body was recklessly unwilling to hit the brakes.

He set his plate down on the porch floor and picked up his wine. "That was wonderful."

Anneliese chased the last of the mustardy arugula around her plate with a roasted sprout. "Thanks."

He swung gently, resting his glass on one bent knee. The radio show changed to a mellow, acoustic playlist. "I wonder if my parents ever do a farm share."

"They do." Anneliese stacked her plate with his. "Your dad asked Nan and me to split it while your mom… Kate said she and Ewan wouldn't use it."

"I had no idea." He was looking at her as though there was a mystery to solve in the use of a farm share. "Come sit with me, Anna."

She did. With her garlicky fingers and grubby hair. She sat when he stopped the swing; she leaned into the open arm he offered. His body was warm and solid, his heartbeat steady in her ear.

He toyed with the ends of her braided hair, pushing the swing lightly with one foot.

When his hand drifted from her braid to the length of her neck, she shivered and stretched to sneak a glance at him. Twilight was falling, returning them to the shadows they'd kissed in on his first night back.

The summer air thickened around them as he lowered his mouth to hers, cupping her head gently. The gentle pressure of his kiss caught a sigh Anneliese didn't recognize as her own. He lingered at her lips, drawing out the tension, stroking the back of her neck, her jawline. Time spun out in a way she forgot it could, while she only let herself feel.

Jack kissed the corner of her mouth, then leaned back, still holding her, searching her face for something. "Is this okay?"

Anneliese slid her hands up his arms. "It is."

She pushed herself up to return the kiss. He hummed appreciatively, and she took that as encouragement.

How long had she waited for the sweet rasp of Jack's tongue tangled with hers, how long had she dreamed of his warm hands against her back? Jack's embrace tightened around her, pulling her into his lap, and she melted against him.

"Anna…" His voice was hoarse in her ear.

She cruised his jaw and shoulder with her lips. "Jack."

He lifted her chin, brought them together with a different, searing intensity. She felt the heat race through her, and her fingers struggled with the buttons of his shirt. She pressed her palms against his chest. Her knees dug into the seat of the swing.

"Come inside," she whispered breathlessly. "Come upstairs."

They left the dishes, the wine. The porch floor squeaked under Jack's feet when he stood, lifting her with him. He hitched her up; she held on, drunk on the scent of him and his breath in her ear. When he set her down on the second step, they stood eye to eye. He held her gaze, waiting, she thought, for her to call it off.

There was no calling it off. Her body ached for him, her heart overflowed. Reason might scold her later, but for tonight Jack Pease would be hers.

She led him upstairs, to her makeshift bed in her makeshift room. The fan in the window whirred over crickets and laughter from next door, flickering the soft light from the hotel's veranda. Anneliese reached for the hem of her shirt and pulled it over her head, laying it aside on a spindly whitewashed nightstand. She had a moment's doubt, standing in front of him in her white cotton bra, her body no longer that of a girl, but Jack was drinking her in with his eyes, and she saw nothing there but desire.

She stepped into his desire and threw her hesitation into the fire she found there. They tumbled to the bed together. With impatient hands, they stripped one another to the skin, fingers streaking over flesh, finding the most sensitive places, lingering where sighs and moans directed.

Her nipples hardened under his touch, his stomach tightened and shivered when she traced the line of muscle that tempted her lower still.

When he cradled her hips in his hands and rocked their bodies together, she shuddered hard. He left her lips to trace a trail of kisses down her belly. He kissed the softness of her inner thighs, whispered something unintelligible across the wet heat he found there, and her first climax hit her.

She panted with the shock of it, and looked down to see Jack staring back at her in wonder.

"Jesus, you're beautiful like that."

His bluntness sent a fresh punch of lust through her, and she fell back against her pillows while Jack's clever mouth brought her up and up and up. When she thought she might fly apart from the pleasure, he abandoned her, but only long enough to stretch alongside her.

"Do you have anything? I wasn't planning on this."

His hands were stroking her ribs and breasts, and it took a moment for his question to sink in.

"In the bathroom," she whispered, glad she'd added condoms to her new house supplies order. She'd cursed herself as an optimist at the time, but she was clear as crystal on the repercussions of irresponsibility. Chad had said no kids; she'd been reckless, so sure a baby would fill the void in her empty marriage.

Jack was back in her bed before she could examine her thought too closely.

She reached for him, marveling at the feel of him in her hands, at the feel of him inside her. She moved against him, smoothed her hands up his back to bring him closer still, opened her eyes to watch his face when he gave in to her.

Gone was the tender control, the gentleness. She met him, harder, faster, driving him to his release with more than a decade's pent up desire, and when they tumbled over the edge together, he cried her name into the quiet.

Jack woke to moonlight mingling with Anna's hair across his chest.

Anneliese's breath hitched slightly when he rolled out of bed. He paused for a moment in the doorway on his return. She sprawled, tousled and soft, in her sleep. Did she relish sleeping alone after years in a bad marriage?

*Of all the times to wonder about her ex-husband.* He never met the man, never had a reason. Anneliese didn't keep any photos of him around. He was as faceless as the imaginary suitor who'd plagued him at the co-op. Jack knew from Joss they eloped when her ex decided to move back to California. That had been while Jack was a summer intern at Kearney-Mulligan.

Anneliese, who always loved weddings, who planned them for others, hadn't had one—not the way Nan or his sister had.

How could a sane man neglect a woman like her, never mind leave her? He'd been with enough women to know one who'd been left wanting for too long. He saw doubt flash across her face when she took off her shirt, as if he might walk out because she wasn't wearing La Perla and offering him a mannequin's physique, and for that he could have knocked the bastard into next week given the opportunity.

*Why did I not see her when she was right in front of me?*

He hadn't, though, and he had no right to his fury at the man she married. She wasn't his. Not to keep, and not to toy with.

He knelt on the mattress, lifting a thick lock of her hair from across her cheek.

"Anna," he whispered. "I should go."

"Mmm," was her only reply.

Jack smiled and pulled the sheet up over her; it was cool now, but the fan still clicked and hummed in the window. He dressed as quietly as he could. He stopped to bring in their dishes, then let himself out through the garden gate.

# CHAPTER 13

Kate found Jack in their parents' kitchen the next morning. From the determined look on her face, Jack was sure she already knew what transpired at the cottage the night before.

He tidied up his notes and stacked them under his laptop. He was on unsteady ground when it came to estate planning, but confidentiality was like breathing.

"What are you doing tomorrow?" Kate bypassed him, heading to the pot of coffee he'd just brewed and pouring herself a cup.

He thought of a dozen scenarios, all involving Anneliese and a day spent in bed, but he kept his counsel. "I don't know, Katie. What am I doing?"

"Anna's taking some furniture from my apartment. I've got almost everyone lined up to move it over to her place." She leaned against the counter and sipped her coffee. "Did you buy the coffee? This is better than Dad's usual."

"It's the last of the high-test stuff I had at my place. I brought it with me."

"Where's it from? I might order some for Sweet Pease."

"Bag's in the freezer." He laughed as Kate simultaneously

rummaged in their parents' freezer and tugged her phone out of her pocket to take a picture. "So, what time are we moving Anna's furniture, and does she know we're coming?"

"Nine." Kate shot him a withering look. "And yes. What kind of friend do you think I am?"

*Hopefully the uninformed kind.* Until he'd considered it, he hadn't realized he didn't want their friends to know. Not until he had time to figure things out with Anneliese.

He toasted her with his mug. "The best kind."

"Are you going to hospital today?"

"I was going to. I have a couple emails to finish for work, then my day is my own. Mom said she liked the reading, so I'll keep reading the Alasdair Sledge books to her."

"You're a sweetie." Kate drained her coffee and set the mug in the sink. "And Ewan writes a rather dashing heroine, doesn't he?"

Jack chuckled. "Cordelia is great. She reminds me of someone, but I can't think who."

"Right?" Kate hugged his shoulders as she passed him. "I'm going over there now. If I don't see you there, I'll see you at Anna's tomorrow."

"Sounds good." He remembered his manners just before Kate closed the front door. "Can I bring anything to Anna's?"

"Nope." Kate let the door bang shut behind her, but it swung open again a moment later. "Actually, you have a good eye. I still need some wall art—about this big—" She held out her arms. "For over the dresser. A surprise statement piece. Make yourself useful."

He shook his head to the sound of Kate's flip-flops on the front steps. Less than twenty-four hours to find a decent-sized piece of housewarming art for a woman you'd known since you were kids, and only recently spent the night making love with. His sister had a high opinion of his talents.

Instead of thinking about Nan's will or the artwork, he texted Anneliese. *You never mentioned you were getting a house makeover tomorrow.*

She replied a few minutes later. *Your sister moves fast.*

*Don't I know it*, he typed. *I'm sorry I left like that. We didn't talk about Chloe. I wasn't sure you'd want me there in the morning.* He waited, but no response came. *You were too sweet in your sleep to wake up.*

Her reply was one word: *oh*

She had been, her hair fanned on the pillow, falling over her face while she dreamed.

Inspiration hit, and Jack opened his laptop. Thornton was small, but it was a college town. He was fairly sure he could get what he wanted on short notice, for the right price.

"WILL IT FIT UNDER THE WINDOW?"

Anneliese directed Joss and Ewan, who were carrying Kate's former couch through from the kitchen. Kate and Ewan had closed on their house, and were in the throes of nesting, including bringing the last of Ewan's things out of storage in New York, and acquiring, as Kate put it, "grown up furniture." It was hard not to envy her friends' good fortune, but she was grateful Kate offered her the contents of her apartment.

"It will," Jeremy's voice came from upstairs, "but you'll want it in the other corner so you can look out the window, and if you ever cave and get a TV, you can put it on the wall opposite. It can make an L with that relic you've already got."

Anneliese looked up over her shoulder.

Jeremy poked his head out from her bedroom. "Seriously, put it in the other corner."

"Fine." Anneliese pointed to the designated corner, and Joss and Ewan set it down. "Are you almost done up there?"

There was a chorus of laughter from her bedroom. Kate was secreted upstairs with Jeremy and Glenn, assembling the bed frame. There had been talk of lamps, bedding, and surprises.

"Almost," Kate called down. "You and the boys can grab the ottoman and end tables."

Joss turned to Ewan with a grimace. "You married her."

Anneliese followed them out to Joss's pickup. They hoisted the ottoman and started back toward the house.

"How's it going?" Nan sat cross-legged on a patch of grass with Chloe, who was making flower crowns for her ponies.

"Kate has taken over the bedroom with Glenn and Jer, and apparently I have to make an L with the two sofas."

Nan laughed. "Sounds about right. Chloe and I were thinking about walking over to the Scoop Shoppe to get some carry-out for everyone. What do you think?"

Chloe looked up from her ponies. "Can we?"

"Of course, baby." She ruffled Chloe's hair, and went to see what was left in the truck.

She grabbed the pair of nesting end tables and started back for the house. Most of the furniture was third-hand, originally given to Kate by her parents, but it was in good shape, and filled out the empty spaces in her little house.

The mattress and box spring she splurged on to replace her inflatable bed would go on Kate's old frame. There would be a dresser for her clothes, like a proper adult's bedroom. While they hadn't had a chance to speak alone since, the memory of Jack in her bed brought a flush of pleasure to her cheeks.

Kate had sent her brother out with a shopping list a mile long. Anneliese still wasn't sure what he was buying. To busy herself while she waited, she took the slipcovers off the sofa and ottoman and carried them to the cellar where the washer and dryer were.

When she got back, Nan, Chloe, and Jack were all in the kitchen. Seeing him there gave her the most delicious swooping sensation, like a perfect secret.

Her mother's voice filled her thoughts, offering wisdom Anneliese knew only too well. *Watch yourself, Anneliese.*

"Hi."

Whatever he was saying to Nan, he stopped. "Hey."

"Mama, me and Nan got four kinds, and we found Applejack. He brought a—"

"Don't spoil it," Nan said, cutting Chloe off. "It's a surprise, remember?"

Chloe's eyes went wide, and she clapped her hands in front of her mouth, which made everyone laugh.

Kate hollered down the stairs. "You can come up!"

Anneliese climbed the stairs wondering what the fuss was all about.

"Ta-da!" Kate, Glenn, and Jeremy all struck poses in her transformed space. Kate reclined across a bed done in Anneliese's favorite soft greens and beiges, with bold, floral pillows in deep purple and fuchsia. Jeremy struck a Vanna White impression with a matching pair of lamps, gorgeous Tiffany-style pieces. Glenn leaned nonchalantly against the dresser, arrayed with framed photos of her friends, family, and Chloe. A huge framed print hung on the largest wall, a soft-focus, black and white photograph of a young girl on a rope swing, long blond hair whipping across her face.

Not just any girl, Anneliese realized with a start. Her. On the rope swing down by the creek on the Fuller's property.

"What? You guys!" She couldn't catch her breath. "Where did all this come from?"

Kate patted the bed. "Glenn had all the pictures printed and framed. They're from all of our phones. I saw the bedding and had to get it for you."

Jeremy turned on one of the lamps. "I snagged these at the flea market a couple of weeks ago. Kate and I are quite a team."

Kate gestured to the print. "That's from Jack."

Anneliese could only stare. "This is all just amazing."

"Mama!" Chloe barreled in and launched herself onto the bed. "Look at your room…"

"I know, Chlo'. Kate-Kate and Jeremy and Glenn did this for me."

Chloe looked at her mother seriously. "Did you say thank you?"

Anneliese looked around the room, overwhelmed by her friends' generosity. "Thank you. So much."

Nan stepped into the room. "Oh, Anna. It's gorgeous. And downstairs already looks so much cozier."

Glenn joined his husband near the door. "We should get back to our place. We've got a thing. Great job, team."

"Bye, guys. Thanks again," Anneliese said.

Nan sat heavily. "I could nap. I never expected to get worn out walking four blocks to the Scoop Shoppe and back. There's ice cream in the freezer, though."

Anneliese gave her daughter a squeeze. "Chloe, can you go down and tell Joss and Ewan that it's time for an ice cream break?"

"Yup!"

"I'll come with you," Nan said to Chloe.

Jack lingered at the doorjamb to let Chloe and Nan pass.

Anneliese's voice failed her for a beat. "Where did you find that?"

"I took it," he began.

It came back to her, fuzzy and piecemeal like a dream. "With that blue kids camera you had. I'd forgotten."

He came to her, putting his arms around her. "I remembered it last week when I was talking to Dad. I had a regular print made for your kitchen wall, but then yesterday Kate asked me to find a piece for this wall, and…well, the photography shop in the strip mall south of town did an impressive rush job."

It was so easy for him, giving gifts, being kind. She wondered if he had any idea how easily he could be thoughtless, too. Still, it was hard to dwell on the hard thoughts when his hands were tracing circles on her lower back, and his mouth was temptingly close. "Thank you. I'd never have thought of myself as an art subject."

"I can't think of a lovelier one." He kissed her, hot, playful, and possessive all at once, teasing out the sweetness with his lips, tasting her sigh when she gave in. She melted into his embrace, clinging to him.

"Mama! Ice cream," Chloe hollered from the kitchen.

Anneliese dragged herself away from the kiss, leaning her forehead against Jack's lips. His smile curved against her skin.

"Ice cream," she echoed.

# CHAPTER 14

"Penstemon, lady's mantle, half a dozen Siberian iris, and..." CeCe Drexler bit her thumbnail and scanned the inside of her shop. "Ferns!"

Anneliese leaned against the counter while CeCe put the bouquet together. She never would have thought to pair the vibrant pink and purple with the delicate pale yellow sprays and the ferns, but the effect was charming—tranquil, but undeniably happy.

"CeCe, you're a genius."

"Honey, I know." CeCe tied the flowers up in clear floral cellophane and an emerald ribbon. "It's my calling."

"Really?" Anneliese fished her wallet from her cavernous bag. "Always?"

"Since I was knee-high to a grasshopper." CeCe rang up Anneliese's flowers. "My Granny Jo could grow anything, and I followed her around the gardens from the time I could walk. I always knew what the flowers were saying, better than I knew what some people were talking about. Granny Jo said plants make more sense than most people anyway."

Anneliese laughed. "I think I'd have liked your Granny Jo."

"You still can. All that breathing sweet air in the garden kept her young. She's 97, and the belle of her retirement community. She still teaches the *young folks* who move in how to garden."

Anna gathered up the flowers and inhaled with a smile.

"She'd like you, too, Anna," CeCe said. "She loves weddings. Had three herself, enjoyed the hell out of all of them, so the stories go. She'd say you have a calling, too."

"Speaking of callings, I might have another gig if you're up for it."

"Honey, I am always up for it. Talk to me."

"I just booked a high profile, has-to-be-flawless wedding for the end of October. The bride is kind of a big deal. I can't get into specifics, but I'd love to have you on the team."

"Tell you what." CeCe swiped Anneliese's card and handed it back. "You put together one of those vision boards you do, and I'll write up an estimate. I do love high-profile."

"Thanks again. These are perfect."

"Give my love to Cora and John."

Anneliese promised, and slipped out the door. An errant breeze teased her with the warm vanilla scent of Kate's bakery. She passed Sweet Peas without stopping, but not without regret. There simply wasn't time for a treat. She was pushing her schedule to the edge by squeezing in a visit to Mrs. Pease between her meeting with the Thornton College chaplain about a vow renewal for an anniversary party, and picking up Chloe.

She made her way past reception and the nurse's stations to Cora's new room, following the signs to the room number Kate texted her earlier.

Anneliese heard Jack before she saw him. His voice flowed out of the room, dramatic, with a touch of affected British accent. Anna paused just outside the door to Cora's room to listen to Jack reading from Ewan's *Mandarin Dragonet*. She'd already read the six existing ebook novellas in a great binge, so she knew what was coming, and smiled as Jack read the reveal near the end of the third book.

"I loved that moment," she said, coming through the door with a soft knock.

He closed the book with a flourish. "Look who came to see you, Mom. And just in time. I have a client in a half hour."

The lingering symptoms of the stroke were evident, but Mrs. Pease was awake and glad to have visitors, if her downturned smile was to be believed. Anneliese scootched past Jack to hug his mother as gently as she could.

"Anna," Mrs. Pease said. "What lovely flowers."

"I see I'm not the only one who thought of them." Anneliese held out the bouquet from Josephine's, grinning at the vast array of flowers spilling out of everything from generic delivery vases to water jugs and borrowed cafeteria coffee cups. "Is there room for these?"

Jack stood and pulled a drooping bouquet from a tall glass juice bottle, tossed the wilted blooms and held the bottle up for inspection. "Will this do?"

Anneliese took it. "I'll get them some clean water."

"Anna—" He touched her hand, speaking quietly. "Can I come by later?"

She nodded, trying to resemble casual, but it was nearly impossible when she could smell his soap on his skin.

Over the running water in the adjoining lavatory, Anneliese heard Jack saying goodbye to his mother. When she brought out the freshly watered bouquet, he was gone. She sat in the chair he'd been reading in, setting the makeshift vase back on the windowsill.

"How have you been? And Chloe?." The words clearly took some effort. "I missed so much."

"I'm so glad to see you, Mrs. Pease." Anneliese took the older woman's hand. "We're both fine. When you're feeling a little stronger, Chloe wants to bring you more drawings for your walls."

"That...would be nice." Cora Pease's words were still labored, but she was clearly willing to fight for them.

Anneliese pulled out her phone and showed Jack's mother some of the images she'd pinned for the upcoming wedding. Weddings were always happy news.

*Happily ever afters? Now those were a gamble.*

"Maybe I'll just reuse all these gorgeous flowers," Anneliese teased. "I think you've got an entire greenhouse in here."

Cora managed a weak half-smile, but her eyelids were growing heavy. Anneliese started to get up, but Jack's mother patted her hand and whispered, "Always good for him."

She gently squeezed Cora's hand, unsure of how to reply. It didn't matter. She'd drifted off to sleep to the clicking and whirring of her monitors.

"Get stronger soon," Anneliese whispered. "He needs you."

On her way to the lobby, she passed John Pease. His wife's recovery was having a positive effect on him. He stood straighter, looked brighter and sharper than he had since Cora's stroke. "Anneliese, what a lovely surprise."

She gave Jack's father a quick hug. "She's resting. I just wanted to say hi, and drop off some flowers."

Mr. Pease hugged her back. "Did you run into Jack?"

"He left. Just after I got there. A client, I think."

There was a particular twinkle in Mr. Pease's eye that understood more than her babbling allowed for. "I'll let you be on your way. Give Chloe a big hug from Cora and me."

Anneliese reached out and grasped his hand. "I will, Mr. Pease. Thank you."

She was fairly certain as she walked away, that he was whistling.

THE WALK FROM THE HOSPITAL TO THE ELEMENTARY SCHOOL LEFT Anneliese sticky and frizzy, but the joyful screeching of the kids in the summer program lightened her steps. Only a week remained before Labor Day weekend, and with it a return to the academic school year.

Kindergarten seemed so grown up all of a sudden.

Grace Mackie was already waiting at the playground with her stroller. From the relaxed little feet peeking out, Anneliese assumed Jax's little brother was napping. Grace waved, causing the man she was talking with to turn in her direction.

The sight sucked the breath from Anneliese's lungs. When the air rushed back in, she began to notice things. His studied disarray, the scruffy beard grown to take the cruel edge off his smile. He had the beginnings of lines around his eyes; his temples were touched with gray, despite being in his mid-thirties, but his body was leaner and more defined.

She'd rather have approached a well-groomed scorpion.

Anneliese squared her shoulders and looked Chad in the eyes. "Hello."

His gaze cruised over her; the lips beneath the careful beard growth curved, but there was no warmth to his smile. "Anneliese. I was just getting to know Grace. It's great to see that Chloe has such good friends."

"I can't believe I thought Jack was Chloe's dad," Grace gushed. "Not now that I know how much she looks like Chad."

*First names already?* Anneliese thought fast; her pulse was pounding, her fingers tingling. "Grace, would you mind giving us a moment? And maybe don't say anything to Chloe. We want to surprise her."

"Oh, sure," Grace said, flashing them a conspiratorial smile and miming zipped lips. She pressed a hand to Chad's tanned forearm. "It was really nice to meet you."

"You, too."

Grace wouldn't notice the lack of real emotion in Chad's expression; he had always been able to hide that. Anneliese whirled and strode around the corner, out of the playground's sight lines, turning on him, knowing he would follow, if only to torment her. "What the hell are you doing here, at Chloe's school, talking to my friends?" The reality of the situation caught up to her in a rush. She glared to hide the fear that was pushing rage out of the way. "How did you know where she was?"

The false cordiality he showed Grace melted away. He leaned in close, speaking low. "You're hardly tough to predict. Same podunk shops, same pathetic walk around town every day."

He followed them? She drew in a deep breath to steady her

shaking fingers and the angry tears that threatened. "Why, after five years, are you looking for us?"

"Can't a man express paternal interest?"

The way he said "paternal" sent shivers of alarm down her limbs. "Why?"

"Congratulate me, Anneliese. I'm getting married."

She nearly got whiplash from his abrupt shift. "What?"

His laugh slithered over her. "My fiancée is just heartbroken for me. My cruel ex-wife keeps my only child from me, after all."

Anneliese couldn't hold back the shaking, and gripped her bag. "That's bullshit."

"Completely," Chad agreed. "But devoted dads down on their luck are so attractive."

She had no words, but it didn't matter. He wasn't done.

"I met her selling real estate. Jocelyn. I'm still doing that, thanks for asking." He straightened, slipping into a shtick. "Funny thing. She's doing a deal on an apartment in San Francisco for this B-list celeb and her boyfriend, and there's a lot of girl talk. Turns out they're getting married in Vermont in the fall, they want to move in after, have the place fully renovated before then. Gotta play interested in the career crap, so I say, 'Yeah? I went to college in Vermont. Met my ex-wife there. It's gorgeous, isn't it?'"

He let the horror of the coincidence settle in.

"Jocelyn talks so much it's a shock her tongue doesn't fall out, but it paid off this time. She's yapping about this *influencer's* wedding and how," he affected a simpering soprano, "the wedding planner has the *prettiest* name."

Anneliese found her voice. "You're *enjoying* this."

"Immensely." The bell rang inside the school. "I figure if you're handling clients like them, you're doing well enough to make it worth my while to stay lost. Weddings are expensive."

The summer classes spilled out the door. Anneliese caught sight of Chloe and Jax making a beeline for Grace. She summoned the steel that had gotten her through the end of their marriage. "I haven't got five cents to spare, Chad. Go home to your new life and leave us alone."

"We'll see." He shrugged, a nasty gleam in his eyes. He rocked forward on the balls of his feet, watching Chloe bounce around Grace and the stroller. "Your friend Grace is right. She does look a lot like me. Maybe from now on you should take my calls."

Anneliese walked away, heart in her throat, stomach clenched. Halfway to Grace and their kids, she turned around, but Chad was nowhere to be seen.

INSPIRED BY THE BOUQUET ANNELIESE BROUGHT TO HIS MOTHER, JACK stopped at Josephine's on his way from the office to Anneliese's cottage. The florist shop was one of many that sprung up n downtown Thornton when he wasn't paying attention. The owner was behind the counter, putting together vases full of ruffled, pale pink blossoms. Their crowded lushness was incredibly sexy.

"What are those?"

The owner looked up through translucent red acrylic frames, her silver-streaked dreadlocks falling over one shoulder. She cupped her hands around one of the flowers and held it up. "Peonies. From my hothouse." She set the bloom down and took off her glasses. "Something I can help you find?"

"I came in looking for roses, but those are exactly what I want."

"These are a sample I'm putting together for a bride, but I can do something similar as a bouquet. Tell me about her."

Jack laughed. "How do you know there's a her?"

"I'm a florist, honey. I know." She offered her hand over the counter. "CeCe Drexler, proprietress."

"Jack Pease. Pleased to meet you." She had a strong grip. He liked her immediately. "You already know her, actually. Anneliese Thompson."

"You've got great instincts, Jack Pease," CeCe said.

Jack left Josephine's with a shallow bowl of peonies and a lighter wallet. He was humming the state song to himself when he let himself through Anneliese's garden gate. He rapped on the porch door and called out to Anneliese.

Her voice came around the door before her, leading with an unexpected sharpness. "Who is it?"

"It's Jack." He reached for the door handle, juggling the bowl of peonies, but she'd dropped the hook and eye latch to lock the door.

"Hey, sorry." Anneliese pushed a stray wisp of hair out of her face and pushed the hook loose.

"Everything okay?" He stepped through the doorway, holding the flowers out, but Anneliese didn't seem to see them.

She was peering over his shoulder at the garden. She dragged her gaze from the street outside to meet his. "Sure."

"Really?" Jack glanced over his shoulder, but the street was quiet save a car passing by.

Anneliese dropped the latch again. "Come on in."

Chloe was kneeling in the booster seat at the kitchen table, crayons spilled out across the table and a coloring book open in front of her with her stuffed clownfish as a paperweight.

"Hey, Ninja Frog," he said.

"Hi, Applejack." She looked up briefly, but went back to her coloring.

There was something in a sauté pan on the stove; the kitchen smelled of pasta and the earthy sweetness of cooking vegetables. "Did I barge in on dinnertime?"

"Hm?" Anneliese was looking out the window through the porch again. She shook her head quickly, clearing whatever cobwebs were distracting her. "No. I mean, sort of, but there's enough to share. If you want to join us."

The invitation sounded genuine enough, but she was looking anywhere but at him. Suddenly every action since they had rushed up her stairs together was suspect. Had he crossed a line? Had he not called, not texted, not...

He was still holding the bowl of peonies, like a fool. "I really just came by to give these to you. I won't intrude on your evening."

"Oh, they're lovely." Anneliese seemed to finally notice him. "Thank you. I'm sorry. It's been a…long day." She took the bowl and set it in the center of the table. "What do you think, Chlo'?"

Chloe looked from her mother to the flowers then to Jack. "Those are fancy. Can I have one for my room?"

"Sure." Anneliese shot him an apologetic smile, and pulled a peony from the arrangement. She floated it in a turquoise plastic cereal bowl with some water and set it down next to Chloe's coloring. "We'll take it upstairs later. What do you say to Jack?"

Without stopping her work filling in a unicorn on the page—he was impressed at her ability to stay mostly within the lines—Chloe said, "Thank you."

"Manners are a work in progress. For both of us." Anneliese went to the pan on the stove, nudging the contents with a wooden spoon. "It's just noodles with veggies and cheese, but we'd love to have you stay."

"In that case, can I set the table?"

"That's my job," Chloe swung herself out of the booster and hopped to the floor. "I'll show you."

He trailed the little girl into the living room, where she dug around in a low cabinet for placemats and napkins, handing them to him like she'd been delegating every day of her young life.

With some direction, he was able to set things to Chloe's standards about the same time Anneliese brought the pan to the table. She tapped Chloe's napkin as she sat, reminding him to put his own in his lap.

"Should we ask Jack our question first today, since he's our guest?"

"Yup." Chloe reached for a large mason jar full of slips of paper, digging around until she pulled one out. She gave it to her mother to read.

Anneliese's smile didn't reach her eyes, despite the lightness in her voice. "How did you make someone's day happier today?"

Chloe followed up. "You have to tell one thing, then it's my turn."

"I don't know if this counts, but I learned something new that's going to help a friend worry less." He looked to Anneliese for confirmation he was playing by the rules.

She tilted her head, obviously curious. "I think that counts. How 'bout you, Chlo'?"

"I traded my yogurt for Jax's fruit snacks 'cause he doesn't like the grape ones."

He couldn't help laughing at her earnestness.

"Mama, you do one."

Anneliese's expression went blank, her eyes stricken, like she'd been caught carrying bad news. "I…"

"Your mom brought flowers to my mom at the hospital, and my mom loves flowers."

His answer appeared to satisfy Chloe, and by the time he looked back at Anneliese, the upset was gone from her features. "That's right, I did. Should we eat?"

After dinner, Chloe talked Jack into a game of Chutes and Ladders on the porch. Anneliese handed him the board game and sent them out to play, grateful for five minutes alone to let her face relax.

Pretending everything wasn't collapsing around her left her feeling jittery and hollowed out. Chad in Thornton. Chad thinking she had money. That ugly veiled threat. Her thoughts raced from one heartbeat of her divorce to another, but she couldn't gather them into any kind of coherence.

She shoved dirty dishes into the sink and let the water run until it was scalding, plunging her hands in and ruthlessly scrubbing plates and cutlery until her hands stung.

"Anna?"

Anneliese looked up to find Jack in the doorframe. "What?"

"Chloe trounced me twice. I thought I'd limp away from the battlefield and see if you needed help." He took in the steam and suds. "I can dry."

"I've got it." The cooking pan settled on the drying rack with an audible thump, and Anneliese winced.

"Okay."

She heard Jack's resignation and sighed. It wasn't his fault she was upset, but what could she say about Chad without sounding like a crazy person? On the surface, he hadn't even been unreasonable. If confronted, she knew he would ooze charm and reason, and she'd be left holding the bag of messy feelings. And what about her daughter? Chloe didn't need Chad's cruelty in her life.

She turned to apologize, but he was gone.

"Jack?" Anneliese pulled her hands out of the sink and dried them.

He reappeared in the doorway. "Yeah?"

"You know what you could do? Help Chloe pick up the game. She's going to need a bath and jammies shortly."

"Already on it, right Frog?"

Chloe slipped around his legs with the Chutes and Ladders box in her arms. "On it."

Anneliese watched Jack follow Chloe through to the living room to put the game away. How could she involve him, when he would be going back to Boston before too long? How could she be thinking of getting in deeper with Jack at all?

They couldn't go on like this. It was unfair to both of them.

It was her own heart to break. There was no money to give Chad. Ruining the closest thing she'd had to a relationship in five years would have to be enough to satisfy her ex-husband's ego.

"Chloe, time for a bath. Head up and brush your teeth. I'll be there in a minute to turn on the water."

She heard her daughter start to push back, followed by Jack's voice, though the words were low enough she couldn't make them out. Heavy pre-K stomps told her Chloe had capitulated. She wondered what kind of deal he negotiated.

Jack stepped up behind her, circling her waist and nuzzling the soft skin beneath her ear. "I could stick around. We could make out like teenagers on your porch swing." He punctuated the thought by nipping at her earlobe. "Drive each other crazy."

She turned to face him, bracing his wrists to put some distance between them. "It's not a good idea—"

"Scared of nosy neighbors?"

"No." She had to look away before he saw how hard this was. "Us. It's not a good idea—and before you tell me we've said that before, I know we have."

Jack took a step back. She missed his closeness almost immediately. "Anna, don't say that. I know there's a clock ticking over us, but we're good together. I—"

"I know." She braved leaning her forehead against his chest. "But it's not just me who's involved, and I don't want to lose your friendship."

"You couldn't."

"Mama, my teeth are brushed!"

She wordlessly thanked her daughter's interruption. "Okay, baby. I'll be right up."

Anneliese stepped back, and the heartache in Jack's eyes mirrored her own.

Eternity came and went while Anneliese's heart crumbled. Jack broke the silence to call upstairs to Chloe.

"Good night, Frog." He turned and walked wordlessly out of her kitchen.

Anneliese ran up the stairs, but she couldn't get the water running fast enough to drown out the sound of the garden gate closing behind him.

# CHAPTER 15

*J*ack hadn't excelled in school by accident. He hadn't been partner track at the firm because of his good looks—though objectively, he knew he made a good first impression in a suit. He was good at information, good at research, good at work—and he threw himself into it with a vengeance.

If he woke every morning with the scent of Anneliese's hair in his dreams, that was his punishment. He'd said as much to Joss. He saw her now, but it didn't matter. Their lives were too separate. She had invited him into her bed, but he couldn't blame her for being conflicted about what happened there. That didn't stop the heaviness that accompanied him from his childhood bedroom to his father's office, to the hospital, and home again every day for a week.

Jack was tired of staying home watching ESPN with his old man. Nan and Joss were checking out some west coast B&B for a few days —a last precious getaway before the foliage season and the baby. Kate was in Montreal overnight with Ewan for a book thing, and he was dodging her anyway. She knew him too well.

Jack finished up a round of emails to connections who might have some insight into elder care and family leave legislation, then dug into estate law.

When his stomach reminded him later that it was midday, he headed for the co-op. After assembling his lunch, he loitered by the produce until Mrs. Thompson's register was available.

"Jack," she said, scanning his take-out box, "how are you?"

"Can't complain." He offered her the smile that had always charmed her into letting Anneliese come along with him and Joss. "How are you and Mr. T.?"

The image of Anneliese's father and the eighties pop culture icon was lost on Anneliese's mother, but it always gave Jack a laugh.

"We're well." She rang up his iced tea. "Will we see you at the Fuller's Labor Day barbecue?"

"You will. Wouldn't miss it." He took a deep breath and went for casual. "Is Anna going to be there?"

Mrs. Thompson's smile vanished. "She's got plans. Sarah and Michelle are coming for the weekend with their children. Why she planned it like that, I don't know."

He'd forgotten. Between the sting of her rejection and his relentless work ethic, he'd completely forgotten how excited Anneliese was to see her two best friends. Michelle, with her vintage glasses and prickly attitude; Sarah, serious and smart. Neither one had ever said much to him in school, but they were always at Anna's side, looking at him like they were waiting for him to say something.

He rose to Anneliese's defense gently. "It's a great weekend for travel, and her girlfriends probably had time off for Labor Day."

It was pure speculation, but it eased Mrs. Thompson's slight frown. "Of course, you're right."

She handed Jack his credit card back.

"Thanks, Mrs. T.," he said, collecting his lunch. "See you at Walt and Molly's."

KATE CORNERED HIM AT THE FULLER'S. SHE BROUGHT HIM A BLUE SOLO cup of Molly Fuller's spiked lemonade and sat on the split rail fence where he'd been leaning.

"Jack, you need to get out of here."

He took the cup. "You told me I had to bring Dad, now I have to leave?"

His sister was, despite their mother's condition, thriving. Marriage agreed with her. Her bakery downtown continued to flourish with Kate's former intern Margot at the helm, Sweet Pease Café at Cooper Vineyard had its legs firmly under it, and Kate was up to her ears plotting to erase the previous owner's questionable taste from her new house.

She poked his cheek. "You're being a growly bear. I'm sorry Thornton isn't exciting enough for you."

*How could it be, once he known the sound of his name on Anneliese's breathless lips when he was inside her?* It wasn't Thornton that had him down. "It's fine. I'm just tired."

"Your pants are on fire, brother dear." Kate leaned an arm on his shoulder. "Mom's doing better, Dad seems back among the living. Take a weekend and go home."

Home? Not his apartment. He'd sublet it for three months. Maybe New York for a few days? Seth would let him crash.

"Maybe I will."

Molly and Walt's front lawn was full of family and neighbors, with Nan's increasingly round belly at its center. Jack's father and Walt were hunkered down at the grill with a supply of cold beer, and Joss was playing a game of Wiffle Ball with some of his cousins and their kids in the side yard.

"So, what's the deal with Terri Beaudette's daughter?" Jack remembered a skinny, Gothy teenager with a chip on her shoulder from Nan's first summer in town. The young woman sitting with Nan, who'd sold Jack yard maintenance supplies weeks before, bore little resemblance to her former self.

Kate squinted in the direction he was looking. "Nan got her the job with Penny at the nursery after that all went down. I guess she likes gardening. She's staying with Molly and Walt this summer, helping out around the farm and working at Coulson's. Getting a degree in horticulture at UVM."

Jack downed the last of his lemonade. It packed a punch he hadn't noticed while he was listening to Kate. "Does the town pay you to stay this informed?"

"No, but they should." She took his cup and hopped off the fence. "Ewan goes to Danielle for all my flowers. He says she's a savant. I told him not to talk like that on Main Street or CeCe will go all *Little Shop of Horrors*."

Having met Main Street's florist, Jack laughed. "Where is Ewan?"

"He was on the front lawn with Nan when I came over here. I suspect Molly pressed him into service. He takes instruction well."

"He'd have to, living with you."

"Stuff it."

Jack wrapped an arm around his sister. "I should go be social. I must have been pretty pathetic to get you over here to bug me."

Kate slipped an arm around his waist and laid her head on his shoulder. "I'd bug you anyway. That's how much I love you."

They started back toward the party together, but Kate paused just before they reached the others. "Jack, seriously? Get out of town for five minutes. You're no fun lately."

IT WAS HARD FOR ANNELIESE TO DWELL ON JACK OR CHAD OR ANY OF IT when her two oldest friends were camped out on her porch. Sarah's three-year-old daughter was splayed across a twin air mattress on Chloe's floor and her six-month-old son snoozed in a Pack 'n Play in the family room.

Anneliese hadn't laughed so hard in years.

"I can't believe it's taken us this long to plan this." Michelle poured a round of frozen margaritas straight from the blender pitcher. "To us!"

She, Sarah and Michelle had survived high school together, and while Anneliese adored her newfound friends, there was nothing like the bond she shared with these women.

"You guys!" Michelle pushed up her cat eye glasses, which were perched beneath blunt cut bangs, dyed cherry red like the rest of her choppy bob. "I forgot to tell you. I was at this fundraiser in D.C., and I ran into Jenna Christensen."

The mention of the Queen Bitch of the Class of '99 gave Anneliese pause. In high school Jenna delighted in making Anneliese feel awkward and small, while Anneliese longed for what Jenna had taken so effortlessly. Namely Jack.

Sarah gave Michelle a deep side eye, pushing aside her long, toasted-almond waves. "Was her tampon on fire, per usual?"

Anneliese grinned. Michelle's biting wit had saved her from humiliation on more than one occasion, and that particular taunt was unforgotten.

Michelle set down her Solo cup and dug into the bagged chips and homemade guacamole spread out on Anneliese's recently acquired porch table. "She was so nice to me, I figured the silicone in her chest had gone to her brain. Credit where it's due, though, she looks incredible. Being a successful politician's wife suits her."

Sarah pursed her lips and attacked the tomatillo salsa with a chip. "She was just sucking up to you because you went viral last year."

"I am an Internet has-been," Michelle agreed, raising a toast to Sarah, "which is almost as prestigious as being a professor of American Literature at a certain institution of Cantabrigian distinction."

Sarah nodded. Harvard really did suit her.

"Almost," Anneliese added wryly, "as prestigious as having made peace with Jenna and become her go-to party planner for Geoff's local events."

Michelle's eyes went wide. "No way."

"Way." Anneliese mimicked a curtsey with just her arms. "I think it was…challenging for her the first time, but I'm good at what I do, and…" *And I'm good at looking cruelty in the face and smiling. Now.* "…we both play grown-ups well."

Michelle clasped their hands across the table. "We are a trifecta of awesome, and I'm so glad we're hanging out this weekend."

Sarah paused mid-margarita sip and turned to Anneliese. "Speaking of Jenna, how's having Jack around?"

"Has he realized he was sooooo in looooove with you in high school?" Michelle teased. "It was just he couldn't see it for all the prom queens throwing themselves at his jumbo-sized ego."

"Not exactly." Anneliese's cheeks were on fire, but she forced herself to play it cool. "He's only staying here temporarily. Living at home for a while and working for his dad. You remember his sister, Kate? She's got two bakeries in the valley now, and her husband is a writer. Anyway, Kate and her friend Nan, who's married Joss—"

"Is Joss still super hot?" Michelle interrupted with a leer.

"Eww. Stop. He's my cousin." Anneliese giggled. "And again, married."

"And Jack?" Sarah looked at her over the rim of her red plastic cup. Michelle was watching her, too.

Anneliese assembled her face into what she hoped was an innocent and uncomprehending mask. "And Jack what?"

"Oh. My. Gawd." Michelle whooped, then clamped a hand over her mouth with a giggle. They all froze, waiting for the squawk of a child, but none came. "You guys did it!"

Anneliese tried to look wide-eyed. "He's my *cousin.*"

Michelle wasn't falling for the act. "Not Joss, dummy. Jack."

Anneliese was out of options. It was pointless to lie to them.

"Holy shit."

Sarah was reserving judgment. Anneliese could sense it.

"Just once, and it won't happen again."

"Ugh." Michelle stamped her feet. "I hate when a guy doesn't live up to his potential."

"What happened?" Sarah set her drink down and slid closer to Anneliese.

For a hot second, she thought about telling them everything, "I can't get involved with him. There's Chloe to think about, and it's not like he's staying."

"Which makes him perfect for a hot rebound affair," Michelle said.

"Miche, hush." Sarah looked to Anneliese. "You nipped it in the bud."

"I told him we weren't a good idea."

"And he didn't come back begging with flowers and ten pounds of fancy chocolates?" Michelle nearly dumped over her margarita in her outrage.

"How do you feel about it?" Sarah was squinting at her in her thoughtful way.

Anneliese wanted to wriggle out of the conversation. "I don't know. Anxious?"

"How was it? I mean, was Jack Pease worth the wait?" Michelle was ready to dish.

Anneliese opened her mouth to put a stop to it, but the truth came out. "Really good."

Michelle pressed on. "On a scale of *Ugh, Chad* to *Hey, Chris Greene?*"

Anneliese sucked up the last of the tequila-scented slush in the bottom of her cup. "I never slept with Chris, you guys know that. And Chad was better than mediocre exactly three times, once of which resulted in Chloe. So pretty much the fact that I had an orgasm at all puts it in the top three."

"Wait." Michelle was pouring a fresh round and waved for her cup. "You really didn't sleep with Chris? I guess I always thought you were lying so we wouldn't think you were a total slut."

"Anneliese was the best behaved of all three of us," Sarah said wryly, "and we were the last, sad virgins of the twentieth century."

Michelle snorted, resulting in margarita up her nose. All three of them laughed so hard they forgot to be quiet until a sleepy complaint from inside hushed them.

Sarah reached across to take Anneliese's hand in the aftermath of the laughter. "I'm sorry for everything you've been through. If we'd known..."

Anneliese squeezed the offered hand. "I know."

Michelle yawned loudly. "Boring. I want the dirt on Jack and really good sex."

This time Anneliese was done with it. "*I* want to hear all about life in the Capitol."

"Ugh, politicians. Let's talk about the time I met Jon Stewart."

Michelle was distracted by her own celebrity brush-ups. Anneliese tucked Jack—and Chad—away in a corner of her mind. This time was hers.

JACK GOT OUT OF TOWN OVERNIGHT. MRS. DRAKE ONLY RAISED AN eyebrow when Jack asked her to reschedule a few appointments. He figured he was making progress with her.

Going back to Boston would have been depressing. His apartment was someone else's for the time being, Iris was conquering Spain with her sister, and he was out of the loop with his team at the firm.

Jack opted instead to crash a little closer to Thornton. As luck would have it, his friend Seth was in Vermont scouting for artists. An art dealer and gallery owner, Seth owned a loft in an old woolen mill near the Winooski River he rented out to tourists when he wasn't using it. The location near Burlington was just different enough to feel like a change, but Seth was familiar enough with Thornton and its inhabitants to offer some perspective.

Seth met him at the door with a beer in hand. "You sounded like you need this."

"Thanks." Jack took the bottle and dropped his bag by the door. The loft was modern and mostly impersonal, except for the art. Large format photographs and bold paintings hung on exposed brick, and the shelves and surfaces boasted museum quality knick-knacks. "Do your renters ever comment about the collection?"

Seth laughed. "I've sold half a dozen pieces to people who've stayed here. I just install something new. Except for that one of Peri's."

Jack knew the reason Seth kept the huge photo canvas that dominated the largest wall space. Peregrine Fowler, photographer and possessor of the most pretentious pun-based name Jack could think of, had been Seth's first discovery. A wiry sprite of a woman with a girlish voice and a skittish nature, Peri helped Seth establish a name for himself as much as Seth had done for her.

In this black and white image, Peri captured the curve of a

woman's lips. Enlarged as it was, there was a shocking intimacy about the shadow where her mouth seemed poised to speak. Her fine skin was evident, even in black and white. The play of shadows in the dent over her top lip reminded Jack of dunes.

"Sara?" Jack asked, knowing the answer.

"She hated having her picture taken, but she loved Peri. And she liked that no one knew it was her."

"Cat's out of the bag." Jack clinked his bottle against the one Seth held. "She was something special."

"Indeed, she was." Seth look a long drink, lost for a moment in memories. "But you didn't come up here to critique my art."

"I wouldn't know the first thing about it."

Seth headed for the kitchen, leaving his beer on the counter. "You came up here because you're in over your head with Anneliese."

"You're as bad as Iris." Jack sat on the sofa and watched Seth dig through the contents of the fridge.

"You still see Iris?" Seth straightened. "There's nothing to eat here. We're going to have to go out."

"Poor us," Jack said. "And yeah. We have dinner every couple of weeks, meet for lunch now and again. She knows Barry from my office, and some of the others on the team."

"You manage to score—and lose—a woman like that, and she still hangs out with you." Seth leaned against the counter, scrolling through his phone. "There's a decent bar on Church Street with a DJ later tonight. We'll get some food and you can be my wingman."

"Can I please?" Jack finished his beer on the heels of his sarcasm. "For the record, I neither scored nor lost Iris. She called every shot."

"I bet Sara would have loved her," Seth said. "Maybe someday I'll date another woman that amazing."

Jack shot his friend a warning look. "You took my sister out, as I recall."

"Hardly dating. She sent me home alone, twice." Seth raised a toast. "And kissed another guy at Nan's engagement party."

"My brother-in-law, it turned out."

"Wasn't he Anneliese's date that night?" Seth was ribbing him.

"And I behaved like an ass about it."

"And now we find ourselves here." Seth grabbed a chair opposite Jack and flipped on a ball game. Jack was grateful for the distraction, but it only lasted a moment. Seth muted the game. "The Reds suck, but that means you can tell me what's going on with you and Anneliese."

He'd known Seth since college, had helped him navigate the crushing grief of losing the woman he loved to an incurable disease. They'd shared an apartment for a few of Seth's darkest years. There wasn't much they could hide from one another.

He was going to have to spill.

# CHAPTER 16

$\mathcal{A}$fter Labor Day, with Sarah and Michelle gone, it was more difficult not to dwell on Jack or Chad. Everywhere she went, Anneliese saw Chad's face in the crowds of college parents clogging the sidewalks, in the market, on the Thornton College campus. Everywhere she watched for Chad, she found reminders of Jack.

Her only real distraction was work. She'd lined up a two-day tour of catered meals and vendor meetings for Lela's wedding. She awaited Lela's arrival with a mixture of excitement and trepidation. If she pulled it off, this wedding could set her career on an entirely new path. *If* she could get through two days with her famous client.

She'd done her research on the reality star.

Lela Tan hit the scene long before she was old enough to drink, creating a name for herself with a carefully curated feed of social media images and viral videos. By the time she emerged as an adult, she was an established member of a tabloid-friendly party cohort who leveraged being beautiful and clever into lifestyle gigs and sponsored lives.

At twenty-three, Lela appeared on *My Nightmare Career: Celebrity Edition*, which as far as Anneliese could tell, meant her publicist nominated her to spend a week doing a job she knew she would be terrible at for the amusement of millions of primetime viewers.

Five years later, Lela had a fragrance, a shoe line, an endorsement deal with a drug store skin care brand, and at least one celebrity television appearance a year—dancing, singing, flipping homes, cooking, shopping.

While Lela and her fiancé had been photographed together, he was rarely mentioned by name, and there was no speculation regarding their impending marriage. By contrast, Anneliese was already fielding calls from Kirsten regarding sponsored products, and while neither *Vogue* nor *Variety* had come through with an offer to cover the festivities, apparently *Entertainment Weekly* was interested. Kirsten said Lela was trying to leverage the interest into a two-hour documentary on a cable network.

Right up to meeting the reality star, Anneliese continued to study Lela's social media feeds while assembling her final proposal.

She met them in the Thornton Grand Hotel lobby. She was no stranger to the hotel's public rooms since her return, but it would always be the site of her senior prom. Though somewhat faded, it still exuded the elegance of a bygone era. For her, it never failed to elicit the sweet uncertainty of first love as a promise, not a broken dream.

Best, given her current circumstances, to set those memories aside.

Lela and her spouse-to-be held hands in the lobby, him looking tanned and relaxed in tailored shorts and a mint green polo shirt, her in a chic mini dress and impossibly delicate sandals. Anneliese raised a hand in greeting.

Lela took the opportunity to have her fiancé frame a selfie for her against the grand staircase before they joined Anneliese. Lela greeted her with a light hug and continental kisses.

"Hello, Anneliese. I can't believe this is really the first time we're meeting. I feel like we're besties already." She had a melodic voice, fine bones, and flawless skin to go with a model's leanness.

Anneliese surprised herself by liking Lela immediately. She turned to Lela's companion. "And you must be the lucky guy."

He shook her hand firmly, like a politician. "Grant Stark. Loulou's date for the rest of ever." He dropped a kiss on Lela's forehead.

Grant reminded her of a pampered, preppy golden retriever. *Loulou?* This woman was not a Loulou. "It's a pleasure to meet you. I feel like we've already met, too, thanks to Kirsten's hard work."

"Kirsten is amazing. She takes all my crazy thoughts and makes me look like an organized person. She told me there was amazing coffee nearby and went to get some. Sweet Pea?" Lela checked her phone. "Should she bring it back here?"

"I know where she is." Anneliese turned to check the portico through the front entry windows and, right on time, a black car pulled up. "I have a car waiting outside. We'll stop and pick Kirsten up on our way to our first stop."

SIX HOURS AND A MEANDERING ROUTE THROUGH THE VALLEY LATER, Anneliese had ticked off all the boxes on day one of Lela's Wedding Tour. From a catered lunch on the terrace at the Damselfly Inn to a hayride at West's Tree Farm to cocktails at Cooper Vineyard and a cake tasting with Kate, she'd worked every angle of her Moonlight in Vermont/Foliage Season concept.

Lela's observations were keen and her eye for detail exquisite. If her opinion of Thornton fell closer to quaint than elegant, Grant's enthusiasm more than made up for it. Anneliese had samples of the best of everything, from textiles to cutlery, to bring together Lela's trendy persona and the charm of New England's turning leaves. The effort had been noted, and she had pages of notes and new ideas from Lela.

She also had an expanded budget.

The car pulled up to an Arts and Crafts-style bungalow tucked into the elbow of the Thorn River. In the fading afternoon light, the gardens surrounding the house were hazy and shadowed. Fairy lights lined the front walkway. A carved sign over the front entry read *The Kitchen Garden.*

"Your last stop," Anneliese said in reply to the couple's surprised faces. "The best kept secret in town. Dinner for two."

Kirsten grinned at her across the back of the limousine; Lela's assistant was an excellent co-conspirator.

"Kirsten," Lela said. "Let's find the restroom while Grant checks us in. You have my bag?"

"Right here." Kirsten patted the satchel she'd been carrying all day before following her employer out of the car.

Grant got out, offering Anneliese a hand. "She's going to have Kirsten touch up her make-up and change her hair so she can do fresh photos for her feed. There's probably an entire outfit hidden in Kirsten's bag…" He trailed off, looking around. "It makes her seem to be everywhere all at once."

"Wow." Anneliese sat down on the garden bench near the porch. "So, what do you do?"

"I'm an architect." Grant pushed his hands into his pockets and grinned when Anneliese didn't hide her surprise fast enough. "I know. I play the boy toy role well."

"To be honest," Anneliese said, "I assumed you were involved in entertainment somehow."

Grant's eyes crinkled when he smiled, despite his youth; Anneliese could picture him on a sailboat. "Not at all. Though I have a film festival to thank for meeting Lela."

"Telluride?" Anneliese guessed. She could also picture him skiing.

"Nope." He was visibly enjoying himself. "I was on a research trip in the south of France—no, really. Studying a Belle Epoque chateau a client wanted to copy, and I held a café door for her. She was in Cannes for the film festival—to be seen, taking some time to shop in a nearby village. I had no idea who she was, just that she was gorgeous. She was wearing this cut-out tee shirt with the word 'Loulou' on it, and I said, '*Excusez-moi*, Loulou,' like I had half a clue about French. She smiled at me, and there you go."

"That's lovely. I'm surprised Lela doesn't mention it anywhere."

"She's really private." Again, Grant smiled at Anneliese's visible incredulity. "She is. Her true personal life is like an iceberg. Her followers and fans only get about ten percent. It's part of why I fell for her." He leaned in. "She's also crazy ambitious, and this wedding—which includes our whole origin story—is a valuable asset."

"How do you feel about that?" She was honestly curious. Privacy she understood, but leveraging your love affair?

"The world can have our wedding footage. I get her."

Anneliese's belly flipped at his declaration. "She's lucky to have found you."

"We're both lucky." He stood again, peering toward the restaurant in search of Lela, then looking back at her. "Would you like to join us?"

Anneliese forced a bright, businesslike smile. "It's not a romantic dinner for two if your wedding planner comes along. I'll drop Kirsten off at the hotel and send the car back for you to use when you leave."

"You're great. Lela always gets the right person for the job." Grant stood and offered her a hand up. "Thanks for all of this, Anneliese."

She stamped out the blossoming envy she felt for Lela and Grant. Love and marriage were her livelihood, not her life.

THE NIGHT AWAY HAD DONE JACK GOOD. SETH HADN'T SOLVED HIS problems, but it had been good to let his guard down somewhere the stakes were lower. Seth had been sympathetic, but in the end, he'd agreed with Anneliese. A fling wasn't worth the collateral damage.

Jack didn't want to be reasonable. He wanted to help Chloe with her bike, or take Anneliese dancing. He wanted to solve his father's issues with the house and managing his mother's therapies.

At least there he was making some headway. Noah Hawes, the district representative in Montpelier, had agreed to meet him for a drink to discuss some of the initiatives being considered in the legislature. Jack figured Representative Hawes might be humoring him, but if he could bend the man's ear, he would.

Noah Hawes owned a mill building at the end of a side lane that wended its way from Main Street down to the edge of the river. Jack couldn't remember if he'd ever walked down there before. He was scarcely a block away from the main drag when he noticed The Kitchen Garden.

His mother had mentioned it in the spring, hinting Jack suggest it to his dad as an anniversary dinner option. Not surprisingly, Kate beat him to that, but he had Googled the place. Upscale for Thornton, a private house turned dining establishment with a killer whiskey list and fresh, locally sourced food, seasonally served on a screened porch that hung over the river. Even as he approached on foot, he could see the gardens surrounding the house, so like the cottage—just the kind of place he'd like take Anneliese.

The golden-haired woman on the garden bench outside the restaurant could have been her.

He figured he was imagining her sitting under the fanciful wrought iron lamps by the front door. Blinking to shatter the illusion, he found it really was Anneliese. And a guy.

Jack knew the guy's type from a half a block away. If he were being brutally honest, *he* was the same type, with darker hair. Fair, with a classic profile, the guy radiated Ivy League, right down to his footwear, and the confident way he leaned in to her. The blueish light in the garden created a hazy filter over the scene. Jack wanted to punch the aquiline nose off the guy's face.

Instead, Jack strode past the restaurant toward Noah Hawes's renovated mill offices. He couldn't help but look back one last time. He'd told Joss he saw her now, but it didn't matter. He'd meant it didn't matter to her.

It mattered a hell of a lot to him.

Noah Hawes answered the door in jeans and a Boston College tee shirt. Jack, still reeling from the sight of Anneliese in the soft, intimate light at The Kitchen Garden, stammered though his thanks.

His host wasn't bothered by Jack's stumble. "I've had a few conversations with your dad over the years. He's a good man. I was sorry to hear about your mother."

"She's on the mend," Jack said. "We all are."

"It's hard," Noah said, gesturing through the main floor of the house to a slider at the back. "Let's talk on the deck. It's too nice a night to be inside."

Jack followed, fascinated by the space. It was an office, a public-facing space, but comfortable. A modern, cantilevered staircase rose to the second level, where Jack assumed Noah lived. He'd done his research. Hawes was semi-retired, his term in Montpelier his only work at the moment.

Noah had become a crusader for families and caregivers when his wife died of an aggressive form of cancer a decade before. Around town, folks admired him for his public service as much as they did for restoring a crumbling mill building and running his political campaigns from a home office with a wide-open door.

The river flowed wide, smooth, and dark below the deck. Jack couldn't settle, so he leaned on the rail, watching the current pick up speed as it surrendered to the gravity of the falls.

"Muriel would have loved this deck," Hawes said, joining Jack at the railing with two bottles of local brew.

"You didn't live here then?"

"Owned the building, but it was just an empty mill office in those days. Muriel and I had a place up near West's. We used to walk in from our place to cut our Christmas trees." The older man took a long drink from his bottle. "It was just the two of us. No one to help out unless we paid them, and I burned through my vacation time pretty fast. All those trips to Hanover for treatments, driving to Boston for clinical trials…"

"So, the bill you're working on," Jack said, "it comes from a place of experience."

"I was mid-level management at the quarry. We got lucky and inherited this place and the land for our house from Muriel's family, so we had some money put by. We were comfortable, but after she got sick, and I started missing work to take care of her, my position at the quarry was 'phased out'. And no one wants to hire a guy knocking on retirement's door. Without her, our homestead didn't feel the same, so I sold it to some dotcom kid from New York for enough to pay down the hospital debts—and that's after the insurance."

"Shit."

Hawes chuckled. "That about sums it up. And I was lucky. This place was structurally sound, if run down, and I played Little League with the building inspector, so maybe I got an occupancy permit before it was strictly livable." He raised his half-empty beer in salute. "Some of those days, working on this building was almost enough to drown out the grief."

"I'm sorry." Jack thought of the fat retirement account he was already accruing, the net value of his apartment, the worry-free health care he enjoyed. "What you're doing, Muriel's bill, it's good work. I want to support it somehow."

"Move home," Noah said, turning to look Jack straight in the eye. "Dig in here, and when the time comes, go to Montpelier and make a difference. You're young, good-looking. It shouldn't, but that can matter. I looked you up. You're a smart kid. You want to help your folks out, make it easier for single moms and the unemployed; you come on back here and make a difference."

The intensity of the older man's passion took Jack by surprise. "Run for office?"

"Start small. Selectman, or assessor's board. A committee. Use that Harvard law degree to fight for the people like me who got 'phased out' or 'downsized' when they had to step back from the rat race to watch the love of their life—or their child—dying."

He thought of Anneliese and Chloe. He had no idea what kind of safety net she had, but the idea that she could lose everything to save her daughter, or that his father's practice—or the house on Chapel Street—might be sacrificed so his mother could get treatment, frightened him. "I never thought."

Noah's voice gentled. "Why would you? You got yourself into good schools. You've pushed yourself since you graduated. Kearney-Mulligan is quite a firm. You earned your good fortune."

"Sure, but I had help." Jack said, realizing as he said it that he didn't often consider it.

"'Course you did. Just like Muriel's family had property. We had help. Pay it forward."

They were both quiet, resting with their thoughts while the river ran ever northward under the deck boards.

Jack broke the silence. "How long would someone need to be a permanent resident before they could consider running?"

Noah's eyes lit up. "Now you're using that Ivy League brain."

ONCE CORA PEASE WAS READY FOR THE COMPANY OF AN EXUBERANT kindergartener, Anneliese brought Chloe over for puzzles, books, and conversation.

They'd driven, straight from school, bearing a stack of drawings Chloe said were of ninjas. Where her daughter got ideas about ninjas, Anneliese hadn't yet figured out.

"How's Mrs. Sosa?" Cora asked Chloe, who had a box of crayons out and was making more pictures for Cora's walls.

"She has a cold," Chloe reported. "We do a Wash Your Hands Parade so we don't get colds, too."

Anneliese hadn't yet heard about the Wash Your Hands Parade. Chloe's anecdotes for Mrs. Pease, who volunteered at the school, gave Anneliese unsolicited insight into her daughter's day.

"Five more minutes," she said. "We have to get you home for supper."

Cora smiled past Anneliese. "Jack."

Anneliese turned; Jack's lean frame filled the doorway. *Why did he always look so damned good?*

"Change of plans, Chlo'. Jack is here to visit his mom. We need to skedaddle."

"Don't skedaddle on my account." He edged past without really looking at her, and kissed his mother's cheek.

"Hi, Applejack." Chloe held up the drawing she was doing for Cora. "I'm drawing frogs."

"Are those tails?" Jack asked, peering at the paper.

"Yup," Chloe said. "Frogs have tails when they're called tadpoles, but then their tails grow off."

Jack peered around Chloe. "Is that what happened to yours?"

Her daughter's musical laughter almost dispelled the awful, hot feeling in Anneliese's chest. She'd told him they couldn't be more than friends. She'd kept to herself, kept her wants locked away with her fears. Why did it have to hurt to see him again? "Time to wrap it up, Chloe."

"I'm not done with my frogs."

"Chloe." Anneliese could hear the sharp edges of her own discomfort. "I said it was time to go. We'll come back another time."

"Anneliese, you don't have to run out," Cora said. "Jack certainly can't mind sharing me."

"Of course I don't," Jack said, but his tone was at odds with his words, and he still wouldn't meet her eyes.

"Still, it's just...best. If we go." Anneliese shook out Chloe's jacket. "Jacket, Chloe Elizabeth. Right now."

"I want to stay with Mrs. Pease and Jack."

Anneliese began gathering up her daughter's crayons, scattering them in the process. Chloe's mutinous expression was the last straw. "Damn it."

"Mama." Chloe's eyes went wide at the curse.

"Anna, you're being ridiculous." Jack reached down to snag a stray orange crayon. "You don't have to leave."

Anneliese shot Jack a frosty look. "You don't get to tell me I'm being ridiculous."

"Anneliese." Cora's tone, though weakened by her condition, was still that of a mother and frequent classroom volunteer. Jack's mother let her gaze linger pointedly on Chloe before gesturing to the hall outside. "Jack. Whatever is bothering you two, I suggest you take it outside for a moment while Chloe finds a spot to hang up this drawing."

Feeling like a scolded teenager, Anneliese slunk out of the room, followed by Jack.

He let the door close softly; Anneliese kept an eye on Chloe through the window while she pressed the drawing up against different spots on the wall.

Jack whistled low. "I didn't know you had one."

"Had one what?"

"A temper."

The words gathered at her lips, flooding out of her in a whispered hiss. "You arrogant, miserable…jerk. You waltz back into town like we're supposed to throw you a parade. I make the mistake of letting my feelings show, feelings you never once in more than fifteen years noticed until it was convenient, we end up in bed together, and that's supposed to make me what? Grateful?"

She knew her cheeks were aflame, and to add insult to injury, two nurses from the nearest station were trying very hard not to watch them.

Jack came back at her with barely restrained passion. "Let me be very clear, I didn't know how you felt about me in high school. I was a stupid kid. A lucky kid who got girls easily. I'm sorry I didn't notice you until it was too late. Trust me, I like what I see now. And, apparently, I'm not the only one. So, we'll stay friends like you want, but excuse me if I don't bounce right back."

*What?* It was as though someone dragged the needle across a turntable, and she was too addled to stop and weigh her words. "What are you talking about?"

"We just shouldn't, you said." Grim satisfaction colored his words. "What did you say to the guy you were cozied up with outside The Kitchen Garden the other night?"

*Now Jack was following her?* It was easier to loose her anger than the sick, sinking fear that shook her. She forced herself to breathe, closed her eyes, then looked Jack in the eyes.

"He's a client. Who was being kind to me after a long day of touring his fiancée around the county." Uncertainty flickered across Jack's face, but Anneliese pressed on. "I need to get my daughter home. I think we should stop before one of says something we regret."

Jack flicked open the door to his mother's room. He made a mock bow in Anneliese's direction, but didn't speak.

Anneliese arranged her face into a smile. "Give Miss Cora a gentle hug, Sweetie, then we need to head home."

Chloe's shoulders slumped. "Okay, Mama."

She clambered up on the bed rail to lay herself gently across the older woman's body. "Bye, Miss Cora."

"Goodbye, Chloe, Anneliese." There was concern in her weary eyes. "I'll see you next week?"

Anneliese mustered her composure. "Of course."

It was impossible to sail past Jack, so she settled for avoiding his gaze as she guided Chloe out of the room.

His mother barely let the door clack shut before she turned her ever-patient eyes on Jack. "That poor girl."

"Chloe?" He blinked.

"You are my only son, and a joy to behold, but you're just such a man, Jack."

"What?" His hands had nowhere to go. He let them hang by his side.

"It wasn't my place to say so when you were traipsing all around the county with Anna and Joss, but that girl was crazy about you."

Hot shame and an adolescent irritation roiled. "I'm not sure you need to be saying it now."

"I could see it in the way she held herself when you were in the room. And you were like a puppy, always sniffing around something, but not her. She was right there, and you never noticed." Cora smiled unapologetically. "I'm old enough now to say what I like."

"Mom—"

"Don't 'mom' me," she said. "Anneliese was left behind when you all went off to college. She was working for her folks and getting her degree, and she was lonely. I only met that awful man she married once. He liked the looks of her, but he was no good."

"He was a fucking idiot," he muttered. *To let her go.* He hoped his mother missed the profanity.

"Be kind to her Jack, and for the love of everything." She paused. "Stay out of her bed unless you can offer her something real. The last thing that sweet woman needs is to have her heart cracked open another time."

Her words were quiet, but they sliced to the core of things. Jack couldn't tell if his mother knew the truth, or was just an excellent guesser. It didn't matter. Cora Pease never raised her voice; her gentle disappointment stung more than a slap.

She patted the side of the bed. "Now, sit down and tell me about your day."

Shaking off the whiplash, Jack sat. "Pretty much the same as yesterday."

"Good," his mother said. "More time for Cordelia and Alasdair. It's time I found out if they get together."

# CHAPTER 17

Anneliese put the scene at the hospital behind her as best she could in the following weeks. On top of weddings and birthdays and a writing retreat to plan, Nan's baby shower was fast approaching.

On the best nights, she fell into exhausted, dreamless sleep before her heart had a chance to linger over the grief of pushing Jack away.

She and Kate had done the heavy organizing, but it was Molly Fuller who pulled the final touches together at the Damselfly Inn. On the day of the shower, Anneliese turned up with her to-do list, meeting Kate to unpack the treats.

"Molly, do you need anything else from the kitchen?" Anneliese carried a huge bowl of tropical fruit salad under one arm and a pitcher of lemonade in the other.

"No, hon. We just need to do the bunting from the chandelier." Molly met her and took the pitcher. "Your mom is finishing up the favors, and Kate arranged the macarons before she stepped out."

"She left?"

Molly fussed with the paper party cups and napkins. "While you were in the kitchen. Said she had an errand."

"She didn't mention anything to me. I hope it's quick." Anneliese set the punch bowl full of fruit in the center of the table. "We'll bring out the warm *hors d'oeuvres* once people are here, the stuff for the games is in that basket by the wing chair, and the gifts can go over there." She took in the inn's first floor parlor with a critical eye. "I think we're done for the moment."

Molly sat. "Good. I could use a rest. Walt was up all night with a sick heifer, so I worked the morning milking with Danielle."

"She got up early to milk cows?" Not only had Danielle come home for the weekend to go to the shower, she'd offered to stay at the cottage playing with Chloe while Anneliese got the party organized. Looking at the time, Anneliese realized they would be arriving soon, as would Nan, Kate, and the rest of the guests.

"She did. She loves those girls. Don't tell Joss I said so," Molly peered comically around the corner, "but I have half a mind to cut Joss out of the will altogether."

"Or maybe your new grandchild is the next Fuller to farm."

Molly's whole face lit up at the mention of Joss and Nan's impending firstborn. A gentle tease was on the tip of Anneliese's tongue when her phone rang. Kate's name flashed from the screen.

"Where are you?"

"Sorry to bail like that, but I'm en route." Kate sounded wobbly.

"Okay…" She mouthed Kate's name to Molly.

"And I have a plus one."

"Huh?" Anneliese switched the phone to her other ear and took a bolt of spring green tulle from Molly.

"Mom was just released." Kate's voice went husky in Anneliese's ear. "She wants to be there. I know she should be resting and will get tired, so I'm just going to bring her over for a few minutes."

"Kate, that's amazing!"

"I gotta go, Jack and I are going to drop her off. He can help with her wheelchair."

The call disconnected, and Anneliese swiped a happy tear from her cheek, blinking back the inevitable sting at the thought of Jack's impending arrival. How was it possible to be overjoyed for him, infuriated by him, and missing him so badly it ached like scar tissue?

"What was that all about?" Molly had been cutting lengths from the bolt while Anneliese was on the phone.

"Cora's out of the hospital. That was Kate's mystery errand. She's going to bring her over for a quick visit."

Molly dropped the tulle and wrapped Anneliese in a bear hug. "It's a good day, Anna. A very good day."

The hug was interrupted by Chloe and Danielle. Danielle took in the weepy, hugging women with a touch of suspicion. "What's going on?"

"Cora Pease is coming home from the hospital. I'm going to be a Gramma." Molly crouched and opened her arms to Chloe, who barreled into them. "And my favorite Chloe is here to see her Auntie Molly."

"I'm your only Chloe," the little girl said, squeezing Molly.

The sound of a car in the driveway pulled Anneliese away from the sweetness. She recognized it as her mother's.

"Chloe, Mere is here. Can you go out and help her carry things in?"

Chloe skipped outside, letting the screen door slam behind her.

Danielle picked up the dropped tulle. "I'll help Molly with this."

Anneliese collected the already cut lengths and a step stool and started handing the bunting to Danielle.

They'd only just finished hanging it when Nan arrived, followed by a steady stream of guests. Anneliese kept an eye on the rooms as people found seats or perused the buffet.

Chloe orbited Nan, drawn like a magnet to the mystery of the baby in her belly. Anneliese had always envisioned having more children; Chloe's obvious fascination with this soon-to-be-born cousin left her feeling hollow and wistful.

Voices from the foyer alerted Anneliese to Kate's arrival.

Kate, Jack, and their mother had come around through the back door, which offered an accessibility ramp. Jack was supporting his mom; Kate followed with a walker.

"Jack." Cora's voice was weak with fatigue, but the maternal tone was still there. "Are we going to linger in the hall all afternoon?"

Jack ducked his head. "Sorry, Mom."

Cora beamed. "Where's Nan?"

"This way." Anneliese led them into the parlor. "I'm so glad to see you out and about."

"Not more than I am to be out." Cora threw Kate a sidelong glance. "This one has been listening to the doctors, so I can't stay long."

"Let me clear a path," Anneliese said. "Everyone's in the parlor."

Anneliese watched Jack with his mother while he and Kate got her settled. She was torn between joy for her friends and Mrs. Pease and fear that the older woman might tire too quickly, or suffer a relapse.

Jack stopped in the doorway; there was an echoing worry written in the tension of his jaw. "Keep an eye on her?"

"Of course." She wanted to offer comfort; her conflicting emotions kept her still. "Kate won't let her wear herself out."

Jack shoved his hands in his pockets and leaned on the wall. "Her doctor will be furious."

"I won't tell," Anneliese said. "Are you staying?"

He glanced over her shoulder into the inn's foyer. "I'm going to run back to my folks' house and see if Dad needs my help, but I'll come back and get Mom and Kate when they're ready."

She noticed Kate watching the two of them from across the room.

"I should get the party games rolling, then, so she doesn't miss anything."

When the last of the guests had gone and the clean-up was underway, Anneliese's stole a moment to collect her thoughts.

She'd been so busy, she hadn't even noticed Jack's return to fetch his mother.

It was a good party, full of warmth, humor and love. Women coming together, as they had since forever, to connect and welcome the next generation into the world.

She hadn't experienced the same goodwill and warmth when Chloe was born, three thousand miles from home, adrift without friends of her own. So cleverly isolated by her husband, she hadn't truly known how alone she'd been.

"Anna," Nan called to her. "Come here a sec."

There was an odd urgency in her friend's tone, so Anneliese set down the tulle she was wrapping around the empty bolt, and went to the couch where Nan had her feet up on a pillow.

Nan took her hand and placed it on the taut fullness of her belly. "She's kicking."

"She?" Anneliese held her breath. She'd loved the shivers of life in her own belly when Chloe grew there.

Nan arched her back slightly. "We don't know for sure, but I just feel like she's a she."

"Pick out boy names, too. Just in case."

Nan placed her hand over Anneliese's. "I like Walter, but Joss says no."

"Uncle Walt is a darling, but Joss is probably right."

Molly came in just as a ripple danced under Anneliese's hand. "Oh!"

"My grandbaby's awake?" Molly picked up the tulle Anneliese had left behind.

"Awake and cranky she missed the party." Nan rubbed the spot where the baby had kicked.

"Nan, you tell that little one we'll throw her a party when she's on the outside. 'Til then, she better stay put. She's not done cooking yet."

Anneliese leaned down to whisper. "Stay put little one, or they'll name you 'Walter.'"

Molly burst out laughing. "They wouldn't dare."

"Who wouldn't dare do what?" Jane Thompson followed from the kitchen with a tray.

"Nan and Joss. Name the baby after Uncle Walt." Anneliese got up to help her mother collect stray dishes.

"Why not? There are worse names."

"It only took thirty-seven years," Molly muttered.

"You're never going to let me live that down, are you?" Jane huffed.

Anneliese rolled her eyes at Nan, who bit back a giggle. Molly and

Walt had been together about that long; Anneliese suspected there was a story there.

"Molly, there are three extra favors." Jane said. "I can take them to the senior center. They'd make a nice addition to the project table."

"Mom, can I grab one?" Anneliese jumped up from the couch. "I don't think Cora took one."

"Do you want me to drop one off over there tomorrow?"

"No, I go right past Chapel Street on my way home."

"Don't bother Cora if she's resting."

"Mom," Anneliese sighed. "I won't. I'll just leave it with John—or Jack—and be on my way."

It was barely supper time when Anneliese pulled up in front of the Pease's house. In all the time Cora was in the hospital—and Jack lived there—she hadn't been to visit. When she stopped to think about it, she hadn't been inside the house since high school.

The ramp was new, as was a small transition at the front door to ease the passage of a chair or walker. Joss's handiwork, no doubt. Anneliese rang the bell, then stepped back to look at the house. She'd always envied the Peases for their storied neighborhood. Chapel Street was one of the original residential streets when Thornton was little more than a settlement, and John Pease's family went all the way back to the founding. Their three-story Mansard Victorian, complete with creaking floorboards, drafty windows, and distinctive roofline seemed luxurious to a girl from the eighties cookie-cutter development outside of town.

John opened the door; she couldn't help looking for Jack over his shoulder. "Anneliese, what brings you around?"

"Hi, John." She held out the miniature bucket full of packets of wildflower seeds. "Cora didn't get a favor from Nan's shower. I thought I'd bring one by."

John took the bucket. "You're a sweet girl, Anneliese."

"No one's called me a girl in a while," she laughed. "How is Cora? We did try not to wear her out."

"She's sleeping now, but she went to bed happy. To be home, and to have been there for Joss and Nan."

Impulsively, Anneliese hugged John. "I'm so glad."

"Dad?" Thumping on the stairs announced Jack as much as his voice. "Who's here? Oh, hey Anna."

*Oh, hey Anna?*

"Hi."

"Anneliese dropped off a party favor for your mother. I'm going to take this to the kitchen. Invite her in, Jack." John stepped aside for his son, with a wink for Anneliese. "We've completely lost our manners without Cora around."

Instead of inviting her in, Jack stepped out onto the porch. "Thanks for thinking of her."

"You and Kate smuggled her out of the party. I didn't even see her leave." Anneliese sat lightly against the railing. "Impressive for a woman with a walker."

"You were busy making sure everyone was having a good time." Jack leaned back against the wall of the house. "You're good at it."

"Still..." She trailed off, unsure of what to say. The ugly things they'd said in the hospital festered between them. "Listen, I should go. Chloe begged for a sleepover with my parents, and I should use the time alone to work on some of my upcoming events."

"Anna, wait." Jack pushed off the wall, hands still in his pockets. "I feel awful about the whole thing back at the hospital. Can we go for a walk, down to the river or something?"

They might not have many more chances to clear the air. With Cora home, John might find he wanted to go back to work sooner, but by any count, Jack would be gone by Halloween at the latest.

Gone back to his real life; safe from the disaster that was hers.

"Okay." She looked down at her pastel ballet flats. "But go easy on my shoes."

At the end of Chapel Street, behind a rusted-out guardrail and between overgrown brambles, a footpath led down to the silty bank of the Thorn River. Jack led the way, but Anneliese remembered.

The trail was dry. The water level was low, leaving a broad, stony beach at the bend in the river. She could hear the waterfall singing as it spilled over the falls behind them.

Jack looked downriver toward the falls. "I was on my way to Noah Hawes's office when I saw you in front of that restaurant." He turned to her, jaw working as he struggled with whatever he was about to say. "I've only been jealous twice in my life, and both times, it was you."

"Me?" She was squinting at him, as though he had something smeared on his cheek.

"That guy you dated at the end of senior year. I hated him for getting to dance with you all night at prom. You were so beautiful, and I felt stupid without understanding why." He let out a bitter half-laugh. "Now I know."

"I wanted you to be jealous that night." Her gaze flicked away to watch a branch float down the river. "But what you saw outside The Kitchen Garden? That was a happy client thanking me. Nothing more."

"I hated him for being close to you when I couldn't be."

"Even if he wasn't a client..." Anneliese sat on a fallen tree, studying him. "You and I are entitled to go out with anyone we want, Jack. Whatever happened between us, we never made promises."

He slapped at a mosquito. "Yeah."

She wrapped her arms around herself. She was entitled, but at that moment, she didn't want just anyone. She wanted the man in front of her. The man she had no business wanting. The man she'd rejected.

With everything going on in her life—Chloe, Chad, her work, Nan and Joss's growing family, and Kate's new house—Anneliese knew she'd made the right decision.

She couldn't be his nostalgia fling while he was playing house in his hometown.

The trouble was, Jack wasn't reading from his usual script. The scene in his mother's hospital room was a perfect example.

"You didn't need to pick a fight with me at the hospital. It was humiliating."

"I'm sorry, Anna. Can you forgive me? I meant what I said at your place. You won't lose my friendship. Please don't say I've lost yours."

If he'd opened his arms, she would have fallen into them. Instead, every fear and uncertainty rushed into the empty space between them, like water over the spillway.

"Anna?"

"It's not so simple for us." She stood, but kept the distance between them. "I've shown you my whole hand. I have a young daughter to consider. You're a swan in a duck pond, just waiting to fly away home."

He turned back to the river.

Another mosquito buzzed around her ear. "But I can't be the reason our friendships with the others suffer. We can't be like this and spend time with the people we both love."

"Then we won't be like this. We'll be adults and put all this behind us."

Anneliese didn't like the coolness in his voice, but she understood the need for it, so she tried for levity. "Pinky swear?"

When he didn't respond, she steadied herself with a long breath.

After a moment, he spoke, but to the water. "Can I still hang out sometimes? I don't want to ghost on Chloe. She's a cool kid."

"She is, isn't she?" Anneliese offered Jack a weak smile. She couldn't blame Chloe for falling for him, too, and Chloe would be devastated if he vanished. "Of course. How could I keep Applejack from his Ninja Frog?"

"Thanks, Anna. That means a lot." His voice hitched. He held a hand out to help her to her feet. "Come on. It's buggy."

They'd made peace, but Anneliese left the Pease's house with a heavy heart.

Her phone rang halfway back to the cottage. It was a local number she didn't recognize. She ignored it twice, but the caller persisted. Her finger trembled over the green answer button, and she answered as though she didn't suspect who was on the other end.

"Glad to hear your voice instead of your voicemail for a change." Chad's voice was like an oil slick. Her stomach turned.

"I wish I could say the same." She couldn't help the resignation. She'd been doubly naive to think she could walk away from him forever. He might not want her, but he'd always want to control her.

"I couldn't get a room at your friend's nice inn last night. All booked up."

"Stay away from them!" Realizing she'd shrieked into the phone, she cast around to see who had heard, then dropped to a stage whisper. "Seriously. Don't."

Butter wouldn't melt in his mouth. "Hey, I'm just a guy crashing in the Green Mountain Motor Lodge, which hasn't been updated since you were a hot little co-ed." He let the backhanded compliment hang for a beat. "Which was so long ago, I barely remember."

Anneliese fought the urge to retch. "What do you want."

"To let you know that these little walks down memory lane we're having are costing me. And I intend to collect."

"I don't have anything to give you. You've seen to that."

"Ouch." Chad didn't sound stung at all. In fact, he chuckled. "Maybe I should petition the court for support from you, little miss celebrity wedding planner."

The anger felt good, singeing away the filth. "Goodbye, Chad."

"I think I'll do that. Maybe talk to a lawyer while I'm in town."

He clicked off the line before she could do anything about it, except hope he didn't make good on his threats.

*How had she ever thought she loved him?*

It was a question even a scalding shower and a tall beer couldn't answer.

JACK WATCHED ANNELIESE DRIVE AWAY, THEN CLIMBED THE STAIRS. HIS dad was whistling in the kitchen, seasoning burgers for the grill and wearing one of the dozen corny aprons Kate gave him over the years. This one read: This Dad is Flipping Awesome.

It surprised him to find there was room inside him for both the lightness and relief at having his mother home resting in her own bed, and the leaden weight of finding and losing Anneliese in only a few short weeks.

"You staying for supper?"

"Sure, Dad. Wouldn't miss it."

It was the right choice. Kate and Ewan came by to celebrate, with pictures of the house for his mom to pour over in preparation for her tour the next day. The laughter in his mother's eyes while they ate together on TV trays on the back deck distracted him from the desire to run full-tilt across the center of town and beg Anneliese for another chance.

But a chance to do what? Wound them both?

When Kate and Ewan left, Jack excused himself and walked over to the office, but he couldn't focus, so he struck out for Temple, hoping the company of strangers might distract him.

Dee was behind the bar, her boyfriend Robbie holding court at the end of the run of stools. He and Robbie had played soccer as kids, had been on the baseball team in high school. He and Joss had played darts with the man. That was enough to share a beer.

"Jack!" Robbie greeted him with a huge grin and a bracing slap on the shoulder.

"Hey, Rob." He pushed a twenty across the bar and pointed to a tap. Dee nodded and swung by to scoop up the cash.

"Dougie, slide over." Robbie elbowed the guy next to him and patted the empty stool. "Si' down. Enjoy your beer."

Jack didn't like the stormy look on Dougie's face. Dee returned with a pint for him, and a round for Robbie's crew. Jack caught a pointed look between the two of them.

"Next one for Jack's on me," Robbie said.

"It's okay, Rob, I'm not staying…"

But Robbie wasn't having it. "Next one's on me. Your sister's the one that got me and Dee together, and your dad kept my ex from taking my shirt when she took the house. I figure I can spot you a brewski."

Jack should've realized Kate had a hand in Robbie and Dee's romance. She and Dee had been tight since their school days; Robbie followed Kate around like a puppy until she'd left town for culinary school. Kate would have loved maneuvering the two of them together years later.

"You a lawyer, too, man?" Another of Robbie's friends, this one wearing a Bruins cap, leaned over to collect one of the drinks on the bar.

"Yeah, why?" Jack picked up his pint glass.

"You know anything about union stuff?"

Robbie put an arm on Bruins Cap's arm. "He's not working, Fitz. Let the man enjoy his drink."

"I am letting him enjoy his drink, I just figured I'd ask. I got that thing going on at work, and—"

"I don't know anything about labor law." Jack nipped the conversation in bud.

The recently evicted Dougie nodded. "He's a suit. It's all banking and shit, Fitz. I told you, you need to—"

"Yah, I heard what you said earlier. I'm asking Robbie's friend here what he thinks."

Jack set the glass down. This was not the scene he'd been looking for. "Seriously, guys, I don't know anything about labor law. I just want to have a beer."

"Nobody asked you to sit down here." Dougie leaned in.

"I asked him to sit here, douchebag." Robbie stood, angling himself at Jack's shoulder. "Settle down, Dougie. Or go shoot darts with Fitz for a few."

Fitz laughed. "I could use some gas money."

"Hey, fuck you, man." Dougie knocked into Jack trying to push past Robbie to get to Fitz. His beer sloshed, splashing the bar and soaking his shirt.

"Jesus, Dougie, you're drunk." Dee materialized out of nowhere. "Pull it together, or get the hell out."

"I was fine until fuckin' Robbie gave up my seat."

Jack saw his opportunity to leave. "Rob, Dee. I'm gonna go."

"Say hi to your mum, Jack." Dee was watching Dougie and Fitz with one eye. Robbie was still between the two. "Sorry about this lot."

Jack ducked out, leaving his half empty glass on the bar. At least Dee got the change from his twenty for her trouble.

About a block from the bar, he pulled out his phone. It wasn't late, Iris might still answer.

She answered on the third ring, voice dusty with disuse. "Jack."

"Hey, what's going on?"

He could hear the sounds of the city behind her voice. Horns, voices, the wind off Boston Harbor. He wanted it to feel like home, but it only felt like music he hadn't heard in a long time.

"Nothing. I just wanted to say hi."

"That's ridiculous. You're not the 'say hi' type." He heard the screech of traffic through her phone. "You're lonely, and you still haven't admitted to yourself that you're in love with…"

"Anneliese."

"Even the way you say her name, Jack."

Iris's even delivery was infuriating, even as it soothed.

"What does it matter whether I love her or not? She isn't interested in anything but friendship."

"She's learned to be careful of you."

"That's not exactly a ringing endorsement." He turned the last corner from Main to Chapel. His parents' house was steps away.

"I'm not being cruel, Jack. Just truthful."

He sat on the steps, keeping his voice low, so as not to disturb the Cartwrights next door, and shifted the conversation away from himself. "Tell me what you're working on."

Iris, never one to beat a dead horse, switched tacks smoothly, and they spent the next half hour talking shop.

"I'm going out on the river tomorrow morning. Time for me to get to bed."

"Sweet dreams."

"Sweet dreams, Jack."

Caught between the remembered scent of the Charles River and the breeze over the Thorn River, Jack suspected his dreams would be anything but sweet, if he slept at all.

# CHAPTER 18

*I*t struck Jack as incredibly unfair that he felt hungover after half a beer the night before. He gratefully accepted a cup of coffee from Mrs. Drake before opening his email. A friend who specialized in estates had emailed back with some advice about drafting a will.

He couldn't help mulling over his discussion with Noah Hawes. Maybe that's what Nan wanted—peace of mind for her family if something happened. Maybe that's how Muriel Hawes had felt.

The retro intercom buzzed. Mrs. Drake announced Joss just as he walked through the door.

"Heard you got into it with some guys down at Temple last night."

"Hello to you, too." Jack looked up from his screen. "Did I do okay?"

"Depends on who's telling it." Joss took a seat opposite him. "Doug Reading says he scared you off 'cause you're a pussy, but I heard from Dee that you were a complete gentleman."

"This town sucks."

Joss leaned back in the client chair. "Maybe I should come back later?"

"Please, either distract me or shoot me."

Joss chuckled. "I have the night off. Nan is helping Kate with fabric and paint swatches. I've been cleaner, but that doesn't mean we can't grab a beer."

"Not at Temple."

When their phones rang nearly simultaneously, both men fumbled for them, but Jack was faster. "Kate? What's going on?"

He half listened to Kate, watching the color drain out of Joss's face as he listened to his own phone.

"Nan's having contractions," Kate said, "but the baby's not due until mid-November. We called the midwife; she said to meet us at the hospital in Burlington."

Joss was already up and out of his chair. "Sorry. I have to go. Nan—"

"I know. Go. I'll check in soon." Jack focused on Kate again. "Drive carefully."

Joss reappeared in the office door. "Can you call Anna? We'll need someone at the inn later, and my mom is in Bennington overnight for a harvest fair."

Joss was gone again before Jack could say anything. "Mrs. Drake?"

She materialized from her front office. "Is everything all right with the baby?"

Jack's heart squeezed, but he kept a calm face. "Just some early contractions. I need to hunt down Anneliese Thompson. I hate to ask, but can you—"

"I'll close up. You go do what needs doing."

He watched her impeccable form retreat; she was truly a treasure. He dialed Anneliese's number uneasily, but she answered right away.

"Jack?"

"Hey, Anna. Where are you?"

He could hear birds and passing cars beyond her.

"On my way to get Chloe at school." He heard a trickle of fear in her voice. "Why?"

"Listen, please don't panic. Nan's having some contractions, and—"

He heard her gasp. "Is everything okay?"

"They're on their way to the hospital now to meet the midwife, but Kate is with them and Molly is out of town."

Anneliese caught on immediately. "I'll call my folks to watch Chloe."

"I can do that."

Anneliese was quiet. "You don't have to…"

"I can get Chloe some dinner and make sure she's entertained for a few hours. Really, Anna. Let me help."

"Okay. Meet me at my house in a half hour, and then I'll head over to the inn."

Relief washed over him, just for finding a way to be useful.

"I'll fill Joss in now. See you in a few, Banana."

He was halfway through a text to Joss before he realized he used the forbidden nickname again.

ANNELIESE THREW TOGETHER A PACKED DINNER FOR HERSELF WHILE Jack examined Chloe's wall of art. A flurry of texts let her know everyone's movements, but no one had any meaningful information. Jack had nothing new to offer.

"There are labeled leftovers in the fridge. Don't let her talk you out of vegetables."

Anneliese was babbling, but there Jack was, filling up her kitchen, less than twenty-four hours after she'd renewed her promise to put distance between them.

"I don't like veg'ables." Chloe frowned, clutching Feesh.

"You do like vegetables. You like tomatoes and carrots and corn and beans." Anneliese ticked Chloe's four favorites off on her fingers. "And Jack is going to call me if you don't eat them."

Chloe looked mutinous and Anneliese quashed a huge urge to pack Chloe up and take her to the inn.

"If you decide to head out for a walk or anything, make sure she wears her warm jacket."

"Anna," Jack said. "I got this."

Her daughter beamed. "Applejack's got this."

"I'm outnumbered." Anneliese grabbed her work bag. "Text me if you need anything."

Jack made an exaggerated cross over his chest. "Promise."

The drive to the inn took no more than ten minutes. Minutes Anneliese spent waiting for Jack's first baffled text. Babysitting was a little different from giving a pint-sized performer a rose. Two-wheelers and digging in the garden wasn't dinner with a persnickety kindergartener. Chutes and Ladders on a warm September night wasn't teeth-brushing and bedtime. Her phone, however, remained silent.

The Damselfly was dark, save for the front porch light, and one glowing guest room window on the second floor. Anneliese let herself in through the kitchen and headed for the office to check the reservations software and the room key board. Once she knew who she might or might not be waiting for, she would get in touch with Kate and find out what was going on at the hospital.

"Frog," Jack said, "there's no sesame chicken in here." There were chicken breasts, tortellini, fruits and vegetables galore, but sadly, no Chinese take-out.

"What's that?"

Jack closed the fridge. Chloe was still standing where Anneliese had hugged her goodbye.

"Delicious is what it is. Let's go have a dinner adventure." He remembered Anneliese's requirement about heading out. "*If* you wear your warm jacket."

"I don't need it," Chloe said.

He fought a laugh at the defiance in her tone. There was a first for everything, including testing boundaries, but he hadn't been leading a team of young associates for a few years for nothing. "Your mom says you do, and if I'm babysitting, she's my boss."

Chloe giggled at that. "Okay."

She shuffled towards the coat closet opposite the bottom of the stairs, but when she came back with a shiny purple puffy jacket, he figured he was in the clear.

He read through Anneliese's babysitter sheet, helpfully pinned to the fridge. No allergies, that was good. Anna's parents' phone numbers. He snapped a photo with his phone, just in case.

"Can Feesh come?"

Jack looked at Chloe's beloved toy. "Tell you what, Feesh should probably stay here, but we'll read...him?" He looked to Chloe for confirmation or denial, and decided no denial was a good thing. "We'll read him an extra story before bed."

"Feesh likes Llama Llama."

Jack had no idea what that meant, but they could cross that bridge when they got there.

He helped her zip the jacket, she Velcroed her shoes, and they headed out. Chloe chatted up a storm, talking about the antisocial ginger cat who lived at the Fletcher Hotel, and that the school frogs had all gone to the pond. When they reached the crosswalk that would bring them to the common, Chloe slipped her hand into his. Her chubby fingers were soft, and he gave them a little squeeze as they stepped off the curb together.

She knew more people in town than he did, he realized. She waved and called hellos all the way around the common, following each greeting with an explanation her mother would have been proud of. Jack met Ava, the teacher helper in the Green Room; they saw Owen and Mia and Jackson and Fawn and three other children Chloe knew from school. Mister Clyde who delivered the mail. The only person Jack knew was the librarian, Mrs. Williams, who waved to Chloe, and told her to take good care of Mr. Pease.

Golden Prawn wasn't very busy, so Jack sweet-talked the hostess into a booth meant for four by the giant fish tank.

"That one's a clownfish," said Chloe.

Jack followed Chloe's pointed finger. "There's a whole circus full of them in there."

Jack wondered how many years in the future Chloe would appreciate being told that her wry expression was identical to that of her mother.

The menu was unnecessary, as far as he was concerned. Prawns Amazing, his long-favorite dish, some sesame chicken, and something—maybe in the noodle family—for Chloe.

While he'd been thinking about food, his dinner companion had struck up a friendship with a slow-moving puffer fish. Her nose was pressed against the tank, and she was singing a little song.

"Do you like noodles, Frog?"

She turned back to him, nose still a little smooshed from the glass. "Yep."

"How about chicken?"

He got another yep from her, but her attention was all for the tank. Jack sent a silent thank you to the genius who'd installed it in the center of the dining room.

By the time the food came, he'd taught her to play tic-tac-toe and she'd shown him how to draw fish. He'd turned his fish into a googly-eyed shark, which won him giggles. Chloe dug into the chicken lo mein with enthusiasm, eating a shocking amount of food for a such a small person.

If she nudged the carrots and celery to the side of the plate, she was thrilled to eat the baby corn. That qualified as a vegetable, didn't it?

She insisted on trying his tea, telling him it needed lots of sugar like her mama drank it.

He paid the check, took the leftovers to go, and decided they'd earned ice cream. Twilight lingered over town, the sky fading from violet to peach, save for the crescent moon. Chloe's steps started to drag, so he swung her up and carried her on his shoulders as far as the Scoop Shoppe.

He split a cookies-and-cream cup with her at a table overlooking the river. She knew more about the river than he had at her age, rattling off facts about it including that it flowed "up." Her eyes were getting heavy, though, so he carried her on his shoulders again.

She'd started to doze during her shoulder-ride home, so Jack took her upstairs. Surveying her room, so clearly full of Anneliese's eye for magic, he hit his first snag.

"Pajamas, Chlo'?"

"I can do it myself. And brush my teeth." She rallied slightly at the thought of showing off her big girl skills, so Jack took himself across the hall to Anneliese's room. He sat gingerly on the end of her bed, trying hard not to remember the last time he'd been there.

"Jack?" Chloe, wearing striped pajamas and carrying her clownfish, was waiting for him in the hallway. "Can you read a Llama Llama book?"

"Can you help me find it?"

She ran to her room, and he winced at the sound of books hitting the floor one by one until she called, "Got it!"

Her bed was crowded once you tucked a person and forty-two plushies into it, so Jack sat on the rug, leaned back against the bed, and opened the book, a sweet story about a young llama and his mother.

In the end, he read three books about the little llama, but Chloe wasn't quite ready to fall asleep, despite her eyelids drifting closed at intervals. He reached up to turn off her bedside table lamp.

"You're good at reading stories."

"Thanks, kiddo. Can I tell you something?"

Chloe nodded solemnly.

"I'd never read anybody a story until my mom got sick, and now I'm reading Ewan's grown-up stories to my mom at home. They make her feel better."

"Mama says I can read them when I'm in high school. That's a long time."

"Sure is." He yawned and stretched his legs. "They're pretty great. I can't wait to find out what happens in the end."

"No spoilers," Chloe said.

A laugh sputtered out despite himself. "Where did you hear that?"

"Jax's mom said it to her neighbor, 'cause he was gonna tell her how the 'vengers movie ended."

"Serious business, that," Jack concurred. "No spoilers, then."

"Can you stay?" she said, petting his hair. "Mama stays until I fall asleep."

"Sure thing." He yawned and let his head fall back and watched the starry sky projected from her turtle nightlight through his own falling lids.

~

ANNELIESE WAS HALFWAY THROUGH A CHECKLIST FOR HER NEXT EVENT— a retirement party at the state park's pavilion—when Joss pulled in with Nan in the passenger seat. She rushed out the kitchen door to meet them, relieved to see Nan home again.

She held the door for them, and Joss paused to hug her. "Thank you."

Nan sat down at the farm table that dominated the kitchen. "Is everyone back?"

"No work until you tell me what happened."

Joss went to Nan's side, pulled there by the gravity that bound them. Anneliese felt a flutter of envy for their connection.

"Braxton-Hicks, they think," Nan said. "But, my blood pressure has been creeping up, and now they want me to do a stress test."

Joss laid a hand on Nan's shoulder. "And she needs to take it easy until the appointment tomorrow."

"I'll let you two get to bed. It's late." Anneliese began gathering up her things. "And Jack is with Chloe. I'm sure he's more than ready to go home."

Nan laughed, wide-eyed. "Our Jack? Babysitting?"

Anneliese slipped her files into her bag. "He's worried about you, and he offered."

"I'm only teasing." Nan's laughter dried up. "And I'm sure he and Chloe are fine."

"My money's on Chloe," said Joss. "Jack's got a soft spot for blondes."

Nan elbowed him, but the damage was done.

"Sorry, Anna." Joss looked at her as though he'd kicked a puppy. "I didn't mean—"

"I know you didn't. Jack's soft spots are no business of mine." She slung her bag over her shoulder, fighting the urge to flee. "On that note, I'm heading out. Call me if you need anything."

She gave Joss a pointed look. "And you, make sure she rests."

The valley was quiet outside the inn, the air heavy despite the nighttime chill. Anneliese pulled her cardigan snug around her waist and climbed into the car.

Jack hadn't texted, hadn't called. *Hadn't needed help?* She'd been tempted to check in on him at least every fourteen seconds, but he'd been so adamant, and she understood the need to feel useful, to feel as though something was in your control. Whether he realized it or not, Anneliese suspected Jack was still coping with the trauma of his mother's illness, and feeling out of sorts in his professional limbo. Being able to help a friend in need, if only by allowing her to keep an eye on the inn, meant something to him.

It would have been easier to write him off as a lost cause, if it weren't for that deep well of caring.

When she parked at the curb, she was surprised to see the first floor dark. Her porch light wasn't even on, but she could make out the glow of Chloe's nightlight through her curtains.

"Hello?"

She called out quietly, walking on soft feet through the kitchen, expecting to find him asleep on the couch. It was empty, the room dark and cool. Anneliese stepped lightly up the stairs; Chloe's night-light stars spilled out her open door onto the hall ceiling.

Her breath left her lungs in a tender *whoosh*. Jack was asleep, long legs stretched out, ankles crossed on Chloe's rug. One arm propped behind his head, dropped back onto Chloe's bed, the other resting his chest. His long, sooty lashes put her own to shame, and in sleep, so much of the boy she loved shone through his features. *He was so beautiful.*

It was Chloe, though, who broke her heart. Her daughter slept on her side, Feesh bunched under her cheek, and one hand tangled in Jack's hair.

Her little girl needed a father, but her father didn't want her. Her father wanted an easy out.

Not wanting to wake her daughter, Anneliese tiptoed into the room and knelt at Jack's side. She gently moved Chloe's hand, tucking it under the blanket.

"Jack," she whispered, placing a hand over his. "Jack."

He blinked, a sleepy smile lighting his features. "Anna Banana."

"Shh." She glanced at Chloe, whose breathing was steady. "You fell asleep."

He blinked, sitting up and rubbing his eyes. "What time is it?"

"Nearly one. I just got home."

"How's Nan?"

Anneliese laid a finger to her lips, then pointed down the stairs.

He scrubbed at his hair, mussing it. Anneliese wondered if there was still a warm patch from Chloe's fingers.

She stood, offering him a hand up. He clasped her hand in his; the jolt that ran up her arm and straight to her heart had nothing—and everything—to do with their lifelong friendship. She dropped his hand as soon as he had his feet under him.

She waited for him to go first, kissing Chloe's forehead and closing her door gently behind her.

He was already in the kitchen, rummaging in her fridge.

She eyed the Chinese take-out containers . "Who around here delivers?"

Jack handed her a carton of sesame chicken. "Chlo' and I walked over to Golden Prawn."

She started to admonish him, but he cut her off.

"She loves lo mein..." He trailed off, fishing a piece of sticky chicken out with his fingers. "And she ate every piece of baby corn on her plate."

Anneliese sighed. "Covered in whatever it is that makes lo mein so greasy and perfect."

"Exactly." Jack offered her the carton. "Want some?"

"Not now, but if there's some left, you can leave it."

He closed the chicken container and stuck it back in the fridge, then ran his hands under the sink sprayer. "I'm sorry, Anna. I know you left stuff, but it was an adventure, and she did great."

He dried his hands on his jeans; Anneliese realized she didn't have a kitchen towel out.

"Thank you." The words came out croaky, but she couldn't help it. It hadn't ever occurred to take her daughter for Chinese food. Or Indian. Or practically anything but brunches with her friends, safe places full of familiar scrambled eggs and toast and juice. "She needs some adventures."

"Hey," he said. It was a careful interruption. "It was fun. She watched the fish and ate noodles and ice cream. I bet she'd love to take you some time."

"Yeah." She swallowed the uncomfortable emotions.

"Anneliese." He wrapped his arms around her and rocked her, swaying slightly, like a parent with a newborn. His hands were still cold from the water. She stretched up on her toes and clung to him.

"Am I failing her, Jack?"

She spoke to the hollow of his shoulder, and he made some space between them to look at her.

"She's amazing," he said. "You're amazing."

She hadn't meant to kiss him, hadn't meant to touch her lips to his with a sigh of longing and heartbreak, hadn't meant to curl her fingers in the short hair at the nape of his neck. She hadn't meant to, but she did, and it was bliss.

He tasted of sleep and sesame sauce; his stubble was sandpaper against her chin and cheeks. He was exactly what she wanted. She coaxed, teased, nipped at the fullness of his bottom lip until the kiss turned hungry: a hot, wet mating of lips and tongue that foretold what she already knew they could be together.

And then he dropped her, pushed her back like she'd burned him.

His jaw hardened. He rubbed at his day-old beard with the back of one hand. "What are you doing?"

"I didn't mean—"

"You didn't mean to kiss me, days after telling me we needed to stay friends. Except when you're feeling grateful? Or you need an itch scratched?"

"What?" She stammered, trying to catch up with the lash of his temper. "No—"

"I don't know how to be around you." He shook his head slightly, as if trying to banish something from his thoughts. "I can't do this."

He was gone before she could gather her wits.

She hadn't even told him how Nan was.

# CHAPTER 19

Jack was halfway home on foot before he realized he'd left his car in Anneliese's driveway.

*Stupid small towns.*

He cursed under his breath and stopped under the streetlight at the corner outside the Mercantile building. The smart thing to do would be to leave the damn car, and go by during the day tomorrow and get it while Anneliese wasn't home. He was parked on the curb, so he wasn't inconveniencing her.

Not that he gave a damn about inconveniencing her. Except he did.

He was tired of doing the smart thing.

He doubled back, his long stride bringing him back to her door in a matter of minutes. She was sitting on the porch swing in the dark, knees tucked up under her chin.

"You left your car."

Jack pushed the screen door open. "The thing is, Anna, I want you. I can't stop wanting you."

Still fueled by the adrenaline of his walk, he closed the distance between them and sat on the swing beside her.

"I think you want me, too, and I'm sure there are a million reasons why we shouldn't, but I can't think of a single one right now." He held himself back, tried not to crowd her, though his hands ached to touch her.

Her eyes were wide, her lips parted. He could almost see the weight she was comparing, desire versus denial.

"Anna." He was begging. He didn't care.

They came together in a blaze, mouths fused, skin warm to the touch. They slipped out of the porch swing, tumbling, tussling on the wide pine boards like the randy teenagers they'd never been with one another.

"Inside?" He leaned up on one elbow, a moment's sanity reminding him they were making out in full view of any unlikely midnight voyeurs.

Anneliese scrambled up, hair mussed from his fingers, lips swollen with kissing. She was exquisite. Her laugh was shaky. "Inside."

They made it as far as the couch, peeling clothes off one another in a frenzy. The sight of her, clutching her half-buttoned shirt to her chest as she darted upstairs and back for the necessary protection, left him hard like a boy in the presence of his first naked girl.

She fell into his arms, all woman, and Jack forgot his youthful self and reveled in her flesh. It didn't take long; they were starving for one another.

When he buried himself in the heat of her, he nearly lost himself then and there. She shifted her hips, humming a little as she moved, and his control snapped. She met him in that wild place, and he bit back a shout when the world went to stars around him.

IN THE SWEATY, HEART-POUNDING MOMENTS WHICH FOLLOWED, Anneliese burrowed against the warmth of Jack's body. She didn't want to speak, certain one of them would say the wrong thing and spoil everything.

That could wait for dawn.

He'd gathered her against his chest and shifted them so he could take her weight. Her head rested on his bent arm, his fingers loosely threaded with hers where their hands lay on her hip. She ignored the chill of the empty room settling over her damp skin.

When Jack broke the silence, his voice rumbled in her ear.

"I know I can't stay. Chloe probably wakes up early."

Anneliese smiled. "Around six. And I don't want to explain grown-up sleepovers to her yet."

His chest rose and fell with silent laughter, and they slipped back into quiet.

"Jack?" The intimacy was like a scab she couldn't leave to heal. "I'm sorry."

"Why?"

"I keep changing the rules on you. It's not fair."

When he didn't reply immediately, she squirmed around to face him.

"I think I broke all the rules by coming home again." He kissed her gently. "This, though? It feels right."

"Are we allowed to have this? Just us? For now? And not completely screw everything up?"

He rolled, sliding his hands around her waist. "Can we try?"

Anneliese saw vulnerability in his eyes. She'd loved those eyes—and the man behind them—since girlhood, but trusting him was a different prospect.

Trusting herself was even more complicated.

"We can."

He smiled, and the clouds lifted from his gaze. He kissed her again, this time more searchingly. The leisure they'd bypassed on the porch unwound around them until she felt it again, that incredible pressure, that primal need. His honesty ignited that fire as much as his touch; she felt him there in the moment with her. The pleasure was heady.

She reached for him. "Could we do that again?"

He nipped at one nipple and she gasped. "If I can get you to make that sound again, I think so."

If his physical reaction was any indicator, he was right.

Jack trailed a path down her body. "Why don't we see what little sounds I can get while I rest up."

He disappeared between her thighs, and Anneliese grabbed for a pillow to catch the not-so-little sounds.

THE PINK AND GOLD HOUR BEFORE DAWN ARRIVED TOO SOON, BUT Anneliese lay on her sofa for a few moments, basking in the warm imprint of Jack's body on the upholstery.

She hadn't felt the warmth of a man in her bed—sofa, but it amounted to the same thing—in so many years. It was almost as delicious as the sex itself, and as impossible to think of letting go.

Tears threatened, so she pushed herself up, pulling underwear and her shirt on to climb the stairs to the bathroom. No stranger to early mornings, she wrote off sleep and climbed into the shower.

Chloe was downstairs coloring in the kitchen when she came down.

"Jack and me got noodles and there were clownfish like Feesh in the tank."

She ignored the impulse to correct Chloe's grammar. "Oh yeah? Did you have fun with Jack?"

"He's funny, but you do Llama's voice better."

Anneliese filled the electric kettle and fixed a mug for herself. "So, you still need me around?"

"Mama," Chloe had perfected an eye roll that belied her five years. "Jack's not my daddy. Of course I need you."

An ache knotted up her chest. *No, he's not your daddy, baby.* She left the mug and hugged her daughter, breathing in the still babyish smell of her hair. "I'm glad. I like this job."

Chloe leaned against her for a beat before going back to her drawing. Anneliese recognized Jack's tall, dark-haired form in Chloe's illustration with a pang.

"So, we should go back to Golden Prawn?"

"Do they make breakfast?"

The kettle was boiling.

"No, but I'll tell you a secret: I love cold lo mein noodles for breakfast."

"Yuck." Chloe's nose wrinkled up. "Can I have Frosted Flakes?"

"Sure, if you have some strawberries, too."

"Yay!"

Anneliese poured her daughter's cereal and sliced a handful strawberries over it, then pulled the take-out containers from the fridge, assembling a plate of cold leftovers despite Chloe's objections. She banished memories of Jack and did her best to focus on getting Chloe ready for school.

The walk to school was full of chatter about her adventure with Jack, and how she was going to tell her class about it at share time. The walk home was quiet, save for the panicky voice in her head screaming over and over that she was insane for even thinking about letting things get more complicated with Jack.

She was still fighting the demon in her ear midmorning when Kate dropped in.

"Anyone home?" Kate called, rapping on the porch door and letting herself in all in one smooth motion.

"In the den," Anneliese called back, setting her pen down on her open calendar. A half-formed to-do list loomed at her elbow, but she was too distracted to tick anything meaningful off.

"My old sofa looks great here, if I do say so myself." Kate plopped down. "Do you have a couple minutes? I want to figure out a rotation to help Nan out at the Damselfly."

"Is there anything new?"

"Basically, her blood pressure's a wreck and the midwife and her doctor want Nan to stay off her feet as much as possible to avoid pre...pre-something."

"Preeclampsia," Anneliese finished for her. "I can certainly take some shifts there doing check-ins and laundry, but you know I'm not in your league in the kitchen."

"I'm going to pre-stock her freezer with pastries for breakfasts and teas. Molly agreed to do weekend breakfasts. I guess Danielle is going to cover the farmer's market circuit for her. I can do some shifts, and Nan was going to call the work-study office at the college... So if a couple of us can cover the other busy times and keep her from fretting while she's taking it easy several hours a day, things should stay running."

"What about Jack? He'll want to help."

"He's got his hands full with my parents' stuff." Kate's eyes narrowed in suspicion. "I got the sense things were weird with you two."

Anneliese steadied her breath. Kate's insight into her brother was a factor she—stupidly—hadn't considered. When Jack had said *just us*, she assumed it meant not parading the sex in front of their friends, but Kate?

"He's Jack. What can I say?" Anneliese attempted breezy. "He was here with Chloe last night as a favor, since I was at the inn. He said he wanted to help, so I assume that would be true now, too."

Kate's expression softened. "He's turning into such a Boy Scout. Too bad it took a catastrophe to get him home again."

"Yeah," Anneliese looked away. He'd been anything but a Boy Scout a few hours before.

"I'll see if he can spare some time away from Dad's office now that Mom is on the mend. He can probably handle check-ins and stuff." She grinned. "I'm sure we can teach him, even if he is a lawyer."

"Maybe," Anneliese said.

"I've got to get back to the café. I left Andy in charge, and I don't want him to figure out that he could run the place blindfolded. He'll leave me for some proper restaurant. Or, god forbid, hospitality school."

"Andy?" Kate's café manager's devoted expression came to mind, and Anneliese suppressed a smile. "He'll never leave you."

Kate gave her a wry look. "Anyway, I left a loaf of yesterday's cinnamon swirl bread on your counter for Chloe. I'll text you later about the inn."

Kate stood, so Anneliese got up, too. When Kate hugged her, she paused, looking hard at Anneliese's face. "If I didn't know better, I'd say you had a touch of stubble burn."

Anneliese snorted. "A likely story."

The lie stung, even though Kate had moved on to the next thing on her mental agenda.

"Oh," Kate said, from halfway through the kitchen. "I almost forgot. Ewan and I are going to throw a big Halloween party instead of a housewarming. You can bring Chloe after trick-or-treating, and she can sleep over. Ailie will be here with Mike and the twins. They can have a slumber party."

"Sounds great," Anneliese said as Kate dashed out the door and disappeared into her pink minivan.

## CHAPTER 20

*M*rs. Drake buzzed a call through at half past four.

"There's a Mrs. Hardy on the phone for you."

The real estate contract Jack was struggling with hit the desk with a heavy, grateful thwack before he picked up the phone. The contract's only benefit had been keeping his mind off Anneliese, who'd been away overnight at a trade show in Albany.

"Jack? It's Jenna Hardy. Jenna Christensen Hardy." The voice was more polished than he remembered, but the husky, come-hither delivery was exactly as he recalled. Senator Geoff Hardy's wife, and the girl he took to his senior prom.

"Jenna." Was it mercenary to ask Jenna if she could get him in to see the senator? He reached for the caregiver information tucked into his drawer. "It's good to hear from you."

"I can't believe you're back in Thornton. Mom says she's seen you around all summer."

"I can't believe I'm here, either, but my dad—"

"I was so glad to hear your mother is recovering. Your parents were always so sweet."

She had developed a glossy way of talking; he supposed it was politics. He did it too, to a degree, with the firm's clients.

201

"Thank you. To what do I owe the pleasure?"

"Geoff got a call from Noah Hawes. Seems he wants to introduce you two. When I heard your name, I was intrigued. I may have mentioned our connection."

Noah wasted no time. Their talk had stayed with Jack as well, but he was surprised the old man followed through so quickly on his promise to convince Jack to stay.

"I hope you left it at prom." Jack kept his tone carefully neutral. They'd relieved one another of their virginity a few weeks later.

Jenna's smooth hum of appreciation told him everything he needed to know. "Water under the bridge. The reason I called, though, is an invitation. Geoff and I will be at our house in Warren next Thursday, hosting a fundraiser dinner. We'd like you to be our guest."

Even if Noah Hawes's machinations came to nothing, he would be a fool not to take the opportunity to get to know Jenna's influential husband. "I wouldn't miss it."

"I'll put you down for a plus-one. I assume you'll bring your...." Jenna let his marital status dangle.

He took the bait, wondering if Anneliese would stomach Jenna for an evening. There was no love lost between them, as he recalled. "I'm sure I can scare up a date. Thank you."

"I'll have someone from Geoff's office send over the details, " she said. "I'm looking forward to seeing you, Jack."

"You, too. Jenna. Give my love to your mom."

He ended the call, only to find his father in the doorway.

"Where are you going that you need to scare up a date?"

"Hey, Dad." He patted the file his father had read. "That was Jenna Hardy. Jenna Christensen, as was. She and Senator Hardy are hosting a thing at their place in Warren next week."

"Dinner with the senator. Planning a run for office?" His dad was teasing, but Jack realized somewhere, deep down, maybe he was. Like Hawes had said. Stay. Put down roots. Get involved locally.

Easier to keep that to himself. "I've never held so much as a student body office. I had a conversation with Noah Hawes about Muriel's Bill. I've been thinking a lot about that stuff since Mom..."

Jack shoved the folder away. "Davis mentioned me to Hardy, Jenna overheard. She and I go back a ways."

His father gave him a knowing look. "Quite a ways, I suspect."

His cheeks went hot. "Dad."

"Okay, okay," John said. "Forget I mentioned it. I came over here to tell you Katie and Ewan invited us to their place for dinner. Ewan's decided to learn to grill."

"Sure. You and Mom want to wait for me, or should I drive over after I finish up here?"

"Your mother's waiting in the car. If you're not ready to go, you can meet us."

Jack looked at the real estate contract and sighed. "I've got to finish that, then I'll grab my car and head out to Kate's."

His father said something on his way out that made Mrs. Drake laugh. Jack had yet to accomplish that feat, but it was rising to the top of a personal to-do list he never would have imagined when he arrived home in July.

ON HER WAY HOME FROM THE ALBANY WEDDING EXPO, ANNELIESE stopped at the office park near Coulson's nursery. The squat, industrial series of buildings with a winding drive, sporting deeply mulched flower beds and outdated signage, was home to Anneliese's dentist, among a handful of other businesses.

According to the email from Kirsten Letourneau, it was now also home to Tan-Stark Wedding Central. Anneliese let herself into Suite 14, and smiled. Kirsten was on a step stool, creating a vision board next to a whiteboard sporting coder-style sticky notes in columns.

"Anneliese!" Kirsten stepped down and opened her arms wide. "It lacks décor, but I've got a handle on things."

Anneliese took in the sheer volume of information Kirsten had laid out. "I wish I could afford to steal you from Lela."

"Have a seat on my free-from-Craigslist couch and we can negotiate rates." Kirsten plopped down on a cheap futon pushed up against the wall. "Okay, I'm kidding. I love working for Lela, but it's not going to be forever. I'm going to remember you said that."

Anneliese sat down. She had her own list of information to coordinate with Lela's right-hand woman. "This is the most recent guest list I have from our bride. Honestly, how much do you think it will change?"

Kirsten scrutinized Anneliese's list, then picked up a tablet and began swiping through some slick organizational software. "I think we can safely say she won't cross anyone off, but she can be crazy generous on set, so it wouldn't shock me to see another ten names before the big day."

"I'll pad the final numbers for the chairs at the inn," Anneliese said.

"Speaking of the inn, I'm meeting someone named Joss over there tomorrow to go over the security team's bullet points."

"The owner's husband. Nan's on bed-rest right now."

Kirsten's eyes went wide. "Oh no! Is the baby okay?"

"Fine, but they both need a little extra looking after. Do you want me to come along?"

"I've got this." Kirsten tapped the keyboard, adding a note to some task. "You must have enough stress in your life."

*Oh, no big deal. I'm sleeping with a man who's going to break my heart, and probably my daughter's too. My ex-husband crawled out from under a rock and slithered three thousand miles to torment me, and the wedding that could ratchet up—or sink—my career is only a few weeks away.*

"Nothing I can't handle," Anneliese said brightly. "I've got to run. I have to pick up my daughter. I'll forward you the confirmation on the flowers and the updated reservation numbers from the hotels."

Kirsten's phone buzzed from the floor near the futon. She gave Anneliese a thumbs-up and answered the call while Anneliese let herself out.

It was officially a high-traffic day if Jack saw even one walk-in client. The man who took the seat opposite him, however, was anything but a welcome distraction. Despite the guy's easy smile and casual dress, he radiated fidgety energy. Not only did his smile not reach his eyes, there was coldness that set Jack's nerves on edge.

"What can I do for you?" Jack closed his laptop and leaned his elbows on the desk. "Mr. Douglas."

"It's Chuck." Chuck crossed one ankle over his knee and relaxed into the space. He would have looked at home on a deck, but the posture looked out of place in an office.

"Chuck," Jack said evenly. "It's rare to get a walk-in."

"I prefer to keep things off the phone until I need to. Little ears, you know."

"Fair enough." Jack pulled out a legal pad and clicked his pen. "Are you interested in retaining counsel at this time?"

"Not just yet." Chuck hedged. "I want to find out whether I need someone who specializes, I guess. Figured it couldn't hurt to talk to a pro about it." He squinted at Jack. "Unless, you don't have conversations."

Jack pulled a breath in through his nose, steadying his temper. Everything about Chuck Douglas pushed his buttons. He looked the other man in the eyes. "I just need to know whether we're dealing with attorney-client privilege here, or whether I'm billing you for a consultation."

Chuck unfolded himself from the chair, expression cool, but Jack saw something dangerous flash there. He tossed his hands up in a defensive motion. "I'm not really in the position to pay for a chat, so I'd better take off. It can wait until I need a custody lawyer."

Jack leaned back now, asserting his position behind the desk. "Happy to give you a couple of referrals if that's your need."

"I'll give you a call. Thanks." Chuck sauntered out, letting the front door bang closed behind him.

Curious, Jack searched every variation of Chuck or Charles Douglas he could think of, even running him through the online directory Mrs. Drake paid a yearly subscription for, but not one hit bore any resemblance to the guy who had just cruised out of his office.

Chalking it up to small-town weirdness, Jack went back to his day. One more case to update, then he could reward himself with a trip to Josephine's. Anneliese would be home from the expo, and what woman didn't deserve flowers when she came home?

ANNELIESE TURNED DOWN HER PARENTS' STREET, A CUL-DE-SAC OF split-level ranches and garrison colonials, all aged into their landscaping over the decades, remembering riding bikes and flashlight tag with the neighborhood kids. For the last couple of years, it had felt like a penance, living with her mother and father again after the divorce. Their scrutiny and disappointment weighed heavily on her, whether real or imagined.

Lost in thought, she very nearly bent the fender of a car with Indiana tags parked in the spot behind her father's station wagon. A frisson of nervous energy sparked down her spine.

Hoping she was being paranoid, she backed her car out and parked it alongside the sidewalk. On the way past, she inspected the car for clues about the visitor.

A sheaf of rental contracts on the passenger seat explained the odd plates, but no amount of peering through the windows could have prepared her for her ex-husband perched comfortably at the bar-height kitchen table, cradling a cup of coffee between his hands and laughing with her father.

Her mother met her at the front door, taking in Anneliese's stormy expression with a frown. "Now, Anneliese, be civil."

"Where's Chloe?"

Her mother glanced over her shoulder. "She's at the Simpsons'. Their daughter is in her class, and they have the sweetest playhouse…"

"Does she know he's here?"

"No. He only arrived a few minutes ago. I made him a cup of coffee." She smiled indulgently. "He's been telling your father fishing stories."

"I don't care what kind of stories he's telling, he needs to get the hell out of here." Her voice went shrill, but she didn't care. A kind of hysteria was brewing behind her breastbone.

"Watch your language, young lady."

"Watch my *language,* Mom? After everything I told you?"

Her mother had the grace to look at her feet, but the small victory didn't make Anneliese feel any safer.

"Anneliese." Chad turned, letting one foot touch the floor, resting his coffee on his bent knee. "You didn't tell your parents I was in town."

Anneliese gritted her teeth. "I didn't know you still were."

Bile rose in her throat; Chad smirked. *Had he been here all along? Had he known Chloe was with her parents while she was out of town?*

*Had he been watching her?*

"I know I mentioned my plans when I saw you. You're busy. I understand if you forget the details." His delivery was smooth and sincere.

"I'm sure I'd have remembered that," Anneliese snapped.

Her parents were watching them from the other side of the kitchen. Anneliese wished she could make them understand, see past the illusion of decency Chad wore.

Chad held up his free hand in a gesture of surrender. His eyes glittered with malice when he laughed. "Hey, of course."

She had to get out of there, get Chloe away before she saw Chad and wondered who the stranger was. "I'll take Chloe's things and get her at the Simpsons. I'll find somewhere else for her to stay until I can be sure he's not going to be here."

Chloe's My Little Pony backpack was already tidily zipped by the front door. For that, Anneliese could be grateful. She shot Chad a warning look and banged out the door.

"Anneliese!" She heard her mother try to call her back, but her little girl came first.

She crossed the lawn and yanked the hatch up to stow Chloe's things in the car, slamming it for good measure before crossing the cul-de-sac to knock on the Simpson's door. She knew the couple casually. Their daughter had been in Chloe's class since the first year of the pilot preschool program.

Meg Simpson answered, wiping her hands on a kitchen towel. The scent of grilled meat wafted through the house. Anneliese could see Chloe and Olivia on the deck, trying to wrestle a brindled cat into a bonnet.

"Hey, Anneliese." Meg turned to call the girls. "Chloe, your mom's here."

"Sorry, Meg. I know you were expecting my mother."

"No problem. I saw they had company." Meg peered over Anneliese's shoulder. Anneliese sneaked a glance at their front yard, where Chad was making his way down the walk with her father.

She tried not to look while Chad loitered across the circle, tried not to shout while Chloe lingered over the Simpson's cat, tying her shoes, saying goodbye to Olivia. Even after all that, Chad was only as far as leaning against the open door of his rental car.

She hustled Chloe down the front walk and into the car, nodding and *really, baby?*-ing along to Chloe's chatter while her heart hammered in her chest.

He watched them from behind polarized Ray-Bans, raising his hand in a mock-salute as Anneliese drove by. An icy ball of fear settled in her stomach, and she checked her rearview all the way back to town, half expecting to see the beige paint and Indiana plates behind her.

Jack turned up on her front porch an hour later bearing wine and daisies—white for her, yellow for Chloe. She'd never been so glad to see him on her doorstep. Chad's intrusion rattled her.

Chloe hugged her flowers close; Anneliese tried not wince when she crushed the petals, but Jack was unfazed. "Can I have them in my room, Mama?"

Anneliese trimmed the stems short and arranged them in a Mason jar. "Sure, baby. But not where the jar might get broken."

Chloe headed for the stairs.

"Two hands," Anneliese called before turning to Jack. "That was very kind of you. The daisies are beautiful."

Jack eyed the taller vase in Anneliese's hands warily. "Why do I sense there's a *but* here?"

She ran the vase under the tap, sliding her flowers into the water and setting them on the kitchen windowsill. "I need you to be careful with her. She's young, and she loves hard. I can live with my choices, but I can't let her heart be broken because of them."

Jack pocketed his hands. "I'm sorry. I didn't think—"

"They're lovely, Jack. You didn't do anything wrong, not really. I'm just trying to be a good mom." Anneliese slipped her hands around his waist. Easier to slip into normalcy and play at being lovers instead of dwelling on her ex. "And I'm happy you dropped by. No one's brought me so many flowers in an even longer time than..."

She was blushing, damn her fair skin, but Jack's eyes sparkled. He touched his lips to hers. "You should have both. Often."

Chloe's feet pounded on the floor, and Anneliese disentangled herself from Jack's embrace.

"Jack, I can tie my shoes." She had brought her sneakers downstairs with her, and she dropped onto the floor.

"I can't wait to see," he said, swallowing his laughter. Anneliese watched her daughter biting her lip as she tugged the laces.

It took her a few tries and more than a few minutes, but she produced a pair of floppy, uneven bows in her sparkly orange laces.

"See?"

"Good for you, Chlo'," Jack bent down to tug at the loops. "Now you can do mine for me."

Chloe squinted at the laces of his wingtips; Anneliese figured those shoes were about a third of her rent. "Your shoes are nice, like Jeremy's."

He looked up, a question apparent in the wrinkles on his forehead. Anneliese laughed. "You remember our landlords, Jeremy and Glenn. Next door."

"Right." Jack looked back at Chloe. "He's got good taste in shoes, then."

Chloe wagged her feet. "Can I watch a show?"

"Sure." Anneliese started to follow her, but Chloe put her hands on her hips.

"I can do the remote, Mama."

Anneliese turned back to Jack who was barely containing his mirth.

"Are you sure she's not a little bit Kate's?"

"Heaven help me."

"Before I forget," Jack said. "Are you free next Thursday?"

"I have to set up an event, but I wasn't planning to oversee the evening." Anneliese peeked into the den, where Chloe was working the remote. "Why?"

"I'm going to a fundraiser dinner at Senator Hardy's in Warren, and I get a plus-one." He rocked a little on his heels. "I'd love to have you there with me."

Senator Hardy and his *wife's* house. Anneliese might have made her peace with Jenna over the years, but she couldn't help wondering if Jenna still carried a torch for Jack.

"Jack, I—"

"Don't worry about Jenna. I know she was pretty awful to you back in the day, but she's a senator's wife now. How bad can she be?"

Anneliese shook her head. "For a man who's been around women all his life, you're shockingly naive about them."

If Jack had an opinion about her remark, he kept it to himself. "Think of the people there who might need an event planner."

"Actually...I'm *their* event planner."

"Oh." Jack stopped short. "Then you're already going."

"Yes. Earlier in the day to set up." Anneliese laughed. "I've done a handful of dinners and small receptions for them since Geoff started campaigning. This one's relatively simple. Just catering and having the tables and linens and stuff coordinated. I can certainly put on a party dress and be your date."

"Oh." Again, Jack stopped short. "I guess I thought…I'm glad you… You're kind of a big deal, aren't you?"

The praise outweighed his initial lack of understanding. She might not be a big deal in her own mind, but maybe she was getting there.

"I plan to be, anyway."

"Maybe we can slip away after," he said, circling her waist and dropping a kiss along her shoulder for every word. "Somewhere with room service and a really big bed."

His lips were erasing rational thought, but Chad's ugly shadow lurked. "One thing at a time."

"I'll start here." He kissed his way to her mouth. She was breathless, desire at war with worry and responsibility. Jack must have sensed her distraction. "Hey, is everything okay?"

"Yeah," she said. "Of course."

"Really, Anna, you don't have to be my date if you don't want to. I don't want to make you uncomfortable at a gig."

"Oh, no." She ran her thumb along his lower lip. "That's not it. I'm just worn out from the expo."

He turned, kissing the palm of her hand. "Can I help?"

He would, too. She wanted to take him up on it. Badly. "No, I'm just going to wrangle some dinner and get Chloe to bed."

"Let me make you dinner." Jack held her hands between them. "Does Chloe like eggs?"

"Yes…"

"Go, sit. Watch TV with your daughter."

Anneliese left him in banging around in the kitchen and snuggled in next to Chloe on the couch. "What are we watching?"

Her thoughts drifted while Chloe recounted the adventures of her current favorite talking animal and its human companions. *Her usual party planner, fade-into-the-woodwork dress wasn't going to cut it.* Kate was a no-go on this one, so Anneliese fired off a text to Michelle.

*S.O.S. Fashion emergency.*

Jack feel like part of a snug little team, making dinner for Chloe and Anneliese, though he envied their language of shared routines and inside jokes. Chloe set the table, Anneliese poured the drinks. Chloe made sure he was caught up on everything she could think to share.

He let Chloe's mile-a-minute narrative wash over while he watched Anneliese. She was more than kind of a big deal.

He'd expected to find her in need of a white knight. Or maybe just glad to have him around because he…why, though? Because he was the sophisticated one? The one with the money and the flashy car? He'd developed a fairly high opinion of himself, hadn't he?

It hadn't occurred to him that Anneliese might be his introduction to Geoff Hardy. He never considered she might know people. If anyone, maybe Kate; but his shy, serious Anneliese?

Once again, he'd put her in a tidy box in his memory and left her there.

"Your eggs are good, Applejack. Did Auntie Molly teach you? She makes the best eggs." Chloe was shoveling scrambled eggs in like they might vanish.

"Chloe, slow down," Anneliese warned. "You'll choke."

"Molly didn't teach me," he said. "My mom did."

"Your mom is Miss Cora," Chloe said.

"She is."

"She missed-ed the frogs this summer. Me and Mama are gonna be ninja frogs for Halloween. Kate-Kate's having a big party at her new house. You should be one too and come with us."

While Chloe stopped to bite into a spear of pear, Jack looked at Anneliese for a cue. She tilted her head slightly, a wry turn and an entertained gleam in her eyes, as if to say, *you're in now.*

Ninja frogs did sound awesome. "What are we wearing?"

"All black with masks and we're gonna make frog heads from sweatshirt hoods and wear masks like this." Chloe put her fingers over her eyes, looking between them.

"I'm in." How could he not be?

Anneliese hid a laugh by getting up to refill Chloe's drink.

"Mama says Miss Cora might not come back to school for a long time, so we have to visit her to make sure she's not lonely."

Jack blinked away a tear, and snuck a look at Anneliese before he answered. "I've got some plans to help my mom get back to school as fast as she can."

Anneliese caught his gaze with a furrow of confusion between her brows.

"Can I help?" Chloe asked.

"Who knows, Frog? Maybe I'll think of a job for you."

He took the dish sponge from Anneliese after dinner, while Chloe went out to water the garden.

"No, the garden doesn't need watering anymore, but she likes doing it." Anneliese laughed. "She'll come back in filthy, but I'll just plunk her in the bath."

Jack handed a clean plate to Anneliese to dry. "She's great. Thanks for letting me crash your Halloween costume."

"If you're going to be here, you might as well be a super cool ninja frog." She polished the plate and stacked it in one of her four cabinets. "What did you mean before? About a plan? That sounds serious."

"Nah." Jack dunked a handful of silverware in the soapy water. "Just some ideas."

Anneliese took the clean cutlery with that same furrow between her brows. "Okay."

He almost confessed the whole half-formed plan right there over the kitchen sink, but the wall Anneliese had put up between them wasn't completely dismantled. He suspected the ideas he was tossing around might spook her, and he liked the place they were at just fine.

She opened the silverware drawer and started sorting away the clean utensils. "Listen, I told Joss and Nan I'd cover the inn tomorrow, so I'm sending Chloe to my brother's place for a few days. Just to be safe."

"Safe from what?" Something about the way Anneliese said *sending* bothered him. "She's not staying with your parents?"

"No." She dropped a fork with a clatter. "I just meant in case my parents are tired of always pinch-hitting for me."

She was rattled. He knew something was bothering her. Maybe she really did feel uncomfortable about being his date for a work thing.

"I bet Jamie's kids are thrilled," he said. Easier to diffuse the moment than press her. "Chloe told me all about them."

"About what?" Chloe burst through the door as Anneliese predicted—grubby, but proud. "I watered the flowers!"

"And now you need a bath. March."

Jack plopped the last dishes into the sink, and then leaned over to kiss Anneliese. "Go give that frog a bath. I'll finish these and let myself out." He trailed a hand down her arm as she walked away, hoping to flirt away the lines of strain around her eyes. "Call me later. I'll tell you all the plans I have for you next time I get you alone."

The blush on her cheeks when she walked away was the sexiest thing he'd ever seen.

# CHAPTER 21

The Damselfly Inn ran like a well-oiled machine, even with its innkeeper on bedrest. Having tucked Nan in with a rom-com, Anneliese camped out in the inn's office with her notes and lists.

It didn't matter how many times she reminded herself that Lela and Grant's wedding was fast approaching, or that the Hardy's fundraiser was days away, her thoughts slipped and tangled like the knots and loops of Chloe's attempts at shoe-tying.

Her schedule didn't work without her parents. There weren't enough hours in the day.

Maybe she'd taken on too much with this wedding, maybe she wasn't cut out for living alone with her daughter.

She was tired of hiding how anxious Chad's increasing pressure left her. The alternative was unthinkable. If he suspected even half the depth of her love for her friends—or her feelings for Jack—Chad would target them as well. Long before his and Anneliese's marriage was over, Chad had driven home the wedge between her and her mother.

Leaving a chasm that continued to widen.

Anneliese dialed the home phone, drawing on the serenity of the

Damselfly when her mother answered. Ever a stickler for manners, her mother completed a short script of small talk before Anneliese could say what she needed to say.

"Mom, I'd like for Chloe to continue spending her afternoons with you."

"Oh?" Her mother let the silence speak. Only the faint drumming of Anneliese's fingernails and the grandmother clock in the adjacent parlor punctuated the quiet.

"I'm going to ask Jack and Danielle to pick her up from school and drive her to your house, but I'm not going to mention Chad to them. I don't want even the thought of him anywhere near them. Or you. Or Chloe."

"Anneliese, I am perfectly capable—"

"I know you are, but I'm Chloe's mother, and I need to be sure Chad's not welcome in your home when she's there."

Anneliese stilled her fidgety fingers until her mother spoke.

"Of course."

Anneliese thought of her parents' neighbor Meg, of Grace Mackie's tendency to trade in juicy secrets, of the way Kate, or Joss, or Jack would react if they knew. "Mom, have you told Auntie Molly or anyone about him?"

Her mother's reply was terse. "Your divorce is no one's business, Anneliese."

"Thank you," Anneliese said, silencing the small voice in her heart that wished they all knew. The people she loved were always better off without Chad's thoughtless cruelty. She was better off not giving Chad the chance to make them question her version of events.

"You're welcome," her mother said, before an audible inhale. "You know I love you and Chloe."

"And we love you."

The conversation with her mother hadn't untangled Anneliese's to-do list. It was a surprise when she rubbed her eyes and looked up to see Joss in the office doorway.

"Sorry I'm so late," he said. "The client needed some hand-holding with her kitchen plans."

"No problem." Anneliese clicked save and closed the site. "Chloe's with my brother and his family for a couple of days, so it's not like I have to race home."

"I bet she's thrilled," Joss said. "No school?"

Her brother's place in Warren was tucked between a hillside and a stony river. He repaired small engines year-round and worked driving a snowcat for Sugarbush during ski season. Anneliese knew Joss had been over to see him about equipment repairs over the years.

"School, but I pulled her out for a day or two." Anneliese breezed past explaining, hoping Joss would be anxious to get upstairs to his wife. *I sent her over there because her father is an awful human being. Oh, I didn't tell you he's been around? And that he's convinced my parents he's not so bad?* "Since Jamie's wife homeschools, I figure Chloe'll probably learn something while she's there."

"Thanks again for throwing your life into the spin cycle for us." Joss pulled up the chair opposite her spot at Nan's desk. "Nan doesn't like this whole arrangement, but we both know we couldn't have a better team."

"Oh, she told me as much. And you're welcome," Anneliese said. "I brought us up a snack and set her up on the couch instead of the bed."

"I'm going to head up and see how she is. Are you all set getting out of here?"

Anneliese checked the time. Nearly eight. "Yeah, I'm fine."

Joss was already half out the door. She listened to his feet on the back stairs before pulling out her phone like a guilty teenager. The quick text to Jack felt clandestine.

Even more clandestine was Jack, waiting for her on her porch swing. He'd opened a bottle of wine, and commandeered an end table from the den on which to serve a picnic dinner.

Autumn was a changeable creature, with days that shifted from crisp breezes to soupy heat without missing a beat, a teasing breath of winter in the evening air, but still the fading velvet softness of summer in the mornings. She wondered what next September would feel like without Jack waiting for her on the porch.

"I had a feeling you wouldn't eat."

She nudged her flats off, leaving them on the mat by the door. It was cool, but Jack had a thick comforter from her bedroom waiting. She slipped onto the seat, into the blankets and his arms.

"How was your day?"

Anneliese could feel her body melting against his. "Better now. Kirsten says the bride changed the sash color for her bridesmaids, which means we need to tweak the flowers…oh that's lovely." Jack's palm was warm on her back under the blankets. She took one of the glasses from the table. The wine was mellow, perfectly paired to the food in a way she never managed—or cared to, if she was being honest. That sophisticated approach was as natural for Jack as waking up.

"I'm glad." He kissed her, leisurely. A question without immediate answer, an exploration. His lips were warm and faintly tasted of the wine, his free hand played with the hair at the nape of her neck. The shivers that coasted down her spine arched her back like a cat.

When his hands drifted under the fabric of her dress, she could have purred with the pleasure of it. Their kisses grew heated, and Anneliese found her way through Jack's shirt buttons. She pressed close to his body, reveling in the thrill of contact.

Cool became cold outside their cocoon, but Anneliese was only aware of the delicious way the air touched her feverish skin.

"Jack."

"Yeah."

Those two words were enough. They abandoned everything and rushed hand-in-hand through her house. Anneliese pulled Jack down with her, into her bed and perilously deeper into her heart.

JACK BALANCED THE BOTTLE OF WINE AND THE FOOD THEY'D LEFT behind, struggling with the plates with the bottle in the crook of his arm, glad he'd made a habit of over-tipping wait-staff over the years.

Anneliese attacked the food. "I don't even know what this is, but I love it."

She'd pulled on a camisole and satiny shorts. A lock of her hair fell over her shoulder, tantalizingly close to the valley of her breasts.

She waved her fork in front of his face. "Are you not going to tell me?"

"Sorry. I was envying your hair." He let his gaze linger where his thoughts had been, enjoying the heat rising in her cheeks. "Roasted sunchokes. I'm surprised you don't have it all the time. Your mom works at the co-op."

A dark cloud passed over her features. "My mother," she said, spearing a chunk of sunchoke, "doesn't care for all the 'fancy prepared stuff.'"

"She seemed miffed that Chloe was staying over at your brother's place."

"She'll get over it. I'm Chloe's mother, not her."

Jack raised a hand in mock surrender. "Hey, just curious."

"Don't." Anneliese's voice went deadly calm. Her eyes flashed with a fury he wouldn't have associated with her, but just as quickly as it came, it passed. She sighed heavily. "I hate when people do that."

"Which part? I never want to cause that look again." Jack crawled over the bed, leaving his plate on the floor, until he sat opposite her. He couldn't quite put his finger on it, but it was almost as though he'd frightened her. "What's going on? Did something happen with work?"

"No." The set of her shoulders relaxed; whatever it was, it wasn't work. "And it was the part where you treated me like a hysterical female who can't control her outbursts."

Jack touched her hair. "I'm sorry. I didn't mean to upset you more."

"You didn't. Just having a rough day. I shouldn't take it out on you." She set aside her food. "Not when I haven't done this...maybe ever."

Her lips curved up, but he sensed the omission of some truth behind the smile. Time to table it for now.

"Note to self," Jack said, reaching across her lap to pick up her plate. "Treat Anna like a princess more often."

She laughed, but her next words cut him to the quick. "Just don't let me get used to it. I'll be ruined."

~

THE NEXT DAY, JACK WENT TO SEE NAN AT THE DAMSELFLY INN. HE found her curled up on the sofa with a stack of books.

He rapped on the door frame before letting himself in. "Hey, beautiful."

"I'm a hippopotamus." Nan shifted to hoist herself up.

Jack stopped her, dropping onto the cushion next to her. "You're a beautiful hippopotamus, who should be resting."

"I feel bad, sitting here doing nothing while everyone else keeps my business running."

"You're cooking a human in there." He glanced at her belly. "That's not nothing."

"That's basically what my midwife says." Nan slipped a bookmark into the novel she'd left open on the side table. "Not that I'm not always glad to see you, but what brings you here?"

"Actually, I came here to talk about you."

Jack handed Nan the folder of documents he'd carried with him in the car like a leaden weight. He wasn't sure how his father did it, drawing up wills and real estate contracts and custody arrangements for the people he saw at the co-op and church every Sunday. "I have a draft for you. I can make changes or rework the language, but I think it accomplishes all the things you want."

Nan took it from him, calmly flipping open the pages and skimming the words inside. "I'll have to read it more carefully and have Joss look it over, but I think this is pretty close to what I want to have in place."

"I'm happy to do it if it makes you feel better." It hadn't made him happy, though. It was unimaginable, the idea of her death. She was his best friend's wife, his sister's best friend, part of his chosen family. She was young and vibrant and alive.

Nan set the paperwork aside. "One of these days, you'll end up settled down, and you'll be asking some lawyer friend to draw up these same documents and it won't seem odd at all. Just a thing you know you have to do."

Jack sat in the chair nearest her. "How is it you ended up so wise, and I'm just catching up?"

"Like I said," Nan tucked the papers under her stack of books. "You'll know."

Jack fidgeted with a throw pillow. He hated wearing his distress on his sleeve. "I think you know a lot of it already."

"Hm." She regarded him for a moment. "It's hard for you to be this unsettled, isn't it?"

He met her steady gaze, feeling some of his restlessness start to drain away. "You're not pulling punches today."

"I'm too pregnant for that." Nan swung her feet up to rest on his knees. "And you—and Anna—mean too much to me to be coy. Sorry about my feet."

"Your feet are adorable." He smiled and rubbed the soles.

She sighed heavily, flexing her feet. "That's divine. Does everyone's lawyer do this?"

"Only the very fortunate," he said, kneading her sore feet. "How are you feeling?"

She *tsked* at him. "Don't change the subject. We're talking about you."

"If you say so." He was being glib, but the truth was, Nan had laid bare the way he was already feeling about Anna and Chloe. Unsettled.

"Oh, wait!" She reached for his hand, placing his palm over her belly.

The skin under the warm softness of her shirt shivered and flexed against his hand.

"Holy shit."

Nan grinned. "Holy shit."

"Are you sure it's not an alien?" He withdrew his hand, but he kept watching the tiny undulations until they subsided. "You're really growing a person in there."

"So did Anneliese." Nan's voice was soft.

"That's the part I didn't expect. I mean, I didn't *expect* to be where I am with Anna, but I never even saw Chloe coming. She's..." Words failed him.

"Magic." Nan finished his sentence.

"Yeah."

It was that simple. There was a little person in there, just as Chloe had been a little person growing safe under Anneliese's heart. Just as another little person might someday grow, and damned if he didn't want to be that someone's dad.

"I should get back to the office."

Nan picked up her book, and Jack wondered if her secretive smile meant she'd seen right through him to the wild new certainty beating in his chest.

~

"I CAN'T BELIEVE YOU DID THIS." ANNELIESE LOOKED AROUND THE southwest-facing bedroom of Kate and Ewan's new house in wonder. Since the closing, she knew they'd been busy, but Kate never ceased to amaze.

Without questioning why Anneliese asked, Kate and Ewan had happily agreed to take Chloe overnight. Anneliese skirted the truth; Jack had sweet-talked her into a night away together after the Hardy's party, but she couldn't leave Chloe anywhere Chad would dare to go.

She couldn't shake the feeling he was still around, lingering in the corner of her vision until he decided that she—and her barely-start-ing-to-be-sustaining income—wasn't worth his time.

Kate, meanwhile, transformed the empty bedroom into a cheerful getaway for the discerning kindergartener.

"Where did you find the bed? And the tent?"

Kate had hung a turquoise and yellow, chiffon and ribbon play tent over a four-poster bed. Gauzy curtains fluttered in the October breeze. It was nearly Indian summer outside, though they hadn't had a proper frost yet, and the fresh air teased at their hair.

"We've got all this space," Kate shrugged, "and Ailie's kids will be here for the party, so I thought, why not make a playroom kind of space they can also sleep in? I got lucky at a yard sale about three miles from here. Poor Ewan had to drag the furniture home."

"So, what's the plan tonight? Trade show? Girl's night?" Kate gave her a saucy look. "Slipping away for a tryst with some hunky man?"

Anneliese laughed too loudly, shocked by the stab of guilt Kate's teasing caused. "Definitely a tryst."

Sometimes the truth sounded like a lie.

She was keeping two truths from her friends, one truth from Jack. Her daughter was spending as many nights elsewhere as in her own bed, and Anneliese was making up excuses faster than she could juggle them.

Kate hugged her. "Go rock your vendor convention or whatever. We're going to watch a movie, and I made kettle corn and homemade marshmallows for microwave s'mores."

"She won't want to go home." Anneliese paused to listen. She could hear Chloe outside with Ewan. They'd been fast friends almost since the moment Kate's husband had arrived in Thornton, and it sounded like he was making up a story for her on the deck. "Especially if Ewan turns her into a space pilot or a warrior frog queen in his next book."

Kate got a little misty. "They're pretty cute together."

"As I recall," Anneliese said, glad to deflect the conversation away from her plans, "he's pretty great with his niece and nephew."

Kate rolled her eyes. "Don't get any ideas just yet."

# CHAPTER 22

The evening of Senator Hardy's party, Anneliese found herself fretting. Her dress—a sale rack sheath her mother hemmed only hours before—was too plain. Her statement necklace was too much. She was too short. Her shoes were trying too hard.

Never mind that she'd video chatted with Michelle while she tried on dresses at Mistle Thrush; her friend declared her *a knockout,* and made her promise to buy something bold from the jewelry case at the craft guild.

Her mother complimented her for *upgrading her work wardrobe.*

Anneliese hadn't mentioned she was finishing her evening off at a luxury resort with Jack Pease. Another omitted truth settled on her shoulders. She'd let her parents believe the overnight in Stowe was work related, which, as Jack reminded her, it could be. The place was a premier location for destination weddings, after all.

She'd wrapped her long, straight hair in a loose chignon, but the teasing tendrils she envied in magazine spreads escaped her. She'd never be effortlessly chic.

A rap at the door halted the downward spiral of imposter syndrome for the moment, and she snagged her heels and padded downstairs to answer the door.

Jack's suit walked the line between business and formal. He'd polished himself up more than she'd become used to. This was city Jack, corporate attorney Jack, moneyed Jack.

Devastating, mouth-watering Jack.

"You look incredible," he whispered into her ear, grazing her jaw with his lips.

She ran a finger down the lapel of his suit. "You, too."

The hour-long trip over the mountain to the Hardy's Vermont home—one she'd already done earlier in the day to inspect the catering, furniture, and linen load-ins—passed more quickly in Jack's company.

The Hardys owned an old farm with a rambling, meticulously renovated and updated New England colonial. At the end of a winding private driveway, Jack turned over the keys to a hired valet.

When took her arm to escort her to the door, all her doubts faded. She was about to walk into Jenna Christensen's house with Jack Pease on her arms. Sometimes petty little dreams did come true.

The senator and his wife greeted new arrivals in the front hall. Jenna noticed Jack immediately, but Anneliese couldn't see any of the predatory gleam her rival had fixed on him in high school.

"Jack. It's so good to see you again. I can't wait to me your—" Jenna's warm welcome cooled when she noticed Anneliese. "Anneliese. you look incredible."

"Thank you," Anneliese said smoothly, glad she'd missed the Hardys earlier, when she'd looked like her everyday self. "Senator Hardy, allow me to introduce you to Jack Pease."

Jenna stretched up on her toes to whisper context into her husband's ear, but Anneliese heard. "Jack and Anneliese and I all graduated from Thornton High together, you remember?"

Geoff Hardy was already turning toward the next guests. "Anneliese, it's wonderful to see you again. Jack, I'd like to speak to you and Noah Hawes later. I'll come find you."

They were borne on the tide of guests and patrons down the hall and into a great room that had been built off the original four-square floor plan. A fire crackled in a huge stone fireplace; servers circulated through the room.

Jack touched her elbow. "Do you want a drink?"

"Sure." She and Jenna had chosen two signature vintage cocktails to compliment the bar. The name was a coincidence, but Anneliese couldn't deny the thrill of satisfaction it gave her. "A Jack Rose."

While Jack headed to the bar, Anneliese enjoyed the view through the massive wall of windows that looked out over the foothills of the Green Mountains. The night sky was clear and cloudless, the constellations keeping watch overhead while warmth and light enveloped the house.

Jenna had done well for herself. Anneliese had envied her success at first. Old habits died hard. Now she understood how hard Geoff and Jenna worked for his constituency, and how demanding their lives were. Maybe she envied the home, but not the life it took to live in it.

The crab fritter she chose from a passing tray was almost as delicious as the sight of Jack crossing the room toward her. The server recognized her from another gig and paused to say hello. Anneliese was asking him about his family when Jack returned with their drinks.

"I like watching you work," Jack whispered.

"You caught me." She took the offered cocktail glass and sipped. It was, like the evening so far, perfect.

"You and Jenna throw a great party."

Anneliese could see their hostess across the room. Jenna had been an impossibly pretty teenage girl, with shampoo commercial hair and perfect skin; now she was one flawlessly chic half of a Washington power couple, and it suited her.

"We do."

The lights caught a flash of brilliance from the diamond on Jenna's left hand, and Anneliese let herself envy the ring even while she cautioned her heart not to wish for it.

JACK WISHED THERE WAS DANCING. IF ONLY SO HE COULD HAVE AN excuse to be close to Anneliese all that much sooner.

This Anneliese was someone new to him, in her elegant dress and impossible shoes. Sky-high heels tortured him with the long lines of her legs. This Anneliese sparkled as she navigated the room. She really had no idea how badly she tempted him—or half the men around them.

At dinner, they were seated with another young couple, a well-known Washington journalist covering the senator's reelection and her wife, and a former colleague of his father's, whose wife remembered Jack and Kate as small children.

Anneliese was deep in conversation with the journalist when Geoff Hardy crossed the room.

"Jack, do you have five minutes?"

Jack stood. "I do."

He followed the senator to a library on the other end of the addition, where Noah Hawes was waiting with a scotch for them all.

Geoff Hardy regarded Jack from across his desk. "Noah didn't mention you took my wife to your senior prom."

"Noah probably didn't know." He shot a sidelong glance at Thornton's family care crusader, but the retiree only leaned against the fieldstone fireplace mantel and contemplated the tumbler in his hand.

Geoff regarded Jack for a moment. "I like the idea of a team. People at every level, working strategically for the state. Noah thinks you have promise."

Jack started to object, but Hardy pressed on. "I think a guy like you —well-connected in your town, with legal experience, and a specific platform that means something to people, would make a strong candidate when Noah steps down. Assuming he doesn't get voted out in the next election, that gives you time to establish yourself as a resident and get involved on the municipal level."

Jack took stock of the two men plotting out a version of his future: Hawes, rumpled and paternal, but clear-eyed, and Hardy, hardly older than Jack himself, but passionate, ambitious, good-looking. He was a rising star on the national stage. Charismatic, smart, a dynamic fundraiser. People talked about him as the future of the Oval Office.

If Hardy was the mold, Jack knew he fit it, too.

"You two have this all mapped out, don't you?"

Hawes chuckled, but it was the senator who countered. "I trust Noah's judgment. He's been an invaluable mentor to me. I see a potential state rep who could angle for the governor's office, or even a senate seat with the right moves." He poured himself another scotch, silently offering one to Jack, who nodded. "Just not my seat. He tells me you're quite the hometown hero."

Jack laughed. "Maybe in high school."

Geoff handed Jack his drink. "Anneliese is a knockout. People love a wife like her."

"She's not my wife…"

Hardy's brows shot up. "No shit? I'm usually pretty good at spotting the wives from the girlfriends. Either way, you guys have a little Camelot going on."

"Look, Senator," Jack began.

"Geoff," Hardy corrected. "Jack, I know. It's not why you went to Noah in the first place, but he and I are working toward something, and we think you could be an important piece of it."

A light knock on the doorjamb distracted the senator for a moment. Jack barely had time to sample the very decent whiskey in his glass.

"Think about it." Geoff was back, but only for a moment. "Time to let you get back to your date. I wonder if Jenna has had a chance to catch up with her yet. Fantastic, all these old friends together again tonight."

Jack followed Senator Hardy out of his office. Noah Hawes clapped him on the shoulder before vanishing into the crowd, while Jack scanned the room for Anneliese and Jenna, hoping he didn't find them together.

∾

Anneliese hardly noticed Jack's absence. She was delighted by the couple seated next to her.

"I've been following him on and off for a year now. It's a plush assignment, for the most part, and Lori's gotten to be friendly with his wife. It doesn't help me much, but it gets us into the parties."

Dana Mulgrew had gorgeous eyes. They shone when she talked about her wife, who managed the D.C. DeVarona Hotel. They captivated when she asked questions, and something about her deep, blue expression invited you into her confidence. It was certainly an asset to her work, Anneliese thought, as she realized she'd been telling them an abridged version of her years in California for nearly the whole time Jack had been gone.

Lori interrupted, laughter in her tone. "She's not a story, Dana."

"You're right. I'm sorry," Dana said. "Everyone loves a small town homecoming tale."

Lori waved as Jenna sailed over.

"Lori, Dana, can I steal Anneliese for a quick minute? I'm dying to catch up."

There was a buttery smoothness to Jenna's voice that suggested Thornton's prying eyes were never truly far away.

"I hope I see you both again before the night is over," Anneliese said, getting up from the table. She straightened her back and looked her former adversary in the eye. "Is there a problem?"

Jenna took her arm and steered her through the crush. "Not at all. You're some kind of sorceress with the details. And you're here with Jack."

Here it was. Jenna was more of an outright bitch in high school. Anneliese had been so certain all that was behind them. Anneliese forced her lips to curve, took a breath, and channeled Michelle's bottomless brass. "I am."

"He always had a little thing for you." Her smile faltered a touch, but not unkindly. "He just didn't know it."

Michelle would die; she and Jenna actually agreed on something.

Jenna snatched a glass from a passing waiter. "I wonder if Geoff will have any luck convincing him to get into politics."

Anneliese felt Jenna's words like a physical punch. *Politics?* He hadn't said anything about… *Plans.* He'd told Chloe he had plans.

Jack would fit right in, taking questions from the press on Beacon Hill; leading marches and rallies on City Hall Plaza. Drifting farther and farther from their little town. From her little life. "I'm sure they're having a very productive conversation."

As if conjured, Jack exited the library.

"Oh, look. There he is," Jenna said. "I'll let you get back to him."

Jenna kissed the air just next to Anneliese's cheek, and released her into the crowd. Anneliese felt like a fish, floundering, gasping for air, as she watched Jack searching among the throng.

Smiling when he found her.

Making his way through the room to her side, tracing the line of her jaw with his palm, before touching his lips to hers. They tasted of scotch, and secrets.

"Hey," he said.

She sighed lightly against his hand. For tonight, she was going to pretend it was all perfect. "Hey."

"You want to get out of here?"

There would be time another day to ask him about his chat with Geoff Hardy.

"I do."

# CHAPTER 23

Jack sped the car toward Stowe while Anneliese typed on her phone.

"Is Chloe having fun with Kate and Ewan?"

"She is. Kate says she let her stay up for a 'late night' dance party before bed."

Jack didn't like the quiver in her voice, as though she were relieved. It seemed unlikely Chloe would be in any distress, but Anneliese was staring hard out the window, lost somewhere beyond his car.

"You're quiet. Did something happen at the party?"

"No. It went off without a hitch." Anneliese was quiet a moment. "Jenna does get what she wants."

Jack chuckled. "She was a beautiful, ambitious girl. Throw in a little luck, and that's what you get."

"Average looking girls with modest dreams and bad luck, on the other hand…"

The sour turn in Anna's voice was unmissable. He slowed for a traffic light, catching her profile in the red glow. He could see the girl she'd been, the way her lashes fluttered in the light. "You were never average looking."

She blew out a breath. "My luck has been fairly awful."

"Anna." His conversation with Noah Hawes and Geoff Hardy still lurked over his shoulder. The clock was running down on his time with Anneliese. Or he could flip his world upside down—and stay by her side for the foreseeable future.

"What?" She was watching him carefully.

The light changed; Jack accelerated through the intersection. A road sign indicated another mile to their destination.

"Your luck has nothing to do with who you are." He centered his hands on the steering wheel. "And I'd hardly call fulfilling your childhood dream a modest ambition."

As they pulled into the resort, the song on the radio changed, and they both laughed as the car filled with heavy guitars.

Jack glanced at her as he parked the car. She drummed along on the dashboard. "Do you remember?"

"Every time I hear this," she said, turning down the volume, "I can smell the interior of your mom's old car. It was playing the night we drove out to the bridge—"

"You jumped in with me. Jesus, the river was cold."

"So cold." She leaned back, letting the music thrash around them. "I'd have gone right back in with you, if you'd asked."

She wasn't flirting; she was serious.

"At least Joss was smart enough to stop us at one jump." Jack cut the engine, ending the song.

"At least," she said; she retrieved her purse from the floor of the car. "Shall we?"

"I'll get the bags."

Jack led them past the main building, along a pathway lined with solar-powered luminaries. The planner in her filed them away for future events. The woman felt the warmth of Jack's hand around hers.

They walked around the pool—gated and covered for the season—and down the path beyond; their feet rustled through the fallen foliage. Just a touch farther north, the leaves were already rich gold and scarlet.

As the path curved, a cluster of small Craftsman-style cottages revealed themselves. One waited with its front porch light on, a curl of woodsmoke rising from the chimney

Anneliese stopped to gape. These were summer cottages; she'd seen them on the website. Pricey weekly rentals that were shuttered after Labor Day.

"Jack?"

With a boyish smile, he dropped the bag, arms falling open as he spun to face her. "Surprise."

"Tell me you didn't get them to open one of these just for us," she said, stepping into his waiting embrace.

"I wanted something special for you."

She felt his smile against her cheek and tilted her head to kiss him. A flicker of something like sadness passed through his expression, but it was gone so quickly she might have imagined it. "Let's see how you did."

Jack turned the key, and ushered her into a fantasy of flowers and lantern light. The single main room was carpeted in petals. Bouquets spilled from milk bottles, old watering cans, Mason jars. From inside another room, an amber glow flickered.

"Oh."

Tears sprang to her eyes, and she let them run over her lashes. It was simply too much.

"Hey," Jack said, catching a stray tear with a finger. "Don't cry." He brushed his knuckle against her cheek, letting his fingers trail along her cheek.

"This is beautiful."

"You're beautiful." From her cheek to her hair, Jack's touch was gentle and reverent. His palms skimmed over her shoulders. "You're cold."

"I'll be fine," she said, reaching up to loosen his tie and smooth back his suit jacket.

Jack shrugged the coat off and tossed it over the back of a nearby sofa, then he lifted the heavy beaded coils of her necklace. Anneliese reached back and undid the clasp, letting the strands fall over their fingers. Jack caught the necklace, laying it over his jacket.

He paused to look at her, and the desire she saw in his eyes shocked her.

Standing a breath apart, she reached back again and drew down her own zipper.

Jack hooked his fingers under the straps and smoothed them off her shoulders, following the fabric with a trail of kisses.

She slipped his shirt buttons through their holes, taking her time, enjoying the work. Jack's warm hands stroked her arms from wrist to shoulder as she unbuttoned, dropping to his sides when she pushed the shirt down in an echo of her discarded dress. She tugged his undershirt free and loosened his belt. When he pulled the shirt over his head, she leaned into his chest, kissing her way up his collarbone to his bared shoulder.

His skin shivered with banked passion; she pressed her body against him, stretched up on her toes to reach his lips. When his hands came up under her thighs to scoop her up, she squeaked, and laughter propelled them to the bedroom and into the bed.

Stray rose petals stuck to her feet. Still laughing, Jack knelt to pull them off. They watched the petals fall to the wood floor before their gazes returned to one another.

Jack took off his trousers, pausing to lay them across the chest at the foot of the bed. His fingers went to the waistband of his underwear, but Anneliese stopped him.

"Let me."

The old bed sagged slightly under their weight where they met on their knees. She'd seen him naked, been with him before, but this undressing felt different. The way they wordlessly traded movements was more like dancing as they removed the last of their clothing.

Suddenly unsure, Anneliese wrapped her arms around him and kissed his mouth, determined to keep her concerns at bay, hold tight to the magic they made together.

Jack broke the kiss, laying back against the pillows and making a space for her. She settled into the curve of his body, achingly aware of the heaviness of his desire between them, but he seemed determined to draw out the moment. His lips cruised her shoulder blades, the nape of her neck. She arched like a cat, rubbing her back against his chest. His clever hands teased her nipples, then glided down over her hips and thighs—a wicked circuit that left her writhing to be touched.

When his questing fingers found her wet and slick, she inhaled sharply. "Jack."

He only increased the pressure at her center, pressing his hardness against her. His tongue traced the curve of her ear. She was coming undone.

The first wave took her, and she bucked against his hand. He groaned, and fresh lust spiked her blood. She rolled, pulling him over her, between her legs. His eyes were glazed with desire; he was as flushed with pleasure as she was. She reached for his face, drawing him down to her. Their tongues tangled, and she rolled against him, seeking out the deliverance they both craved.

"Hold that thought." He unwound himself from her and vanished into the other room, returning with his travel kit. "I hope you don't think I'm too presumptuous?"

"Come here." The growl in her tone surprised her, but then he was with her again, his skin hot against hers.

When he filled her, she held him still for a moment, with her body and her gaze. After a beat, she moved under him, setting the pace. The tempo built and they led one another into the giddy, whirling finale.

In the quiet afterward, she lay in his embrace, his heartbeat slowing under her cheek, their fingers twined. Jenna's words slithered into her ear, poisoning the sweetness of the moment. She shuddered, and Jack reached for the blankets. She snuggled against him, to ward off her own uncertainty as much as the cold.

In the morning, the concierge pointed them in the direction of a popular breakfast spot. They shared an omelet and a decadently oversized Danish; Jack ordered a cappuccino in a deep bowl with inch-deep froth, and asked the waitress for extra sugar for Anneliese's tea. She didn't ask how he knew her tea preference. Neither did she mention what she'd heard from Jenna the night before.

Jack picked up the Burlington Free Press to read while they lingered over the meal. Anneliese's heart squeezed. Framed by the picture window and backlit with October sunshine, leaning in his chair to accommodate the news, Jack was a vision she would remember for the rest of her days.

Even if there weren't many days left for her when it came to Jack.

He squinted at her as he flipped the page.

"What is it?"

He dropped his voice and leaned over the table. "Your client has arrived."

"How did you know?" *Had she said something? Violated her contract?* She didn't think so, but Chad's threats had left her more distracted than normal.

Laying the newspaper down on the table, he pointed to an above-the-fold column on an inside page. A photo of Lela Tan and companion shopping on Burlington's Church Street topped an article speculating on the reality starlet's presence.

"I put two and two together, and got Lela Tan."

Anneliese fished in her purse for a dollar. "Can I get attorney-client privilege?"

"I won't tell a soul," he promised. "You don't need to pay for my silence."

"She planned to be here a few weeks ahead of the big day. Kirsten's got a couple feature editors on hooks. She hasn't said much to me beyond that, but we'll have last-minute things to move into place if she gets one of them, additional security and..." She trailed off. Jack was looking at her as though he'd never seen her before.

"You really love it." He folded the newspaper. "I mean, you've been talking about weddings since forever—"

"When you and Joss would let me get a word in edgewise."

Anneliese laughed. "To be fair, though, you two weren't exactly my target audience."

"This one, though. This is the big case, the big client. I didn't put that together. Maybe because," he paused, a sheepish downturn to his smile, "I assumed planning a wedding was like throwing a cocktail party in a movie."

"I wish." Anneliese cradled her mug. "Details, lists, spreadsheets, phone calls and emails."

"And romance. You see couples, see their love and their promise and make it tangible."

She couldn't help her surprise at his insight. "I guess I'm not the only one at this table who's seeing something new."

Jack paid the check as an afterthought, signing the credit card receipt with the kind of throwaway nonchalance she aspired to. He left a generous tip, and the neatly folded newspaper for someone else to read.

"Tell me," he said, taking her hand as they crossed the street. "What happens after this wedding?"

"I'm not foolish enough to think this one event is going to solve everything, buy us a house or a nice car, but if it goes well," she pulled down her sunglasses, "and I think it will go well, it might mean access to another tier of contacts."

"If my education taught me anything, it's that knowing the right people matters."

Jack certainly had the open doors that came with degrees from Williams and Harvard, with working for respected judges and attorneys. Even here he had somehow managed to draw the attention of their local state representative and a United States senator.

Jack opened her door when they got back to his car. Anneliese couldn't help but hope he would mention his talk with Jenna's husband at the party, but he slipped the car in gear and pulled into traffic without a word on the subject.

The news item about Lela piqued his curiosity about her job, and he kept her busy with questions and ruminations on her work for most of the drive home, only changing the subject about ten minutes north of town.

"If there's anything I can do to help with Chloe or anything else, you'll tell me?" He glanced at her between long stretches of road. "I have a lot of time to make up for."

That surprised her. "Jack, you don't owe me anything."

"Anna Banana," he said, seriously, despite the childhood nickname rolling off his tongue, "I could spend the rest of my life working at it and never make up for the way I've taken you for granted."

He reached across the console to cradle her cheek in his palm. The tenderness in that touch felt like words neither of them could say.

When Anneliese stopped by Sweet Pease for tea and avocado toast on Monday morning, Kate joined her in the booth, a to-go cup steaming between her hands.

Kate pinned her with a look. "Are you sleeping with my brother?"

"How did you know?" The panicked question rushed out before she could consider. *She'd never been a convincing liar, but did she have to be such an open book?*

Kate leaned back, bracing her hands on the end of the table. "Holy shit. You are."

Anneliese closed her eyes and let her head fall back against the booth's vinyl seat.

Kate leaned in. "Since when?"

Without opening her eyes, Anneliese started to defend them both. "Kate, I—"

"I'm going to kill him."

Anneliese's eyes snapped open. "What?"

"I'm going to kill him. I can't believe he just waltzed into town and seduced you."

"Both of us had something to do with it."

Jim set her toast and tea on the table. "Hey Anneliese."

"Thanks, Jim." Anneliese grinned up at him, a manic sort of glee in her throat. She turned back to Kate as Andy departed. "The more I think about it, we've been heading toward this since I came back with Chloe."

Kate mulled it over for a moment, a dozen different reactions playing out across her features before she spoke. "Fine. But I'm still going to kill him."

The rush of adrenaline at being caught started to fade, and Anneliese studied her toast. "Can we not make a big deal about it? It's not like it's a long-term thing."

Kate scrutinized her face. Anneliese struggled to keep her expression neutral, so Kate wouldn't see she'd tumbled headlong in love with Jack, and it would shatter her like glass when he went back to Boston.

Whatever arrangement of facial muscles she produced, Kate seemed satisfied.

"I won't say another word," Kate said, but Anneliese was certain Ewan would know in a matter of hours.

"Good. You can tell me about Nan instead. Any change?"

"Nothing to report. She's had her feet up for days, and it's making her crabby." Kate hunched down over the table. "Now. Back to you and my brother."

"Not another word, hmm?" Anneliese insisted. "Okay, fine, but how did you figure it out?"

Kate leaned back in her seat, arms crossed smugly. "Ivy Brennan was in the café yesterday. She said she'd met my brother at a political thing for one of Sterling's clients on Saturday night. 'Isn't he handsome?' Ivy said. She went on to say Jack mentioned staying at some place in Stowe she'd always wanted to go to. She also said she saw you, but didn't get a chance to say hello. Thus, I deduced you left Chloe with us because you were going to Stowe overnight. With my brother."

Kate paused to draw breath. "It was Ewan who looked at me when I laid out the evidence, and said, 'I've been waiting to be right about that since Nan and Joss's engagement party.'"

The memory of that night was fresh, despite the two years that had passed. Ewan was Anneliese's date. Jack had gotten drunk and flirted with the wedding photographer, and Ewan and Kate kissed in the catering tent.

Anneliese cut her toast into triangles and pulled the teabag from her mug, laying it on the plate. She studied the drop of tea that fattened at the corner of the bag before rolling down the lip of the plate to pool against the crust of her toast.

Kate tapped the table with her fingernail. "Are you in love with him?"

"Of course not." Anneliese met Kate's gaze. "We weren't going to talk about this."

"Okay." Kate frowned, then popped the lid off her coffee and downed the remains as she changed tack. "Back to the Damselfly. The doctor and the midwife are letting Nan walk around again, but no lifting or heavy exercise, so I want to keep the inn-sitting schedule going so she doesn't try to overdo it."

"Agreed," Anneliese said. If Kate was ready to drop the topic of Jack, so was she. She bit into her toast and sighed. "Where did you find good avocados around here?"

"They're imports, obviously, but they looked fantastic, so I bought a flat from the produce guy." Kate's smile turned sly. "He had extra. He delivered a bunch to the catering company in Woodstock that did Senator Hardy's party."

Anneliese swiped her finger through a stray smear of avocado, and gave up. Kate was relentless. "There *was* an avocado roll that was pretty amazing."

Kate settled into her seat with a satisfied exhale. "I can't believe you two finally got over being weird and got together, and didn't tell anybody."

"Can't you?" Anneliese gave her friend a wry look. "And I promise you, we're a million years from 'getting over being weird.'"

# CHAPTER 24

Jack's father was at his desk in the office the next morning. John Pease looked up from a pile of files with a steady expression.

"You aren't half bad at this small-town stuff, son." He straightened the edge of the manila folders against the desk and slipped a stray pen into the pen cup. "I guess you're about done with it all, and ready to get back to the city."

"If you still need me around, Dad..." *My schedule could be wide open.*

He was giddy with possibility. He could stay on as long as his father needed—or wanted. He could consult. He could work at the co-op, or hang up a shingle. He could do what Noah Hawes wanted and run for a local office.

"You've given me a gift, Jack. I'm grateful." His father stood and looked out the window. The view to the common was starting to wear its autumn colors. "Your mom's improving daily, and between her therapists, the health aide, and her church group, she doesn't need me hovering all day. It's time I got back to it, at least for a few more years."

Jack started half a dozen sentences, but no words came out. When he'd arrived, sick with worry and buried resentment, all he'd wanted was to head back to his life in Boston, and here was his father cheerfully offering him exactly that.

"What if I told you I can stay on? Part-time, or just when you need a hand with something." Jack blurted out the question. He could almost see his words lying on the floor, naked, vulnerable between them.

His dad blinked. "Well, of course you can't stay on. I've kept track, son. You're expected back in Boston. Your mother and I wouldn't dream of—"

"I'm not going back." The dam broke and all the plans he hadn't fully formed rushed out. "I'm going to find a place, maybe stay with Kate to get out of your hair for a while. I don't know what I'm going to do for work yet, but I've got the means to figure it out."

He was almost breathless with it, this freefall into the future.

John Pease's smile spread—slowly at first as the meaning of what Jack said unfurled, then dawning all at once. "Jack!" He spoke his son's name in a choked laugh. "Are you sure?"

His own smile mirrored his dad's. "I wasn't—I don't think—until I said it."

"Does your mother know?"

"Like I said, I didn't even know for sure until just now."

"So." His father peered past them toward the doorway. He gave Jack an arch look. "Anneliese doesn't know?"

Jack laughed. His dad teasing him about girls was a good sign. "She doesn't. I guess I should tell her."

"Maybe not until later. I heard something about her having a meeting this morning."

"You're worse than Kate." Jack shook his head, reaching for the notebook he'd left on his dad's blotter. "How do you know that?"

"Anna stopped by the office earlier with some brownies from Jane. Mrs. Drake wanted to hear all about this secret wedding she's cooking up."

"She told you?" Jack couldn't keep the surprise out of his voice.

"Just the stuff Evangeline cares about. Fabric and flowers. Champagne."

Evangeline Drake cared about fabric and flowers and champagne. Wonders never did cease.

The giddiness of his decision swamped him again, but he was buoyed by the tenderness of the woman he loved bringing his father sweets and conversation. "Of course."

Anneliese found Nan and Kate upstairs at the Damselfly Inn. Nan, tucked into the fairytale bed Joss made for them, looked cross. Kate was bustling around the room picking things up and running a commentary.

"… and Danielle came in the other day to see about a job on the catering staff. She's still pulling regular shifts for Penny at the nursery, but with school starting up, she wanted to add another source of income." Kate noticed Anneliese in the doorway. "Hey, Anna."

"I stopped by the library." Anneliese set down her bag and offered a stack of books to Nan as a distraction. "I brought half the new releases. Mrs. Williams wasn't pleased with me, but she likes you."

Nan reached for the books with a genuine smile. "I just finished Ewan's latest manuscript, so I need something new. Thank you."

Anneliese sat on the bed. "How is it?" She shot a look at Kate. "He doesn't let me read them until there's a proof copy."

"He took pity on the pregnant lady. I only got to read it just before he let Nan." Kate shrugged. "What can I say? He's a monster."

"Agreed." Anneliese took note of the pile of laundry Kate was collecting. "Are you…doing laundry?"

"I'm helping." She held the small bundle of clothes at arm's length. "Hopefully there aren't any of Joss's boxers in here."

"You're safe," Nan said to Kate's back as she left the room.

Kate's voice drifted back up the stairs to the kitchen. "Back in a sec."

Anneliese tucked her feet under her legs. "How are you feeling?"

Nan shifted awkwardly. Anneliese remember the feeling of trying to get out of her own way to be comfortable. "Tired of so much bed rest. Impatient for this little one to be on the outside. Terrified that might actually happen before it should."

Anneliese reached out to take Nan's hand, but spoke to her belly. "Stay put, little one. We'll wait."

Nan puffed the pillow behind her head. "Kate says you slipped away overnight with Jack."

Anneliese's guilty heart thumped. "He took me to a political fundraiser."

"And one of the more exclusive resorts in Stowe, from what I hear."

"Yeah." Anneliese fought the flush she felt rising on her cheeks.

Nan's steady gaze forgave everything before Anneliese could even confess. "Are you in over your head there?"

Anneliese gripped her fingers hard. "Probably."

"That can't be easy." Nan laid a hand over hers. "Especially with Chloe in the mix."

"What gave me away?"

Nan shifted again, pulling her knees up. "Chloe, actually. The way she's taken to him; it seems as though he must be around a lot. And the way Jack looks at you. It's always been obvious there was something between you two, but I never wanted to pry."

"There was never anything between us but my idiot teenage crush."

Nan squeezed her hand. "I don't think that's true. From the first time I saw you two in a room together, back during the first summer I was here, it was pretty clear to me feelings were tangled up in the spaces between you."

"I've always been half in love with him," Anneliese muttered. "Stupid me."

"I don't know about stupid," Nan mused. "Jack's a good man. Have I ever told you about the first time I met him?"

"No..." Anneliese leaned against one of the bedposts. "Was it while you were at school with Kate?"

Nan nodded. "Kate dragged me off to Boston for a long weekend. I had only been once, despite growing up two hours from there, and she was full of plans. We'd crash on her big brother's couch—he was a pain, but he wouldn't say no—and go out dancing, do some shopping. She had a list a dozen deep of restaurants she wanted to try.

"He was—and I'm just being honest—hot. I was tongue-tied. I'd never considered speaking to a guy that good looking before."

Anneliese didn't argue. "Yeah."

"He teased Kate mercilessly, but there was this protective adoration there, too. You know how they are. But me, he dazzled. He flirted—harmlessly, but also mercilessly. He walked right up to some invisible line Kate had drawn around me. Kate didn't know there was no need for that. I was so unequipped to deal with a charmer like him, I'd have run like a frightened mouse if he'd made a real move.

"For all that, though, the flirting, the dazzling, he was always kind to me, and not like annoying-sister's-friend-so-I-have-to-be-nice. He wanted to win me over, and he did, which meant he got another sister.

"When I ran into him again at the Pease's house, I saw him with the rest of his family, and decided I wanted nothing less than someone like him. Not *him*, but…"

Anneliese sighed. "And you found the only other one in existence."

Nan laughed. "Probably not, but I did find one. I guess I'm saying I know Jack's a player, and he's had a lot of good things come to him relatively easily, but he's capable of so much love." She rolled again to accommodate her belly. "And it's official, I've become an armchair philosopher trying to keep this baby from popping out early."

Kate came back in. "No coming out of the oven early. Aunt Kate is an expert on cooking times, and she says you're not ready yet."

Nan grinned. "Aunt Kate is correct."

Kate hugged a basket of folded laundry to her hip. "So, what are you two up here plotting? I can see it in your faces."

Nan flashed Anneliese a look of shared secrets. "Just girl talk."

Kate narrowed her eyes in their direction, but there was no malice. "Like how Anna's seeing my brother and didn't tell us about it?"

Nan shot Kate a pointed look. "Would you?"

"Fair enough." Kate set down the laundry basket. "Now that we all know, though, she can tell us all about the Hardy's party."

Anneliese chose the superficial details. Maybe the heavier, darker things she kept from her friends would feel lighter if she indulged in some easier sharing. "The usual. Jenna looking fit and polished. Geoff glad-handing and winning folks over…."

"Boring." Kate leaned against a dresser. "What Jack didn't tell me, was how he got invited to that."

Anneliese channeled her irritation with all still left unsaid between her and Jack and took the cheap shot. It was that, or spill every secret in her heart, and once she started talking, she wasn't sure where she'd stop. "He never said exactly, but the senator's lovely wife seemed pretty happy to see him."

Kate took the bait, rolling her eyes. "Ugh. Jenna. Her family is so nice, though. Maybe someone dropped her when she was a baby."

"Kate." Nan scolded, but they all ended up giggling.

"I FEEL LIKE I'M IN AN EPISODE OF A PRIMETIME FAMILY DRAMA." EWAN handed Jack another box of tile and started up the stairs. He and Kate worked some miracles with the garish decor, but it wasn't without labor. "All the menfolk building things while the ladies tend to the pregnant woman."

"Write a pilot," Jack said. "This time next year we'll all be watching people prettier than us play ourselves."

Ewan shot Jack a look over his shoulder. "Is that a dare?"

Joss was on hands and knees setting tile in the master bathroom. He pushed up to kneeling and wiped the sweat from his forehead. "What are we daring Ewan to do now? He already married Kate."

It was good to laugh with them, his oldest friend and his brother-in-law. "The writer in the family noticed we resemble the cast of a feel-good network hit."

Joss gave the thin-set a stir. "This episode gets terrible ratings. No one wants to see a guy tiling his friends' bathroom."

"Depends on who plays you." Ewan put down his box of tile. "I showed Kate the demo reel for the guy they just signed to play Alasdair Sledge. I think she's contemplating an upgrade."

"No shit? They hired someone?" Jack perched on the sink counter. "It's really happening."

"I'm going to London to meet the writing team next month." Ewan said. "My agent says we'll get to see the soundstage where they're filming the interiors, which means I might get to meet the guy."

Ewan's stories were fresh in Jack's memory. "Who've they got to play Cordelia?"

Ewan lit up. "Jessica Strand."

"It's going to make a killing," Jack said. "She was hot as hell in that future jazz-age assassin movie."

"I'm banking on it," Ewan said to them both. "I need to be able to pay the contractor."

"Speaking of," said Joss, "I need you guys to get started pulling out the cabinets in the downstairs bath while I finish this."

Ewan mock saluted and headed down the stairs.

"Jack, hang on."

Jack paused in the bathroom doorway. The set of Joss's jaw was a warning; his friend was chewing on something.

"What's the deal with you and Anna?"

Jack contemplated covering their tracks, but he couldn't. Neither could he confess his change of heart. Not yet. Not until he'd spoken to Anneliese. "I don't know." He turned to face his friend. "Neither of us really knows."

Joss nodded. "It's none of my business—"

Jack could hear Ewan banging on something downstairs.

"It's really not." He kept his tone mild. "That's why we didn't throw ourselves a parade."

"It's not like we all get together without you and talk about it." Joss sat back on his haunches. "But you're not fooling anyone anymore. And I feel compelled—guy code—to tell you I'll put you on the floor if you break her heart."

Joss's tone was mild enough, but Jack took it at face value. Guy code.

"Shit." Jack blew out a breath, but the curse was passionless. "I should go down there. Ewan and I together are just barely useful to you, and I have to head out in half an hour. I'm picking Chloe up at school and driving her to the Thompsons'."

"That's good of you."

He straightened, feeling Joss's scrutiny.

"I know what you're thinking, and yeah."

Anneliese had said it aloud, the fear he might hurt Chloe by becoming important to her. He knew it, but he was determined to stay important to her—and to her mother—even if this summer's folly didn't play out like he was beginning to hope it might.

"Hey." Joss turned back to the thin-set. "I know I just warned you about Anna, but… Take care of yourself, too."

Jack paused at the top of the stairs. "It's funny how those seem to go together now."

His cell phone rang halfway to Chloe's school.

Desmond Chambers was a warhorse of a corporate attorney and the managing partner at Kearney-Mulligan Boston. He had a voice like gravel in a trommel, and was a bit of a relic, but he ran a tight ship. Jack had always enjoyed his company.

"Jack, where the hell are you?" Jack sat up a touch straighter in the driver's seat, though he knew the old man couldn't see him.

"Still in my hometown, Des."

"I know that," Des boomed. "How's your mother?"

"Better. I've—"

Des cut him off. "I need you back here, Jack. I had Stephanie overnight you information about the case I gave your team. To bring you up to speed."

"About that," he began, negotiating around a hay baler making its easy way down the country road, "I don't think I am coming back."

Des was silent on the other end of the line. Jack let it play out a moment, easing the car over the last hill and past the hospital.

"I know I have to give notice, and of course, I'll come back to fulfill my obligations, but this is me telling you to start looking for my replacement on the team."

"Hot damn. Your girlfriend was right." Des was laughing.

"My girlfriend?"

"With the flower name. The one who looks like Audrey Hepburn."

"You discussed me with Iris?" Jack didn't bother to correct Des's impression. "How did that happen?"

"Don't sound so betrayed, Jack. She knows your whole team. I met her at a charity thing. You came up. Myra loved her, and we got to speculating. Iris bet me dinner at Argonaut that you'd end up staying there."

Jack heard a muted conversation behind Desmond's voice. Life at the firm would go on. He was replaceable.

"She eats like a horse. Don't say I didn't warn you."

Des guffawed. "I'll miss you, Jack, but if you're determined, I'll have Stephanie get in touch to formalize the transition."

It sounded so antiseptic: the transition. His transition out. Some hungry young associate's transition in. In six months, no one would give him a second thought. He let the unexpected lightness of that thought carry him out of the car and into the school vestibule where Chloe's sign-out sheet waited for his signature.

"THIS IS THE THIRD TIME THIS WEEK," JANE THOMPSON SAID. THE Thompson's fussy living room pressed in on him, but Anneliese's mother insisted he stay for a little something.

"This client is a great opportunity for Anna. It's no big deal to help out with Chlo' so Anna can work."

If he wondered why Anneliese was so adamant he drive Chloe from school to her grandparents' home, he chalked it up to his willingness to help. Any of them would have done it if they'd had time.

Anneliese was up to her ears in details, finalizing checklists, organizing security and hotel reservations, limousines and coordinating the crew from *US Weekly*. It wasn't *Town & Country Weddings*—apparently that, or Oprah, had been the goal—but Anneliese said Lela was satisfied.

The complicated workings of single parenthood had never occurred to him before this summer. Anneliese's parents both worked, as did their friends, Anneliese's hours were changeable, and yet she made the endless juggling look effortless and gentle.

If all went according to plan, he'd be the one to help her with those arrangements. For the long haul, if she'd have him. One by one, the pieces of the revised future he wanted dropped into place. He never dreamed it would be so simple.

Jack sipped at a metallic diet iced tea and hoped Chloe would demand her Mere's attention sooner rather than later.

"You know, Jack, the way you and Anneliese were always together as kids, I used to hope you'd get married." Jack very nearly spit tea across Mrs. Thompson's cabbage rose wing chairs. "But you didn't, and things turned out differently. I guess that's life in a nutshell, but it pleases me to see you're still a good friend to her."

"It's my pleasure, Mrs. T. Really." He hoped he didn't sound as shaken as he was.

"I know it's just for the summer, but it's lovely to see Chloe respond to a positive male role model. I worry, with just the two of them..." Mrs. Thompson trailed off. "It's too much to hope Anneliese will establish some kind of truce with her ex-husband. She's so stubborn sometimes."

Anneliese was certainly stubborn, but Jack was beginning to understand the kind of scars Chad left on her heart. "I don't know the guy, but from what I hear, he doesn't exactly sound like the fatherly sort."

Jane adopted a long-suffering expression. "He made some mistakes, but when he was here a few weeks ago, he was charming and kind. He made a good case for himself."

Jane pressed her lips together and glanced furtively around the room, missing Jack's shock following her news. Anneliese had to have known her ex made an appearance. How could she not have confided in him?

Still, Anneliese deserved better from her own mother.

"I don't think Chloe's lacking for good men in her life." He fought a losing battle with the edge to his voice. "She's got Joss and Ewan, your husband and Walt. She's smart and funny and charming, and perfect just the way she is."

*Perfect just as Anneliese is raising her.*

Mrs. Thompson gaped at him for a moment, before regaining her composure. "Of course," she sputtered. "I only meant…"

Jack set his rapidly warming glass aside. "I know what you meant, but Anneliese deserves more credit. She's made a good life for herself here, and I know how grateful she is for the help you've given her."

"Well, I—" Anneliese's mother started and discarded a few replies before her carefully composed expression faltered. "You're right."

Jack stood. "Thank you for the tea. I should get back. My mom wanted to try some cooking tonight." He tried for a sheepish grin to dispel the tension. "My father is definitely not the kitchen wizard in the family. I have no idea what I'm headed home to."

"Of course, Jack." Mrs. Thompson showed him out. He saw her linger by the front door as he drove away.

Her words played back in his mind while he drove the few miles back into the village. He'd always casually dismissed Anneliese's discomfort with her family as a lingering teenaged impatience with their strictness. They always appeared so supportive and loving, and his own tight-knit family was the template he applied to everyone.

Cataloging Mrs. Thompson's opinions on his past with Anneliese and Chloe's upbringing showed a different, more critical side to their family dynamic.

That Mrs. Thompson seemed more concerned about spilling the beans than by Anneliese's ex appearing in Thornton sent ripples of anger through his blood.

Parked in his parents' driveway, Jack loitered in his car long enough to text Anneliese and let her know he was thinking about her, and that Chloe had left from school with painted miniature gourds, which were currently adorning the front porch at her grandparents' house.

The accompanying photograph earned him a string of starry-eyed emojis. The simple *thank you* that followed left him feeling like an accomplice as he went in to see how his folks were getting on in the kitchen.

He just wished she'd told him. He'd have been a willing one.

"YOU ARE AN ABSOLUTE MIRACLE WORKER. I LOVE IT." LELA TOOK Grant's hand across the table that occupied Kirsten's temporary office space.

Anneliese and Kirsten had decorated it with samples from Sweet Pease and Josephine's. Kirsten played Lela's favorite songs from a desk speaker, and they'd scattered the room with the luminaries Anneliese had loved in Stowe. They'd put up interior and exterior shots of the wedding venues on easels.

Grant leaned over and kissed his future bride. Lela's career and ambition might appear frivolous, but the two of them were the real deal. She recognized the light in Lela's eyes. It matched the glow she saw in herself when Jack was nearby.

"Lela, I've got a feature editor at *US Weekly* Skyping in fifteen. I know it's not *Oprah* or *Vogue*, but I think you'll like her." Kirsten was all business, pulling out a flat iron and a color palette.

"Anneliese, you are wasted in this tiny town." Lela gave her a sly smile. "You should be in San Francisco where I can hire you for parties and dole out your number to the deserving."

"No." Realizing she'd been curt, Anneliese backtracked. "I'm just too much of an East Coast girl."

"New York, then." Lela conceded, chasing her vision. "Champagne brunches and rooftop garden teas. Girl's weekends and..." Here Lela batted her lashes at Grant. "Baby showers. We could launch a whole entertaining brand!"

Kirsten, despite her youth, intervened maternally, just as Anneliese would have redirected Chloe. "Lela, we've got to touch you up."

The two women left. Grant gave her an easy smile as he swiped open his phone.

A life in New York sounded like nonsense, but Anneliese indulged in a daydream while she waited. A snug little apartment in Queens or Brooklyn, Chloe growing up immersed in theatre and music and the chaos of city life. She imagined them traveling by subway, sharing coffees with clever names in SoHo cafes, spending lazy weekend afternoons in Central Park.

Kirsten chose that moment to reappear. "Grant, she'll be ready in five, and she wants you on the call."

"Gotcha." Grant stood, straightening his chinos and running a hand through his blond hair. "The lady calls."

Kirsten touched Anneliese's shoulder. "You know, Lela's not wrong. You'd be great at her version of this."

"Not you, too." Anneliese laughed. "I'm not getting caught up in this fantasy."

"Not necessarily a fantasy. I was working a concierge desk in Las Vegas when Lela found me. I took a leap and relocated a few years back, and it worked out. Lela's a bit magical that way."

"I have a daughter," Anneliese countered.

"I'm just saying, Lela's got great instincts. Unless there's something keeping you in this town, you might want to give it some thought."

Anneliese did give it some thought as she drove to her parents' house to collect Chloe.

Was there something keeping her in Thornton? She'd come home because her family was here, and she'd had nowhere else to go. She'd stayed because she built a life here. A life now filled with Jack—on her porch, dancing with her at Founder's Day, in her bed, in his suit at the Hardy's fundraiser, high-fiving Chloe in the yard. He was everywhere, but when he left, her life would pick up where she'd left off in July. Quiet nights at home. Work, school, friends. Nan and Joss would be new parents. Kate and Ewan had their house. She and Chloe would have a new appreciation for Chinese food, and hole in their hearts.

Turning onto her parents' street, she found herself searching the cars in the nearby driveways for any unfamiliar cars. Chad might have switched to keep her from noticing him, but there was nowhere for her to hide.

Lela's enthusiasm for New York took on new meaning. She and Chloe could vanish there, be swallowed up in the lights and color, and Chad would have a harder time getting past the gates of city schools.

With no sign of her ex lurking near the house, Anneliese let out a breath she hadn't been aware of holding and shook off the fantasy. She would keep hope that he would bore of harassing her, hope he would give up his delusions regarding her finances, hope he never tainted her friends' lives with his presence.

# CHAPTER 25

Ith his dad's help, his mom had managed a simple weeknight supper, after which Jack sat with her at the table, talking over his change of direction.

Accomplice or not, he'd set the wheels in motion.

"What will you do with your apartment?"

"It's worth a small fortune right now if I sell—"

"If? You can't go telling Anneliese you're staying if this is an *if*."

"That's not what I meant," Jack countered. "And what do you mean, I can't tell Anneliese?"

"That girl's been in love with you since you grew armpit hair. Fine if you don't feel the same, but I don't believe that, and she's had her heart broken enough. Jane never said much, but I've seen the hurt you get when life deals you a bad hand on Anna's face."

Jack glanced at his father, but John only shrugged helplessly.

His mother gathered her shawl around her shoulders. "Are you in love with her?"

Jack nearly spit out his beer. "Mom."

"I can't imagine raising a child on my own, and then to think about dating?" Cora shivered delicately. "You need to be fair with her."

*Like she'd been fair with him?*

Jack glanced at the lights on in the kitchen at the Cartwright house, wishing he could flee this conversation. Rosie next door might be more sympathetic.

*Out with it, then.* "I am in love with her."

"What about Chloe?"

It was easier to answer that question. "She's incredible."

His mother smiled. "Then get on over there and tell them."

Jack planned to do just that. He'd ask her for the truth about Chad. Set his hurt feelings aside, and let her know he was in her corner. With that out of the way, he would tell her everything.

He helped his dad clean up the dishes and get his mom settled in their fancy new adjustable bed, then left the lovebirds to their recorded television. His mom was still catching up on what she missed while she was in the hospital.

Anneliese would be expecting him. Such was the rhythm of their days: the easy companionship, the mutual avoidance of his timeline whenever their evenings at home allowed. He struck out on foot, a bounce in his step as he imagined how the future would play out.

They could get married. The idea nearly stopped him in his tracks, but he liked it. He could be a father to Chloe.

Chloe had a father, for better or for worse. Jane Thompson's earlier words danced in his ears: *He made some mistakes, but when he was here, he was charming and kind. He made a good case for himself.* Joss's assessment of the man told a different story: *he just took her apart and it was all she could do to drag her pieces home afterward.*

Chad had been around. Did that mean he was making noise about parenting Chloe? Had he threatened them?

The pieces fell into place as he walked. Anneliese had been uneasy to the point of distraction, irritable and fearful. Chloe's trips to her uncle's house, and to Kate's while they were in Stowe suddenly made sense, but clarity brought no relief. Not only had Anneliese hidden Chad's presence, she hadn't trusted Jack enough to confide that she was afraid.

There wasn't time for him to examine those thoughts further. He was at her garden gate. He rapped on the porch door, aware now of the hook dropped in the latch, trying to place when it had first been that way.

Anneliese opened the kitchen door slowly, drying her hands on a towel. Warily, he imagined.

"Oh, sorry." She lifted the hook from its eye, letting it fall and swing while she tossed the kitchen towel over one shoulder. She opened the door and invited him in, head cocked like a sparrow. "What is it?"

"Why didn't you tell me your ex came around?" He blurted it out, without forethought, finesse, or any of the hallmarks of his adult self.

Anneliese stepped back. A hitched breath, a slight widening of her eyes. He saw her tells, and they were damning. "Jack, I—"

"I could have done something. I could have helped." The last word caught in his throat.

"How?" she asked quietly, addressing the air on the porch, unable to meet his angry stare. "What would you have done? Answered the burner calls I didn't know were from him and told him to leave your woman alone?" With a glance over her shoulder—he'd forgotten Chloe was home—she continued. "Escorted us home from the school every time I had to pick her up, to scare him off? Slept on my parents' front steps to keep him from coming around?" Her voice rose, taking a hard edge. "Tell me, Jack. What exactly would you have done that wouldn't have escalated an already awful situation, before hopping in your beautiful car and driving off to your beautiful life, leaving me behind to pick up the pieces?"

"I could have at least been aware you were dealing with that." He couldn't deny the surface truth in her tirade, but the end hurt. "We are friends, aren't we? As well as..."

*Lovers.*

"Yes," she sighed. "And for the sake of that, for the sake of your career and your family, for our friends, I didn't tell anyone anything. He's a shark, Jack. A predator. I didn't understand that, even when our marriage ended, but I know it now, and I won't allow him near you, near your parents, near anyone I love."

"Even his daughter?"

"Especially her. He's been lurking at the edges of my life for weeks now, quietly making it clear he thinks there's something to be gained in extorting me. Talking about his flesh and blood as though she were a commodity. If you got caught up in that, it could destroy your career." She paused, drawing a brittle breath. "Or your political aspirations."

"Screw my political aspirations." He wished he could take back the words as soon as he'd spoken them. *How had she known?*

Anneliese must have seen the realization in his eyes. "I'm not the only one keeping secrets, am I? I thought you were just having another one of your charmed moments, getting invited to wine and dine with the senator. *Connections*, I thought. *Jack's got connections.* Turns out, Jack's thinking about a run for office and needing some well-placed advice. I'm sure Massachusetts will adore you. You're practically a Kennedy already with your gorgeous face and your ridiculous charm."

"You've got it all wrong." He backpedaled frantically, trying to figure out where she'd gotten that idea.

"I don't think I do." She was blazing, furious and hurt, and he was still helplessly lagging. "You're arrogant enough, coming into my house accusing me of lying to you, when you've been plotting your bright—solo—future for weeks."

Any cool he had snapped. "Is that really what you think of me?"

"Mama?" Chloe stood in the open kitchen doorway, dragging Feesh along by his fin. "Jack?"

"I think you should go." The venom was gone from Anneliese's voice. Jack didn't like the emptiness which replaced it.

"Okay." He turned to Chloe, who was regarding him with open uncertainty. Her guarded expression sliced through his chest like a blade. "I'm sorry."

"Me too." Anneliese turned her back to him and went to her daughter, nudging Chloe back into the kitchen. "Come on, baby. Inside."

He heard Chloe's questions as they retreated, but couldn't make out the words. *Just as well.* He didn't want to know Anneliese's answers.

Jack walked right past his parents' house and down the trail to the river bank. It was quiet there and mosquito-free since the chill of October had killed off the worst of the insect population. He sat on a rock, keeping his feet out of the water. Clouds obscured the moon, breaking to allow glimpses of starlight, and the low-rush of water over the falls muted the sounds of the village nightlife. He could have been alone in the universe.

He felt alone in the universe.

He'd gone off to Williams with the idea of a law career—just like the old man, but Jack wanted more. It had driven his major, his summer plans. He'd gone straight to law school, falling in love with the high stakes and hard living at Kearney-Mulligan from his first week as an intern. He'd never questioned belonging there, never questioned any of the pieces of his personal puzzle as they fell into place.

All his life, he'd chosen a path and followed it with confidence and clarity.

Like the river—tumbled and churning from its fall—he was facing a bend around which he couldn't see the future. He knew what he wanted, and it didn't look like the map he'd charted in his head for years. His heart was at the helm, and his heart was content to navigate blind.

His heart wanted Anneliese and Chloe and the cottage. His heart wanted to take a stab at serving the town he loved. His heart was on the verge of being crushed because he was too blinded by his own ego to give Anneliese what she needed.

It was time, Jack realized, to cut his old life free and trust the new navigation. He got to his feet and jogged up the trail where the porch light waited at his boyhood home.

His parents tried to slow him down, but he knew what he needed to do. He ignored the flurry of texts from his sister. Their parents must have enlisted her help. Car keys, an overnight bag, a cold soda for the ride, and his wallet and phone, and he was on the road.

He was halfway to the New Hampshire border before he considered how Anneliese would take the news of his departure.

Not well, he surmised, but there would be time, he hoped, to make it up to her. To explain things.

Jack drove straight to Iris's apartment.

"Good thing I'm not entertaining this evening," Iris said after he buzzed her door.

"I didn't think," Jack said. "I'm sorry. I can crash with one of the guys…"

"You're always welcome, Jack" Her tone turned playful. "I'm a little surprised you're here. I keep waiting for you to tell me you're not coming back."

"I'm not coming back." The words felt good—right, even.

"Come in." Iris held the door for him. "I'm going to open a bottle of wine, and you're going to tell me the whole story."

"I could really go for a shower."

"You know where it is." Iris gestured down the hall. "Meet me on the deck. There won't be many more warm nights."

Fifteen minutes later he climbed the stairs to Iris's roof deck. The long drive, the late hour, and the emotional rollercoaster of his sudden departure all conspired to leave him feeling untethered. Three stories above Boston's West End the illusion of floating loosened his tongue.

Two glasses, fogged with condensation, rested on the glass top table between two vintage lawn chairs.

"You've upgraded."

Iris looked up from her phone. "Mmhm. I found them at an antique sale in Brimfield. Promised the seller I wouldn't dare repaint them. After I bargained him down forty percent."

Jack eyeballed the hot pink paint job—one Kate would have admired. "That was dishonest."

Iris shrugged. "He got paid. I got my chairs."

Jack knew he didn't need an invitation to tell his sad tale, but the available wine lubricated his storytelling.

"I'm in love with her—Anneliese." He swallowed, encouraged by

Iris's open expression. "We've been…together for a few weeks, and her daughter…Chloe's just amazing. Funny, adorable, fierce—you'd love her."

"The daughter?"

"Really. She's fantastic. But Anna and I…" He paused. "We went into it with our eyes open, I swear, but I didn't realize…"

"I always wondered what you'd be like in love," Iris mused, topping off Jack's nearly empty glass then propping her feet on the table. "This is better than I imagined."

"Shut up." He leaned back, enjoying the way the city's ambient light played with the wispy clouds in the night sky. "Along the way, I realized I loved being home. More than I ever imagined. And they need me, my people." He looked her square in the eye. "It's nice to be needed. "

Iris regarded him over the rim of her glass, but she said nothing.

"I ended up talking with this guy, the state rep from my town, about elder care and family leave, and he suggested I think about staying on, running for office. The next thing I know I'm at a fundraiser for Geoff Hardy."

"Exalted circles," Iris murmured.

"His wife Jenna was my prom date."

"Of course."

"I'm going to do it."

At this, Iris set her glass down. "Far better than I'd imagined."

His head swam. He was giddy with confession, but Iris needed to hear all of it. "I might have fucked it all up."

"I doubt that." From a small chest cooler nearby, Iris withdrew another bottle, which she uncorked and poured.

"I didn't tell Anna about it. I wasn't sure. It's crazy." He looked to Iris for confirmation. "It is crazy, right?"

"Insane."

"I told Des I was leaving the firm. I talked to a real estate agent on the drive south. I've got an appointment tomorrow." The wine was going to his head. "I was going to tell Anna everything. I think I was going to propose."

"I hope not," Iris said with a small smile. "I'd expect better than a haphazard ask from you."

Jack ignored the smug turn of Iris's lips. "I was helping Anna out, dropping Frog—Chloe—at her grandparents' house, and Mrs. T.—that's Anna's mom—starts talking about how Anna's ex has been around."

"Exes do have a way of doing that," Iris said mildly.

"This one hasn't so much as seen his daughter since they split up, but suddenly he's turning up across the country, and I didn't realize it until after her mother said something, but he's got Anna all riled up. I think she's scared, and she didn't say anything."

"And you didn't ask."

"I lost my cool. I wanted to slam Anna's ex's face into a wall, but I yelled at her instead."

Iris sipped delicately from her wine glass. "Perhaps that's exactly why she didn't tell you."

"Shit." Jack downed what wine remained in his glass. "I hate when you're right."

Iris was chuckling softly to herself.

"What?"

"You used to be so...smooth."

JACK LEFT THE REAL ESTATE AGENT'S OFFICE THE FOLLOWING MORNING. and made his way a block over to the Commonwealth Avenue Mall. It was crisp in Boston, blue skies and turning leaves overhead, and the faint scent of autumn wafted over the less savory aromas of urban life. The only thing missing was Anneliese by his side, but they would—if he had anything to say about it—have years for trips to Boston. And New York, and London, and Zihuatanejo. Everywhere.

He fought the urge to call her, text her, beg her to hear him out. He wouldn't make the mistake of crowding her, not with their future on the line. He was simply going to prove to her that he was serious.

After that, he'd grovel if need be.

His condo would be listed as soon as his sublet moved out. It would be staged with his furnishings, and those would go into storage once it sold. Given the aggressive market in the city, he didn't think it would take long.

His next stop was a meeting with Des at his Kearney-Mulligan office. An exit interview, and hopefully an endorsement. Jack hoped the old man would look favorably on his plans.

He'd missed all of late summer in the Public Garden. The heat had only been settling in when he left, and now it was full-blown autumn. The evergreen hedges were more prominent now, the elms and maples bare. Mums and leafy purple cabbages lined the walkways. Jack stopped for a moment on the bridge, but the Swan Boats were long gone from the water.

The thought of bringing Chloe in the spring lightened his step. He crossed Beacon Street and plunged into the midday crowd on the common. The firm's offices were in a high-rise a few blocks from the other side of the park, and Jack could just make out the silhouette of the building as he approached Park Street Station. Behind him the Frog Pond was empty, waiting for colder weather and ice skating.

Another reason to bring Anneliese and Chloe to the city.

By three that afternoon, he'd have handed in his resignation and met with his team so they could move on with their projects without him. Iris had made reservations for dinner, and in the morning, he would go back to Thornton.

Home.

He would go home, and start looking for some place to live while he mapped out this new rest of his life.

ONE SHOT ALWAYS TURNED INTO TWO. JACK HAD FORGOTTEN THAT. TWO shots blurred into a long night when you'd been out of the whirl for a summer and most of the fall.

His friends at work had gotten wind of his meeting with Des and invited themselves to Iris's dinner reservations. From there, loose plans were established. They presented him a goodbye party—*fait accompli*. Promising himself he'd go straight back to Thornton in the morning, he left the high-rise where Kearney-Mulligan's offices occupied ten floors, along with every member of the team he was leaving behind.

It quickly became a roving festival, as they moved from bar to bar as a cohort. Good friend that she was, Iris supervised Jack's return to her apartment after last call.

Jack collapsed onto Iris's sofa. "I need to call Anna Banana."

"It's late. And you're fairly drunk." Iris was a gentle scold.

Jack opened one eye. Aside from a pink glow high on her cheeks, Iris was cool and composed, as always. "You're fairly sober."

Iris shrugged. "My father says he spiked our bottles with Aquavit."

"Bullshit." He laughed at her inability to keep a straight face. "I've met your father."

"So you have."

"Shit."

"What?" Iris's brows knit in concern.

He hadn't checked his phone all night, caught up in farewell revelry and expensive tequila. "My sister called and texted a bunch."

Kate answered her phone on the first ring; he could hear the anger in her voice. "It's two a.m. Where the hell have you been?"

"Boston, like I said." He shook his head slightly at Iris, who was watching his side of the exchange. "Didn't Dad say anything?"

"He said you went. He was suspiciously quiet about why. I was stuck in a meeting all afternoon, and Andy went home sick, so I was covering the kitchen at the winery. I called about a zillion times to ask you myself." Kate paused to draw breath. "And you decide to return those calls now?"

He was sobering up fast, or so he thought until he stood and all the blood rushed to his head. "I made some decisions, so I went down to talk to Des and my team." *And I let them treat me like a prince for a night because I was feeling sorry for myself after fighting with Anna.* "I wanted to tell Des—"

"You're drunk," Kate said. "I can hear it."

"I had a couple drinks after the meeting. I didn't know—"

"Well," Kate cut him off, "while you were having a few drinks, did you lose sight of our housewarming Halloween party in less than twenty-four hours? Chloe said you promised to go as a ninja with her and Anneliese. Cutting it close there, Brother Dear. Let's just say, I know a few things you don't think I know, and if you hurt that little girl's—or her mother's—feelings, I will bake you into something tasty and serve it at Thanksgiving."

Too late, he thought, wondering insanely if he'd make a good substitute for the ground pork dressing the Fullers always served at Thanksgiving.

"Did you just giggle?" Kate's anger ratcheted up to furious.

"Sorry, Katie. It's been a long night."

"Don't be late, Jack."

Kate hung up, and Jack couldn't help but think he was years too late already.

"If I sober up and leave right away, I'd be in Thornton by sunrise."

"I know you want to get back to your friends," Iris said, "but I'm certain your sister would agree that the last thing anyone needs is you wrecking yourself on a late night run up the interstate."

Jack cradled his swimming head in his hands. "I came down here to make everything right. Why do I feel like I did the wrong thing?"

Iris straightened a stray lock of his hair. "You've come entirely undone."

He caught a hint of a smile around her eyes. "You think this is funny?"

"Not funny." Iris leaned back in her chair. "You're falling apart, but I think perhaps this is the best of you. Your Anneliese makes you better."

"She does."

"I can't wait to see how you put yourself together." Iris got up and stretched. "You should sleep."

Jack stood and the room tilted a bit. *So much for a clearer head.* "I think you're right."

∾

Anneliese cursed Jack even as she missed him. It was maddening. He'd vanished the evening of their argument and no one knew when he planned to return. Two days later, Halloween dawned without a word from the third member of their Ninja Frog trio.

Chloe was quiet at breakfast, despite assurances that grownups had arguments, and Jack would certainly still be a ninja with them for Kate's Halloween party.

Over Frosted Flakes with bananas, Anneliese very nearly texted him to ask, but the hurt was too fresh. What she needed was get herself and her daughter out the door. Kirsten was meeting her at the inn to go over logistics, and then they were going back to Kirsten's office to finalize the to-do list. Lela's big day loomed even larger than Kate's Halloween party.

Hopefully larger than the gaping hole in her heart where Jack had taken up residence.

The need for tea and sympathy drove her into Sweet Pease after she dropped Chloe off at school, but Kate was working on royal icing lace appliqués for Lela's wedding cake and, from what Anneliese could tell, mainlining coffee.

"I didn't sleep well." Kate yawned. "Since my brother called at two, and I need to get this lace perfect."

Anneliese's already throbbing head banged in time with her pulse, but she bit back the flood of curiosity. If Jack didn't want to tell her where he'd gone, she wouldn't ask.

"If you and my brother are an open secret now…" Kate set down an empty piping bag. "I can ask you what got him all hot and bothered that he raced off to Boston."

Anneliese drew another tea-infused breath. *Must be nice to move your temper tantrum three hours away to friends who would take your side.* "No idea. News to me."

"Crap." Kate lifted the tip of her piping bag with a little flourish and tilted it. "I probably wasn't supposed to tell you." Her expression hardened. "He was pretty drunk late last night. Probably out with the boys."

"Mmm." Anneliese hoped it was as simple as a night out with whatever boys he had. And hated herself for caring either way. "I've got to go. I don't want to keep Kirsten waiting."

"See you tonight!" Kate went back to her icing. Anneliese's phone pinged; she swiped it open impatiently, hoping it was Jack but finding a string of text bubbles from Lela, Grant, and Kirsten.

She groaned, reading back. Group texts were the worst.

She left the message thread to pile up; Lela's updates were best read in a digest. Meanwhile, her black pants and sweater were ready at the cleaners, and she was going to need them for Kate's Halloween party in—she checked the time on her phone, which was still bubbling with messages from Lela and company—eight hours.

# CHAPTER 26

*J*ack woke when the midmorning sun poked him in the eye. While he'd slept off his goodbye party, a family of elephants moved into his cranium, and they were renovating.

Iris left a tall thermos of coffee with a note telling him to lock the door behind him. Her postscript wishing him luck made him smile. It was good she was rooting for this new him; he needed the moral support. He scribbled a response, grabbed his keys and wallet, and went to find his car.

He was in the lane to jump on the Zakim Bridge when his phone trilled.

"Jack? Brian Washington here."

It took Jack a telling moment to recall Brian Washington was his downstairs neighbor. "Hey, what's going on?"

"Heard you're selling." Brian's voice was accompanied by the crackly voice of the MBTA. "Lauren and I will give you ten over asking. Cash."

Even given the aggressive market, Jack was impressed with the offer. Even more so that Brian knew before the listing had gone live.

Brian asked if he could come by to take a look.

"I can be there in ten. Fifteen, max."

Jack swung the car over one lane and edged onto already congested Storrow Drive to head toward Back Bay. Why bother with showings and open houses when the Washingtons downstairs wanted it that badly?

Jack called his tenant, who was at work and unbothered by an impromptu showing, since the housekeeper was there anyway.

Wanda answered the door at the apartment. Her glossy pile of curls was wrapped in a bun on top of her head, and her dust-streaked tee proclaimed her a member of Red Sox Nation. "Mr. Jack!"

"Just Jack," he reminded her.

"Are you coming home? The renter, he's not a good tipper like you."

He looked around. The space was familiar, of course, but it didn't feel right. Someone else's sweatshirt tossed over the couch. Someone else's snack left out on a plate on the coffee table for Wanda to clean up.

"Actually, I'm selling. Maybe to the Washingtons on the second floor."

Wanda grinned. "I clean for them, too, so, maybe I won't miss you too much."

"I'll miss you. Turns out I'm a grown man who can't make his own bed."

"You'll learn when you need to keep house for the right woman." When he blushed, a broad smile lit her face. "You found one!"

He would never have described himself as the type with his heart on his sleeve, but maybe this new Jack was that kind of guy.

The Washingtons were late, arriving after Wanda left. Out of deference to his tenant, he waited on the landing, watching the extra hour tick by. If he got on the road within the hour, he'd still be back in time to change and meet Anneliese and Chloe at the cottage.

If fate smiled on him, he could apologize to her and still be part of Chloe's trick-or-treating.

The Washingtons were sweating, despite the wind gusting down the Commonwealth Avenue Mall.

"Sorry, Jack. Our train was delayed, so we walked from Fenway," Brian said.

"More like ran," his wife said, still breathing hard.

The Washingtons looked over the updates to the kitchen and bathroom while Jack messaged the real estate agent to cancel the listing. As Lauren cooed over his view, which she thought was better because of the extra story, he contacted a woman he knew from Kearney-Mulligan to ask if she could handle a private real estate transaction for him.

Storrow Drive looked like a parking lot, so Jack headed into Cambridge, figuring he could make his way through Somerville and pick up I-93 north of the city.

There was still time to make the party.

GRANT STOOD WHEN ANNELIESE PUSHED THROUGH THE DOOR AT THE Jalapeño Grille. With a week before the event, Lela and Grant planned to depart for pampering in New York before returning for their big weekend; this would be Anneliese's final face-to-face before the wedding.

Grant held Anneliese's chair, smoothly seating himself on the bench opposite to take Lela's hand. Kirsten glanced up from her phone, her fingers never slowing over the keyboard.

"Lela and I just wanted to thank both of you for all your work," Grant began.

Lela cut him off. "Most people write me off, like I'm just the shallow party girl I show to the public. Grant is special, and I'm glad he talked me into having a simple, small-town wedding, and having someone he thinks so highly of handling the details with Kirsten."

Anneliese thought of the lists, the permits, the endless text threads and the sheer amount of money spent on this "simple" wedding, and suppressed a bubble of hysteria. "It's been amazing, and I can't thank you enough for trusting me with your wedding."

Kirsten set her phone down and jumped in her seat, giving a little celebratory shimmy. "I did it!"

"What?" The reply came from all three, almost in unison.

Kirsten turned the phone's screen to show them an email.

Lela squealed loudly enough that two concerned faces emerged from the kitchen to check their table. "*Modern Bride* wants to shoot my gown!"

"Does this place have champagne?" Grant asked. "Even I know *Modern Bride*."

Jalapeño Grille didn't have a liquor license, but that didn't stop the small group from basking in Kirsten's success over their lunch. When it came time to say goodbye, Anneliese stopped Kirsten.

"There's a housewarming and costume party tonight at Ewan Lovatt and Kate Pease's home tonight. I'd love if you'd come as my guest." She thought of Kate's musings about a guest spot on the Food Network. "We can break the good news to Kate—and Nan —together."

"I'd love to." Kirsten blew out a breath as Lela and Grant stepped into their hired car. "I can't wait to put them on a plane to Bali for two weeks."

"Vacation?" Anneliese walked Kirsten to her rental car. The bright blue hatchback somehow suited Lela's funky assistant.

"First one I've taken in a year," Kirsten said. "I've got a flat in Mayfair booked for a week, then I'm headed back to San Francisco to coordinate the finishing touches on their new apartment, so it's ready when they get back."

"I truly can't imagine," Anneliese said, "but London sounds amazing."

"A party at Ewan Lovatt's house sounds amazing," Kirsten countered.

"It's probably not the kind of party you're used to. Kids every-where, a bonfire, pumpkin painting."

"I'm so there. They're incredible. He's one of my favorite authors, and I have about four pounds of Sweet Pease croissants on my hips."

Anneliese took out her phone, texted Kirsten the address, and shot a message off to Kate, hoping her friend would forgive the last minute plus one.

She said goodbye to Kirsten and walked back to her house. She needed to put the finishing touches on their costumes—and to believe somehow Jack would come through for Chloe, if not for her—but it was Lela and Grant's wedding that occupied her thoughts. Television, print, online…one of her weddings would be actual news. Niche news, but her name might get a mention.

All she had to do was pull the whole thing off.

As she passed Vellichor, she noticed a teenage girl loitering outside the bookshop. She was reminded of herself at that age, waiting for a ride in front of Marian Muse's store. Time had dulled the edge from the memory of waiting for Chris Greene to pick her up in his mom's shiny Lexus.

Her golden boy for a spring. A troubled kid from old money, balancing on the knife's edge of idealism and cynicism. He had been ready to take her with him, no matter which way he fell.

She was foolish enough to think they'd land, if only for a heartbeat.

The long-ago spring they were almost lovers, she thought they would be together forever. For one wild weekend, she believed herself capable of running away with him. She and Chris had made plans. Delicious, secret, crazy plans for a life they would never pull off.

In the end, she knew that wasn't who she was. She let Chris go, denying their connection to make it easier for him, just like she denied her feelings for Jack to protect herself.

All those pent-up emotions had been her downfall. Chad exploited her wounded heart, leading her to where she was now.

Peering down Chapel Street, she noted the continued absence of Jack's car in his parents' driveway, but a spark of hope endured all the way to her garden gate, where it sputtered to death, smothered by fear and outrage.

The only man waiting for her was Chad.

Bold as brass, he sat on her steps, elbows balanced on spread knees.

"Enough bullshit, Anneliese." He was beyond greetings, his practiced demeanor gone. Here was the man who came so close to hurting more than her heart and her confidence. "Just give me what I want, and I'll get out of your pathetic little life."

Anneliese forced her body still, kept her voice level. He would know by her shaking how afraid she was. "Please leave, Chad. I don't have what you think I do."

"Jesus, Anneliese, you're a cold fish."

She held her tongue, loath to give him satisfaction of an outburst.

"You were all hot for it when it was flowers and dinners and candles and shit. Looked at me like I'm meant to be looked at. I figure, what the hell, I'll marry her." Chad stood, taking a stride through her garden toward the gate still shut between them. "You got a ring, and boom. I've got blue balls and you're nagging me for a kid."

"Just go." She couldn't help the tremor in her words this time. "You don't want Chloe. You never did. And I. Don't. Have. Money."

He walked right up to the gate, reaching over it to grab her wrist, twisting hard. "You're about to, then. I know what that Tan bitch and her boy toy are worth."

Her bones ground together in his hand, pain radiated up her arm, but she leaned in, used the pain to stay mad instead of scared.

"How many times have you flown out here, rented a car, slept in some motel, to harass me?" She hissed at him. "You could put that toward your wedding. But you never understood common sense or delayed gratification, never saw past your next impulse, your next selfish want. I was naive and insecure then, and I fell for it."

Anneliese grabbed him with her free hand and slammed his arm down on the picketed gate. Chad howled and let her go, but he was still in her garden. Still between her and the cottage.

"Everything okay over there?" Glenn appeared at the end of the hotel driveway, pruning shears in hand. Anneliese didn't know how, but he seemed to inflate, growing taller and wider as he snapped the shears closed.

"My guest was just leaving," she said weakly, flipping the latch on the gate and pushing inward so Chad would have to back up.

"It looks that way, doesn't it?" Glenn said, planting his feet—and the tip of the shears—in the soil at the end of his driveway.

Chad beat a hasty retreat, attempting to preserve some dignity by glaring at her as he shoved past. Anneliese noted he had parked far enough away from her place to avoid notice, and shivered.

When the rented car turned at the end of the street, she let out a breath, flushing at the hitching sob that followed. Glenn dropped the shears and jogged over, wrapping her in a hug.

The shaking and the tears hit hard and fast. Glenn held her through them, patting her hair and rubbing her back.

When her tears ran dry, he asked, "Honey, should we call the police?"

"No. What do I tell them? My mean ex made veiled, non-specific threats and called me names, and he wants money I don't have that he's not entitled to?"

"Anneliese, he was trespassing. On my property. I saw him. I'll call them for that if you want."

It hadn't occurred to her that her landlords could do that. She felt foolish and small in the face of his kindness and her own helplessness.

"Would you? His name is Chad Davis."

"Consider it done." Glenn gave her a squeeze. "And between you and me, if that's your ex, your taste in men has improved. That guy you're seeing now is a dish."

Anneliese didn't know whether to laugh or weep.

Joy is a verb, his mother said, but joy was hard to do when everything conspired to keep you from it. His phone's charging cable was back at Iris's place, which he only discovered a half hour northwest of Concord, New Hampshire, on a lonely stretch of I-89 where the poor cell signal killed his battery.

He wouldn't have needed his phone at all, though, if he hadn't hit huge weekend traffic snarls at every major interchange between Boston and Bow—and that didn't count the series of long lights, pedestrians, and roadwork keeping him from getting across Cambridge. He regretted taking the extra time to show his apartment to the Washingtons; he was nearly two hours behind.

He ran numbers, calculating drive times and mapping roads in his mind, but it came up short. He was going to miss most of the party.

His chest hurt as he pictured the look of disappointment on Chloe's face.

He considered taking the extra time to get off the interstate in search of a gas station or diner where he could maybe buy a charger or borrow a phone, but losing more time searching for a gas station off the interstate in the wilds of New Hampshire without GPS wasn't worth it.

Even finding a phone to borrow wouldn't help. The only number he had memorized anymore was his parents' landline, and, like everyone else he knew, they would be at Katie and Ewan's, dressed up for Halloween. His mother, sporting a cane instead of the walker, had threatened to dress as Fred Astaire, with her husband as Ginger Rogers. Jack wondered if they had gone for it.

He would never find out at this point. Kate would murder him before he had a chance to see his mother again.

ANNELIESE SAW CHAD'S SHADOW AROUND EVERY CORNER, HIS SNEER IN every reflection she passed, though the man himself never materialized.

Halloween in Vermont wore its favorite costume: a magazine-quality autumn day. Crisp, dry air teased the fallen leaves along the roadsides, and the last vestiges of the season's painted foliage still clung to the maples and oaks. Oblivious to the glorious weather, Anneliese picked up Chloe, already wearing most of her ninja frog costume, with a leaden heart. Her steps dragged under the clear blue sky and western-trailing horsetail clouds.

"It's okay, Mama." Chloe consoled Anneliese as they wrapped their belts—complete with scabbards for plastic ninja swords—around their waists. Matching green fleece hoods hung down their backs, with Kermit-like frog eyes affixed to the tops. These would be combined with black eye masks once they got to the party. Ninja frogs, just as Chloe and Jack planned. "Jack is going to come. He wouldn't miss it unless he really had to."

"I hope you're right," Anneliese said, wishing her daughter wasn't quite so optimistic. Jack's departure felt like a herald of things to come.

No one had heard from him since his late-night conversation with Kate. He hadn't called again, or texted. Kate only said she'd tried to reach him midday, but had been busy getting set up for the party after that. Anneliese wished she knew how to reach Jack's friends in Boston, even as it stung to realize she didn't know them.

Chloe collected her plastic pumpkin basket and trotted downstairs with Feesh in her free hand. Her stuffed clownfish was settled at the kitchen table to await their return.

"Hoods up," Chloe announced, tugging her own lopsidedly into place. Anneliese secured hers and grabbed her purse.

Together they made the rounds of their block, trick-or-treating at the Fletcher Hotel and a handful of their neighbors' houses, before making their way around the town common.

Anneliese scrutinized every man on the street. When Chad wasn't among them, she began to hope he'd slunk back under his rock when she hadn't given in.

Chloe's earliest Halloweens were confined to the cul-de-sac her parents lived on; this year she was delighted by the variety and adventure of a downtown trick-or-treat. Anneliese was determined not to spoil the experience.

Halloween was second only to Christmas in the village. Every business on Main Street and around the common was decked out in spiderwebs and ghosts. Jack-o'-lanterns lit the pathways through the common. Shopkeepers and employee's handed out treats in costume, including Jim and Moira at Sweet Pease, who slipped Chloe an extra handmade chocolate pumpkin.

Anneliese let her work her way down to the bridge and back,

wanting to prolong the heartbreak of Jack's absence at Kate's house as long as possible.

On Chapel Street, the porch light was off at the Pease's house, but they stopped at Rosie Keller's next door. Rosie was Anneliese's art teacher in middle school; she taught at Chloe's school now, and Chloe was excited to show off their frog hoods.

"My friend Jack was supposed to come too, but he got busy," she said with easy certainty. "He'll come to Kate-Kate's party instead."

Rosie's eyes crinkled. "Your friend Jack wouldn't be my neighbor Jack by any chance?"

"Yeah, that's him," Chloe said, looking at the Pease's dark house.

"I've known him practically since he was born." Rosie crouched down, offering the candy bowl to Chloe. "He was the wrinkliest little baby I ever saw."

Chloe giggled, but thoughts of Jack and wrinkly babies did nothing to cheer Anneliese. She pushed the thought aside and joined in. "You were pretty wrinkly yourself, Chlo.'"

"I was?" Her little girl inspected her fingers and palms, then turned to Anneliese in wonder. "Will Nan's baby be all wrinkly?"

"I bet they will."

"Jax says Peyton was really red and scrunchy."

Rosie Keller laughed. Anneliese sighed.

"Happy Halloween, Mrs. Keller," Anneliese said, steering Chloe off the porch. They waved and were off. "Let's get the car and head out to the party, 'kay?"

The crowd of masked and costumed strangers milling the lawn outside the Lovatt-Pease homestead sent shivers of unease racing along Anneliese's arms. Kate—in a shimmering sequined go-go dancer dress, silver vinyl thigh-high boots, fairy wings, and a tiara— met them at the door and fussed over Chloe's costume, dispelling Anneliese's nerves.

"This is amazing, but—" Anneliese waved a hand up and down Kate's tall, glamorous form.

"But what am I?" Kate shook her head, revealing a pair of dangly, glittery earrings shaped like sugar plums. "I'm the—"

"Sugar Plum Fairy," Anneliese finished. "Of course you are."

Her own modest costume felt frumpy. Black pants, black sweater…

"Mama! Your frog hood!"

*And that, too.* With a wry shrug, Anneliese pulled her hood over her French-braided hair and followed Chloe inside. Her little girl found Ewan's niece and nephew straightaway and the three of them raced off to explore the party's offerings.

Anneliese found Nan and Joss holding court on the upholstered window seat in the breakfast nook. Nan was bolstered and cushioned, with a buffet of snacks and drinks around her.

Anneliese gave her a stern look. "Does your midwife know you're out?"

"She and the doctor signed off as long as I stayed put, drank lots of water, and kept the candy to a minimum."

"Love the frog eyes," Joss said.

"Your turn will come," Anneliese replied. "Just you wait."

Anneliese was deep in conversation with two couples who taught at Thornton College and had kids at Chloe's school when Kirsten arrived, dressed in a hodgepodge of animal print and sequins, with a bubblegum pink Marie Antoinette wig perched on her head and a beauty patch over one dimple.

Anneliese excused herself and wove through the room to welcome Kristen. "Look at you!"

Kristen took in Anneliese's ninja frog getup. "Love the amphibian superhero vibe."

"There's a smaller one around here somewhere," Anneliese said.

"I can't wait to meet her."

"Speaking of meetings." Kirsten peered around the room. "Will you introduce me to Ewan Lovatt?"

"Where did you find it all?" Anneliese wondered aloud at Kirsten's costume. "And sure. I think he's in the kitchen."

"The wig was at a costume shop in Burlington. I walked by last week, but had to go back for it when you invited me to this. The rest is all from the thrift shop south of town." Kirsten did a little spin, gaze coming to rest on Kate's three-mile legs vanishing up the stairs. "I'm no disco fairy goddess, but I did okay."

"You look amazing. Come on." Anneliese led Kirsten through the great room to where Ewan towered over a small crowd, some of whom Anneliese recognized from the college.

Ewan caught sight of her and excused himself, hugging her and squashing the frog eyes with his chin. "Anneliese."

"Ewan, this is Kirsten Letourneau. She's working with me on the beg wedding."

"It's a pleasure." He shook Kirsten's hand and she flushed scarlet.

"I'm such a fan of your work. Thank you so much for letting me gatecrash. Your house is just gorgeous. Your wife is just gorgeous." Kirsten clapped a hand over her rouged lips. "Oh, shit. I'm sorry," she muttered through her fingers.

Ewan laughed. "She is. And thank you."

"I hear Jessica Strand is going to play Cordelia," Kirsten continued to gush. "I can't wait. Honestly. She's just amazing. Your characters just slay me..."

A gaggle of pint-sized superheroes and mythical creatures barreled through, interrupting Kirsten's praise. Anneliese caught the word donuts and figured the school-aged entertainment was starting.

"Where's Chloe?" Anneliese asked, as Ewan's niece and nephew ran past.

"I bet Ailie's got her," Ewan said.

Anneliese gave him a grateful smile, letting him lead her to the donuts-on-a-string.

KNOWING THE PARTY WOULD BE IN FULL SWING, THE DRIVE SEEMED TO lengthen as Jack traveled farther north. He would owe Chloe big-time for not having his ninja frog costume, but at least he would get to see hers.

Chloe, who tucked herself neatly into the fabric of his life when he wasn't looking. He loved her. It was enormous and simple all at the same time, and he gripped the steering wheel harder to ground himself.

Of course, Anneliese was likely to be even more furious than before he left. He had botched the whole thing.

Iris was right. He used to be so smooth.

ANNELIESE COUNTED THE KIDS LINED UP UNDER THE DONUT STRING. None were wearing a green frog hood and bandit mask. She turned to Ewan; Kate materialized at her shoulder.

"Where the hell is my brother?"

Anneliese's heart skipped. "I don't know. And I can't find Chloe."

Kate adjusted her wings. "Let's see if she's finishing up the scavenger hunt with Ailie."

Through the mounting panic, one name beat against Anneliese's ribs like a kick-drum.

Chad.

"Kate." Anneliese grabbed at Kate's arm. "Chad has been in town. He was giving me a hard time. I didn't want to—"

"Chad?" Kate's face paled. Her grip tightened on Anneliese's arm. "Why didn't you tell us?"

"Jesus." Ewan raked his hand through his hair. "I'll go look out back."

Anneliese wrenched her hand back. "It's like I said to Jack. He's terrible. How could I expose you—any of you—" She looked around the room, fear stealing her words. "I just wanted him to go away."

"Jack knew, too?" Kate's temper flared. "I'll kill him."

The knowledge Jack had kept her secret flickered against the darkness crowding Anneliese's thoughts.

They found Ewan's sister on the screened-in porch.

"Is Chloe with you?" Anneliese's voice was tight.

"She should be out back on the lawn with Ollie and Gen. Some of the kids decided to play flashlight tag with glow sticks while the first group did donuts." Ailie scanned the room, looking for Anneliese's missing child. "I can call them back…"

"Chloe!" Anneliese hollered, using the voice her daughter never ignored. The chatter around them stopped, but her little girl didn't appear.

Ewan rushed in. "She's not in the barn or the shed."

Ailie put a hand on Anneliese's shoulder. "Let's get some people together, walk the property. Maybe she got disoriented playing tag in the dark." Ailie was pale with worry. "I'm so sorry I took my eyes off her at all."

Anneliese forced her mouth to form words. "It's not your fault."

Kate wrapped them both in her arms. "Let's check the barn and shed again. If she got spooked, she might not have come out."

Fear solidified to terror in Anneliese's chest. Chloe loved Ewan. She would have gone to him as easily as she would to Jack.

Shaking off thoughts of Jack, Anneliese took a deep breath and plunged into the October darkness with Ewan and the others.

# CHAPTER 27

*Of all the nights for a moose and her calf to be taking a moonlit stroll through Catmint Gap.* Jack lost another five minutes waiting for a gangly baby to cross the road.

He could still make the tail end of Kate's party. Chloe was supposed to have a sleepover with Ewan's niece and nephew, so he might even have a chance to apologize to her in person before she went to sleep.

That thought warmed him as he forced himself to slow down through town, but his foot nudged the accelerator once he cleared the Thornton College athletic fields, and he raced his regrets into the inky night.

Valley gave way to forest about a mile from Kate and Ewan's homestead. Jack flipped on the high beams and let the light lead him along the rolling, curving road. Cresting a small rise, he caught sight of the house in the distance, lit with torches and string lights against the increasingly longer nights. He could just make out flashlights winking from all sides of the house.

A pang of sorrow pressed his foot harder on the gas pedal. He was missing all the fun.

The same sorrow nearly caused him to sideswipe a sedan parked off the side of the road. With a curse, he swerved neatly across the median line.

"Ever consider hazard lights?" he muttered, righting the car in its lane.

The sedan wasn't the only one pulled over on the shoulder. It looked like half the population of his hometown was at his sister's house tonight. Cars lined the country road, and his high beams revealed a similar line of parked cars leading to her driveway.

Remembering Kate's VIP entrance, Jack eased the car left down the cart road leading around to the barn. The undergrowth brushed his car. Deep ruts played havoc with his suspension, but he had made a promise to Chloe, and damned if he would lose time hiking a half mile in from the last parked car.

The high beams caught a flash of movement ahead and Jack tapped the brakes, wary of a second wildlife encounter in one day. The critter that burst out of the undergrowth was on two feet, dressed in dark clothes. Jack's stomach clenched when he realized the figure was wearing a huge pair of green frog eyes on its head.

He slammed the car to a stop, leaped out, and rushed to the shoulder of the road.

"Chloe?" She tumbled and sprawled in the scrubby grass at the edge of the woods. "Is that you, Frog?"

"Jack?" Her sweet little face lifted; she pushed herself up and ran to him.

He swung her onto his hip. "What are you doing out here all alone?"

"You forgot your hood." Her lip trembled and she burst into noisy tears, burying her face in his shoulder. He held her tight and rubbed her back, murmuring to her while his heart raced. Without his phone, he had no way to call Anneliese. She must be frantic.

The flashlights.

"Hey, Frog, Let's take a ride to Kate's house and find your mom, okay?" A nodding motion from the hollow where his neck and shoulder met Chloe's damp face confirmed his suspicions.

He felt a little of the tension drain out of her small body, but she froze again, heartbeat thundering when the underbrush thrashed, maybe ten feet from where they stood. A cell phone flashlight beam cut through the darkness at ground level, followed by a vaguely familiar voice.

"Dammit, Chloe. I just wanted to show you the horses."

Chloe whimpered into Jack's shoulder.

Jack edged back toward his car, holding Chloe tight to him as Chuck Douglas burst out of the undergrowth carrying Chloe's ninja sword and a glow stick.

*What the hell?*

"Hey." Chuck skidded to a stop, leaning over and breathing heavily. "Thanks, man. My daughter. She just took off."

It all clicked into place. Chuck. Chad. That sleazy visit to his office. Anneliese's asshole ex.

"*Your* daughter?" Jack stepped into the beam of his headlights and watched Chuck Douglas go bone white. "I think I know whose daughter she is."

Another swath of light appeared over the rise from the direction of Kate and Ewan's house.

"Chloe? Chloe!" Jack recognized Joss's voice and his knees went weak in relief.

"Joss, it's me. I've got her," Jack called, "but we've got company."

Joss ran down the cart path, coming into the light just as Anneliese's ex tried to bolt. Without missing a step, Joss tackled the bastard. The two men hit the ground with a series of grunts and thumps.

All around them, the costumed search party emerged from the woods carrying flashlights, glow sticks, and illuminated phones. Jack cradled Chloe's head against his shoulder when Joss's fist connected with what sounded like cartilage.

The faraway blare of a siren sang out over the chaos, but there was one face Jack needed to see before he could relax his hold on Chloe.

He squinted into the beams of light and shadows but it was Chloe who found her mother first, picking her head up and reaching out.

"Mama!"

Like someone had hooked his heart and hauled on the line, he spun just in time to catch Anneliese in his free arm.

~

JACK DROVE THEM HOME IN HER CAR.

Anneliese rode in back, cradling Chloe against her. Chloe had fallen asleep in Kate and Ewan's living room while the police were interviewing guests, never waking when they moved her to the car. In the rearview mirror, he could see the smudges of exhaustion under her eyes.

Jack's thoughts raced.

Chad's aim had been to extort Anneliese. Jack figured Chad wouldn't have actually taken Chloe, but if his own terror was any indicator, maybe the threat alone would have brought Anneliese around to some kind of arrangement.

Probably using the same cart road Jack had, Chad hid somewhere in the shadows, intending to seal whatever sick deal he thought he was making.

There was a flashlight scavenger hunt in the backyard for all the kids. Chad tried to lure his daughter away by suggesting they visit the horses.

Chloe was smart. She knew Kate and Ewan didn't have horses, knew better than to go with someone she didn't know.

She was also only five.

When the ruse failed, he put himself between Chloe and Ewan's sister, who was supervising the event. Chloe panicked and ran into the woods. Her tearful explanation that she thought she could go around the barn in the woods and find a grown-up she knew but got *losted*, tugged at Jack's heart.

His ninja frog got losted, and he was there to find her only by sheer luck. The enormity of it was enough that his hands were still shaking, hours later.

The police escorted Chad off Kate and Ewan's property. If nothing else, he was trespassing. Jack overheard one of the officers mention a similar report from the landlord. Jack mentally filed away the information.

Anneliese would have a couple of hard days ahead—and she would need an attorney. Jack was already considering who to ask for at Kearney-Mulligan's San Francisco office.

He pulled into the driveway at the cottage to find Anneliese asleep too. Jack negotiated the booster seat's harness buckles and scooped Chloe onto his shoulder for the second time that night.

He woke Anneliese with a gentle shake. "Come on, Anna. Let's get you both inside."

# CHAPTER 28

nneliese woke with a gasp, yanked out of a nightmare of darkness and flashlight beams. Her skin was clammy, her heart racing. The night's events still held her heart in a vice.

Her daughter slept in the bed beside her, Feesh under her chin. Chloe was still wearing her ninja frog leggings and turtleneck. Anneliese's phone told her it was nearly dawn. Mouth pasty with sleep, she held her breath a moment, waiting to see if she had woken Chloe.

Anneliese let out an audible whisper of gratitude. To Jack? To the Universe? Her mother's god? She didn't know. Only the house's familiar creaks and sighs whispered back.

The nightmare was still there, lurking in the room's shadows, playing out in still frames every time she blinked. The white-hot fear, like her heart had been torn from her chest. Her daughter safe in Jack's arms. Joss restraining Chad by the side of the road. Anneliese tucked a stray curl behind her daughter's ear. It would be a long time before she slept soundly again.

Pushing the covers away to let the cool of the room dry her damp skin, she realized she was bare-legged and wearing her U2 tee shirt. The door was open. A glance at the chair in the corner showed her the black pants and sweater from her costume. How had she even gotten to bed?

The police had come. They took Chad away. There were questions, her statement. Chloe clung to Jack like a burr when Anneliese had to relinquish her own hold; he remained near while she spoke with the police.

He had bundled the two of them into her car and driven them home, but she had no memory of downtown, of the driveway, or the house.

She told herself she was checking the lights and locks. She paused at the doorway to her bedroom, fingers worrying at the hem of her shirt.

He had tucked her in—tucked them both in.

And camped out nearby.

Across the hall, through Chloe's open door, Jack slept on Chloe's floor, Chloe's pillow tucked under his head and one of her afghans over his legs.

Anneliese crouched, touching his stubbly cheek. "Hey."

He sat up so fast they nearly collided. "Is everything okay?"

She straightened, the sudden motion leaving her dizzy. "Chloe and I are fine. She's asleep. I don't remember you putting us to bed."

Jack leaned back against Chloe's bed and rubbed his eyes. "You were out cold. I couldn't leave you."

*But you will.*

He rolled his shoulders as if they were sore.

"You didn't have to sleep on the floor. Kate's old couch is..." But Jack knew where Kate's old couch was.

"Too far away from you. Both of you." He touched her hand— just a brush of contact. His eyes were haunted. "How're you feeling?"

"Like I never want to let her out of my sight again."

Jack curled his fingers around hers. "I know the feeling."

The heat in his eyes took her breath away. She could swear he wasn't only talking about Chloe.

"Anna," he said, pulling her out of her thoughts, "you're asleep on your feet. Rest. I'll hold down the fort." He hoisted himself to standing and cradled her face in his hands. "Rest."

She was too tired, too unsteady, to do more than nod and let him walk her back to her bed. Chloe snuffled and curled in against her, and Anneliese slept again.

J ACK PAUSED IN FRONT OF A NNELIESE'S BATHROOM MIRROR, CERTAIN the last twenty-four hours had given him his first gray hairs. When the only gray his reflection offered back was his skin color, he splashed some cold water on his face and moved along.

It was nearly dawn; he had barely slept after driving all day with a bear of a hangover, and he was sure the encounter with Anneliese's ex cost him five years of his life. Chloe and Anneliese slept curled together on Anneliese's bed. He only meant to sit down somewhere quiet for a moment after tucking them in, but Chloe's floor proved sufficient for a few stolen hours of sleep.

Jack meant what he said. He didn't want to let either of them out of his sight anytime soon, but they would all need to reestablish normalcy in the coming days.

He was done sleeping for the moment, his whirling thoughts replacing unsettled dreams. Falling back on his legal training, he pulled up the internet browser on his phone and skimmed information about California's divorce and custody laws.

Anneliese would need to make some difficult choices, he reasoned, and here he could help. Or at least he could help her find the right attorney.

He emailed Iris a sketch of the situation without naming names, knowing that any gaps in his professional circle, she could fill. Knowing she would see through his nameless client and never say a word.

Handling logistics felt good. Being useful felt good. Jack tidied the family room, then moved on to the dishes left in the sink after an obviously hasty dinner the night before.

He found a broom in the closet under the stairs and swept the floor. His jacket hung discarded on the newel post, so he grabbed a coat hanger when he put the broom away.

He still had Anneliese's car keys.

A car in the driveway startled him. While he'd played house, the sun crept over the mountains, and with its arrival the Thompsons were checking on their daughter and granddaughter.

A heavy dew soaked the mums on the front steps of the cottage when Jack lifted the latch on the porch door.

"Jack," said Mrs. Thompson. "Where are they?"

"Sleeping." Jack ushered Mr. and Mrs. Thompson inside. Mr. Thompson wore a fleece jacket over sweatpants and a tee shirt. Her mother looked put together as always, despite the hour, a pair of dark smudges under her eyes the only indicator of strain.

"Bobby," Jane said, "can you get the bag?"

The bag in question appeared to hold breakfast fixings. Anneliese's father hefted it and followed Jane inside.

She set to work immediately, rifling through the kitchen like an expert. She kept a steady stream of one-sided small talk, mostly expressing gratitude for Jack's part in the events.

Mr. Thompson sat in the family room with a newspaper, but Jack noticed his eyes tracked the stairs more than the newsprint.

Still attuned to the sleeping woman and child upstairs, Jack was the first to hear Anneliese's bedroom door creak open, and a small voice in the stairwell.

"H'lo?"

"Oh, Chloe!" Mrs. Thompson dropped her whisk and rushed to meet her granddaughter. Her husband folded his paper and made his way to the bottom step.

Given the racket, Anneliese would be awake any minute. The last thing she needed was Jack lurking in her kitchen.

He gathered his few belongings, realizing as he did that he'd forgotten to borrow Anneliese's power cord overnight.

He would need his car. And a phone charger. First stop, Kate's house to collect his car, scrounge some breakfast, and enlist his sister and brother-in-law to return Anneliese's car to the cottage. He knew Kate would appreciate an excuse to check on Anneliese. He hoped Mrs. Thompson was really listening when he told her where he was going with her daughter's car.

Once the rides were sorted out, he would make himself useful at home. Give Anneliese a chance to breathe before he told her everything.

And begged for a chance to prove himself.

Through the haze of waking, her mother's voice registered, but Anneliese was too cozy to let reality intrude right away. She heard Chloe downstairs helping with breakfast, which smelled like apples and cinnamon.

Chloe.

Her heart jumped, and she fought back a wave of panic. Her mother was downstairs. With Chloe. Who was safe. She forced a few steadying breaths, and then swung her feet out of bed. There was nothing to be gained by freaking out in front of her daughter, and there was breakfast in her future.

Meals were how her mother showed love.

Anneliese took a few steadying breaths before she stepped off the stairs and into the living room.

Her father rose from the sofa and without a word wrapped her in a hug. "Sweetie, I'm so glad you're both okay."

Anneliese let herself relax into her father's embrace. "Me too, Daddy."

"Your mother and I had a long night," he said quietly. "We made some mistakes, and we're sorry."

Anneliese let out a long breath, leaning back to look up at her father's face. "Thank you for that."

Her father kept his voice down. "I just hate that it took something like this to show us we were wrong."

A strangled sort of half-laugh rose in her throat. "I guess you'll just have to trust me a little more?"

"A lot more." Her dad hugged her again. Then he returned his voice to a normal volume. "Now, let's see what the chefs have for breakfast."

She let her father usher her into the kitchen, where the apple spice pancakes Anneliese smelled were nearly ready. Her eyes were all for her daughter—barefoot, with her My Little Pony apron tied around her favorite striped pajamas. "This looks great."

"Mere and me made pancakes." Chloe waved a batter-sticky whisk over the bowl.

"Mere—" Anneliese began, her mother speaking in concert.

"And I," her mother finished.

They would never see eye to eye on everything, and it wouldn't all be resolved right away, but she was her mother's daughter, and every-thing—even family—took practice to get right. Anneliese inhaled deeply and met her mother's gaze. "Morning, Mom."

Her mother reached out and squeezed her hand. The gentle pres-sure gave Anneliese hope.

"Jack left after we got here," her mother said. "It was good of him to stay the night."

Jack. She had almost forgotten his tenderness and care the night before, and how he was there when she woke in the early hours. If her mother suspected anything more than square dancing had happened between them, she was playing it close to the vest.

"Mere," Chloe interrupted, "the batter is making bubbles."

Anneliese's mother released her hand. "Then it's time to get cooking."

If she wished Jack had stayed for her mother's pancakes, Anneliese could play it close to the vest, too.

SOME POET ONCE SAID SOMETHING ABOUT THE BEST LAID PLANS, JACK recalled with a grumble, when he found his sister and her husband weren't at home. Ewan's truck was missing from the driveway, and the house was dark, but his car was waiting for him next to Kate's hot pink van.

Kate wasn't one to sleep late; more than a decade of pastry kitchen shifts made her a creature of dawn hours. His knock went unanswered, but he knew his sister kept a spare key under a pot of mums.

Since his phone was still dead, Jack grabbed a notepad from Kate's fridge and wrote his sister a note. He left it with Anneliese's car key on the counter, then moved to the second part of his plan: a new phone charger and making himself useful at his parents' house.

Jack started to head towards Robidoux's Hardware, but he wasn't ready to answer questions or overhear gossip—well-wishing or not. Instead he swung the car around the common and headed south to the town's only strip mall, located down the highway about a mile, where a worn-down chain department store still held out.

When he returned to town, he found that useful wasn't as simple as he thought. His parents weren't home, the house was spotless, and a teenage kid Jack recognized from down the street was raking leaves in the yard. The kid nodded from under a huge pair of headphones, but didn't stop to chat.

In the house, he found a note his parents left letting him know they knew what happened the night before and tried texting, but they had an appointment with a private practice therapist in Hanover that couldn't be moved. His mother's new, shakier scrawl would take getting used to, but it was good to see she was working on it.

Left to his own devices, Jack sat on the sofa in the den. He reached for the remote, thinking he could catch up on the World Series. It wasn't every year the Cubs looked this promising, and if his Sox weren't in it, he could root for Chicago.

When he woke, his neck was stiff and his left foot asleep. The slanting, golden light told him it was late afternoon. His newly acquired phone charger still lay in its bag. His phone was just as much a brick.

Jack plugged in the phone before scrounging for food. He was halfway through a container of cold grilled chicken when his phone powered up, pinging and chiming like a celebratory cuckoo clock.

He left the food to retrieve his phone, nearly dropping it when he read the list of texts from Joss, from Kate, from his parents. Nan had gone into labor later that morning. He checked the timestamp of the most recent message from his sister, saying Nan was close. He called Kate first.

Kate answered on the first ring. "Where have you been?"

"Asleep with a dead phone. Mom and Dad are in New Hampshire, something about a therapist. Are they okay? Is the baby okay?"

"I know where our parents are, dork, and yes. Everyone's fine. It's a girl. She was born about an hour ago."

Jack felt burst of raw happiness and relief at the news. "Name?"

"Haven't heard yet. Ask Joss when you talk to him. And Jack?" Kate paused. "Someone should tell Anneliese."

"She doesn't know already?"

Jack heard a smug satisfaction in his sister's voice. "Nope. I told Nan I'd let her know, but I think you should be the one to tell her."

ANNELIESE USHERED HER PARENTS OUT THE DOOR WITH PROMISES TO come for dinner the next day. The sun was gone behind the trees, and pearly twilight crept over the mountains. They had stayed all day, picking up the slack while Anneliese snuggled her daughter, while she spoke with the chief of police when he dropped by.

She lingered in the garden, while Chloe diligently overwatered the impatiens Jack gave her. It had long since stopped flowering, and the first frosts had come and gone, but Anneliese didn't have the heart to tell her the flower was dead.

Longing for Jack filled the empty space around her. The love she felt for him now blazed like a thousand of the torch she carried for him when they were teenagers. Leaning on the fence to take in the view of downtown, she wished desperately for him to stroll down the sidewalk and push open the gate, to hold her and lend her a little strength.

It was so hard, being strong enough for two all the time.

The sight of a tall, dark-haired man coming around the bandstand on the common set her heart drumming. Anneliese shook her head to clear the vision, sure she was imagining him. She had an awful day and a half, but there was no time for her to fall apart.

His smile when he saw her was as real as the pickets under her hands.

~

THE STREETLIGHTS WERE JUST COMING ON. JACK WANTED TO STOP AND savor the sight of Anneliese and Chloe in the garden, the crisp, cool autumn night falling around them.

Under a sky like that, it was hard to believe anything bad could happen.

But it had, and Jack had no illusions of heroism. Dumb luck and grim determination to get to Anneliese and Chloe for his own selfish reasons put him in the right place at the right time.

He wanted to be in the right place because it was where Anneliese wanted him, where Chloe wanted him.

"I come bearing news," he called out.

"Applejack!" Chloe ran right up to the gate, but stopped short. "Mama, can I?"

Anneliese rocked back on her heels. "Jack can come in."

"New gate protocols?" Jack asked Chloe, glancing at Anneliese for confirmation.

"Mama says that bad man is my father 'cause he and Mama made me, but nobody taught him to be good, so he doesn't get to be my daddy, and he can't come in." Chloe looked at her mother for reassurance. "Because fathers and daddies aren't always the same."

"Your mama knows her stuff, Frog."

"What's the news?" Anneliese kept her tone light, but Jack heard a trace of worry.

"It's a girl! I just talked to Kate and Joss. I came straight here." He crouched to tousle Chloe's hair. "You have a new cousin."

"What's her name?" Chloe asked.

"Phoebe. Phoebe Victoria Fuller," Jack said.

"Can we go see her?"

"Not yet, but soon. She's a little underweight and will have to hang at the hospital to finish getting strong enough to come home, but she's healthy and so is Nan." He swiped open his phone to show Anneliese and Chloe the pictures Joss sent.

They were so close, Jack could reach out and touch the spot of soil on Anneliese's cheek.

Satisfied—if a little disappointed—with the information available, Chloe went back to her chalk drawings.

"Victoria was Walt's mother's name," Anneliese said. "Jed and Tory ran the farm up until Jed died. Remember Mr. Cartwright used to talk about how his cousin Walter was born the same year he came back from Korea?"

"I didn't until just now, but yeah." He didn't know how to begin. "Anna—"

"Chloe, can you go inside for a couple minutes? I need to talk to Jack. Grown-up stuff."

"Can I watch the frog show?"

Anneliese laughed. "Sure."

"Frog show?"

"A National Geographic documentary on some crazy South American frog." Anneliese stood and peeled off her gloves. "I'll never hear the end of it."

"Anna—" He needed to begin to apologize for bungling it all so badly.

"You saved her. I'll never be able to thank you enough for that."

"Oh, the hell with that." It burst out of him before he could think twice. "I love her. I love you. I made a royal mess of it all, but there it is. I love you both, and I'd have done whatever I had to keep her safe last night."

❧

The earth tilted. Anneliese would swear the ground lurched. The fierceness of Jack's expression should have frightened her, but it did the opposite. She reached for him, framing his face between her palms. "Say it again."

"I love you, Anna. I love Chloe. I want to be her dad." His voice faltered. "Because fathers and daddies aren't the same."

"I've loved you as long as I can remember," she whispered. "But what do we do about it?"

The heat in Jack's eyes took her breath away.

"I don't even know where to start, Anna, but I need you to know I'm not going anywhere. I resigned from Kearney-Mulligan and listed my condo while I was in Boston."

"You did what?" The planet was definitely off its axis.

"It might have an offer already. That's why I was late. Someone in my building—"

"Jack."

"I hit traffic in Cambridge, at the 95 interchange, twice on 93. I left my phone charger at home." He showed her his phone. "That's where I went this morning. Well, after figuring out the cars…"

"Jack."

"I've got ideas about the future, but none of them are as important as having you two in it."

Her head was swimming. "I thought you wanted to be a partner at the firm. And what about Noah Hawes and Geoff Hardy? Politics?"

"I did want the firm and all that, or I thought I did. Turns out, small town family practice has its charms. And I really can't leave until I can get Mrs. Drake to crack a smile." His eyes crinkled with amusement. "Maybe things won't work out, but I'm going to see about running for office here somewhere down the line. Be the guy working with Noah and Geoff to protect families and seniors and single moms." He held their hands between them. "This week, I want to be the guy who helps out with Chloe while you're putting the finishing touches on the wedding of the year."

She could feel the weight of his hope between them.

"What do you say, Anna Banana?"

"Can you forgive me for keeping the truth about Chad from you?"

"Can you forgive me for being clueless and blind for twenty years?"

Anneliese took a deep breath. The anger and uncertainty she harbored only days before seemed small in the face of the swamping love she felt when she found him by the side of that country road, holding her missing daughter like a dad. The rightness of him eclipsed their argument, and their secrets were laid bare now.

"You're really staying."

"I'm really staying."

His palms were warm against hers, his fingers gentle. Anneliese stretched up to seal the future with a kiss.

The rest they could wade through to find solid ground.

Together.

# EPILOGUE

"This suits you." Iris hung a long, flowing scarf over the back of her chair and took in the view of the Fuller's pastures and the blue-gray smudge of mountains on the western horizon. Late afternoon sunshine and muggy September warmth welcomed the crowd on the lawn at the Damselfly Inn.

"It had better," Jack said, leaning in to kiss her cheek. "I just won a primary. I'm in it for the long haul if all goes according to plan."

"I have no doubt you'll do well." Iris snuck a glance back at the house where Mrs. Drake was badgering one of the catering staff. "Your campaign manager isn't going to let you fail."

"She's a treasure. There was no way I was letting her retire completely when my dad did. I'd be sunk without her."

Iris looped an arm through his. "It doesn't matter how many times I visit. This place is almost too lovely to be real."

"I'm still considering taking on a partner. *Björnsdottír and Pease, Attorneys*, has a certain ring to it…"

Iris patted his arm. "You're charming, but not as charming as a city with a symphony orchestra and fresh sushi."

Jack spotted his friend on the terrace. "The photographer is waiting for me, so I'm going to leave you with Seth. Maybe he can talk you into it."

Iris raised a hand in greeting. "Not likely, but he's always good company."

Leaving Iris, Jack mused happily on the assembled partygoers. Barry from his old team at Kearney-Mulligan and his wife Emily were talking with Seth. Emily hugged Iris and enfolded her into their conversation.

His family was on the inn's front porch. His mom, sitting on one of Nan's rockers, her walking stick the only physical reminder of the ordeal that brought him home. His dad, ever by her side, stood with Molly and Walt Fuller, catching up on whatever news the village had yet to share with the valley. Molly was holding Phoebe on one hip.

Kate popped out the front door carrying a paper plate. He heard her call out to Ewan, who was giving their eighteen-month-old daughter, Maisie, a shoulder ride.

Joss caught sight of Jack first. "Mom, I need Phoebe. Jack's here for the picture."

The photographer shuffled everyone onto the inn's front steps, centering him with Anneliese and Chloe, and arranging Kate, Ewan, Joss, Nan, and the kids around them.

Anneliese stretched up to whisper in his ear. "This one will go on the kitchen wall."

He kissed her quickly, but the telltale click of the camera lens told him he was caught. After that, the photographer brought in his parents, the Thompsons, the Fullers. They could hardly get everyone to look at the camera at the same time, never mind stop laughing. The noise drew the guests from the backyard around to the front.

A sea of faces, some less familiar than others, but everyone precious in the moment. Noah Hawes talking to Geoff and Jenna Hardy—not too far away, their detail officer talking to no one. Jenna's parents, deep in conversation with friends. Rosie Cartwright talking to Anneliese's brother Jamie. CeCe Drexler and Penny Coulson holding what appeared to be an impromptu Chamber of Commerce meeting with Marian Muse and a few other local faces.

Satisfied with the shots she had, the photographer released them.

Jack reached for a nearby glass, abandoned with someone's snack plate on a table on the porch. He tapped it with an equally abandoned fork. The crowd quieted, all eyes on him. The pride in Anneliese's expression carried him into his speech.

"Thank you all for coming today. This was originally supposed to be a simple potluck fundraiser for my campaign, but it's gotten a bit bigger than that. More like a friends and family reunion." He took Anneliese's hand. "Most of you know I married the love of my life a couple years ago, but I'm a come-home-and-go-big kind of guy." The crowd took their cue to laugh, and he dropped to one knee to speak directly to Chloe. "Can I tell them?"

Chloe's gap-toothed, third-grade smile beamed. "Yeah."

He stood again, hugging her close. "Earlier today, we finalized Chloe's adoption. I'd like to take a moment to congratulate myself on being lucky enough to have both these wonderful women in my life forever." The applause went on so long that Chloe got shy, so Jack held out a hand. "My sister made a cake, which I'm told is being cut out back, so before you all vanish—I don't have a glass, but if you do, raise it to family, to Thornton, and all the great things we're going to do together."

He waited on the stairs as the party scattered. Anneliese joined Sarah and Michelle, who swung Chloe up and around in a hug.

His mother made her way down the front steps to join him. "I've never been prouder of you, Jack."

He hugged her. "I love you, Mom"

"I'm going to find some cake and a nice shady seat in the backyard. Go kiss those women you love. There's no better time for it than right now."

"You're right."

"I always am."

She was, but what struck him was the memory of another thing she had always been right about. Something he had to learn the hard way. He sought out Anneliese and Chloe, his breath catching when the sun kissed their blond heads, thick in conversation.

*Joy is a verb.*

Turn the page for an excerpt from
SUGARING SEASON: STORIES FROM THORNTON & BEYOND

# SWEET BASIL

## A THORNTON VERMONT STORY

# AFTER THE EVENTS OF FAMILY PRACTICE

"Andy, I literally couldn't have done this without you."

Kate Pease's hair smelled like vanilla and lemon when she kissed his cheek. Five years, he'd worked for Kate at her two locations—first in her downtown pastry shop, then as a manager at her café at Cooper Vineyard—and every day of those five years he'd slept with that distinctive scent in his dreams.

Kate's husband (because of course if you're going to nurture an unrequited passion for your boss, she should be blissfully married) was launching his latest novel at Kate's vineyard café in—Andy checked his smartwatch—fourteen minutes, and so far he'd kept a handle on every detail.

"No problem, Kate. We're all really happy for Ewan."

Kate swept away, the swishy folds of her skirt brushing up against the long legs he'd admired since he was a college freshman.

"She's too old for you."

He hadn't seen Danny—*Danielle*, he mentally corrected himself. Someday he'd remember that she was going by Danielle now—in weeks, not since she'd gone back to school after spring break, but there she was beside him, a tray of bud vases for the buffet tables perched on her shoulder. She was right, but that didn't mean he didn't fall in love with Kate again on a daily basis.

"Shut up, Danny."

"Whatever." She shrugged and continued past him.

She'd cut her hair—short—and dyed it platinum blonde since her last shift. He'd liked it long and dark, especially the secret shocks of violet you only saw when she put it up, but this suited her, too.

"Andy?" Margot, who ran the downtown location, peeked out from the kitchen. "Can I borrow a couple of staffers? I need to bring the cake in from the van."

"Sure thing, Margs."

And just like that, it was showtime. Kate was counting on him.

Events meant keeping his head in the game, but two hours in without a hitch meant he could step back and breathe. He paused by the bar to survey the room, his eyes lingering on Kate, who swayed with her husband on the rented dance floor.

Danny wove through the tables collecting empty glasses, stopping to deposit her tray on a folding stand nearby. She elbowed him playfully, following the direction of his gaze. "If we weren't such good friends, I'd say something about how good they look together."

He eyed the tray of glassware.

"Yeah, yeah. I know." She hoisted the tray. "You coming out after?"

He shrugged, but Danny was already pushing through to the kitchen. He looked at his watch. An hour to go.

Kate always stopped in the kitchen to say goodnight to the staff after a function, and tonight was no different. He watched her depart, hand-in-hand with her husband, and wished desperately for his other vice.

Satisfied that Margot had a handle on things, he slipped out into the vineyard and down to the dock the owners kept for summer lake traffic.

He let his legs dangle over the edge, lit a cigarette, and listened to Lake Champlain lap at the wood beneath him, knocking his ashes carefully into a paper cup.

He could hear footsteps on the dirt path above. He'd thought the vines hid him from view, but he hadn't counted on Danny..

"Those things are gross. Girls won't want to kiss you."

"Jeez, Danny, are you thirteen?"

"It's a good thing you're grandfathered in. People call me *Danielle* these days." She plunked down next to him. "And I'm twenty-one, as you well know. You were at my birthday party."

She'd thrown back every shot anyone bought her, including an ill-advised round of schnapps. He'd held her hair back while she threw up in the ladies' room, then driven her out to Fuller's Dairy, where she stayed when she was home from school. She'd changed all his radio presets, but she hadn't puked in his car.

"How did you know I was down here?"

She wiggled her fingers like a sideshow mystic. "I see everyyy-thinggg."

"Weirdo." He put out a hand to nudge her, but the playful gesture felt wrong somehow.

"I saw you attempt a subtle exit after Margot clocked us out. When you didn't come back, I figured you were hiding, or you finally drowned yourself because Kate Pease is still married to Mr. Tall Dark And Broody."

"Nice, Danny." He rubbed out the cigarette, dropping the butt into the cup. Burning down his place of employment—or the terraces of Marquette and Frontenac grapes—wasn't on his to-do list for the evening. "Don't you have someone else to torture?"

"Actually, no." She tilted her head and batted her lashes. "And I need a ride."

He sighed. Danielle Beaudette was not a flirt, but her thick, black cat-eye makeup and sooty eyelashes made a convincing argument in her favor nonetheless.

"Come on." He hoisted himself up and grabbed his soaking filter, swimming in its cup. "For all you know, I have a hot date to get to after I drop you off with the cows."

Danny laughed heartily at his back all the way up the hill to the staff parking lot, but she was uncharacteristically quiet during the ride out County Road.

"You okay?"

She tucked her hair behind her ear, her face deeply shadowed in the dark car. "Yeah. Just thinking."

He swung into the Fullers' driveway. The farmhouse was dark, except for a light in the kitchen window.

She gathered up a grimy messenger bag from the floor of his car. "You want to come in? I didn't eat before the party, so I'm going to make some food."

He thought of the older couple who owned the farm. "I don't want to impose."

"Oh, Walt and Molly are next door tonight visiting their grandbaby." She opened the car door, climbed out, then leaned back in. Andy couldn't help appreciating a brief view of unexpected lace and curved flesh. "So?"

He *was* hungry. "Can you cook?"

"Enough to feed myself."

He killed the engine and followed her to the back porch. She fished out keys, let them in, and pointed him to a basket of slippers before unlacing her black combat boots, toeing off her socks, and sliding her feet into a pair of green suede moccasins. "Molly doesn't like shoes in the house."

He poked around until he found slip-on fleece house shoes that sort of fit and shuffled after Danny, through a cozy den and into the kitchen.

Danny was already banging around the kitchen. She'd pulled out a cast iron skillet, some bacon and a loaf of Sweet Pease honey-oat sandwich bread.

"BLTs?"

It struck him as odd, seeing Kate's bread on someone's counter. He'd made countless sandwiches at work over the years, but rarely considered that people who bought whole loaves might do the same.

"Earth to Andy?" Danny rapped on the skillet with a pair of tongs, then waved at him with them. "Can you stop thinking about the boss for four seconds and open that cabinet? Plates."

A violent flush rose up his neck. "I wasn't—"

"Thinking about Kate? Liar. Your face gets all weird when you do." She rolled her eyes back and let her jaw go slack.

He fetched the plates, then reached for the single tomato resting on the windowsill. Danny laid the bacon out in the hot pan, and handed him the serrated knife from the block by the stove top.

He sliced the bread, then the tomato, thick like he would have for a customer. "Toaster?"

Danny kicked at a lower cabinet door. The toaster was inside on a shelf, its cord coiled around it.

He had to cram the bread in a little, but he got the toaster going. Danny was flipping bacon. The kitchen smelled amazing.

Andy opened the fridge, looking for mayonnaise, and found the jar on the door. What interested him more was a stack of glass storage containers. There was a beautiful collection of cheeses in those containers.

"Are we allowed to eat the cheese?"

Danny laughed, pulling the last slice of bacon from the pan. The toast popped. "Yes. Look." She slid the skillet off the burner to cool and wiped her hands on a kitchen towel. "I live here. Walt and Molly stepped in and offered me a place with them when things at home were... not good. This is the place I think of when someone says home. If we want to eat the cheese, we eat the cheese."

While Danny started assembling sandwiches, Andy pulled together a plate of cheeses. He glanced back at Danny, who had laid the sandwiches out open faced. "Where's the lettuce?"

"Still in the garden."

She picked up the plate with the sandwiches, reached into the fridge for a glass bottle of milk, and breezed past him.

"Where are you going?"

"Bring the cheese. We're going to get the lettuce."

He tromped after her, delayed by changing back into his shoes. Her slippers lay abandoned by the door, but so too were her heavy, black boots.

He'd expected a practical vegetable patch. Instead, Danny waited for him on a whimsical bench fashioned from what looked like driftwood, amidst a maze of trellises and raised beds. A lush jungle of edibles slept in the blue darkness. Andy smelled damp earth and growing things.

He recognized Danny in that scent. This garden, it was hers.

"You got any basil out here?"

She laughed, pointing to a nested stack of round pots. "Over there. Top tier."

He wound his way between the beds. Pea vines, leafy bean bushes, and taller climbing squashes, blossoms closed against the night. Flowers were artfully tucked in with the food.

"Did you do all this?"

Danny's voice floated back to him. "Sort of. There's always been a kitchen garden here. Since before Walt was born. He and Molly have helped me with building the boxes and stuff, but yeah. It's what I do, or at least what I want to do."

He often forgot that about her, since he only saw her at work, or when the Sweet Pease gang went out after hours. She'd worked at Coulson's nursery, too, before starting college, and still did in the summers. He pinched off a handful of sweet basil leaves and brought them back to her on the cheese plate.

"Better than plain old lettuce."

She shook the dew off the leaves and spread them on the sandwiches, patting the bench next to her. Her feet were bare, toes curling into the stone and dust.

It was only just dark enough for stars thanks to the late summer sunset. He let the living quiet settle over him while he tucked in. The valley chorused with peeper frogs and crickets, the occasional car or truck on County Road, and the barely perceptible sleep-sounds of the dairy herd.

"You were right about the basil." Danny set down what remained of her sandwich, and scooped up a bit of soft cheese with her finger. "I hope you don't mind my fingers in the food."

He didn't, now that she mentioned it. "We did eat unwashed basil."

"Unwashed basil, fingers in the cheese. We are adventurers." She licked her finger. "That's really good."

He didn't want to be intrigued by her bowed lips, her fine-boned hands that were always slightly chapped, at odds with her pin-up girl makeup and ever-changing hair.

"I've been paying attention to the vendors."

"Impressive, since Kate's usually around for that."

He set his plate down too hard, nearly sending his half-eaten sandwich into the gravel path. "You never let up. What is it to you if I like Kate?"

She leaned back and leveled him with a cool look that reminded him that she wasn't just the sarcastic kid Margot had hired a couple of years back. "Maybe I don't want to see you miss opportunities while you're pining for someone who is never going to feel that way about you."

"Yeah," his laugh turned bitter. "Like who? It's not like I've ever been a girl magnet."

Danny pursed her lips—with a healthy dose of side-eye—and returned to eating her sandwich, snagging a slice of another cheese and sliding it between the bread slices as she did.

Andy left his food, the bench, and Danny's infuriating snark and wandered into her garden. Through the fir stand ahead, he could make out the shadowed silhouette of the grand Victorian house next door. Around a corner of the building, he could just see the flickering glow of firelight, and if he stretched out his ears, he could hear laughter and low music.

Kate—and her husband—might very well be there. The owners were her friends.

"I lived there for a while when I was younger."

Danny's voice was soft—wistful—and he felt sorry for taking a verbal swing at her.

"I didn't know that."

"My mom was Meg Swift's home health aide before they moved to be closer to her grown kids. They let us stay in the apartment over the garage." He hadn't heard her get up, but she appeared next to him among her plants. "I was always happy there. I mean, I was a teenage jerk to my mom, and I had stupid taste in boys, but things didn't get bad until we moved in with my uncle."

Andy slung an arm around her, hugging her to his side. "You seem happy here, though."

She shifted slightly, leaning into him a little. He liked the way she fit there.

"I am. I have better taste in men now, too."

He wondered who the lucky guy was just as he realized he was holding another guy's girl, then let his arm drop away.

"You're not even going to ask."

He turned at the sharp wonder he heard. Her expression was fierce, her body suddenly rigid with tension.

"You, you idiot."

*Him, what?* He had just enough time to blink before she stretched up and kissed him full on the mouth. She let her lips linger for a beat against his; his body responded before his head could catch up.

He caught her arms, sliding his hands down to hold her hands, leaning in to let the kiss play out between them.

She tasted of basil leaves. Her skin was impossibly soft, right down to her palms, but he could feel the calluses on her fingers. The scent of earth and rain clung to her like perfume.

She rocked back on her heels, pulling away from him, but holding him in her gaze. "You."

He reached up to touch her cheek and she pressed her face into his hand. The gesture was so unabashedly tender, so unlike Danny. A pang of longing squeezed his chest.

"I didn't know." He whispered it, feeling every inch the idiot she'd called him.

Danny tightened her hold on his other hand. "Now you do."

～

Read the rest of **Sugaring Season**
https://books2read.com/SugaringSeason

# ALSO BY CAMERON D. GARRIEPY

Thornton Vermont

Damselfly Inn

Sweet Pease

Family Practice

Sugaring Season: Stories from Thornton & Beyond

Bread & Promises (Yuletide)

The Best Laid Plans: A Socially Distanced Thornton Vermont Romance

Green Mountain Hearts

Ambitious Heart

Unbound Heart

Troubadour Heart

Green Mountain Hearts: the Complete Series (paperback only)

Standalone Romance

Buck's Landing

Short Fiction in Anthologies

Valentine (Metaphysical Gravity)

Requiring of Care (Echoes in Darkness)

Christmas Mini-Romances

Tempests & Temptations: Two Christmas Romances

Bread & Promises (Yuletide)

Cinnamon Girl (Wish/Sugaring Season)

The Soloist (Joy)

Star of Wonder (Merry Little Christmas)

Santa's Photographer (Secret Santas)

Merry's Christmas (Atlantic to Pacific)

Twelve Days 'til Christmas

CHILDREN OF THE PARALLELS
SPECULATIVE MIDDLE GRADE SHORT FICTION

Parallel Jump

Parallel Hunt

THE CROWBOURNE CHRONICLES
FANTASY, ADVENTURE AND FAIRY TALES
SERIALIZED AS ISLA BRIGHTON

Silvertongue *(coming soon, Kindle Vella)*

The Golden Quill *(coming to Kindle Vella)*

Songbird *(coming to Kindle Vella, 2022)*

The Physician & the Siren *(coming to Kindle Vella, 2022)*

# ACKNOWLEDGMENTS

None of the Thornton crowd has dogs, which is a shame, since dogs have been part of my life for as long as I can remember. In May of 2019, our family lost Maurice, our thirteen-year-old pug, and I would be remiss if I didn't thank his sweet, goofy soul for hours of unwavering support and snuggles while I wrote this trilogy.

Thank you to Mark and Felix, always.
Living with a writer might be challenging.

Bottomless gratitude to Patti Stevens for hours of wine and sympathy on Patti's Patio (and for the inspiration for *My Nightmare Career: Celebrity Edition*). Your friendship has been a gift these last few years.

Special thanks to my Facebook reader group for helping me name a few other things along the way:
Roxanne Piskel, Nancy Campbell, Tara Lagana, and Angela Amman inspired the Thornton Founder's Day Festival. Angela and Tara named Chloe's plushies Bear and Bubbles, Roxanne came up with the Jalapeño Grille, and Kirsten Piccini originally named Nan and Joss's daughter—unfortunately, I had to change it at the last minute because of a four-legged houseguest.

On that note, thank you to Lucy Breguet for being just the guest pug I needed to finish this book.

Thank you to Words Aptly Spoken authors Jennie Goutet, Korinthia

Klein, and Julie C. Gardner, for reading this book in its early stages. I have the best village.

There aren't numbers large enough for the thank-yous I owe to Mandy Dawson and Angela Amman, without whom I'd be adrift in a sea of imposter syndrome and abandoned ideas.

Thank you to Maine State Senator Heather Sanborn (D-Cumberland), for whispering in Jack's ear, when he was frustrated by his parents' situation.

And to all my lawyer friends, I've taken great liberties with your profession, but Jack and Iris especially represent everything I love best about the lot of you.

Dear, marvelous Roxanne Piskel, you are the baddest editrix in all the land, and I love you for it.

Thank you to Daphne du Maurier for *Frenchman's Creek*.

And to everyone who's waited so patiently for this book to tell this story, thank you from the bottom of my heart. I'm going to miss Thornton a lot.

Which means I'll probably come back someday…

ABOUT THE AUTHOR

Cameron D. Garriepy attended a small Vermont college in a town very like Thornton. She's missed it since the day she packed up her Subaru and drove off into the real world. Some might say she created the fictional village as wish fulfillment, and they would be correct.

She is the author of the Thornton Vermont series, and the founder of Bannerwing Books, a co-op of independent authors. Prior to Bannerwing, Cameron was an editor at Write on Edge, where she curated three volumes of the online writing group's literary anthology, Precipice. Cameron appeared in the inaugural cast of Listen to Your Mother – Boston, and irregularly contributed flash fiction to the Word Count Podcast.

Since her time at Middlebury College, Cameron has worked as a camp counselor, nanny, pastry cook, an event ticket resale specialist, and an office manager. Cameron's ghost-writing and editing hides in the tech and finance sectors. In her spare time, she is an archer, a baker, a gardener, a knitter, and a reader of a lot of romance novels.

Cameron writes from the greater Boston area, where she lives with her husband, son, a very silly pug, and four naughty hens.

Connect with Cameron online at
www.camerondgarriepy.com
Hear first about sales and new releases via Cameron's newsletter—
subscribe at
bit.ly/smartsexynewsletter
Join the conversation in Cameron's Facebook group at
bit.ly/thorntonfbgroup

# ABOUT THE PUBLISHER

Bannerwing Books is a writers' co-op founded in 2012 by Cameron D. Garriepy, and completed by Angela Amman and Mandy Dawson. Currently residing on Slack, somewhere in the ether between Boston, Detroit, and Paso Robles, Bannerwing presents works by Stephanie Ayers, Ericka Clay, and Liz Zimmers, as well as collections featuring Andra Watkins, Kate Shrewsday, and Kameko Murakami.

www.bannerwingbooks.com

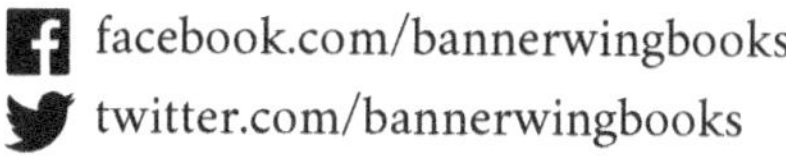

facebook.com/bannerwingbooks
twitter.com/bannerwingbooks